The Last Irish Goddess

A Novel

Steve Delaney

PLAIDSWEDE PUBLISHING

Concord, New Hampshire

Designed and composed in Minion Pro at Hobblebush Design, Brookline, New Hampshire (www.hobblebush.com)

Printed in the United States of America

Cover artwork by Judi Calhoun

ISBN 978-0-9962182-6-9
Library of Congress Control Number: 2017942612

Published by:

PLAIDSWEDE PUBLISHING

P.O. Box 269 · Concord, New Hampshire 03302-0269
www.plaidswede.com

For Lisa
Welcome to a where/
when that might have been

The Last Irish Goddess

Steve Delaney

"You're never really dead until your descendants forget your name."

—Heard at an Irish wake

Contents

Foreword

One of the endearing mysteries of the Irish soul is its flexibility. It enables a people whose brand of Christianity was suppressed for well over a century not only to thrive as the most devout nation in all of Catholicism, but to retain traces of belief in the older Celtic faith displaced gently by St. Patrick and his successors.

I believe "gently" is the key word here. There was little or no "convert or die" coercion when Christianity appeared in Ireland in the Fifth Century. Tolerance of the old faith and its believers lasted for centuries, and there's still a wink and a nod about the absence of strict orthodoxy in the practice of religion. An entire well-formed belief system is now called superstition but still exists as references to leprechauns and pookies, to banshees and Otherworld.

So there's a cultural readiness to embrace a bilateral belief system, room for World and Otherworld to exist cheek by jowl. And in the time of Teagan and Conor, it was still all right for him to call himself Oisin the Avenger, and it was easy for people to bestow the title goddess on her.

The Setting

The Last Irish Goddess evolved after I retired from a five-decade career in broadcast journalism.

That's important only because it marked a change in how I write. It was a huge discovery that novelists are not as tethered to facts as journalists are, not nearly. That discovery was exhilarating and still is. It allows the building of a personal world, especially if the tale is set in another time. But writing about a time and place that really existed re-imposes some of those fact-fences on the text.

The end of the Seventeenth Century and the beginning of the Eighteenth framed an era of unusually intense turbulence, even by the standards of the thousand-year struggle between Celt and Saxon for control of Ireland.

The notorious Penal Laws were as described in these pages, an English effort to use the law as a club to suppress the Irish.

The smuggling of wool was real but a few years later than described.

The great landmarks, Dunguaire and Doonagore Castles are real. Dunguaire is often visited. Sir William French is fictional. So are the Baileys of Doonagore. It is now a private home. The clifftop fortress of Dun Aonghasa, and the ancient Poulnabrone gravesite in the Burren also exist and are described as they would have been understood at the time of Teagan and Conor.

The efforts to improve the road past Dunguaire and the Kinvara harbor are also historically true, but again a few years later than in the story. Turlough O'Heyn the priest lived in Kinvara during Conor's time.

Finally, the High Sheriffs of County Clare served one-year terms in those years, and are identified accurately. However, I have given them personalities of my own devising.

The Irish language also has a personality of its own. It contains more sounds than English does, and efforts to weld those sounds onto the Latin alphabet often look awkward to non-Irish eyes and sound opaque to non-Irish ears.

The glossary on page 269 is an attempt to clarify some of that strangeness.

Characters and Locations

Prologue

When the Egyptians were learning to use pictures to move ideas from one mind to another, and the Assyrians were poking holes into wet clay for the same reason, something weird happened in the northwest marches of Europe, and for a very long time nobody noticed that something profound had occurred.

There is no easy death for stars. They rip themselves apart in cataclysms of crushing gravity and massive explosions. The surviving fragments go hurtling off through the Universe on random tangents. One such fragment moved so fast when it met the edges of Earth's atmosphere it skipped off, like a flat stone on a pond. But the collision scraped a bit of dead meteor material off the wanderer, and those particles fell through the thickening air.

A north wind herded the orphaned star-flakes into a glittering shower that fell onto the greenest land in a place where it folded into ridges, valleys and modest peaks. The few clusters of people who lived there didn't notice the extra ingredient in the rainfall that day on the south slope of a modest mountain that later men would call Ben Cullagh, one of the Twelve Bens of Connemara.

The star flakes worked their way into the soil and thus into the food chain. After a few generations the people of Ben Cullagh noticed that they were getting shorter and that some of them now had red hair. They also found that some could bring light to the night, that some could move heavy rocks with the touch of a hand, that some could sense forces and powers unseen, and that the laws of logic and physics could be bent.

They tried to hide those abilities from the neighboring tribes but it didn't work and the Ben Cullagh Irish began to be shunned. When the Celtic invaders arrived with their iron weapons, the gifted ones withdrew into their remote homeland and pondered the name the newcomers gave them: People of the goddess Danu, or Tuatha de Danann.

Every once in a while they become curious or annoyed at the doings of ordinary people and on rare occasions some of them turn up in a world where they are regarded with awe or fear, or both.

The Last Irish Goddess

1

Malachi

A grieving man sat alone at a table in his tavern and tried not to weep. *I think there's been water enough on this sad and rainy day.* A small girl with bright red hair came in from the kitchen. She pulled a chair across the bumpy floor and reached for her father's hand.

"We'll be all right," she assured him, not sure she believed her own words. "Och, lass, ye may be right, but it's hard, very hard, so it is." Malachi Moran reached out to smooth an unruly red curl and tried to smile. Teagan Dearg, he called her, Red Teagan. All the friends who had come back to the inn on this soggy funeral day had left, unable to lighten his mood. Only his Tay remained, the tangible harvest of the dozen joyous years shared with Kate.

"Well, Tay, it's just us now, us against a world gone cold." He looked down at his muddy boots, but she increased the pressure on his hand and drew his eyes back to hers. "Take them off," Teagan said. "I'll clean them in the morning, but they'll pass the night outside this door. Now let me draw you a cold pint of ale, just one, mind you, and we'll close this sorrowful day, so we will."

"Whisht, lass, you're only ten. What do you know of the drawing of ale?"

"Mother was my teacher, and you will see how well she taught me."

Malachi watched with surprise and pride as his daughter stepped to the tap, drew a just-so pint and placed it in front of him. "Sláinte," she said.

3

"We must speak of this again, Tay, but I have a question for you. Do you think you can still live in a place where your mother's presence echoes so?"

"Papa, this is our home, my home. I learned to walk in this room and I want to stay here. It smells of warmth and love, so it does."

Her eyes are pinning me into this chair. I'd forgotten how intense she can be.

When Kate was dying, she made me promise to look after Teagan. Of course I will, especially since she's such a slice of her mother. He raised his drained mug and smiled at her.

Och, look at how my smile works on her face. This child is both perceptive and transparent. When she's older, she'll shield her expressions but right now I'm glad to see her mind reaching for normal, even if it's a new kind of normal.

"Mother Boyle told me we'll have sunny skies in the morning," she said with a glance at the window. It revealed only a reflection of the room's lantern. "I like this room. Mama told me once it's a place where laughter dwells."

"Don't listen too much to Sinead Boyle, Teagan," Malachi said with an upraised finger. "But in truth tomorrow must be a better day and I am ready to meet it." He slapped the empty mug down on the table and got to his feet.

"If I ever forget to tell you, you are the only treasure I have left, and I love you more than I can say." He blushed at the candor of his words and went upstairs.

Teagan flipped her hair out of her eyes and let a small smile reshape her slightly triangular face. She picked up the empty mug and took it into the kitchen where she washed it without really seeing it. *Tomorrow will indeed be a better day, so it will. Oh, I wonder if I'll sleep tonight. I can still hear clods of dirt falling on my mother's casket.*

◆ ◆ ◆

The sun slanted up slowly, rising above the limestone landscape of the Burren, the stony ground that covered so much of County Clare. It lightened to beige the gray of Doonagore Castle, the English stronghold above the village of Doolin. Sunlight flowed on to brighten the village houses and so to the shore where it gave color to an unsettled sea.

In the middle of the morning the gates of Doonagore opened for two figures on horses. Sir Edmund Bailey was off to tour his holdings in and around Doolin and his son Arthur went with him on a smaller horse.

The heir to Doonagore was thirteen years old and had never been described as handsome. Most people thought he had a feast of nose and a famine of chin. Some noted his hair and hands never seemed clean and his eyes were too close together. Arthur Bailey was learning the arts of occupation from his father. Sir Edmund was the landlord of almost every holding in Doolin. Among his tenants there was not a single Englishman nor a single Protestant. Edmund Bailey told his son repeatedly how primitive the Irish were, how lazy, and how frequently they invented reasons to rebel or resist the natural order of things. "We English rule and those Irish serve."

"Where are we going this morning, father?"

"To see the publican Moran first. I have ears in the village and I hear he's been encouraging the restless among the Irish peasants. I'll warn him of the folly of resistance and then I'll raise his rent. We can't have these people think they can resist English rule."

Arthur's mouth moved in what he thought was a smile. *The innkeeper has a daughter whose hair is brighter than any I've seen. There are a lot of redheads in this rainy land, but most of them are all freckled and ugly. This one is so bonny. She's three years younger, but I can wait. My father says, what is it? "Anticipation is the better part of acquisition." Yes. She will be the first in a long string of Irish women I will have. After all, I'm of the ruling class and she's a mere peasant and not even English. Today I will see her again and tonight I'll think about her eyes, brown with flecks of gold. When she learns how much I want her she'll be so flattered. She's not the only girl in the village, but she is by far the fairest. She will thank me for picking her out from the others. Maybe today I'll learn her name, not that it matters.* He trotted happily behind his father anticipating a very good day.

Malachi and Teagan were sipping tea when the tavern door crashed open and Sir Edmund Bailey strode in, followed by a swaggering Arthur.

"The inn is not open," Malachi said with a sour look on his face. "It's always open for me," Bailey said.

"Not today," Malachi said. "Yesterday I buried my wife and today I do no trade."

"I'm not here to order that swill you call ale," the lord of Doonagore said. "I am here as your landlord and as lord of these lands all around. I am here to warn you off this business of stirring up rebellion against the Crown. And to drive home the point I am increasing your rent by half, starting at the change of the month."

Malachi slapped his teacup down on the table so hard the handle snapped off. He shook off the hand Teagan put on his arm.

"You English understand nothing. You know naught of managing the minds of men. When your subjects come in here and complain, they are letting off steam the way a teakettle does. If not for that vent, they may go forth burning and pillaging. Believe me, dissent is better than destruction. In truth, what I do here does more to keep the peace than all the harsh orders you issue." He watched Sir Edmund's face turn red.

"And while I'm being candid here's another thing. Your Arthur has an unhealthy fixation on my daughter, who does not enjoy his attention. Look there, he's drooling over a little girl! If that spawn of yours ever harms my Teagan, I will kill him on that day.

Now, as I said, the inn is closed. You are unwelcome here, as is this weasel who bears your name. Please close the door as you leave."

"Watch your tongue, Moran, or you'll be lashed in front of your own inn."

"If you do that no one here will pay your rents and men will die in the uprising you will have caused. You are not entirely a free agent here, Sir Edmund. I hope you are wise enough to know that. By the way the new rent will be paid on time." Malachi stood and opened the door. The lord of Doonagore stalked out into the drying mud, followed by his son. Teagan evaded Arthur's effort to touch her hair as he passed.

Malachi closed the door and turned to Teagan.

"He's disgusting, so he is," she said with a shudder.

"They both are," the innkeeper agreed. "But I will say this to you, my dear. As long as I live, you will be safe from that boy. I believe he is defective in some way.

There's a chance, and a pretty good one, young Arthur will annoy the wrong man, and will not live to inherit these lands." He saw on her face the new thought that followed her mental dismissal of Arthur Bailey.

"Papa, if we're to keep the inn, you must allow me to help. As you said, it's now us against a cold world."

"You are my partner in this, and I will teach the skills you need."

As they sat over a second cup of tea the door opened again for Sinead Boyle and her son Patrick, who was twelve. He and Teagan had known each other all their lives.

Malachi did not smile or rise to greet the widow Boyle. Sinead had decided their children were well matched, and missed no chance to promote that notion all over Doolin.

Teagan thought young Patrick was pleasant but not exciting. *He's too much under his mother's thumb, and now I think she's got another campaign going. My poor mother is barely cold in her grave and already the widow woman is trying to replace her. And she'll go at it like one of those English bulldogs, all teeth and no tact. Smothering Sinead, my father called her once.*

"Malachi, poor man, and the wee Teagan too. We are here to see what we can do for you. You shouldn't wallow alone in your grief. Isn't that so, Patrick?"

Teagan saw Patrick's face change. *Sinead is intruding here and doesn't even know it, but Patrick is embarrassed for her.*

"Sinead," Malachi said with a touch of asperity. "I am not wallowing, nor is Teagan. Rather we are discussing how to run the inn from now on. Yesterday we looked back in sorrow. Today we look ahead to what's next. It has already been an interesting morning, so it has. I think I'll open this afternoon, so Tay and I can try out our new partnership in Malachi's Tavern. We'll make it the best in the West, and what think you of that?"

"I'm sure you'll try," Sinead said. "But you'll need help, and Patrick and I are here to offer it." Teagan stirred in her chair. *Wrong answer. She should have said it's already the best in the West, but she's not smart enough to know that would cheer my father somewhat.* She rose and took the teacups into the kitchen. Patrick Boyle followed her.

"Mother does not dance well," the boy said with a shrug. "Rather she stamps around like she's squashing cockroaches."

Teagan smiled at her mental image of the bulky Sinead dancing over the corpses of insects. She knew Patrick was trying to apologize and she felt sympathy for him, not for the first time.

"Patrick, her timing is poor. She has a good heart, but Papa has just buried his best friend, and I my mother, just yesterday. We're trying to look forward but the past is close behind us, so it is. We need some time."

"I do know that, but she doesn't steer well."

Red Teagan again smiled at Patrick, a small smile. *Some day, some distant day, I will have to pick a man. Will there be a prince on a white horse for me, or must I choose between one who's growing up cruel and one whose inner light has been shaded by his oh-so-busy mother?*

2

Sean

Kinvara sits at the southern edge of County Galway and at
the tip of one of the fingerlings of saltwater that form the eastern end of
Galway Bay. The village is about twenty-five miles from Doolin and has
always been a port with good shelter from the friskier Atlantic winds.

One of its great landmarks is Dunguaire Castle, built at water's edge
on a slight rise that may be the rubble of its ancestors. In the first years of
the eighteenth century it was an oversized toll booth on the only decent
road between Galway, the shire city of the Irish west, and the scattered
coastal towns of County Clare.

◆ ◆ ◆

In the year Teagan Dearg Ni Moran was twelve a man and a boy crept
around the Dunguaire Castle toll station and made the long trek to
Galway City. Conor O'Canavan was glad to see The Claddagh, the fishing village on the edge of the waterway that spilled into Galway Bay.

"The man we seek will find us here," said Rory Donovan, the retired
soldier who was teaching Conor how to use a sword. They sat on benches
shaded by a tree at an open-air tavern and Rory rubbed his tired legs.

"They named this place for what they could see," Conor said. He
pointed at the stony beach and fought the urge to hold his nose. He

grinned a little. "They should have named it for what they could smell. Maybe breantas, or lofa."

"It's a fishing village. People here think it smells like money." The voice came from behind them, and they turned to see a tall, gaunt man in a gray hood, a man who was trying to smile.

I don't think he finds much humor in his life. His smile is a harvest of great effort. "Iss misha Conor," the boy said. "And here is Rory."

"I know Rory and he has told me of you. He says you may have the makings of a warrior, and he wants me to help him learn if that is true. Oh, I am Sean, and I am an archer, so I am."

Rory ordered mugs of the dark local stout for himself and the archer, and cold milk for Conor. The boy wrinkled his nose. Sean tried another smile. "Drink it, son. Our people become far too fond of this quaff," he said, holding his mug in the air. Conor subsided and listened to the gossip. Sean's face seemed to retreat into itself as he stared at the nearby walls of Galway City.

"I asked to meet you here because this is real Irish ground. There's been a settlement here for more than a thousand years, mostly because there's shelter from the storm winds." He nodded to the walls. "Back there it's all English. And these new Penal Laws they've passed are going to make it even harder on us." He looked at Conor. "We will need men to keep us from being destroyed by foreigners, our language, our customs, our faith, and most of all our honor. The grand question is, are you to be one of those men, Conor?"

"Sean, I am thirteen years old."

"You will get over it. What will you become as the new century develops? Tell him what will change, Rory Donovan."

"Some of it is already the law in this sorrowful year of 1695. As a Catholic, you cannot vote, cannot hold public office, cannot own a horse worth anything much, cannot buy or inherit land from a Protestant, cannot build a stone church, or teach school or possess a firearm. There's more, but that's the heart of it."

"But this is our land! It's not fair!" Conor shouted.

"Of course it's not fair. And yet their army defeated our army, as a side issue in a religious dispute. Now they bleed this land with impunity."

"But we have to do something," the boy muttered, scowling at the men. They glanced at each other and Sean nodded.

"We will," he said. "We will annoy them and make their occupation of this land as expensive as we can, in the hope they will relent. For Rory and me the time is ending for us to act as rebels and for you it has not yet begun. So we can still teach you how to resist, mind, body, and spirit."

Conor glared at him, blue eyes shedding ice behind the cascade of black hair. "You'll not find mind or spirit lacking, but the body needs help with weaponry."

Sean stood, his eyes bringing Rory to his feet, and Conor, too. "Follow me," he said, moving north along the waterfront. "This is where the City of Galway was founded, here where the River Corrib enters the bay. The city has moved inland along the river, and now the bank is much the same as in ancient days."

They came to a place where a horseshoe-shaped sand dune stood about six feet high, with its open side facing the distant city wall. "What is this place?" Conor asked. "An old pen for animals?"

"This is an outdoor classroom," Sean said, unwrapping his cloth-covered staff. He tugged at one end of the staff and a bow slid out of the cavity that ran the length of the pole. "And this," he said with a flourish, "is what you will study." Sean reached into his pouch, came out with a string, bent the bow and attached the string to notches in either end. He touched the string and it thrummed.

"May I touch it?" the boy asked, his eyes open wide.

"Aye," Sean replied, grinning. "It's yours once you prove you can care for it."

"What about arrows?" Conor asked, itching to get his hands on the weapon that looked to him more like art than arms.

"Soon enough," Rory said. *I told Sean this boy has energy and focus, and Conor is proving me right.*

Sean stood beside Conor and issued instructions. "Here, put this leather pad on your left arm, from the wrist up. It will keep the string from scraping your skin. Now, you put your body into the bow. Push it away from you with your left. You hold the arrow in place with your right, just like this. Here, try it."

Conor examined the arrow, a metal tip on one end, and a notch for the bowstring on the other end, behind three feathers. They were bound and glued to the shaft. He touched one. "What kind of feather is this?"

"It is from a wild goose," Sean answered, as the crinkles grew around his eyes. "Maybe that's fitting, since the common people are now calling your father one of the Wild Geese, the Irish nobility expelled by the English after their resistance collapsed a few years back. I almost went with them."

"Why didn't you?" Conor asked.

"Because I can't resist the English in Ireland from France."

Rory went to the closed end of the U-shaped earthen berm and fastened a white sheet to the end wall, so the black circle in the middle of it was visible. Then he walked twenty paces back toward the others and drew a line in the gravel.

"Try it from here," he said.

Conor held the bow in one hand and the arrow in the other. "I have watched men shoot," he said. "Sometimes there is a contest near the market." He looked at Sean and grinned. "But I never noticed which side of the bow the arrow goes on."

"Do not be flustered," Sean said, crinkling up again. "Right hand, right side of the bow. For the left hand, use the left side. And you will never forget that."

I have put this off long enough. Maybe I will look foolish, but Rory says I have done that before. All right, now. He pushed the bow away with his left hand, held the arrow near his ear with the right, and released it. It fluttered through the air and skidded along the ground, nowhere near the target.

Conor's face reddened as he kicked the dirt. "Made a bollocks of that, right?"

Rory shook his head gently. "Conor, you can only curse when a shot fails to meet your goals. Since you don't have any goals yet, don't curse. Just shoot."

He shot until his arms were sore, glad to have the protector on his wrist. The results were better, not with each shot, but measured over what he thought was a very long hour. *This is discouraging. I know what should happen but it doesn't.*

How does anyone ever learn this thing? The dejection must have shown.

"Whisht, lad," Sean said. "We all remember our first shots, and our first disbelief when the arrow would not fly true. Men practice a lifetime to become good archers and eventually you will be one. Not the Robin Hood of English legend but good enough to gain respect. For now, gather up the arrows and then off with ye to Ceann Mhara. I will visit to see how you are faring."

Conor walked about picking up stray arrows. He turned a corner in the berm and was startled by a boy of his own age who held two more arrows in his hand.

"If you would paint King William's head on the target," the boy said with a grin, "then you would shoot straighter."

"Aye, I will try that," Conor said. "Iss misha Conor. Conas a ta tu?"

"Ta me go maith. Ish me Ronan, Ronan O'Malley. My people have fished these waters since Brian Boru was a puppy."

"That's a long time," Conor said. "Speaking of puppies, who's this?" He pointed to a red and white hound wagging his tail and half his body at Conor.

"This is Sea Dog. He crews with me. He's in charge of rat control on my uncles's lugger, the *Moira*." Ronan shrugged. "The Claddagh has always sheltered men of the sea. If you have time I will show you our boats, boats we call *Gleoiteog* for their beauty."

"Ronan and I are off to the port, Rory. I'll see you at the tavern in an hour."

Rory waved and the two men watched the boys walk toward where the bare masts of the fishing fleet swayed to a tune called by wavelets in the shallow water.

"The boy Ronan shows promise," Sean said. "And I suspect your Conor is too busy most of his days to grow many friendships."

"That is true, my friend. And it will be good for him to learn of an entirely different kind of Irish life thriving along this shore."

On a sunny day in July of 1696 Deirdre O'Canavan pulled Rory aside. "D'ye know aught of those boys who are always clotting my door? And is it safe for my Conor to play among them?"

"Aye, lady, it is," he answered. "I've been watching since he first met those lads five years ago. If he's to be a leader, he must lead, and they are his first command, at fourteen. Just consider it another form of warrior training. A man either has or has not the ability to persuade his friends that what he wants of them is what they ought to do, aye, what they want to do. And Conor can already do that without even knowing it." Rory stopped and rubbed his throat. The woman smiled and went inside for a mug of stout.

"Ah, the soul shouts its thanks," he said, after putting a serious dent in the pint. "I can tell you the day after we got back from archery training in Galway one of the lads suggested they all scout through the woods and pretend they were the legendary Fianna. Nobody thought that was a good idea. And then twenty minutes later Conor stood up and said, 'Come, my warriors. Let us hunt the boar in the forest.' The young O'Brien got to his feet and said, 'Your warriors? Do you then claim to be Fionn Mac Cumhaill?' Your clever son said, 'No, I am Oisin. Now, let's be off. The woods await!' And off they charged, six or eight of them waving sticks and pretending they knew the ancient Fianna war cry."

He stopped for another assault on the mug and a cheek-wrinkling grin. "Of course Conor had to rush out front and lead the way. And this very morning one of them called him Oisin, who was the Fianna's war leader. It's straight out of legend, lady, but when a leader can get men to do his bidding on an idea that has just been rejected, the art of command is at work, and he will show it again."

"So he's growing properly then, inside and out?"

This time there was pride in Rory's smile. "Aye, he is. The lad has been under my wing for five years now, and he's beginning to stretch his own wings, as he should. After a very few more years he will be as well launched as I can manage."

"And it's quite well you've done for him and for yourself, Rory, so it is. You have been taller and leaner, as if stretching to set him an example."

"Aye, and at my age 'tis an effort, lady, an effort indeed." He drained the mug and set it down with a loud, satisfied, "Ahh."

3

Sinead

In the summer of 1697 Teagan Dearg Ni Moran was fourteen years old, leggy and coltish. She had a light sprinkling of freckles across a nose that stopped just short of turning upwards, and a few more across her hands and arms. Her teeth were white and straight, and she had a sunny smile. But it was still her hair that drew the first glance and usually the second. It was the brightest shade of red anyone in Doolin had ever seen, and the sea breeze would not leave it alone. She was quite simply no longer the ten year-old child whose hair and eyes had so captured Arthur Bailey when he was thirteen.

At seventeen Arthur was still infatuated. He would ride into Doolin and trot up and down the main street in hopes of seeing her on some errand. Once he cornered her near the Boyle cottage, where Teagan had gone to ask if Patrick could help Malachi with some chore.

"You know you are my destiny," he said, and blocked her way with his horse. "You shall be the first harvest of my lordship over Doolin. You should be flattered. Let me see that nice smile, and take a deep breath while you're at it."

"I'll do no such thing, you overgrown rodent." *He wants to see my bodice rise when I breathe. He's leering. He makes my skin crawl.* "Now out of my way."

Arthur Bailey did not want to move, but his horse skittered aside

15

when Sinead Boyle erupted from her kitchen door and jabbed him in the ribs. Arthur almost fell off.

"You stay away from my Teagan, you Sassenach snake," she yelled, bringing other women to their doors and then into the street. Three of them stood hands on hips and glared at young Bailey. The widow Boyle was just getting started.

"By the Saints and Powers, where do you think you get the right to come into our village and intimidate our people? I tell you right now, you will never have this girl, and if you haven't noticed this yet, you will. Red-haired Irish women are not sheep. Now, get your sick self gone before I take this broom and break it over your head. It's a wonder to me anyone would claim paternity over such a sorry specimen of man as you!"

Bailey reddened and kneed his horse. "Mark my words, old woman! I will not be thwarted by peasants. Never!"

The women closed in on Teagan, touching and murmuring. *This is almost as bad as being ogled by Arthur, but smile and thank them. It's not the time to tell Sinead I am not* her *Teagan, not while she's basking in the praise of her friends.*

Sinead Boyle just happened to visit the tavern one day while Malachi was down at the port helping to unload a shipment of Galway ale. "Good morning, child," she said with a warm smile. "Is there a half-pint of cheer perhaps cooling for me?" Teagan moved quickly to the tap and placed a glass under it. When the amber liquid filled it the girl took it to the widow Boyle. *She wants to talk to me again, probably about Patrick. She thinks I forget she sees Patrick and me as a "nice couple" and she's trying to train me for the role of Madam Boyle.*

"Sit with me, dear, and let's talk, shall we?" Sinead said. "I think you need to be more careful about how you dress and how you wander around the village alone. You're old enough to begin learning how to be a lady, not a tavern wench."

"Mother Boyle I am not a tavern wench!" Teagan felt real anger. "And my father has appointed no one to train me, not even you. I'm young but I am a free person. Now, would you like another? Yours is gone and you haven't yet told me I should marry Patrick."

"No, dear, I must run," the woman said, and moved heavily toward the door.

Malachi came in a minute later with young men carrying barrels of ale. "I saw the widow Boyle leaving. Is she still telling you how wonderful Patrick is?"

"We never got to that," Teagan said. "This time it was all about how I should be more lady-like." She shrugged and wrinkled her nose. "I let my hair loose," she said, a phrase they used when the Teagan Dearg temper flared. "I always know what's on her mind, maybe because it's always the same theme. I told her you had not appointed her to train me to be a proper wife. Papa, I think she has eaten Patrick's spirit. She'll not get mine, no matter how hard she tries."

Red Teagan Moran walked out of the village of Doolin every day or so when the weather permitted, tasting the salt-flavored air and trying to whistle the songs of the seabirds. Slowly she learned the landscape and saw the Atlantic kiss the rim of County Clare, sometimes with passion and sometimes with tenderness.

One day she found a special place north of the village. The Burren's network of underground streams came to the surface here and there. This one formed a pond where it emerged. Cool water rippled under a light breeze in the midday sun.

Teagan took off her shoes and wiggled her toes in the water. Then she had a better idea. Looking carefully around her, she took off her clothes and sank into the pond. *Ooh, cold, but so refreshing.* She waded out until the water covered her neck and then kicked back to the edge. *It's so magical. I'll keep this a secret, and when I find a man to marry, I'll bring him here.*

4

Eamon

In a land where free-swimming salmon were royal property and deer were forbidden to common men, a lot of royal creatures went missing, a few at a time. When he was fifteen, Conor watched the trial of a man who had shot a deer with one of the forbidden muskets. Clearly he'd been beaten before coming to the dock, and the prosecutor tried to make his life forfeit. Instead Eamon O'Shaughnessy was given twenty lashes and fined a year's pay. That was excessive, Conor thought, because the man had no work and had been beaten into such a ruin he could do no work. Eventually O'Shaughnessy was released to the village, where he nearly died of neglect. On a chilly November night a week after the trial there was a knock on the man's door, such as it was, and a hooded stranger stood there, his face hidden.

"I have done nothing," O'Shaughnessy cried. "See, I can't possibly get into any more trouble. Just look at what they've left of me." He dragged one stiffened leg across the uneven floor.

"Do not mistake me," the voice within the hood said. "Just hold the door."

He stepped away and appeared again with a well-grown deer over his shoulders. He plopped it down on the rough plank table. "Do you know the dressing of such beasts?" the stranger asked, wiping some blood off his left arm with a cloth he found on the table.

"Aye, that I do, my lord. I was once a butcher."

"I am not your lord. He is much harder to see. Get about butchering then, Eamon, and show me how while you're at it." He threw back his hood and the cripple gasped.

"But I know you, you're the boy who trains with Rory the Warrior."

"Eamon let me explain about your eyes. You don't see me. You haven't seen me since your arrest. And tomorrow you still haven't seen me. Isn't that true?"

"Aye." Eamon touched the deer. "How long has this lovely beast been dead?"

Conor thought about that. "Perhaps an hour. They are not found close to the village except where the fruit trees grow."

Eamon let out a grin that gave his bruises exercise and shook his head. "Well do I know that, young Robin Hood."

Conor's head came up sharply. "Eamon, if you ever again call me an English name, you will never see another deer. If you must label me, call me Oisin."

Eamon tried not to smile; it still hurt. "The son of Fionn Mac Cumhaill? The one who lived three hundred years in a magic land without aging? That Oisin?"

"Do you know my own name, or am I just that boy who runs around the village?" There was silence while Eamon scuttled around for knives and cords.

"So. I too am the son of a famous father, but until my own fame glues my name to your tongue, just call me Oisin. Now, what shall we do with this buck?"

For the next two days, O'Shaughnessy hobbled around the village with small paper-wrapped packages. No one could believe he was offering venison. "Oisin gave it to me," the cripple said, staring through the disbelief on other faces. No one refused the meat.

"There's a rumor in the village," Rory told Conor on a rainy afternoon few days later. "They say the cripple O'Shaughnessy is giving out free venison to the poor of Kinvara. It's clear that he can't hunt, and he doesn't say he did. He says Oisin gave him the meat." Conor could see Rory's eyes crinkle. "Do you know aught of that, my lad?" Rory asked.

"The O'Shaughnessy are a big family in this parish, and they have vivid imaginations. But if Oisin is doing such a thing, it may be because it annoys the English. And annoying the English is more and more appealing these days."

5

Turlough

"These Penal Laws are killing us," Conor declared. "It's hard to be Irish if you have to speak English, and can't have a church or a school, and can't vote or do a lot of other normal things. Rory, you talked about this, you and Sean, when we went to Galway. I'm noticing more about how they control us, and it's getting more urgent for me to resist English oppression."

They sat in Seamus Hogan's tavern after another of the old soldier's lessons in arms. Rory smiled at his protege. "There's a man you should meet, lad. Perhaps he can teach you how to annoy the English without getting hanged."

"Iss misha Turlough." The man's gray hair leaked out from under an old wool cap. "People say you are the priest."

"Sometimes people say true things. I do not hide."

"You are forbidden to be a priest," Conor said. The man stopped cleaning a chicken coop and wiped his hands on a cloth that had been washed too long ago.

"Even discrimination has its rules, lad. I am a secular priest, not a Benedictine monk or a Franciscan. So by the rules that apply here I can say Mass, marry couples, and baptize their children. But I'm not supposed to record any of it."

Did he just wink? "But only the Church of Ireland is legal, not the Catholics."

Turlough O'Heyn sat down on a box and waved Conor to another seat. "I told you I know the rules. I was already here when Sir William French took over the castle and I went to see him. Once my own family held this lovely corner of Ireland, and Sir William knows we've been here a thousand years. He is a rational man and he knows almost nobody here shares his faith. Some of the earlier Frenches went Protestant just to keep these lands in the family. So, we are not enemies. I don't build stone churches, and he doesn't hunt me through the bracken."

Conor almost flinched as the priest wiped his face on his greasy rag. "Now we come to you, young O'Canavan. I have been watching you, some others and I. And I tell you this. You can annoy the English, to use the words you spoke to Rory, and still keep your contacts civil."

"How do I do that?" Conor wasn't sure he wanted to keep his contacts civil.

"What do you know of this crisis in the wool business?" O'Heyn asked, trading a question for a question.

"Wool?"

"It's politics, and you must keep up with it. Politics will define whether you can live under these people, or force them to kill you." *Hah. I have the boy's full attention now.*

"For generations the merchants of Galway have been in the wool trade," the older man continued. "Wool from flocks in Headford and Tuam, even from the Burren and the wilds of Connemara, it all goes through Galway on its way to the European market. But this year the English have banned wool exports from Galway to any market except England, because too many of the leading families of Galway have shown signs of discontent with London, including the Frenches. And so the English pay low prices for that wool, since there's no competition for the fleeces. Now does that suggest any course of action to you?"

He is testing me, trying to learn how I think.

"If I had a fresh shearing of wool, I would look for a better market."

"Ah, but this is an island, and there's only one buyer here."

Conor thought about that. *But boats are not island-bound. Boats and ships . . . Ronan! He has boats, or at least his family does. Those fishing boats can't go to Europe, but a ship can. And that's where I'll need Sir William. It might fit nicely.*

"The workings of your mind are all too visible on your face," Turlough said with a twinkle. "You must learn to shield your thoughts, although at sixteen, having thoughts is enough in itself. Now harvest those ideas for me."

Conor fidgeted, hoped the old man would not use that filthy rag again, and stalled to align his half-formed thoughts. "All right then. If I have a boat I can load it with fish or with wool. I know where to get a boat, for the right price. Now I need to get the word out to shepherds or their landlords. They can sell for higher prices through me. But to do that I need the indifference of the authorities, and in Kinvara that's Sir William French. Since he's being squeezed as well I can probably get it. Now the last thing is a foreign ship to lie up somewhere off the Connemara coast so a fishing boat can meet it there. That's as far as I've gotten." He looked up shyly.

"It's a start," the old priest said, "and a good one. But you must break the shackles of smallness. Schemes that fail usually do so for lack of reach rather than for lack of grasp. A foreign ship, say from France, would never come here for a fishing boat full of wool, which may not arrive while it's here. But if there were twenty fishing boats, or forty, that would be bait enough. Talk to Sir William French about attracting foreign ships. Talk to your friend in The Claddagh about boats and where they should pick up the wool. And seek restive men in the countryside who can take the wool to some hidden landing where the boats can load it."

Conor processed all that and grinned. "It will be nice to see some real money move from hand to hand among the poor people of this land."

"You can't sell, you must trade," Turlough O'Heyn said firmly. "Too much gold floating around will give the English yet another excuse to squeeze the Irish. Trade for goods that cannot be found here."

"Why are you guiding me to do things that would not occur to me?"

"Och, lad, 'tis a grand question. William French is English, and I have said we are not enemies nor are we close. As for the rest of the English, they are my foes and yours, and the foes of every man who yearns to guide his own life and worship his own God. I have vowed to harass the English intensely, and you are among my instruments."

Conor felt a scowl pinching his features together. "I am not in this for religious reasons, but because they banished my father and indirectly widowed my mother. I shall snap at them until I am strong enough to rebel, and then I shall take back my land."

This boy is fierce and a clear thinker, and when he grows into his anger he will be too dangerous for the English to tolerate. In the meantime, I can use him. This smuggling business will focus his energies, and there's a low risk of capture.

The old priest watched Conor walk away in a gust of wind-blown rain. *I think this venture will turn out well.*

6

Jeremiah

"It's been a good harvest in Doolin, Malachi, so it has. All the greens and most of the grains came in above my hopes. That's worth a second pint, my friend, all the more because Bailey has been pushing the Doonagore staff harder then ever." Jeremiah Danaher took a mighty swallow and grounded his empty mug.

"We have felt it as well here in the village," Malachi agreed. "The truth is, Jeremiah, the castle does not control enough land to make it a successful British holding out here on the edge of the world. That's why Bailey strives so hard. That and Arthur, the poor crazed heir. It's lucky he sent the boy to Dublin to try to make something of him. It's been easier for Teagan without him sniffing around her and drooling. And so, my friend, because things are not as bad as may be, we will toast the harvest, on the house. Tay! Two mugs of that good Dublin ale, please."

She brought the ale with a light step and a cheerful smile. Her bright hair was gathered in a single braid that fell across her right shoulder like a living rope.

"Teagan, you know Jeremiah Danaher, don't you?"

"Aye, you are the gardener of Doonagore. A warm welcome to you, sir." She turned with another smile and went back to the inn's kitchen.

"I have watched her grow up, Malachi, ever since her mother died," the old man said, lifting his mug toward the open kitchen door. " What is she now, sixteen? Seventeen? She was always pretty but now she's a true beauty, and that smile is like honey on a wheat cake."

"I can take no credit for that, my friend. But she's also a very nice young woman, and I hope I've had a hand in that part of her growth. Fathers always fret over daughters, you know." He breathed in the peat-scented air and sat back.

Danaher raised his mug to the innkeeper. "I don't know about that, truly I don't. I've never been graced with a child, let alone a girl child. But you have done well. What are you going to do when she leaves?"

"Leaves? What are you talking about?"

"Malachi, young girls marry, even those who are not as stunning as Teagan Dearg. She will attract every eligible young man in the west of Ireland, and quite a few ineligibles as well. You can't tie her here just because you need her."

Malachi shifted in his chair. "Jeremiah, you make the truth a discomfort, so you do. I shall not refuse the right man for Teagan, but who is that man? I look around. Patrick Boyle has no spine and there's no one else in the picture."

"Malachi, I am a gardener, not a prophet. But I need no special powers to know someday a man will come for Red Teagan. Who can say whether he'll be rogue or rascal or the prince that young girls find in their dreams."

By the time Teagan turned nineteen Malachi thought the old gardener's vision was flawed, that the girl would wither on the edge of the world. Men had come and gone through the tavern but no one got more than politeness from his daughter.

Sometime he winced when Teagan would make some sharp-tongued comment that rebuffed a would-be swain's efforts to charm her.

As he did frequently in quiet moments, Malachi Moran thought about his daughter. *It will take a strong man to win her and to keep her. She does not accept foolishness. It makes me wonder whenever someone new comes in for the first time. I'm not exactly brooding but most girls her age are married by now or at least betrothed. There she is serving up plates for Patrick and Sinead. I don't want her to spend her life doing that.*

Patrick has found work on the waterfront and seems to have an understanding of the shaping of stones. He's helping to improve the quay so visiting boats will be a bit less battered by the Atlantic waves when the west wind blows in.

Patrick Boyle, whose hair was rapidly turning white at age twenty-one, had been gone for about a half hour when the door opened and two young men came in carrying packs over their shoulders.

Overnighters. They'll need supper and a room. Oh, I know one of them.

"Welcome, young Rowan. Your father must be loosening your tether these days, to let you voyage alone. And who is this brawny lad?"

"It's Ronan, sir, my name is Ronan."

"Iss misha Conor Mac Cormac O'Canavan," Conor said.

"Ah, you're the one!" the man smiled. "Seamus Hogan sent me word of you, but I didn't think you'd be here yet."

"I borrowed a ride with Ronan and his good friend, Sea Dog." He saw confusion on Malachi's face. "Oh, Sea Dog is a dog, sir, one of Ronan's crew."

"Malachi, young Conor. Call me Malachi. Sir is a word reserved for pretentious Sassenachs, and I have no love for them. The two of you will stay the night, and I do not brag when I say the fare is fine here. Now, a pint for each of you." He waved them to a table and yelled into a back room. "Tay! Draw two pints for the lads, and quickly!"

The girl came out with a mug in each hand, not moving especially quickly. "Ah, here you are. You've seen Rowan before, and this is Conor."

"They stink," she declared.

Conor thought her comment was dismissive and it annoyed him. "We have been at sea, colleen, but tomorrow we shall smell like fresh-cut hay. And what about you, tomorrow? Will you still be snippy?"

"Iss misha Teagan. Teagan Ni Moran. And I don't care the weight of a mouse dropping whether you think I am snippy or not."

As she stood over the table, hands on hips, Conor saw the taproom's firelight reflecting off her bright hair.

"Oh," he said. "You have red hair and brown eyes." *Is she the one? Is this sharp-tongued girl to be the mother of my son, as my father predicted?*

"Congratulations," the girl was saying. "You may be smelly and stupid, but at least you can thank the Powers you are not blind."

Ignoring the girl, Conor turned to Ronan. "Is she always like this?"

"I've never noticed, but then I haven't been here for about a year. I don't even remember whether she was here back then. I think they call her Teagan Dearg because of her hair, or maybe it's her temper."

Red Teagan stamped her foot and shook her hair. "You are beastly, talking about me as if I'm not here or invisible!"

"Invisible would be nice," Conor said with his most irritating grin. "Then we couldn't see you. Does it mean we couldn't hear you? What a blessing that would be."

"I will serve him," Teagan said, her voice and her color rising as she pointed at Ronan. "But you come swaggering in here like the lord of Doonagore. You will starve before I bring you so much as a crust of bread. And when the harper comes tonight, I will ask him to play you his harshest insult song. And I will smile while he ridicules you. And . . ." She broke off and fled into the kitchen. *Oh, why did I let that man get me so flustered? He's just another stranger in the inn. But he does have a nice smile, and his hair sometimes falls in front of those very blue eyes, and his hands look strong. His ears, I didn't even notice his ears, and usually I do. I'm so ruffled! It's just not like me, and I scarcely noticed the other one at all.*

Ronan clapped his hands when she'd gone. "You are smitten, my man, and so is she. Even I can see that."

"Not so, Ronan. Your mind is drowning in your ale, so it is. She is a redheaded shrew, and I'll have naught to do with her. Nothing. Do you hear me? And no smirking."

Malachi Moran wiped an invisible spot off his bar and looked at the doorway his daughter had stormed through. There was a small smile on his face.

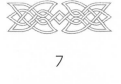

7

CONOR

CONOR O'CANAVAN slept poorly on the night of his arrival in Doolin. The redhead's pretty face would burst the peace of his slumber and change his heart rate. He saw the wicked smile she had shown him while the bard sang of how wretched a man he was. Conor tried in his sleep to envision that smile ignited by joy but failed. Earlier than he had planned he was up and outside to wash his face in the water bucket by the well.

Wind from the west. I hope Ronan and Liam will have an easy passage out of the harbor. Och, it's early to rise to stay ahead of the summer sun. There it comes, slanting up the sky north of that tower, Doonagore. And Red Teagan said I came swaggering in like the lord of Doonagore. Teagan said. Red Teagan smiled. Teagan Dearg swirled her hair. Teagan stamped her foot. Come on Conor, clear your mind.

The tavern door opened behind him and Teagan came out. She held a bucket of dirty water and sloshed it out before she noticed Conor. "I missed," she said, with yet another variation on her trove of impudent grins. She went back inside and slammed the heavy door behind her.

When he went through that door a few minutes later Malachi Moran was in the taproom laying out a quick meal for Ronan, who wanted to catch the early tide.

"I fear I leave you in mortal peril, my friend," the young fisherman said.

"I am not aware of any enemies here," Conor said.

Ronan smiled. "It's not enemies, my man, but rather more subtle attachments."

"What are you talking about?" Conor asked. "You make no sense."

"This morning you wouldn't know sense if it were a club," Ronan said with a grin. "Walk me down to the quay and see me off. At least one of us can escape the trap." He clapped Conor on the shoulder, leaving the new exile with a frown. *What in the name of Brian Boru is wrong with him today? He's babbling nonsense.*

The wind had backed off a few points toward the southwest, perfect for the departing lugger as Conor pushed it away from the quay. He watched as the sails slid up the mast and shook in the breeze until Ronan brought them taut to the wind.

This is hard to watch. It's like when Mother and I stood on the quay in Galway, and watched my father and his ship getting ever smaller.

It was everything normal being slowly drawn away from me and today is the same. I know I will see Ronan again, since we have so much wool smuggling to do in the spring. Besides, he's really a good friend. But here I am alone and on my own. Don't like this part of it. Maybe separation and solitude are the real price of exile. Come on, Conor.

Think ahead. What's behind is not going to change, and what's ahead can still be bent to a shape that pleases me. A shape that pleases me. Why do those words bring Red Teagan to mind? And why is my mind such a cluttered place today? Breathe the good sea air, Conor, and think about your future. Ignore Red Teagan.

◆ ◆ ◆

Less than a mile away the iron gate of Doonagore Castle squeaked open and two men left the little fortress on the path to Doolin.

"Consider it a scouting trip, Thomas," the younger one said.

"Call it whatever you will, young sir. You just want to see that girl again."

"Ah, Thomas, she is so bonny. She'll be the central gem in my collection."

"Arthur, you can't have women in bundles. And slow down a bit. Don't blunder your way into another misadventure. Your father's not here to fix it."

"But you are. It's why my father hired you, Thomas. He told me that we English are in charge here by right of conquest, and in the natural order of things that means as overlord in Doolin I can claim whatever little treasures there may be. And so destiny gives me the girl. I need only claim her. My father said so."

Back from the harbor, Conor opened the brightly painted tavern door. *Doesn't Malachi ever leave this room?*

"Ho, young Conor. Is your friend safely away?"

"Aye, that he is, and on a breeze blowing fair toward his destination." He sat down at the table. "I wish my own course were as clear, so I do."

"Aye, lad, we must fashion a future for you. Now, what skills do you have that may earn you your food and shelter?"

Conor shrugged. "I've been making a list, but it's a short one. I am a semi-trained warrior in a land where the last uprising was so long ago it fades from the memories of old men. I have some skills as a fisherman, fewer as a sailor or navigator, and socially I am a large and clumsy puppy. That sums it up. There's not much in my treasure chest."

"Don't scoff at yourself, lad. You have energy and brains and a healthy body.

Many a man has made much with less. And as for the warrior part, the absence of battle is not peace. They push us hard here on the coast and in the Burren proper too, though the visible blessings of this land are not abundant. An English commander sent here to put down an uprising fifty years ago wrote back to London that the Burren is a country where there's not enough water to drown a man, nor wood to hang him, nor earth to bury him."

Malachi laughed at his borrowed words and Conor joined in, mostly out of politeness. *I'll need somebody to have conversations with now that Ronan is gone, and it's surely not going to be that Teagan.*

The innkeeper was still talking. "The point is that the Burren is no Garden of Eden, but nor is it the stone desert it's been called by the English. When the limestone dissolves and dirt forms in the cracks, it's rich enough to grow a good livestock fodder."

"I still don't see how I can stay here in Doolin," Conor said. "I have no skills in the managing of beasts."

Malachi started to answer but stopped when the door slammed open. Conor saw a tall young man stride in, followed by another, who appeared to be a servant. The youth pulled off a cloak with a swirling motion and dropped it on a chair.

"Ale, wench," he shouted toward the back room. "Ale for two." The pair sat at the other end of the table where Conor and Malachi were talking.

"It is early for ale," Malachi said.

"Ale I have ordered, and ale I will have. And we need this table," the leader said.

Conor stared at him and did not move.

"You may use that end of it," he said. "But this end is not yours to claim."

The newcomer spoke coldly. "I claim what I want, and I get it. When this land is mine I will teach you peasants how to honor the gentry. Thomas," he called and snapped his fingers. "Throw this lout out, preferably into a mud puddle."

Conor stood up. "Malachi, your village has a pimple. Does it have a name?"

"He is Arthur Bailey, and his father is lord of Doonagore Castle, and landlord of almost every holding in this parish."

"He is a churlish oaf," Conor decided. He waved a dismissive hand at the far end of the table. "Young man," he added for emphasis. "I do not like you."

"Careful, lad," Malachi Moran said, his brow wrinkled. "He has no humor. And the man Thomas, here, is his protector."

"I suspect his job keeps him busy, if his master lurches about as a habit."

"Innkeeper! Who is this peasant who dares be so impudent to his betters?"

Conor took a close look at the youth who was acting as if he were the King of England. He saw blue eyes set too close together under a thatch of untended sandy hair, and a nose and chin sadly out of balance on his face.

"I answer for myself, Sassenach," Conor said with a smile untouched by mirth. "Iss misha Conor Mac Cormac O'Canavan, and as to whether you are my better, Celt and Saxon have been contesting that for seven hundred years." He watched Teagan approach the table timidly with two mugs of ale. *She's afraid of this creature. I wonder why.* "Thomas," Conor said. "Sit and enjoy your quaff. You're not well enough armed to carry out your master's orders."

"I expect a smile with my service," Arthur Bailey said, putting a hand on Teagan's arm. She jerked free, and some ale splashed into the man's lap. Bailey sprang up cursing and stepped over his chair, an arm raised to strike her.

Conor stood between them. "The spill was your own fault," he said quietly. "Now, pick up your chair and sit back down."

"Nobody tells me what to do!" Bailey shouted.

"That's obvious, and a shame it is. And an apology would be nice. Thomas, is it your duty to train this puppy as well as to protect him? You must need your position."

"Aye, I do. And some days are harder than others." He stood next to Arthur Bailey and put a hand on his shoulder. "If this gets out of hand I cannot be sure you will be safe. This young man is no peasant, and he moves like a warrior. I cannot bring you home damaged, and if there's a fight all of Doolin will stop paying rent again. The last time it took years to restore order, and lives were lost. A dram of spilt ale must not start another uprising. We should just leave now."

Something in his voice got through to the young hothead. "But I'm not paying for the ale. And as for you, papist heathen, I will have my revenge, you will see."

"I have not touched you, rodent. If I had you would leave here on a litter. So no revenge is due you, since you have not been wronged. Besides a man cannot be papist and heathen at the same time. Listen to your man Thomas and just go away. He is wiser than you know."

"But don't you see?" Bailey asked. "God made the Irish to bend to the will of the English. My father told me so."

With Thomas guiding his arm, Arthur Bailey left the tavern. After four paces he stopped and shook his fist. "I will burn this house and all within!"

Inside, Malachi Moran sat down heavily at the table, laughing.

"What? Am I missing some joke?" Conor sat down too, as his anger receded.

"You said you have no skills in the managing of beasts," Malachi said, wiping his eyes. "You have just proven that you do indeed have those abilities. Teagan! Perhaps it's not too early for ale after all."

She came quickly with two pints and sat when her father pointed to a seat. "Teagan, you fear that wastrel. Why?" Conor asked, locking eyes with her. "I do not wish to say." She dropped her eyes to the hands in her lap.

"You must."

"Conor, do not tell me what I must do," she snapped.

"Daughter, the man has threatened to burn down the tavern and us within it. I take that seriously and so does Conor. We must know what drives his rage."

The girl avoided her father's eyes but looked into Conor's. "It's about me. He says I am exotic, and he wants to know me better. For the past year he has been touching me, breast and buttocks, when I serve him and my father is not in the room. I hate it. And he's never clean." Her hands rose to cover her face.

Malachi leaned toward his daughter and spoke softly. "This has been going on for a year? Why have you never told me?"

"I was ashamed. And he is powerful."

"He is nothing," Conor said. "His father has power but there is a limit to it. And I tell you this." He waited until those eyes sought out his. "That man will never again lay his hand upon you. Never. That's my promise."

The girl watched and listened, sitting absolutely still. After a moment she got up from the table. "I may have to change my mind about you, rover." She walked around the chairs, bent over and kissed him on the cheek as her fire-colored hair whisked across his face and left another redness there. He didn't even notice his blush as she took his empty mug to the back room.

"We get flies in here sometimes, boy. Close your mouth." Malachi's command was softened by a big smile.

"A long time ago," Conor said, and tried to switch the talk to a new track. He cleared his throat and started again. "A long time ago, we were talking about what I might do here in Doolin for the next five years. That is, beyond accepting the occasional kiss on the cheek from Teagan."

"Lock that moment into your memory, Conor," the girl said, plunking a full mug down in front of him. "It might not happen again."

She tossed her hair and went back to the other room. Conor looked puzzled, and Malachi smiled again, clearly enjoying the younger man's confusion. "You're about to say you can't make sense of the lass," he said. "She wants it that way. If she didn't like you there would be no doubt. I think all women learn this kind of behavior when they're very young. We men never learn to unlock the mysteries of the female mind, but they are nice to have around. I miss her mother every day."

"What happened to her?" Conor asked.

"It was some kind of illness," Malachi said with a shrug. "I don't even know if it has a name. One day my Kate was vibrant and happy. The next day she was tired, and on the third day she was sick. Three weeks later I wept over her grave. Teagan was ten years old and since then it has been her and me against the world. Mostly we've been all right, or so I thought until this morning. I'm not sure I'm ready to be father to a grown girl."

"I think you're doing very well," Conor said. "She's smart and she's very pretty, when her temper allows. Now, can we figure out a future for me here?"

"Surely, lad. I'm going to send you down to the port, and you will ask for White Patrick Boyle. He's leading an effort to extend the breakwater to block some of the worst of the Atlantic waves. It will help protect the boats tied up at the quay. He will need help. He expects you, and I've said you could be a useful pair of hands. Can you swim?" Conor nodded.

"Better yet," Moran said. "And after this morning, I've decided that you can be more than just a strong back in whatever you undertake."

◆ ◆ ◆

Over the following weeks Conor went from confusion to soreness to confidence as his body and mind got used to the work and to the concept behind it. The newest stone-worker saw the benefit of the small rocky island that lay just offshore: how it blocked some of the wind and helped keep the Atlantic surge out of the port.

He cut the inn's firewood into cubes and used them to teach himself how the stone blocks in the harbor were fitted to reduce the waves that battered the quay when the wind blew hard from the Aran Islands.

"See, Teagan? It works this way," he'd say, exercising his new enthusiasm.

"I see," she'd say, not quite following the demonstration. *But I like the way his face lights up. It's a nice face. Sometimes his eyes capture mine and it's hard to look away. And sometimes I can almost sense what he's thinking before he speaks. How does that happen? It doesn't with my father or with anyone else.*

"Stone is the symbol of true civilizations," Malachi said one night. "Ireland is old, my young friend, very old. How do we know that? Our island is dotted with stone structures, graves and forts that may be older than the ancient wonders of the world." He let that sink in and sipped more ale. "In fact, one of them is right over there on Inishmor. It's called Dun Aonghasa, and it's a cliff fort, huddled right against the top of a three hundred-foot sheer drop to the sea."

"I would truly like to see such a place," Conor said with a sleepy fuzziness in his voice. "But not tonight."

"Tomorrow then. It's Sunday and there's no work on the sea wall. I know a man who's sailing to Inishmor, and he will find room for two more."

"Three more," Conor said. "I said Arthur Bailey would never again put a hand on Teagan." He turned and captured those eyes with his. "And I can't keep that promise if I leave you here with that animal prowling about."

Teagan's face reddened again. "You don't have to do that."

He produced that grin that annoyed her as often as it intrigued her. "Teagan, don't you know what a promise means? It means that as long as that man is a threat, you are under my protection. And we'll speak no more of it."

The girl stood up suddenly, hands on hips. "You don't own me, young O'Canavan.

So don't try to tell me what I can speak of!"

She looks so beautiful when she's angry and her eyes flash like that. Wouldn't it be terrible if that were her normal mood, if she were always angry?

Malachi Moran moved to ease the tension. "Teagan, don't let your hair loose." She tried to look contrite. "Now skip down to Mother Boyle and ask if she can spare Whitey to mind the inn tomorrow and Monday. She'll agree, I think, mostly to get him out of the house. Whitey considers Sunday a day of rest, but I'll wager he won't mind resting with a pint of ale wrapped in those great paws of his."

That night Teagan put herself to sleep imagining romantic variations on an excursion with Conor. In one dream he was an armored knight on a white horse who slew the dragon that menaced her. She woke up wondering why the dragon's name was Arthur.

8

Dun Aonghasa

The boat danced across bumpy blue water toward the Aran Islands and Conor noticed that he liked the motion better than ever. *And look at Teagan, sniffing at the air like a prettier Sea Dog. Much prettier. Redder hair. Better smile.*

The dent in the shoreline that was Doolin receded. South of the village the vertical Cliffs of Moher rose hundreds of feet over roiling surf on the port side. Ahead lay the islands, rocky outcroppings akin to the limestone waste of the Burren, and lightly populated. *We'll pass north of the first two and make for the main port, the village of Kilronan.*

There was another stone quay like the one in Doolin, but longer. Conor noticed how well the stones were fitted. *Until a month ago, I would never notice such a basic thing as a harbor wall. I can see a lot of it now at low tide.*

"Conor!" The captain shouted. "Heave the line to Tobin there in the blue shirt!

Toby!" He called even louder. "Here comes the mooring line! Throw, boy!"

Conor did, landing the weighted line just in front of where Tobin waited. He watched as the man snugged the line two turns around a bollard and hauled in the slack as the boat eased closer. Conor put out the bumpers and turned to help Tay up the vertical iron ladder, but she was already above him, leaning down with that smile. Conor tossed up the sacks and packs that held their fresh clothes and scrambled to the paving stones. They connected the quay to Kilronan's best pretense at a road, a cart track that led to the left around the harbor to the village square.

"There's an inn just there," Malachi said and pointed toward a thatch and stone building that overlooked the harbor.

"Malachi, you old thief!" A man shouted when they were still fifty yards away. "I keep hearing how you cheat the innocent into paying full fare for room and board at that malodorous sty you've got in Doolin. But here, as you can see, even the most refined of my guests sing praises of the service and the rooms."

"Finbar, your bragging embarrasses even you. I'll have two rooms for tonight, please. The lass here is too old to sleep with her father and too young to sleep with this unpolished youth, who is not yet her husband."

Conor was shocked. *Husband! Where did that come from? We are simply on a sightseeing trip together.* He glanced at Teagan and saw her give her father an incredulous glare, and noted a fresh redness not explained by the sea air. *I'll have to learn to read those changes in her face, but the keys seem very complicated.*

Teagan would not look at him. *I've never been so embarrassed. What must he think? What was my father thinking? He's just an ordinary young man, and a stranger at that. But he does have a way about him. And he has confidence and a very nice smile.*

Down, girl, your imagination is boiling over. Again.

The trip to Dun Aonghasa began only after a heated discussion about the fare for a round trip. All the villagers who were not busy joined in the haggling, and that seemed to Teagan to be most of them. *A lot of these men are just here to stir the soup. This is the best entertainment they've had this week. Suppose Papa just steps back and asks if anyone else wants the work?*

The bargaining ended when Malachi offered a pint of ale for each leg of the trip, collectable at the village tavern upon their return. It took the pony cart less than an hour to reach the foot of the hill that led to the Dun Aonghasa fortress.

"The road ends here," the driver said, pulling needlessly on the reins. The horse had already stopped where he always stopped on such trips, and Conor gave him a pat on the neck. *Good thing you know your way, little horse. Your master was so charmed by Teagan he never gave you a single command in the entire seven miles of this jaunt. She was a sight though, red hair tossing in the sea-scented wind, and brown eyes flashing.*

She's captured that man completely. Conor, you know the bait she uses, protect yourself. Aye, but do I want to protect myself?

He watched as Malachi and the driver shrugged through a rough cloth at the front of a hut. *I'm sure there's ale for sale inside, and those two are telling each other how hard the trip here has been, and how much they need a restorative.*

A wind-stunted tree grew where the path to the fortress began, and under it an even more distorted bush clung to a space between rocks. The bush was twitching and Conor was fascinated. *Every few seconds a leaf trembles in the still air. I used to think the* sidhe *were teasing those leaves; the Little People making them jump. My grandmother said that's not true, but it's a lovely thought anyway.*

"Look, Teagan, the leaves on that bush. See how they wiggle and jump when the wee people tickle them!"

"Och, it's daft ye be, young Conor. It's raining is all, and the raindrops fall from the tree to the bush, so they do. Besides, there are no wee people, and well ye know it." She ended with a toss of her hair and a dismissive smile.

"No little people!" Conor gasped. "But men see them all the time, leprechauns and pookies. Our stories are full of them."

"Hah!" she said, thrusting a practical mind between Conor and his legends. "Old men see the wee people all right, and lovely visions they are. Most of those sights occur when those men leave my father's pub. Wait here while I fetch him."

She turned, smiled the rebuke out of her response, and went inside.

She doesn't seem to have any magic in her vision. If my own mind were so tightly bound to facts, would I ever have become the man I am? And doesn't every Irishman believe at least a little in the unseen?

The girl was soon back, her step lighter than ever, and her face caught in some middle ground between sulk and smile.

"What's wrong?" he asked, again unable to interpret her face.

"Nothing," she said, her features still in careful balance. "My father says he'll not be going up there. He says he's seen those stones before, and the ale here is better and cheaper than he recalled." She stopped and twinkled at him. "We may have to pour him into the cart on the way back, and aye, into the boat as well."

"Do you still want to go, unescorted?"

"Do you think you frighten me, refugee?" The pout was gone, wiped out by a teasing grin. She stepped out on the path, her eyes flashing back in challenge.

Conor was stunned. He'd thought his question reflected only his concern for Teagan's honor. But it seemed clear she hadn't heard it that way.

The land rose gently but not smoothly. Their path was barely more passable than the rock-strewn landscape on either side. Here and there sheep harvested greenery from where cracks between the limestone slabs held a little soil.

"Teagan, why don't the sheep eat the flowers?" He pointed to a sprinkling of purple blooms that accented the grayness of the ground.

"Maybe they don't taste good," she chirped. Conor tried to figure out whether her smile was appealing or annoying. *The wind dances with her hair and the rain has stopped. A patch of blue sky pours sunlight onto the sea, and here I am adventuring with the prettiest girl I've ever seen. What could be better?* Conor looked for the skylark exulting above but could not see it.

The long-deserted fortress loomed ahead, its bulk hiding whatever might lie beyond the modest little tunnel that pierced the inner wall and controlled access. Teagan led the way into Dun Aenghosa's central refuge. Thick stone walls rose in a curve on three sides of the structure, the land-facing sides. The enclosed grassy area measured fifty yards at the ends of the arc and thirty yards from the gateway to air. Only space defended the fourth side of the ancient fortress.

Teagan ran to the unprotected edge and peered down to where the Atlantic waves battered at the sheer cliff almost three hundred feet below. Conor, terrified, charged after her and snatched her away from the rim.

"What are you doing?" she demanded and struggled in his grasp.

"Saving you! If you should get dizzy and fall into the sea, what would I do?"

"You mean how would you tell my father you lost his only child?"

"No," he said, moving the arms that held her. *Her eyes are so deep and her skin so clear. And her lips . . .* The kiss intensified when Teagan put both arms around his neck and pulled herself in until there was no space between them. *She is so warm and soft. Can I breathe and still do this? Yes! Her eyes are closed. Her hair washes my face. Why can't I hear the surf or the wind or the birds? Just the thumping of my heart, a little like hard exercise but so much different.*

At some point Teagan broke the kiss, put both hands on his cheeks, and kissed him again, lightly, on the nose. She stepped away with a smile and skipped up a flight of stone stairs built into the massive wall. She reached back for him from a ledge once used by the fort's defenders. "Come," she called. "We rule here, let us survey our domain." Conor stood behind her on the rampart, his hands stretched out to cover hers where they rested on the top course of stones. Teagan leaned back and tucked her head into the curve where his neck and shoulder met.

"It all changes now," he breathed as the wind pulled her hair across his lips.

"Nothing changes," she said, snuggling closer. "I knew I would kiss you up here when my father said he'd stay below. I didn't know it would be so powerful."

"Powerful indeed," he said, and tightened his arms around her. "You literally took my breath away. May I have it back now?"

"Yes," she whispered, and then tensed in his arms. *What just happened?*

"If you were not so man-stupid you would already know everything I am or ever will be is yours. What do you think that kiss was, some game? I was pledging you my whole self, soul and body. This body!" She grabbed his hand and held it to her breast, and he could feel her heart pumping through the fabric of her bodice.

"You shall have all of me, and soon," she said, turning again to look over the wall. "But not here. I know another magical place to give you the gift of me."

"You told me you decided to kiss me before we came up here. But I was the one who kissed you."

"Hold that notion until you're old; it's a harmless illusion." Conor didn't know what to say so he nudged her hair away from her neck and kissed the bare skin he'd exposed. That seemed to work. She sighed and melted even closer.

"See?" she asked, freeing one hand and pointing. "There's that poor

horse, waiting down there in front of that hut where the ale is flowing. And way beyond is the second island, Inishmaan, and the little one,
Inisheer and the Cliffs of Moher. And somewhere to the left is Doolin,
about where that smoke is rising." Conor was lost in the geography of
Teagan, and ignored her words. He felt her body move with her breathing
and cherished the intimacy of that contact.

"I wonder what's burning?" she asked idly and felt Conor tense
behind her.

"That Bailey said he would burn the tavern and all within it. Do you
suppose . . . ?" He stopped when he saw the fear in her face.

"We have to get back!" she shouted.

"Tay, listen. It will take hours to get there, maybe until dark. And if it
is the inn it's beyond our help, right this minute. Besides, we're not sure
that's what's burning. But aye, let's go down and sail back to Doolin. Now
take a last look at your domain. It may be a while before we can revisit
this magical place."

There was urgency in their descent from Dun Aonghasa. On the way
they agreed to keep from her father their fears for the inn and to avoid
telling him about their discovery of each other.

"I think he has a strong heart," Teagan said. "But let us not test it today."
It took them both to get a recumbent Malachi into the cart, and the driver
needed some help too. Conor twitched the reins. "Go home, horse."

The little horse whuffled and shook his head as if he had seen such
things before. He made a wide turn in front of the ale hut and trotted
down the track toward Kilronan. During the ride Conor and Teagan
invented new ways to communicate with handholding and soulful stares.
*I thought her eyes were brown but there are flecks of gold deep inside. I never
saw that before. Maybe it's because I'm seeing her in a way I never did before.*

"You won't be able to see if the inn is safe until we walk there from the
quay," he cautioned Teagan, sensing her tension on the long sail back
to Doolin.

"I know," she said, giving his hand a squeeze. "It's just that going back
seems to take so much longer than the run out to Inishmor."

"Tay, it's not just that you're anxious. The wind is blowing from the
Burren into our faces and so it takes longer."

9

Tim

When the boat rounded the unfinished jetty and snugged into the quay Teagan knew they would be unable to keep their suspicions from Malachi. Gloom threw a dull sheen off the faces of an ad-hoc welcoming committee.

"Look," Conor whispered. "That man has a look on his face that says: 'Something bad has happened and you're going to hear it first from me.'"

"That's old Bad Tidings Tim Toomey," she answered. "He's Doolin's authority on calamities, probably been waiting here since the fire. Oh, Conor, this confirms all my fears. We have lost everything!"

"No, we have not," he asserted. "We have found each other, and even better, you were not here when whatever happened was done. Suppose we had not gone to the fortress? Here comes that Toomey, so full of himself. Let's go stand by your father."

Bad Tidings Toomey stepped up to greet them. The little man was wringing his hands and shifting from foot to foot. "Och, Malachi, Malachi! A dark day in Doolin it is, a dark day indeed. It's bad I feel for you and the lass, very bad, aye."

Malachi wished Tim Toomey would simply take his place alongside the other symptoms of a hangover but he knew that would not happen. "Tim, stop wailing and speak clearly, man. You're not making any sense, none!"

White Patrick Boyle spoke, his long face caught between sorrow and shame. "Malachi, I have failed you. You trusted me with your inn and now I have lost it."

"Whitey, what's all this?" Malachi demanded, anxiety raising his voice by an octave. To Teagan the seabirds, too, sounded more urgent as they swirled around the quay. Boyle raised his head and looked Malachi Moran in the eye.

"The three of you had been gone just a few hours when young Bailey burst into the pub with four armed friends. He shouted, 'Who are you?' I told him, and he drew a sword. 'Where is the girl, and the old man, and the young one who insulted me? I will have the girl and kill the man, and as for the old innkeeper, he will have to find other work. Now get out. I have no need to kill you, but you will burn if you stay in this hovel.' Malachi, the man had spit running down his chin. He wanted to be sure I would tell you what he said." White Patrick Boyle stopped and blinked into his memory. Teagan and Conor held up a stricken Malachi Moran.

"Then they held us outside at sword-point while Bailey set the tavern on fire. I tried to go inside to fight it, but one of those young hooligans ran the point of his sword into my shoulder." He slid out of a coat and exposed a bloody bandage.

"He laughed when the thatch caught fire, so he did, and he danced when the rafters collapsed in a cascade of sparks. As he and his friends were riding off he stopped and pointed his sword at me. 'I will kill the man,' he said again, and his eyes had a wild look. 'And I will have the girl, and have her and have her, and then I will share her with my friends until none of them wants her any more. I will not be thwarted by peasants,' he yelled, and they galloped off."

"White Patrick," Malachi said as his face struggled with what he'd heard. "I'm so sorry you're caught up in this. It's not your struggle, this evil thing. It's mine to fight."

"Ours," Conor said, his face as grim as Teagan had ever seen it. She reached for his hand and found it clenched into a fist. "Come, then," she said. "There's some hidden whiskey we may yet find. There's no reason to delay our inspection."

It was a solemn little procession up the path from the harbor to where the hamlet of Doolin sheltered from the Atlantic winds behind the shoulder of a hill. Solemn but for old Tim Toomey, who scuttled ahead so he'd be able to scan their faces on first sight of the still-smoking rubble.

"It's all gone. By the Saints and Powers, I am a ruined man!" Malachi wept.

Conor's anger redoubled as he watched the older man crumple to his knees as tears ran down his weathered cheek and got lost in his beard. He turned to see Teagan standing with her father in wide-eyed shock.

"It's the only home I've ever known," she cried into the hollow of Conor's shoulder, as he wrapped one arm around her. The gesture was lost on her grieving father but not on Bad Tidings Toomey. He noted the relationship between the two young people had changed. He didn't know how to turn that into bad news, but he would work at it. He did not see the change in Red Teagan's face as the wrath within her boiled up.

"Conor, this cannot stand," she declared, straightening up and glaring at the ruins. "We cannot be bullied this way. The injustice stinks at the gates of God!"

"Nor will it stand," he promised. "We will rebuild on this site, and we will secure reparations for the damages done. The old Brehon laws of Ireland demand compensation, and I'm sure the laws of England do too."

He turned to the others. "Whitey, would you poke through all this to see if there's a dram or two for you and Malachi, and even for Tim. There's a cellar for ale and spirits, under a trapdoor behind the bar. Teagan, come with me. We have other treasures to find."

Fifteen minutes later they were back. Whitey had found a barrel of ale, and had tapped it on a ledge of stones that stood on what had been the gable end of the tavern. Bad Tidings Toomey asked for seconds.

"Look at the wee toad!" Teagan was livid. "It's like he's toasting tragedy!"

"No, my heart," Conor said. He tugged at a red curl freed by the wind. "You need a focus for your grief and rage, but it's not Tim. This day will become legend and Bad Tidings Toomey is the story's father. The ale simply lubricates the tale."

"Well, he's creepy and vile, and I don't give a mouse plop about legends."

"You will, since it's the legend that will help us recover from the damage."

White Patrick Boyle stared at them over his mug of ale. Conor had a sword on his right hip, a strung bow over his left shoulder, and a quiver of arrows on his back. Teagan carried a long, cloth-wrapped package that appeared to be heavy.

"Those are the tools of a warrior," Whitey said. Deep in his second pint, he shaped his words carefully. "Not those of a stone mason. And is that a musket?"

Conor grinned. "How could that be so, Whitey? You know Irishmen are not allowed to possess such weapons. And as to the sword and the bow, my home has been attacked. The next raid will not succeed."

Malachi stirred for the first time since his outburst on seeing the damage. "Do you think he will come back?" Conor was struck by the passivity he heard in the man's voice. *He is older than he was this morning. I hope it's just shock and not a permanent change, a decay of the spirit. Teagan has enough to cope with.*

He spoke into the oncoming dusk, intending that they all should hear. "Aye, I do think Bailey will attack again. Today he achieved only part of his goal. There is still my life and Teagan's honor, and I say this: He shall not have either."

Conor heard Teagan gasp and spun around to face Thomas, the servant from Doonagore. He spoke to the man in English. "Thomas, if I see a weapon, you are a dead man. Is your hand in this shameful act?"

"It is not, Conor, although I do have shame. I refused to come with them this morning, and now I'm a man with no station. I have failed in my charge to turn young Bailey into a decent man. I think there is a sickness in him, an incurable dark place in his heart. I only came to express my regret for what he did."

"You are showing far more nobility than your lordling," Teagan said with her first smile of the afternoon. "Tell me, Thomas, do you speak Irish?"

"A little, miss," he answered in halting Irish. "I had an Irish nurse in Dublin, where I grew up as a somewhat sickly child."

"Then stay and help us rebuild. We'll not be bullied by that prancing puppy."

"Aye, Thomas, sit with us," Malachi added in an oddly soft voice. "And maybe Whitey can find an unbroken mug for you."

Thomas looked at the heavily armed Conor. "You will have need of your weapons," he said. "Young Bailey will want to check off the rest of his list now that he has tallied the inn. You must protect yourselves."

Conor smiled and shook his head. "You have not sat among us long enough for me to tell you how we intend to face another raid."

Malachi wiped his face, clearing the last dribbles of ale from his beard. "There need not be another raid," he said. "Tomorrow I shall present myself at Doonagore and seek justice under the old Brehon laws of this land and under English law as well. No legal system anywhere allows such abuses as we have suffered. I shall take White Patrick Boyle with me as a witness to the truth. You two will not go," he added, pointing at Conor and Teagan. "The young man's ire seems to be centered on you, and I have no wish to ruffle waters that are far from still."

Conor felt Teagan's hand slip into his. *She wants to calm me with that little squeeze. But my calm is the cold stillness of pent-up anger. It's the same as I felt when I set out to avenge Rory Donovan, but this time I think the wrath is stronger.*

"Malachi," he said. "We must go with you. I cannot let you face the madman alone. And I will not let Teagan stay behind in a place where there is no lock that can be thrown to keep that animal at bay. So, we are going." She nodded assent.

Malachi Moran said nothing. *I am being overruled in my own home, or what was my home until this morning, but he sees the threats clearly, and she agrees with him. True it is, they are smitten with each other, and I am at peace with that. He is strong enough to make a good protector for her unless his passions get him killed. But if he lives I think she'll be cherished.*

The quiet gathering around the barrel of ale ended abruptly when Sinead Boyle heaved her bulky self into the group and began issuing orders. Two women who seemed to Conor to be acolytes stood behind her, hands on hips.

"Up with the lot of ye, ye great pack of louts, there is work to be done. You men sift the ashes and clear the rubble to see what might be saved. Ladies, let us examine the living quarters. And if you want any more ale," she told the men from behind a waggling forefinger. "It means more work. Now, set yourselves to it!"

Conor stared. *I think I'm afraid of her. Look at them all jumping up and scurrying around, even Teagan. Everything she says is a shriek. It's a wonder that White Patrick can still hear. And now I know why his hair has turned so young.*

He lost track of the women, caught up in the heavy labor of salvage. He and Thomas and Whitey and even Tim Toomey heaved and lifted and shoveled and swept. Malachi did not help. "I will protect the barrel," he said, opening the tap.

"If any man claims to have seen me with a broom in my hand," Bad Tidings Tim grumbled. "I will deny it and curse my accuser."

"Well, Tim," Whitey said, "then why are you helping?"

"Because your mother terrifies me. And I'll deny that too."

When they had done all they could they went back to the ale barrel where Teagan found them. Conor gave her his best smile. *That smudge on her nose makes her look prettier than ever.* She grinned back with a little wave. *He's been so grim since we got here, but with a big sooty mark on his chin he just can't look stern.*

"What have we left?" Malachi asked. The question startled Teagan. *It's so odd for him to ask for an accounting. He's always done for that for himself.* Her confusion became a quizzical glance at Conor, but she could tell he didn't know how to read that look.

"Well, we each have the clothes we packed for our return from Kilronan tomorrow. We found three changes of clothing for you and two for me. One has a scorch mark on the bodice that I will wear proudly as a badge. We also found some bedding."

Malachi was clearly not thinking about shirts and sheets. He turned to Conor with a blank face and a detached voice. "And what of the tavern?"

"Not much left there. Whitey says Bailey splashed brandy all over as he set the fire. But the storage shed is intact. We can take things from there for now."

"Tomorrow," Malachi said with an airy wave. "Tomorrow justice will be done, and I shall have money to rebuild my home and my trade."

Teagan and Conor traded another look and this time he had no trouble seeing the concern on her face. *She's afraid all this has eroded the vitality of his mind.*

Malachi stood up and put one hand against the stones to steady his legs. "The pub is closed for the night," he said. "Whitey and the rest of you, thanks for your help on this day, and we're off to Doonagore in the morning."

"Come, Papa," Teagan said, tugging at his sleeve. "There's a fire and we have some bedding. The sky is clear and you'll sleep well in the open air."

Conor moved his weapons to the other side of a low wall that once defined the inn's little courtyard. "If someone comes in the night," he told Teagan, "I will not permit entry. We have no door to lock, so I will be the door and you can consider it closed." He smiled and moved some bedding that smelled of smoke to a spot where tussocks of grass had been clipped by sheep.

10

Teagan

As the stones gave up the last of the heat the sun had lent them, Conor lay on his back under his covers, staring up at an almost-full moon rising over the Burren. His mind was filled with the day's events. He did not linger over the deep sadness he had felt when he'd realized how hard some ancient Irish tribe had worked to thwart invaders, and how hard-pressed those old warriors must have felt, to have penned themselves into a stone cage on the edge of infinity.

He did not dwell on the evilly set fire that had so deflated Malachi Moran. Instead he drifted into a private space his mind saw as a green meadow beside a woodland pond, where brightly colored butterflies and dragonflies fluttered in the sunlight and where his vision was just as free. Again he felt the welcome red spiderweb of Teagan's hair flowing across his face.

How soft her lips were. How deep her eyes, and where did those golden flecks come from? When she took my hand and held it to her bodice, how warm she was within that covering. And that promise: "You shall have all of me, and soon." All the troubles I've ever had just dissolved in that pledge. I must keep her safe from that sick English rodent. I must . . .

Teagan made sure that Malachi was comfortable in his bedding near the fire. *I can't believe I'm tucking my own father into bed. Somehow that seems backward. It's been years since he tucked me in, and now I realize he held back when I began to become a woman. Maybe Conor will be the next to tuck me in, and what would that be like?*

She eased herself into her own bedding but could not fall asleep in spite of the day's exertions. *So much has happened. A day that began in joy is ending in sorrow. But what joy there was up on those ramparts. I thought he would fall down in shock when I pulled his hand to me. I want it there again, and even closer. And I know he shares my concern over my father. I wonder what he thinks we should do?*

Teagan Dearg Moran got up, wrapped herself in a robe and paced around the space that had been the taproom just hours ago. *It's hard to say I envy my father, because most of the time I don't. But tonight he's sleeping and I'm not. I wonder if Conor is awake.*

She stepped around the little wall and saw him lying beside it in the moonlight, his face at peace and looking young in his sleep. Teagan leaned over to touch his face.

"Conor?" Instantly he was on his feet, sword in hand, scanning the courtyard for danger. That was only part of what frightened her. "Conor, you're naked!"

"Aye, that I am," he agreed, his sense of humor quelling his sense of danger.

"But . . ." Conor tried very hard not to laugh. *For once in her life she is speechless.* "Tay, I'm sorry to startle you, but I don't sleep in my clothes, so they smell fresher in the morning. But should I have waited to dress before seeking out a danger that may have been the cause of my awakening? Fortunately that cause was you, and I don't think you are a danger, and least not an immediate and mortal danger." As he said that, Conor wrapped himself in his blankets and sat down in the moonlight.

"What keeps you awake? Surely we have had a long and busy day. In fact I fell asleep while I was thinking about you."

"You did? I was thinking about you too, but my worries over my father pushed you to the back of my mind. I came out here to ask what you think we must do about the changes in him."

"Come, my heart," Conor said, and patted the ground next to him. "Sit with me and let us consider Malachi Moran." She sat down shoulder to shoulder, but quickly swiveled around so she could see his face. She also saw quite a lot of his chest and noted a little tuft of hair in the center. She pulled her focus back to Malachi.

"I'm so afraid," she whispered. "And I'm not used to being afraid. My father was always my refuge, my shield. I'm just not sure that's true any more. So now what?"

"Now what is me," he said, making that simple statement sound like an obvious and eternal truth. He reached for her hand and held out his other hand too, holding it in front of him until she put hers into it. "I will be your refuge and your protector. In a way I already am. At some point it will be natural for me to take over from your father, and I think that time is now. It's not just Arthur Bailey and his sick mind; it's all the buffeting of life. I stand between you and your troubles and I always will."

"You are sweet," she said sliding her fingers along his cheek.

"Don't say that aloud," he said with a grin. "My friend Ronan would tease me endlessly if word should get out that I'm sweet. He thinks sweet and soft are the same."

Teagan watched him recapture the hand she had freed to touch his face, and she decided she liked that. *Here we are holding hands in the moonlight and grinning. And there's nothing under that blanket but him. Why does that thought keep coming back to me? I guess it's because I never saw a grown man naked before. Could it be that I was more fascinated than shocked? Wicked thought, tavern wench, wicked. And delicious.*

She tried to shiver away those thoughts but Conor misinterpreted the gesture. "Are you cold?" he asked. Teagan nodded with a light squeeze to the hand that held hers.

"Move around and lean back against me." He chuckled. "Right now I think there's enough heat in my body to warm us both."

They sat watching the moon and trying not to overdo the contact between them. Conor's blanket-covered back rested against the stone wall. *It's only my robe that keeps me from touching the body of a naked man. That's probably dangerous, but it's Conor and so it's exciting too.*

Conor leaned forward until his lips touched her ear. "When I touched you out on the island," he whispered softly. "My breath would not flow and my heart moved within my chest. I would know that feeling again."

She sighed and replied in a voice so soft he could hardly hear her.

"Conor, from this moment when we are alone, you need never again ask if you can touch me. Now what are you going to do about that?"

She heard a catch in his breath and she felt his hands unclasp where they met across her waist. Her breathing went ragged as each hand crept slowly but steadily toward its warm and rounded target. "Mmm," she heard. *Did I say that or did he?*

"Wait," she whispered and sat up straight. Conor heard a light rustling and his breathing changed as one shoulder and then the other emerged from her wrap and straps slid down her arms as she pulled free of the fabric. "I am not yet ready to have you inside me, but short of that, I deny you nothing."

Conor said nothing, but lay on his back and pulled her torso onto his chest. He raised his neck and kissed her deeply and at length while his hands ran lightly up her sides until he reached the swelling of her breasts. Teagan raised herself to give those hands more room.

Mmmm. His fingers are rough from all the stonework he's done, but so gentle. His touch warms me all over, but if I touch him back, and I so want to, my "not tonight" pledge will melt like snow on a May morning. I have to stop, and it's now or never, and even though never is so tempting . . . . Teagan rolled off Conor's chest and settled herself alongside him, while his fingers continued to trace her curves and shorten her breath.

"My love, I told you I have a better time and place to finish this magic we have started, and remember, I said it will not be long now. And I promise you it will be worth the wait." She sat up and wrestled her garments back into place, then leaned into him for one more long kiss.

"Tay, right now I am the luckiest man who ever lived. There are stories of men who discover great treasures, but in you I have outdone them all. I want no awkward moments to dim this glow, and so I will wait, and I cannot tell you how hard it is to wait. Now go get some sleep. There's not much night left, and you can't be found here by some stray early riser. Damn, girl, I'm speaking with more nobility than I'm feeling. So, off with you now."

Conor fell asleep with a smile on his face, and it did not fade as he snored into a light duet with the village roosters.

11

Arthur

The sun was two hours above the limestone landscape when the little procession walked out of Doolin, headed for the higher ground where the mini-fortress of Doonagore pushed above the stony skyline.

Malachi insisted on leading. "It was my honor demeaned and my inn destroyed."

Conor and Teagan walked side by side, not quite touching but very aware of each other, sleep-deprived and glowing. White Patrick Boyle never noticed. He thought about how to fill the witness role Malachi asked of him. But Bad Tidings Toomey noted the glances and smiles and decided there was no gloom-and-doom angle here. He was not a specialist in love stories. He considered such tales simple gossip and below his standards. Toomey was there over Teagan's objections. "He's a leech!" she hissed to Conor. "How can I respect a man like that?"

"We need him to spread the legend, however this ends," Conor replied. "Take the long view on this one, my love, and try to be nice to him."

She turned on him. "Do not think that because I love you I would give my own judgments over to yours. You cannot make me like this man."

"I don't care if you like him or not. But tolerate him because on this day the simple truth is we need him."

"All right, but don't think you can tame me with a kiss. Or many. I forget how many. And weren't they delicious!"

"Tay, I'm not blind. I see your red hair and I know a temper goes with it. But there's passion too, so here I am. Let's see what we can do for your father."

She stared at him. "What is that thing on your head?"

He smiled and touched the gem at the front of the gold band circling his head. "It's a good luck charm. You know my people are from Connemara, and we believe in luck, but we try to help it a bit. This has been in my family for a long time." Where the tiara rested on his forehead there was a four-spoked wheel, and where those spokes met a large moonstone glowed in the morning light.

The walk to Doonagore covered a bit less than a mile and Malachi Moran set a pace so brisk that Tim Toomey wanted him to slow down, but didn't dare say so. He was afraid Moran would order him back to Doolin and Teagan's fearsome young man would enforce the order.

Approaching the structure's south-facing gate, the hikers stopped beside the long shadow thrown by the morning sun. Conor scanned the fortress, starting with the defensive wall that enclosed a modest courtyard. Several men watched them over the wall's top. A round tower three stories high formed the heart of the stronghold, and there were men up there as well.

Archers. We're very exposed here. I don't like this at all.

Malachi Moran took a step forward. "I come seeking justice for my loss," he shouted to the men on the wall. "I would speak with Sir Edmund Bailey."

"You will deal with me," Arthur Bailey called from the top of the tower. "My father is away, and I am in charge here. We English rule and you Irish serve. That is the natural order of things. Now be gone, peasant, and take your rabble with you. You Irish vermin will get nothing from me. I owe you nothing, do you hear me? Nothing!"

Conor looked around to see how the others reacted to Bailey's rant. *There's something unsettling in that laughter. I do believe we are facing a madman here.*

Malachi did not accept the dismissal. "I claim restitution for my loss according to English law and the old laws of Ireland. Justice must be done, and since I was harmed at your hand, I say you must go into your treasury to make me whole again. After all, I am the injured party here."

Arthur Bailey turned to the man beside him and shouted, his neck veins standing out and his hand trembling as he pointed.

"Chester, let this animal feel what it's like to be injured. Shoot him!"

The man raised a bow and fired. His arrow bored through Malachi's foot, pinning him to the ground. Before Chester could nock another arrow he was dead, falling backward off the upper rampart with Conor's arrow in his throat.

Conor jerked the shaft out of Moran's foot, causing him to cry out. "Tay, you and Whitey get him away before they shoot at us again. And give me the musket."

Bad Tidings Toomey, aghast at seeing real bad news close at hand, was already scooting down the lane back to Doolin. Conor ducked behind a shed outside the walls.

He could hear Arthur Bailey scream curses at his men as he ordered them to open the gate and slay everyone except the girl, who was to be brought inside the stronghold undamaged. As soon as the portal opened, Conor fired his musket. *I'm too far to hit anything, but between the noise and the hole the ball will make, it might stop them until we can get fair away.*

There came the sound of shouting behind the suddenly slammed gate and Conor could hear some of it. "He's already killed one of us and he has a musket! He still has his bow and a sword as well. You want us to charge out there and slay him? You lead the way and we will follow."

"Kill him! Kill him! You saw it all, he's guilty of murder! Better yet, bring him back here and we'll hang him, just like those old Spanish sailors from the Armada. We'll watch him swing to the breeze, and dance while he dies, dies, dies!"

"But Arthur, what would your father do?"

"He's not here. The man must die and I will have the girl. Now, go!"

"We will not," one of the entourage said.

"Then you are dismissed! Off with you, all of you!"

Conor could hear one of the men start to laugh. Another spoke up. "And if we are not here, how long do you think it would take that young warrior to come in here and carve off your stones with a dull knife?"

Not very long, though the idea had not occurred to me. I think they'll squabble long enough for us to reach Doolin.

He took up his weapons and trotted down the pathway to the village. Within a quarter of a mile he caught up with the hobbling Malachi. Conor and White Patrick Boyle fashioned a rough chair out of interlocking hands and carried Malachi between them while Teagan watched their rear for signs of pursuit between glances at her man. Teagan looked for Tim Toomey but he was so far ahead she could no longer see him. *Conor is not wearing his little crown thing any more. Maybe it just comes out of his pouch when he anticipates danger.*

When they reached the tavern there were already a dozen villagers drawn by Toomey's inflated version of what had happened at Doonagore. Teagan looked sourly at the blackened rafters above her. *Thanks to a spate of rain off the ocean, the place now stinks of wet ashes. But we won't be here tonight.*

Malachi sat with his foot propped up, in the smothering care of Sinead Boyle.

White Patrick scuttled around the village for things the widow Boyle thought she would need to keep her patient in comfort.

"Should we rescue him?" Conor whispered to Teagan.

"No, my heart. I think he enjoys the attention and she wants to do it. Besides, someone will have to look after him while we're gone."

"Gone? Where are we going?"

"Och," she said in fake sadness. "Conor, life with you will be interesting indeed.

You are a lion in crisis, but in between spurts of bravery, you have the wits of a puppy. Of course we must leave, they will set the sheriff on you for the death of that Chester." She stopped to produce one of those impudent grins that Conor was beginning to recognize as the onset of amusement. "But I don't have to go, I didn't shoot that man. I could just wait here for Arthur Bailey to come down and apologize for the injury to my father. And perhaps he'll bring me roses. Don't you think that would be nice?" She ended with a sidelong glance enhanced by the wispy red halo of hair encircling her head.

"Teagan, I'll have to ask after the local custom for fixing the age when children become too old to spank. I'm sure Mother Boyle has a thought or two about that, or more likely, many thoughts." Again, he had missed her mood.

"Conor Mac Cormac O'Canavan, if you ever strike me in anger you will die in your sleep, and never you forget it!"

How quickly she can go from banter to blazing wrath. Why do I feel a little off balance when she does this? But I can't go around on tiptoe, in fear of her next outburst.

He put on his best insincere smile. "But Tay, my dear. It would not be in anger, but in education. I would be trying to teach you how to behave as an adult, and the spanking would simply be a way to re-enforce the lesson."

"All the same, my lovely beast," she said as she glared at him. "Do not overreach, or you will place your favorite body parts at risk."

White Patrick Boyle trudged into the tavern's courtyard with a pack-horse. He and Conor had an intense conversation about what should be loaded onto the packsaddle.

Teagan already knew what she would take and quietly made a small pile near the courtyard wall. Her thoughts kept drifting back to her father.

How will he get along without me? It's not fair. My life is so rich now, and his will be so empty. That Widow Boyle has had an eye on him ever since my mother died, and now she'll think she's got him for sure. But what can he do? There's no home for him here, no money to rebuild, and no restitution for the damages.

The girl walked away from the bustle around the tavern, on the road that led north along the coast. She found a convenient roadside rock and sat on it. *No shortage of rocks around here, or in my life either. Where will we go? What will we do? When will we be back? What will change here while we're away?* She scuffed her shoe idly against the gravel under-foot. *Oh, what's that? The road was empty a moment ago. Where did that woman come from?*

The walker was small and dark and kept a lively pace along the rough road. She wore black clothing and had a small pack slung over one shoulder.

She's looking at me and smiling. Och, she's stopping. Now what?

"You are Teagan Dearg," the woman declared in a warm voice.

"Aye, I am." *That sounds pretty silly, but there's something about those eyes. Who is this stranger who knows me?*

"I am your husband's grandmother." The woman smiled, and Teagan saw good teeth and only a few time-etched lines in her face.

"But I have no husband!" Teagan was deeply flustered.

"By the time tonight's moon rises you will be married in all the measures that matter. Now let us see what manner of lass my young Conor has acquired."

She took both the girl's hands in hers and pulled her to her feet. Teagan almost flinched. *She has the most intense stare out of those black eyes.*

"Aye, ye'll do, like Deirdre before ye. Now, I have some things for you."

She swung the pack down and pulled out two carefully wrapped packets. "There are herbs in these, herbs that do not grow here. This is for Malachi. His wound will fester. A tea brewed from this will help. Tell that woman to make him drink it. He won't like the taste, but he can wash it down with ale." Teagan held the little package as if she feared it would burst and be lost if she should drop it.

"This one is more personal. This is for you. You will pound these leaves with a pestle and moisten the remnant with water. Then apply the cream to him before each time he enters you. I've made up a little in advance for tonight, and you will need it. Every time, no exceptions."

"But I've never even touched his manhood, and I only saw it once, and that was an accident!" Teagan's face was almost as bright as her hair.

The older woman chuckled, a pleasant sound, Teagan thought. "You will see plenty of it, starting this day, and you will enjoy the touch of it. It's not for nothing you have all that red hair."

"But, my lady, what does it do?"

"I am not your lady, my lass. Conor once called me Mathair Crionna, or you can call me Bridie. As to what this potion does, it prevents pregnancy. You and my grandson should get to know each other for a couple of years before you start dropping babies all over County Galway."

"But we're in County Clare."

"Not for long, my sweet. Now get back to your village. You must greet those who have come to help before you leave here."

"But Mathair Crionna, how do you know there are people here to help? You haven't reached the village yet."

"Teagan," the small woman said with a small smile. "It's really hard to explain how a person knows things, but in my family there's a tradition of knowing things others cannot sense. We are a very old family, and you are about to join it. I welcome you with joy. And my first gift to you is easy passage into womanhood."

"Will I see you again?"

"Child, I cannot see into the far future. But if you ever need me, go alone into an open pasture under the full moon, raise your arms to the sky and think my name. And I shall hear though soft your thought may be."

"Wait. You have not said how you know there are people in Doolin to help."

"Whisht! Too many questions, lass. Be off now, and take care of my boy."

"But don't you want to see him?"

"My girl, I see him always, but he does not see me, and for now that is fitting. Go along now, and remember, you are both under my protection."

Teagan took five steps toward the village and then turned. Mathair Crionna smiled and waved her on. The girl, holding her herbal packets carefully, took another twenty steps, and turned again. The road was empty.

But the tavern courtyard was as busy as Teagan had ever seen it. Conor was trading slaps on the back with five young men of his own age. Some of them were shouting, "Oisin, Oisin!"

Teagan was unaware that her mouth was open. *Oisin indeed! I'll have to get to the bottom of this!* She saw Conor greet two older men with a bit more reserve.

"Seamus Hogan, it's welcome you are. You seem to have exported me into a hornet's nest. And you, sir, I know your face but not your name."

"I am Andrew Molloy, a builder. These young puppies have been calling me Handy Andy, and I've decided that I don't mind the title at all. It might, umm, come in handy in my work. As to why I'm here, Seamus promised ale and hard work." He stopped and the grin on his face faded. "Conor, I am sorrowed by the evil that has struck here. Are you hale in the wake of all that?"

"Aye," Conor said. "But it's worse than you know. This morning Malachi Moran went to the castle to demand restitution for the inn's loss, and the young heir ordered an archer to shoot him. I killed the archer, but Malachi was struck."

"Conor," Seamus said. "When you sent that boat to Kinvara last night with news of the fire, I sent another boat to the Claddagh, to get young Ronan. I said we would need timbers for rebuilding, since there are none here. He should get here tomorrow. Now, these Fianna lads I brought for labor have all brought their weapons. The inn is as safe as if you were staying here. By the way," he added, drawing Conor aside. "Do these people know you have gold?"

"Not a one of them, Seamus, and I'd like to keep it that way. I can almost pay for the repairs myself from the smuggling profits. I didn't worry over that."

"Your mother did, and she asked me to bring you some of the treasure as well as her love. You won't get it in front of all these people but you shall have it."

"Seamus, if you can stay a while it's better that I'm not connected to the funding of this project. If you act as overseer and paymaster, I can stay out of it."

Hogan gave his head a vigorous scratching. "Why is that important?"

"I am about to kidnap Moran's daughter, the redhead over there. In law and custom it's abduction, though the victim seems willing. But the English have banned the old Irish abduction custom, so there's a bit of risk involved."

Hogan began to laugh. "Haven't you got this backward? You just killed one of their archers, and now you worry about their law against kidnapping brides?"

Conor had to grin. "It is an oddity, so it is. But I'd like to keep the abduction and the rebuilding apart. Can you stay until Molloy and the Fianna boys get started?"

"Yes, you recall young O'Brien, one of your lot? He's not here because I asked him to keep the tavern for me in Kinvara, and then I asked your mother to keep an eye on him. And between her and Mother O'Brien, my tavern will be safe without me. Now I'd like to see what sort of creature has you in her net."

Seamus and Conor crossed the patio to where Teagan watched Boyle pack the horse. He almost gaped. *This girl is dazzling. She has bright red hair, perfect skin, golden brown eyes, and she's tall enough to be a match for this lucky lad.*

"Teagan, this is Seamus Hogan. He's a friend of your father's, an innkeeper from Kinvara. In fact, he was the one who told me to come here."

"Well, Seamus Hogan, should I thank you or chase you with a stick? Just when I think he's wonderful, he does something that's annoying."

Conor grinned. "She treated me badly when I first got here as a refugee, but lately her disposition has improved, a little."

The girl stamped her foot and scowled at him. "A little, indeed!"

Hogan was still stunned. *How can a glare so intense it should boil water, look so provocative? This young fellow is going to have his hands full with this girl and I wonder if he even knows it.*

12

The Burren

Within an hour there were handshakes and hugs and a teardrop or two. Finally a grinning Conor took up the lead rope and the horse began moving under its neatly stowed load. After a last wave and one more shouted "Slan anois!" they left.

"Oh, where are we going?" he asked. "I have no destination in mind."

"We're off to find a future," she smiled, throwing out her arms and spinning around in the road. "That's the grand plan. But for now, north along the coast road until we are hidden from watchers in the village, and then east into the Burren."

"But Tay, there's no water there, nor wood."

"Aye, so ye've heard what we tell the English. There is water enough, just not a lot of it in the same place. The Sassenach never get off the main roads, not even their sheriff, who will come from Ennis in search of us."

"Tay, does it bother you to flee justice beside a man who's now twice a fugitive?"

"That's a silly thing to say, my man," she said, grinning and twirling again. "I'm only sorry you did not rid the world of that Bailey instead of his man. Besides, my future is now linked to yours forever, and I do not chafe in those tethers. At least, not yet."

Conor caught the grin she used to soften her words. He reached for her hand and relished the living warmth of it as they walked along enchanted by each other.

"Tay, we're walking out onto a peninsula. Not a good place for fugitives. We could get trapped out here by any pursuing force. I don't like it." *There's that grin again. The one she uses to persuade me to do something her way. But still, this is not a sustainable defensive position.*

"You will like it," she was saying. "In a moment we'll drop over a ledge and become invisible to anyone who's not in a boat. And there's a surprise there, a place I've been waiting to show you." The horse balked at the footing and they looked for an easier way off the ledge.

"You should know first, limestone is soft for stone," Teagan said, "and second, water erodes it pretty easily. The result here in the Burren is a system of underground streams and caves. And this," she pointed with a flourish, "is where one of those streams comes to the surface."

Water bubbled up from a spring in the middle of a pond, a flooded sinkhole at the foot of the ledge. It was roughly circular, about forty feet wide and surrounded by low-growing plants, some of them rare beyond the Burren.

"It's beautiful," Conor said. "How did you know it was here?"

"After my mother died my father was lost in grief and his work, and I just ran loose. One day I found this and kept it secret, even from my father. In those days Sinead Boyle was always at me to act ladylike." She wrinkled her nose at the idea.

"When did she give up on that?" Conor asked with a twinkle.

"She has never given up trying to reform me. She warned me against you four times in the first week you were here."

"Well, you didn't listen very well, did you?" he teased as he began loosening the straps on the horse's packsaddle.

"Oh, I listened. There was no escaping her," Teagan said, hearing the echoes of old conversations. "She'd back me into a corner of her kitchen and go on in that screechy voice about the wild boy from up in County Galway, the landless fugitive who would drag us all into crisis."

Conor considered those labels. "Was she so afraid of me? Did she ever say?"

Teagan sat by the pond's edge and took off her shoes to dangle her feet in the cool water. "I think she saw you as a threat to her plans. Mother

Boyle always thought her Patrick and I would 'make a nice couple,' as she put it. But I never thought of him that way for two reasons. One, I would never be free of her, and two, I just don't think White Patrick cares much for girls. He used to talk about the priesthood but not so much recently. I think his mother so frightens him that he's not free to express his own thoughts. He's a good man, but I would want someone who's more in charge of his own decisions." She glanced up with one of those impish grins that always captured him. "Someone like you with all your well-known faults."

"What faults?" he asked, pretending to be indignant. "My lone flaw is a weakness for red hair and a sharp tongue." *She has a way of rolling her eyes and crinkling her nose that would be comical if she didn't have such a lovely face.*

"Oh, Conor," she said with an exaggerated sigh, wiggling her feet in the water. "Even a listing of your faults would take so long we would lose the sunlight and the heat reflected onto these rocks. There's a better way to pass the afternoon. I have not bathed since before we went to Dun Aonghasa, and I don't think you have either. Now's our chance." She pulled him to his feet with a smile and started to take off her clothes. "What's that odd look on your face? If you don't wear clothes when you sleep, do you then wear them when you bathe?" She stopped and tilted her head to one side, sniffing. "You do bathe, don't you, Conor?" His laughter was muffled as he pulled his shirt over his head and tossed it aside.

"Aye," he whispered. "But I've never thought about it as a public event. Can you teach me how to undo these strings and fasteners?" He'd begun tugging at the blouse she wore, one that showed a bit of cleavage.

"You do this and this and this. Besides we're not in public and the horse won't care." Teagan wriggled and fabrics fell away into a little heap around her ankles. Conor was stunned and then smiled. He reached out gently to touch skin he'd never seen.

"You're not the only one making discoveries," she said as she leaned her hips into him. "There seems to be something between us." Conor took a step backward. "You do this and this and this," he said as he worked the buttons on his pants. A bit bemused, he allowed himself to be pulled into the water. *Cold! Damn, this is cold.* Teagan didn't seem to notice. She waded in waist-deep and then dove under, emerging halfway across the pond with only her water-darkened hair and white buttocks above the surface as she dog-paddled to the other side.

Conor was a better swimmer and caught up with her at the far edge of the pond. They turned toward each other, and then it was not so cold in the water. She wrapped both arms and legs around him. Conor held her bottom in both hands and pulled her to him until they could get no closer. If the sun moved, neither knew it. If the wind blew, neither felt it. If time passed, it passed outside their realm of kisses and touches, some of them quite intimate.

"Tay, I have never felt so alive or so needy," he whispered. "This can only end in one way. Are you ready for that?"

"I will be in a moment. Let's get out and dry off a bit, and then . . . well, I think it's time for me to become a woman."

She led him by a convenient handle to the pond's edge, close to their clothing and the packs he had removed from the horse. She found some rough cloths and then a small container she placed next to the linens.

"Come out of there, I want to dry you off," Teagan said with a smile. "You must be chilled because you don't look very relaxed." She stood before Conor with water dripping off her breasts and rubbed the make-shift towel across his chest. He lay down on his back and smiled. She put her small hands on his center and touched, the towel forgotten. "Just a moment," she whispered, and crawled a few feet away to the vial. He saw her hips and breasts sway as she moved. Conor drank in the sight of her. *I think "not very relaxed" is an understatement.*

"What is this?" he asked as she twisted the lid.

"Woman-magic," she said with that enchanting grin. "Trust me. Just close your eyes and try not to wriggle so."

Later, perhaps much later, she stirred from her favorite spot in the curve of Conor's neck and breathed into her lover's ear until he shivered. *I thought this place would be special when I was a little girl dreaming of coming here with the man I'd wed, but I had no idea it would be so perfect. No idea.* "My treasure," she whispered. "There is no shelter near here, but less than an hour away, an old woman runs a small inn near Lissateaun and we can get there before dark."

"The hill of the fairy fort? I don't want to go. I don't need any fairies, I've got a magical creature right here in my arms."

"That's nice, my love. I see which of us will be the practical one. We have to go.

They are hunting for us, and when shepherds bring their flocks here for water in the evening, we should not be here."

"Oh, all right. Where's horse?" he asked.

"Over there in the bracken. Horse has a name, my man. It's Pookie. Conor, can I just put on shoes and go like this?" She ran her hands down the sleek curves of her body, sending his imagination into spasms. There was lightness and joy in his laughter. "Tay, I would have to fight everyone we'd meet, because if they get a look at you like this, there would surely be trouble. A man cannot use his lance and his sword at the same time."

She giggled at that idea and helped him pack the horse, still wearing only her skin. *She's teasing me, and there's that impish grin. It's magic she is indeed.*

13

Maeve

The lingering daylight had tinted toward blue when Maeve Curran looked out her kitchen window to see two people and a laden packhorse approaching from the West. Her small inn was tucked into the foot of a hill topped by the remnants of a circular defensive wall made of earth long ago. *They're the first guests in three days and I'm glad to see them, but they do upset my plans for supper. And do I have enough ale?*

Conor slowed his steps as they approached the door. "The sheriff will be looking for a red-haired girl. Let's make sure that nobody here can say they ever saw one. We'll make them think we are old and not at all interesting." He took the tiara out of his pouch and put it on.

Teagan blinked as the crownlet disappeared and so did Conor's youth and proud stature. In their place was a weathered bearded man whose hands appeared work-worn. So did hers, and she wondered what her own face looked like. When the door opened Teagan saw a short elderly woman who held tightly to the door latch. "Good evening, madam," she said. "We are bound for Gort Inse Guaire by way of Corrofin, and we had trouble with the horse. Now the light is fading and we seek shelter for the night. Have you a place for us?"

"Can you pay?" Maeve asked in a crackly voice that carried more than a trace of suspicion. "You do not look rich, and I must see some money before I let you in."

Conor reached into his pouch and pulled out a small fistful of copper and silver coins. Teagan suppressed a smile. *Those are the coins from my father's tavern. I wonder if they still smell like smoke. Clever fellow, this man of mine. He asked me to swap some gold for those lesser coins. He said paying in gold would make people remember us.*

"There is enough," the old woman said. "You'll bed down by the fire, after some cheese and bread and a bit of ale. Ale is extra. I am Maeve, and welcome here."

"I am Oliver, and this," he gestured dismissively, "is Elizabeth. And we will each have a pint of ale, if you please."

"Please," Elizabeth said in a whiney voice when Oliver went off to see to the horse. "Can you tell us the tidings? We have been in the Burren for days, and the rocks do not whisper."

"Nor do the trees, where there are trees," Maeve said. "But a man came this afternoon, a Sassenach, and said to watch for a young couple fleeing the sheriff."

"Oh," said Elizabeth. "Oliver doesn't see well, but I do. We passed some people on the boreen today. Of course a bigger road would have more travelers. But what were these people running from, and how did they look? We may have seen something."

"Well, they were Irish, of course, and the man killed an Englishman with a bow.

And he had a musket. I heard he was young and strongly built, like a warrior."

"He sounds fierce," said Elizabeth, shaking her head. "And the woman?"

Maeve frowned in concentration. "He said she was young and fair, with bright red hair. She is pledged to the heir to Doonagore Castle, over by Doolin."

Elizabeth scratched herself. "I will ask Oliver, but I think we greeted a young couple on the boreen that leads to the Hole of Sorrows up in the Burren."

"Poulnabrone? They say Fionn Mac Cumhaill himself built it. Do you think they can hide there? People say it has many evil spirits as a stray dog has fleas."

Oliver came back into the room and complained of a shortage of food for the horse. "The stable boy doesn't seem to know very much."

"Oh, Francis. He's my sister's nephew. He's a bit simple, but he does what he's told. It's so hard to find that in young people these days. Not like when I was a lass. Well do I recall the torment we got when we misbehaved. That discipline turned us into good solid adults, so it did."

Oliver made a sympathetic noise and asked for more ale. "We have been a long time on the road, Mother Maeve, and we must cut the dust."

"All right. And bless the weary, your Elizabeth says you may have encountered a pair of fugitives on the road today." Conor/Oliver scratched his beard to obscure his grin. "We saw few travelers, but there were two people, young people, who seemed to look over their shoulders a lot, if you know what I mean." *Good. She's a fish with a fat worm.*

"Oh yes," the innkeeper said, clearly avid to hear more.

"There was a shifty look in their eyes," Teagan/Elizabeth chimed in. "But even so, there was an arrogance about them, wasn't it so, Oliver? It's as if they were too good to be chased, and, besides, that red-haired wench wouldn't even speak to the likes of me. I hope she gets what's coming to her." She made a vicious slicing motion across her throat, and reached for the ale. Conor blinked. *She's quite the actress. I'd better make note that she can do things like this. She certainly has the old lady's ear.*

When Conor and Teagan spread their bedding he told her to keep her feet toward the fireplace. "If your feet are warm the rest of you will be too."

"Well, I hope for more than smoky peat to warm me during the long night hours."

"You can rely on me to keep you in comfort, Tay, even if I must sacrifice."

Teagan hesitated before removing her clothes. "Conor, what will happen when you take off that crown thing? Will we go back to looking like ourselves? I'd hate to have old Mother Maeve come stumbling in here to catch you making love to a red-head."

"Truth is, I don't know. I think I should leave it on, just to be safe. Do you think you could accept sleeping with a bearded man you've never seen before this day?"

"We all have our burdens to bear, my dear, and I must do my share. But when I feel like screaming for joy, how do I stay quiet and avoid having the old lady hear me?"

Conor chuckled as he laid his clothes aside and crept into the blankets.

"Will power, my dear. The holy men say the spirit must overcome the urges of the flesh, so they do. Perhaps we should not play this night."

"Not a chance," she said with a grin as she slid in beside him, moving as close as she could. Twenty minutes later they interrupted some lazy fondling and tried to listen to the urgent words coming from behind the door to Mother Maeve Curran's room.

"Ride you to Doonagore as fast as you can . . . fugitives in the Burren . . . seen going toward Poulnabrone . . . Maeve Curran of the inn at Lissateeaun . . . reward for information. Francis, harken to what I say! Off with ye now." The fugitives hugged each other and grinned as they heard the stable-boy gallop away, his way lit by a full moon above the limestone landscape.

◆ ◆ ◆

"I'd rather see you as I know you are than as I see you now," Conor said as they trudged north and east the next day. He took off the tiara and caught his breath once again at his companion's transformation. Gone was the aging drudge who called herself Elizabeth, and glowing in the morning sun was Teagan Dearg, his love. "I prefer you like this," he said with a smile.

"Conor," she replied with her own grin. "Would you prefer me even more as I was after our, umm, bath yesterday?" She twirled around, played with the fasteners on her clothes and smiled when his eyes lit up. "My man, I like you too, a lot, but I don't know much about you."

His eyebrows went up and he stopped walking. "Tay, my heart, in the last two days haven't you grasped all there is to know about me?" He was learning how to tease her into a blush.

"Not your body, silly, although that is a lovely toy, and I relish the learning of it.

Your mind, your past, those are the things that are mostly blank. You just turned up at my father's tavern one day like a chunk of Atlantic driftwood cast up on the shore. While we move toward Kinvara, can you tell me how you came to me, and why?"

"Aye, I can and I will. You deserve to know what sort of man you have chosen." He looked into the distance, where richer soils marked the northern edge of the Burren, where trees grew taller and in greater variety, although still forced to bend to the wind.

"I was a happy child, cherished at home, allowed to explore the world around me, and schooled in language and numbers. Then everything changed when my father was exiled after the siege of Limerick failed in 1691. I was nine years old, and that day is locked as firmly into my memory as the day we went up to Dun Aenghosa. I'll tell you the tale as we move along. You too, Pookie."

Pookie responds to Tay but ignores me. What's behind that? Oh, well . . .

"When we were exiled from our lands near Galway City we sought shelter with my mother's cousin in Kinvara. Our cart was stopped at Dunguaire Castle to pay the toll, and a brutish guard tried to pull my mother off the cart. I jumped on him and bit his ear, but I was only nine, and he threw me off. His name was Dillon, and he said he was going to skewer me on his sword. But another guard named Rory Donovan stopped him, and Sir William French intervened to prevent bloodshed. He was the lord of the castle, so he was, and still is."

Conor stopped to look into his memories and felt Teagan's hand squeeze his. "The lord of Dunguaire let us go without paying the toll and Mother gave that tiara you admired to the old soldier for helping us. Oh, it has powers that neither of us then realized, and Rory gave it back on the day she hired him to look after us and to teach me the arts of war. He became a sort of second father to me.That day seems like a very long time ago."

Red Teagan Moran stopped Conor in his tracks and kissed him softly. Almost instantly the tenderness ignited into passion as the lovers lit each other's emotions. Teagan sighed. *His life has been so full and yet there's an emptiness in it.*

"Conor, I love you. I love you more every day. And your story moves me so. Losing your father and your home, it must have been so hard for you. And for your mother."

He looked at the teardrop running down her cheek.

"Wait, my heart. There's more. Rory was already in his sixties when he came to us, and gradually he got older and less active. There was something wrong with his leg he would never discuss. One day when he was a crippled pensioner he went to Seamus Hogan's for a pint, and on his way home he was struck down by that ruffian Dillon and a henchman named James, a one-eyed man. They once demanded money from merchants in the marketplace until Rory ran them off. Dillon rubbed dirt into the sword cuts he had given Rory after James knocked him down with a club. I still get angry thinking about it."

She examined his face and saw only hardness.

"Seamus brought him home in a wagon and we eased his pain with whiskey whenever he awoke. A woman went to the holy well and brought back some water that seemed to help, but poor old Rory died within the hour."

His eyes are seeing horrors that had been tamped down in his memory, but I hope he can feel the squeeze from my hand.

"A few days later I learned where they were hiding and killed this James with an arrow. Just after that I challenged Dillon and killed him with my sword. It's odd, but in the middle of all that I had a vision of my dead father, who told me how to fight Dillon. After that Sir William French banished me from Kinvara for five years, and Ronan brought me to you. Best thing he ever did, and best thing that ever happened to me."

"So, my man, you've traded one enemy for another, Dillon for Arthur. Oh, and if you're banished from Kinvara, why are we going there?"

"Mostly because I want you to meet my mother. But I also want to get Father Turlough O'Heyn to marry us, and because I can offer Sir William French a plan that will cause him to cancel the banishment. At least I hope so," he added.

"And that's how I got to be the man you met in Doolin," Conor said as they moved toward Kinvara. "Pookie says he wants a drink and a bit of rest in the grass. We're not in a rush, and we can take the time. Maybe you and I can find something to do besides watching Pookie chew."

Much later, as they walked north and east Conor reached for Teagan's hand again. "You claim I improved after our first meeting," he recalled. "But that didn't happen quickly. Do you recall the next morning when you regretted not pouring a bucket of dirty water on me?"

"Aye," she said, reddening a little. "That was the day you first met Arthur Bailey."

"I prefer to think of it as the day you first kissed me," he said with a smile.

14

Deirdre

During the purple phase of twilight, two travelers led a pack-horse into the quiet streets of Kinvara and Conor knocked on a certain door. His heart jumped when Deirdre O'Canavan opened it. She gasped and fell weeping into Conor's arms. "I thought I would never see you again," she said while hot streaks of joy ran down her cheeks.

He held her tightly and looked over her shoulder to see Teagan also weeping quietly. "I told you when I left you would live to see your grandson running through your house. And you will." He reached out to Teagan and pulled her to his side.

"Mother, this is Teagan Dearg Ni Moran, from Doolin."

Deirdre looked from Conor to the stunning girl beside him and reached for her with both hands and a wide smile.

"You are welcome here, my dear. Conor, does Teagan have anything to do with me becoming a granny?" She watched, trying not to smile, as both young people blushed.

"Not yet, but I hope so. By the way, is Father Turlough well?"

"So then, you need a wedding. Yes, he's doing well, so he is. And I'm very happy for you both. Teagan, I know more about you than you think I do."

"What do you mean?" the girl asked, wide-eyed and a little annoyed with herself for feeling intimidated by this older woman.

"Look at my hair," Deirdre said, lowering her shawl. Teagan stared. *It's bright red, exactly like mine, except there are silver threads running through it. And her eyes are brown too, but darker than mine. What should I think about all this? Is my Conor trying to marry his mother?*

"Tay, my father told me on the day he was expelled from Ireland," Conor said, "that eleven years hence I would meet a girl with brown eyes and red hair, and she would be my love forever. That girl is you, my heart. Mother, I'm off to Hogan's to bring home some ale. While I'm gone my two favorite women in this old world can get acquainted."

He picked up the ale bucket and slipped out the door, grinning.

"How did you read that little act?" Deirdre asked as she ushered Teagan into the little household's best chair.

The girl caught the lightness in the question and smiled. "I can almost hear what he's thinking. 'This is an elegant escape. I'm not sure I'd want to be there getting sliced up while the two of them compare notes about what sort of man I am. On the other hand I'm dying to know just what their consensus is.'"

Deirdre laughed aloud. "You've got him pegged perfectly. I think you'll do."

Teagan produced a little frown and leaned forward. "That's the second time I've heard that judgment in less than a week."

The older woman raised an eyebrow and Teagan took that as an invitation to proceed. "During the morning of the day we left Doolin I got a little overwhelmed by the sudden changes in our lives. I was worried about leaving my father in the hands of a carnivorous widow, worried about whether I'd made the right choice to go with Conor, worried about becoming an outlaw in the eyes of the English, and worried, too, about the threat to me from the crazy man whose father is the lord of Doonagore." She stopped to blink away those images and folded her hands.

"Anyway, I went for a walk and sat on a roadside rock feeling a bit sorry for myself. I noticed a woman approaching from the north. She called me by name, though I'd never seen her before. She said, 'I'm your husband's grandmother,' and I said I didn't have a husband. She brushed that aside and . . .'"

Teagan stopped. Deirdre had turned pale and was gripping the edges of the table. "Describe this woman," she demanded, with no trace of politeness.

"She was small and wore dark clothing. She had bright eyes, quick steps, a nice laugh and a sense of assurance. She stood me up and said, 'Come and let us see what manner of lass my young Conor has acquired.' She locked me into those black eyes and I thought I was going to fall in. Then she smiled and said, 'Ye'll do, just like Deirdre before ye.' I wasn't aware what she meant at the time."

"Did she identify herself, this grandmother woman?"

"Yes. She said, 'Iss misha Bridget Ni Mullaly O'Canavan, and my Conor used to call me Mathair Crionna.'"

Deirdre gasped, still stunned. She shook off Teagan's outstretched hand and spoke, her eyes nowhere near the girl's face.

"Once I told someone that she was an unusual woman. I had no idea. One day she said, 'Take this tiara. It will keep you safe.' The next day she was gone, and I have never seen her again." She paused, staring into her past. "Conor has it now. Have you seen it?"

"I think so, a golden headband with a big moonstone mounted on a wheel in the front? He puts it on when he thinks we are in danger, and the other day it muddied our appearances so a woman who ran an inn would be unable to identify us as a fugitive and his red-headed woman."

"I never knew it had power, that kind of power," Deirdre said. "Once I tried to give it away as a thank-you for a favor done to us. But now I have reason to believe it is as old as our Celtic legends, perhaps the work of the Tuatha de Danann, perhaps a bit of Otherworld. I've learned that it's from the valley between Ben Cullogh and Ben Brack in Connemara. It's among the most remote places in Ireland, a place where the things we know as certainties may not be so certain. By the way, does Conor know you have met Mathair Crionna?"

"No," the girl said. "But we've been a little busy." She blushed at her own words, and Deirdre smiled broadly.

"If he's anything like his father was, I can be sure you were busy. And sore?" she asked, one eyebrow arched.

Teagan blushed again, to more laughter, light friendly laughter.

"My girl, we're going to get along just fine," Deirdre said. "Welcome to my home, it's now yours as well. Conor will bring you great joy, and it seems as if he's already doing that, but there's a chance of great sorrow, too, so there is."

◆ ◆ ◆

Conor walked through the narrow, darkening streets with the empty ale bucket in his hand. *I haven't really been out of Kinvara that long, but the things I recall seem to be from a very old collection of half-forgotten memories. Here is the alley where Rory Donovan was attacked, and down that way is the path to the shack where Dillon was hiding. Ah, here it is. Seamus Hogan's tavern is a place where my memories are warmer.*

He walked in and sat by the door. "What can I bring you?"

"Paddy?"

"Oisin? What are you doing here?" Paddy wasn't very discreet with his greeting and Conor was glad there was no one else in the place.

"Weren't you banished? Seamus and all the others sailed off to help you down in Doolin three or four days ago."

"I killed an Englishman, and so we're outlaws."

"I always thought you would be the first of us to do that. What happened?"

"How about some ale first, Paddy. And how do you like your new career?"

Paddy O'Brien scratched his head for a long moment. "I like it better than I thought I would," he said with a trace of surprise in his voice. "And by the way, who's we? You did say, 'we're outlaws,' didn't you?"

Conor's smile broke the Kinvara wide grin record. "Teagan Ni Moran. Her father Malachi is the innkeeper of Doolin. You will see she is a creature of magic. The heir to Doonagore Castle, which controls the lands all around the village, coveted Teagan. When he was rebuffed, he burned down Malachi Moran's tavern. The next day Teagan and I went with her father to the castle to seek damages, and young Bailey ordered an archer to shoot him. The man hit him in the foot, and I shot the archer and killed him. That was less than a week ago, and now the High Sheriff of County Clare has stirred himself out of Ennis and is hunting for us along the main roads. We have stayed off those roads and have dulled Teagan's bright red hair, and until now we're still free."

"But can that sheriff reach you here, in County Galway?"

"We'll see, Paddy. It depends on how Sir William French reacts to a

search being conducted here. I'll see him tomorrow. What kind of mood
is he in these days?"

Paddy wiped a ring of condensation off the table where Conor's ale
sat untouched.

He didn't want to say that as an apprentice publican who should have
been keeping his ear tuned to the talk across his tables, he didn't know
how the local winds were blowing.

"I'm thinking he's pretty calm for a man with enemies in Galway City.
The smuggling of wool goes well, his marketplace is running without
intimidation, and the town is prospering. He's even lowered the road toll
in recent days and says he's going to use the toll revenue to improve the
road. So he's pretty happy, I would say."

Two men came in and sat where they could see all the tables and
the doors to the kitchen and to the outside. Conor noticed. He put
both hands on the table and raised one finger and one eyebrow toward
the newcomers.

Paddy O'Brien caught the gesture and responded with another sig-
nal from their Fianna days. He took his smallest finger and invaded his
left nostril, twisting it as if harvesting something. To Conor, the vulgar
motion meant, "don't trust."

"On my way here," he said, "I saw a red-sailed boat under five stars."

"I've seen two of them recently," O'Brien nodded with a very slight
eye-dart toward the door and the two men who sat near it. The boat and
the stars were on a heraldic shield representing the English stronghold
of Galway City, and Conor understood the pair were suspected of being
Galway's eyes on the restive town of Kinvara and its disaffected lord, Sir
William French.

Conor got up and went behind the bar. *Thanks to living with Malachi
all those weeks I know how to draw ale.* He filled two pints and took them
to the table by the door.

"Here, gentlemen, my treat. A token of your last visit to Hogan's tavern."
Well, they're scowling, so I must have their attention.

"Who are you? We don't know you."

"On the contrary," Conor answered. "I have lived here for many years,
and I don't know who you are. But I know what you are, and you are a
danger to this town and its people. So drink up and leave. Not just the

tavern but the town as well. Your errand here is over and your masters will find you easy to replace."

"Now see here!" the taller man blustered. "You can't make good on your threat, young man. Do you know whose agents we are?"

"And since when," the other man demanded, "since when did the serving men in this tavern start wearing swords to pour ale? And you clearly don't know how to use it."

"Let me tell you a little story, Englishman. Not long ago, two men collected extortion money from the merchants in the market, and sometimes they robbed the shoppers as well. They were expelled at swordpoint, and to this day the market operates without stress." They stared stone-faced while he paused.

"A few weeks ago a soldier attacked and killed a crippled old man, with the help of a one-eyed henchman. Within days the henchman was dead of an arrow in the eye, and then the soldier, a man named Dillon, fell to a sword cut. Someone stuck his head on a pike just outside that door. Ever hear that story?" *Hmm, I think the little one just blinked.* "There's a moral to those stories. We patrol here. We control here. The Crown does not, the city of Galway does not, and its agents have no role here. So, as I said, enjoy your quaff and then leave."

The taller man gathered his indignation. "Young man, you are talking insurrection, rebellion against the Crown."

"I am doing no such thing. But in this town I am telling you to keep your prying eyes out of our business. Look, if there ever is an independent Ireland, the movement to create it will not start in Kinvara. Go back to Galway City and tell the ruling families we will be better citizens without their feet on our necks. Those feet are coming off these necks, mister spy, and the rulers of Galway have the first chance to remove them. We reserve the right to act if they don't. That's all I'm saying."

"Don't you recall when the English armies rolled over the Irish? Your lot lost, young man, and the consequences are real. And by the way, just who is making all this noise about self-rule and non-interference in the affairs of a worthless hamlet on the edge of the world?"

Conor smiled at them and opened the door. "You may call me Oisin."

"Oosheen? What kind of a name is that?"

Paddy O'Brien, who'd been wiping down the bar and listening with

mixed feelings to the talk, burst out laughing, and pointed at his departing customers. "You don't know as much as a gobbet of chickenshit about
us, Sassenach. None of you do, and so in the end we will win and you
will lose this land."

When the door closed, Paddy went to the tap and poured two fresh
pints. "Well," he said, sliding a mug toward Conor, "Do you think you
have rapped hard enough on the bees' nest to provoke a reaction?"

"I'm going to have stop having political conversations in taverns," Conor
said between sips. "But I don't think the lords of Galway are in position to
clamp down on us. London is still annoyed with them, and the smuggling
is having an effect. Galway can't just go running off to London and say,
send the navy and send the army, because Kinvara is restive. I hope I'm
reading the situation properly, because if I'm wrong, we'll be quite busy
here over the next few months. Perhaps we should call the Fianna home
from Doolin in case the Galway lords try to swat the Kinvara fly on their
own. Anyway, it's time for me to go back with a full pail."

◆ ◆ ◆

*Have I been gone too long? Will I find the two of them staring at each other
in stony silence? How awful that would be. And I have to go to Dunguaire
tomorrow. My road seems to be pretty rocky just now. Well, the lamps are
on and there's a bit of turf smoke rising from the chimney. Here goes . . .*

"Good evening, ladies."

"You were gone quite a while," Teagan said.

Conor turned on his best grin. "Ah, so you missed me then."

"No," Teagan said. "But we missed the ale you promised an hour ago.
And now that you're here you can pour some."

Deirdre sat by the fire and allowed her grin to spread to its natural
limits. She *is going to be so good for Conor, especially when he gets full
of himself.*

"Mother, Paddy O'Brien was at the tavern. He's minding it for
Seamus Hogan."

"I know. Seamus asked me whether he would be a good minder, and I
said between his mother and me, we would make sure of it."

"We also had two English spies in the place, and I told them to leave
town."

"I thought we were coming in discreetly," Teagan said, showing confusion. "Yes, Conor," his mother chipped in. "Did your passions rule you again?"

Conor sat down and let his shoulder slump a little. He was way beyond putting on airs for these two. "My father told me that I would not be strong enough to resist fighting back against the indignities done to me and to the people here." He allowed himself a rueful grin. "I think he was right all those years ago."

Teagan reached for his hand. "What I think is, our challenge now is to direct your anger and your sense of violated justice in a way that allows you to do something positive without giving the Sassenach an excuse to hang you."

Deirdre nodded. "And it begins tomorrow with your visit to Sir William French. You've been gone less than two months of a five-year banishment, but my boy, what a busy time you've had!" She reached out to hold Teagan's other hand. "It's not exactly us against the world, because we surely have friends, but the scales are ever tipped and our path is ever uphill."

She shook her head as if to erase her last words. "Now, to practical matters. Into the bedroom with you two, and I shall make do where you once slept, in this room."

"No." Conor's rejection was firm, and Teagan nodded in agreement. Deirdre answered them with a small smile. "My son and my new daughter, hear me. You are not the only ones for whom life has moved quickly in these few weeks. Conor, I'm not yet forty, and have been a widow for one quarter of my years. My life surges within me, and I do not wish to be a widow for the next twenty or thirty years." She stopped and looked through the window without seeing.

Conor stirred in his seat, the ale forgotten. "Mother, what are you saying?"

"I know," Teagan said, tightening her grip on Deirdre's hand. "She has found love again, and it surprises her as much as it shocks you."

Deirdre looked at Teagan and nodded and at Conor and spoke. "She is right. Oh, it is not the burning passion that the two of you share, or that I once had with Cormac your father, but it is yet a flame, and if it's closer to peat than to pagan bonfires, it is still steady and warming."

Conor and Teagan could not mistake the glow on her face as she looked within herself and drew on memories to enhance her words.

"You will ask who has captured this aging heart, and I shall tell you. It's Seamus Hogan." Deirdre flushed as she said the name.

Before Conor could speak Teagan jumped up and drew her almost mother-in-law into a hug. "I have met him," she said. "And I think he is a good man."

Conor missed the flash of understanding between the women. *How do I deal with this? My mother and Seamus Hogan are together as lovers? Come on, Conor, dredge up a little of the approval she wants.*

"I must say I am surprised. Not shocked, but surprised. Somehow a man never thinks of his mother as a woman, a creature of flesh and blood, part St. Bridget but part Viking Valkyrie as well. For what it's worth, I approve. Seamus is indeed a good man and has offered good counsel to me. I truly hope that he gives you some of the happiness that you've missed ever since my father was banished."

"Conor, you great oaf! Hug her!" Teagan said. He did.

"I think I need this ale more than ever," he said after sitting down again. "Mother, how far has this thing between you and Seamus gone?"

"Exactly as far as this 'thing' between you and Tay has gone, and that only recently, just before he left for Doolin." Teagan caught the hair-twisting and rising color in Deirdre's cheeks. Conor was too busy adding things up.

"So that's how he knew about the gold. I should have figured it out."

"What gold?" Teagan asked.

"She doesn't know? You didn't tell her?" Deirdre asked her son, her tone half accusatory. Conor's face went blank.

"My dear," Deirdre said, and captured Teagan's hand again. "We were once a family of note, before the English penal laws were enforced a few years ago. We were thrown off the family's lands, but I was able to hide some of our gold in the false spokes of an old cart we used to move our things to Kinvara. Seamus took some to Doolin, since we thought Conor might need it. We didn't know about you then," she added with a grin aimed at Teagan.

"Conor, why didn't you tell me?" Teagan seemed hurt. "I thought there were only the two or three pieces you had me change in the tavern's taproom."

He shrugged. "That knowledge may have influenced the way we related to people around us when we were very vulnerable. But now you know," he said with a smile. "And so now I have one less thing to hide from you. And here's another. I am up to my ears in this wool-smuggling business that started a few years ago, and has furnished me a separate income. Not a fortune, but perhaps enough to support you."

"So now I see! You go around threatening English heirs and spies, you're on the run for killing another Englishman, and now you're a smuggler. And we're not even married yet!" Her eyes flashed and her hands went to her hips in a pose he'd seen before.

Conor looked at his mother and saw a twinkle override the carefully neutral expression she wore.

"Tay, you said yourself that life with me would be an adventure. I hope you meant that, because we're right in the middle of it."

She was still peeved. "Don't you ever undervalue my loyalty, young Conor, I'm in this for the rest of my life, no matter what. Back to the real world now. Where are we sleeping tonight?"

A passerby would have heard light laughter rolling out of the modest cottage on the edge of Kinvara, and when the lamps went out, Conor and Teagan cuddled impossibly close on the floor in front of the dying fire, and Deirdre lay in her bedroom with a grin that did not fade until she slipped into sleep.

15

Sir William

Sir William French sat in his castle and measured his assets against his obligations. Financially, that was easy enough. The wool smuggling netted him an unexpected income, one that his overlords did not know about. His marketplace thrived, and his toll collection brought in more revenue. In addition, the traditional rents he charged his tenants were being paid without much squabbling. *So, I'm on the plus side as far as money goes. But it's the political equation that's so troubling. Galway is out of favor in Dublin and London, and the Frenches are out of favor in Galway. That's mostly because of my stupid cousin Gerard, but it's easy for them to turn on me, too. I may have to use some of my new profits to sand off the rough edges of my relationship with the First Families. Now, if I could improve the road and bring some shipping to Kinvara, I could raise money and afford to bribe the Lords of Galway to leave me alone, at the very least.*

"Sire, a moment, please." Eoin, the garrison commander, came in, hat in hand. "Do you recall that young man you banished a few weeks ago?"

"You mean Conor O'Canavan, the one who killed those thieves?"

"Aye, sire, the very one." Eoin tried not to remember letting O'Canavan pass the toll station without paying. "Well, he's at the gate this morning, and says he must speak with you. I told him you were busy and he threatened me."

"Oh? Just what did he say, Eoin?" *It wouldn't take much of a bluff to sway this nice simple man. Too bad I can't appoint Conor as my garrison chief.*

"Sire, he said he would see you even if he had to step over my lifeless body to do so. I thought his mission must be urgent, indeed, and said I would tell you he's here. Sir William, I do not know what he'll do if I say no to him." *The man is twitching and sweating. He's terrified.*

"Just send him up, Eoin. I'm curious to hear his story."

"Aye, sire. Should I muster the garrison and arrest him when he leaves? After all, he was banished, and yet he's here."

"No, let's just hear him." *What is he thinking? Conor could kill half his men before they could produce weapons they've never used. Ah, look at the relief on Eoin's face.* The castle master could barely hear Conor moving quickly and lightly up the stone stairway.

"Well, young Conor," he said as his guest reached the main chamber, " it looks as if you have turned five years into five weeks, or is it six?"

Conor smiled, knowing his grin would irritate his host. "Sir William, it's about seven weeks, maybe eight. But I must thank you for the exile, because I have met the girl I'm to marry. We're staying with my mother, with your consent, of course."

"Why should I grant my consent, when it seems as if I just threw you out of Kinvara yesterday?" French was half peeved and half intrigued by this confident young man.

"I can think of many reasons, such as harmony in the marketplace and ridding the village of Galway's spies, peacefully, of course. But that's not the main thing. What you have here is a chance to turn Kinvara into a significant seaport, and all it would take is a quay, where ships can tie up. The water here is calm in most winds, so we would not need a protective breakwater. Here, let me show you what I have in mind."

French watched his visitor pull out a sheet of parchment and draw on it. The lines became a quay, a safe harbor for all but the biggest vessels.

"And how do you know of such things?" There was skepticism in the lord's voice.

"I have spent weeks on the construction of a protective breakwater in the harbor of Doolin. I understand the fitting of stones. Maybe it's in the blood. My Irish ancestors built strongly in stone. Have you seen the fortress of Dun Aonghasa, out on Inishmor?"

"No," French said. "But those who have say it is impressive, and ultimately sad, that a people should pen themselves up to avoid their foes."

Conor retained his grin, but somehow it had become less ironic and friendlier. "The same thought occurred to me when I saw it not long ago," Conor said.

The lord of Dunguaire stirred in his chair. "What a mountain of labor it must have taken to turn that rocky wasteland into a sanctuary. Working with stone is still a challenge, as I have thought many times about the building skills that went into the making of this little castle. Now Conor, where do you propose to lay hands on enough stone to build this quay of yours?"

Conor let his inner imp off its leash. "Well, this is the biggest pile of stone around, and it's already cut into blocks of a size that can easily be moved."

Sir William blinked. *I'm not used to being teased by Irishmen. At least I think he's teasing, his eyes are a little crinkled in their corners.*

"Find another pile, funny man," French said with a thin smile.

"All right, what about the remains of that old fortress just west of the town center?

The last time I saw it, the birds and rabbits were making homes for their young in the rubble of the house of O'Heyn. Besides, the locals have mined it for stone for a long time. There may not be much left for what we need but it's a start, and it's yours."

Sir William French got up from his ornate chair, went to a cabinet, and tipped a few ounces of mead into two small goblets. *I don't think I've ever offered a drink to an Irishman, but it seems our fates are somewhat linked. How did he know I was thinking about improving the harbor?* "You said not enough for what we need. Why do you think you have any part in this?"

"I know how to build it, and nobody else here has that skill. You may not want to go around Galway City asking for stonemasons. I think we can reach an understanding, just as we did in the wool business. Thanks for the mead; it should help us smooth out a few little details. Now, here's what I have in mind."

Twenty minutes and another goblet of mead later, Sir William French leaned back in his favorite chair and looked at his young guest. *I can't think of him as a boy now. His mind is sharp and he has a leadership quality that anyone would envy. But what am I to do with him? He has turned banishment into a demonstration that I need his skills. But look, his face is troubled.*

"Conor, I think there's something you're not telling me."

"There is. I tried to hide it but I do have some troubles that may concern you."

"Well, out with it, then. Now I'm doubly intrigued."

Conor sat very still on his little bench. "Do you know the Bailey family who control Doonagore and the lands around Doolin?"

"I know of them, why?" Conor didn't quite squirm as he seemed to search for the right words, and the lord of Dunguaire read his posture as uncomfortable.

"The day after I got there the young heir burst into the tavern where I was staying and terrified the owner's daughter. I suggested he leave, and he did, but soon after that he came back with some other young Englishmen and burned the tavern down. I was over on Inishmor at the time with Malachi Moran the tavern keeper and his daughter, Teagan. The next morning we went to Doonagore and demanded reparation for the loss, according to English law and the old Brehon laws of Ireland. Bailey ordered one of his cronies to shoot Malachi, and the man put an arrow into his foot. I killed the archer, an Englishman, with an arrow of my own, and we left while they were shouting at each other inside the fortress. The heir then called on the High Sheriff of County Clare to run me down, so Teagan and I left and found our way here, arriving last night." He shrugged and stared through his host, as if he were revisiting the events of the past week.

"It's been pretty busy, and in the middle of it I fell in love with the innkeeper's daughter. She's called Teagan Dearg. She has the reddest hair I've ever seen. Anyway, one of the reasons we came here was to ask Father Turlough O'Heyn to marry us, but I haven't seen him yet."

French sat still for a moment, pondering what he'd heard. "You seek my protection against an officer of the law in the conduct of his duties?"

Conor shrugged. "You asked me what I had not told you, and that's it."

"The Sheriff of County Clare has no authority here in County Galway," French said. "And hearing the Doonagore heir is unstable is not a surprise. It's hard enough keeping a lid on a quarrelsome people like you Irish without providing you with just cause to rise up again. Here in the west of Ireland our control is not as firm as in most of the island, and that's not a surprise to you. The ruling families have no influence in County Clare, and young Bailey is not their problem unless he ignites another uprising in the Irish west."

Conor's thoughts roiled his mind, so he got up and went to stare out the narrow window at the restless water of the bay before he spoke.

"Sir William, I believe the flaw is much deeper than a passing phase. It goes beyond the entitlement he feels as an heir, and I think it centers on his flawed belief that because he is English, the normal rules don't bind him in Ireland. On a deeper level I believe there is a dark place in his mind that none can reach, a place that hatches evil. And I must stand against that evil."

I know his father was old Irish nobility, but the son inherited well. It's so sad that my Isabel died so young. I would have liked having a son such as this man.

"All right then. You stay out of Doolin and I will hold the hunters at bay. And together, we shall make a marshy shore into a harbor."

Conor walked back into Kinvara village, noting that some work had been done to widen and level the road between town and castle. *Sir William is trying to carve out a way to make a living from his holding without squeezing the tenants too hard. Too bad he's an Englishman, he's got good instincts. And he serves as his own steward, which is the best way to stay in contact with his people. Now we'll see what happens when the sheriff comes knocking on his castle gate.*

He slipped through the village he called home, toward the house where Turlough O'Heyn lived. The priest, in his usual old work clothes, was in his garden.

"You were exiled, so you're not here," the man said from among his beets.

Conor grinned. "And a fine sunny day to you too, my friend. Now I can't recall why I was looking forward to seeing you again."

"You want to bask in the glow of my cheerful nature," the priest said, trying on a smile that he hoped was benign if not beatific.

"You haven't been excommunicated for being an old grouch, have you? Or for your views on strong drink?" Conor asked with a dry throat gesture.

"No. I'm still marrying and baptizing and burying, and once in a while dispensing a mug of ale to my friends. Tell me what any of that has to do with you."

"I need your professional services. I want to get married."

"Have you got a victim?"

Conor grinned. "Aye. Her name is Teagan Ni Moran, and she's from Doolin.

Everyone likes her, and even you will approve."

Turlough O'Heyn pulled a weed and leaned back on his haunches. "Son, you've been gone for less than two months, and you're supposed to stay gone for five years. Are you sure this urge to marry isn't due to some romantic accident?"

Conor knew the priest would get right to the point, and he was ready for it. "Father, we've taken to sleeping together in the past few days, but I can tell you that we've started no new life that I know about."

"Well, then, down to business. The banns will have to be posted for three weeks, and by the way, why don't you marry this Teagan in her own parish?"

"One, there's no priest in Doolin these days, and two, if we go back there I will be arrested for killing an Englishman, and Teagan will fall into the hands of the crazed heir to Doonagore. The story always dries my throat, Father."

O'Heyn smiled and lurched to his feet. "That's the second hint you've left about a drink. You're in luck because a guilt-stricken parishioner has just left me a bottle of that good whiskey from County Antrim. Come, I'll pour you a dram."

An hour later Conor walked home. *I'm getting better at this. The story grows nicely with each telling.* He swept Teagan up into a feet-off-the-floor hug and whirled her around. "The priest says he will marry us, though he feels sorry for you," Conor was almost singing, his voice full of joy and mischief.

Teagan boxed his ears lightly. "Put me down, oaf. What did the master of Dunguaire say, and did you tell him everything?"

◆ ◆ ◆

In the morning, a breathless small boy knocked on the door and said Paddy O'Brien had sent him to tell Conor that five young men had arrived by boat from Doolin. Conor gave him a coin, and he and Teagan went down to the waterfront, where the Fianna were unloading the *Moira*.

"Welcome back," Conor said. "And thank you all for going down there to help.

How is the project going?"

"Almost finished," one of them said. "And that Handy Andy is really good at directing work crews. The beams are up, the thatch is back on the roof and now he's finishing up the furniture and the bar counter."

"Good. And where is Seamus?"

"He's helping Andy finish up, Oisin. He should be back in a day or so. The lugger is sailing back there this afternoon. Oh, by the way, we'll start patrolling again tomorrow, but this is a day of rest, and you may find some of us at Hogan's, telling Paddy O'Brien all that he missed."

Conor waved them off and turned to Teagan. "Come, my love, let me show you around your new town. We'll pass the old O'Heyn castle on the way to the biggest oak tree I ever saw."

They strolled hand in hand through the village, aware of the old women who stopped their gossiping to stare at the vibrant young couple. "They'll have something new to chew on," Conor said with a smile. "Like who are you, and why are you with me, and they'll decide they've never seen a prettier girl, or one with redder hair. Then they'll decide they don't like you because you outshine their granddaughters."

"Conor, you have an overactive imagination. Oh, I think I see the big tree you were talking about. We don't get big trees in the Burren, the wind bends them over so."

He thought back to when he and his mother had hired Rory Donovan under this big oak, and how his life had changed in the years since then.

This old tree hasn't changed at all as far as I can see. I suppose a dozen years or so, or even the beginning of a new century, is not much of a notation in the life of a tree like this one. I understand why the old people used to venerate oaks. This one is so dense that there's nothing growing under this carpet of last year's leaves.

But out at the ends of the branches, where the light gets through to the ground, the wind shoves the leaves around and tilts the tussle between sunlight and shadow for control of a few patches of grass. "Look, Tay. Near the trunk nothing grows in the deep shade, but that's not true out where the light gets through."

She reached for his hand. "And where are we in our own struggles? Are we caught in some great dark or are we getting enough light to make a difference?"

"Hmm. Here's what I think. The English oppression is the great darkness you spoke of, and freedom is nourished by the occasional burst of sunshine. Now, O wise woman, how do we make use of that?"

"You mean without being hanged for bringing light into the dark," she said. "Let's begin with our own troubles before we start another revolution."

Conor drew his girl to her feet and led the way toward the rubble that had been the once-ruling O'Heyn clan's stronghold. "I told you I had made an agreement with Sir William French to build a quay here, in exchange for his protection against the Sheriff of County Clare. Here is the raw material for that quay. This rubble was once a fortress for the O'Heyn family. I'm going to ask White Patrick to come up here and supervise the placement of stones, once I get them down to the shore."

Teagan squeezed his hand and smiled. "Maybe White Patrick will thrive in Kinvara, out from under Sinead. Do you know any girls here who might like to meet him?"

"Some of my friends have sisters. Let me think about that. Now we have to get your father up here for the wedding. Is there anyone else from Doolin you'd like to invite? I mean aside from Arthur Bailey," he added with a teasing laugh.

"Don't laugh so hard," she said. "If he sees us wed and realizes that I am no longer a virgin prize, he may relent." She looked up at Conor with a hopeful glance.

"The sun will rise in the west before that happens. Remember the old story of the dog in the manger? He'll think that if he can't have you, then no one else will, especially me. I think we're in danger as long as that rabid rat is a force in the west of Ireland."

16

Seamus

On the day Conor began freeing stones from the O'Heyn rubble, White Patrick Boyle arrived in Kinvara on a Galway lugger.

"How is your mother, Whitey?" Conor did not expect his polite question to generate an eye-roll from the newcomer.

"She's like a cat that's just eaten a bird. And the bird is Malachi Moran. She's been after him for years, and now he can't even run, and she's moved into the tavern. She says that enables her to take better care of him. The poor wee man, we should hold a wake."

"But Whitey," Teagan said. "Aren't you glad she's found a bit of joy?"

"Aye, but it comes at your father's expense, and I like your father, so I do."

Conor grinned and reached for Teagan's hand, which never seemed far away these days. "Then you'll be happy to see him. The banns of marriage are posted for Teagan and me, and Malachi will be here for that in about two weeks. By the way, where's Seamus?"

"I don't know. When we landed he just walked off. Didn't say whither bound."

"I know," Teagan said with a twinkle. "Should we go and greet him, or is that being done far better than we can imagine?"

Conor grinned. "Oh, we can imagine. But let's go to the tavern. It's the secondmost likely place he'll want to check on. And maybe Paddy

93

O'Brien will draw us a little ale. White Patrick, would you like to join us in a bit of cheer?"

"Of course. I've learned a lot about taverns in the past few weeks and a little about ale, too. So lead on, my friends, the quay can wait."

They trooped into the tavern and sat where the English spies had once posted themselves by the door. "Ho, Paddy!" Conor yelled. "Ale for three, please."

"Here you go," the temporary bartender said. "Conor, is this the fabulous Teagan?"

"Aye, so she is. And this is White Patrick Boyle. He'll be your new best customer.

He's here to work on the quay."

"The what? Kinvara doesn't have a quay."

"Soon it will," Conor said. "Whitey and I are building it for the lord of Dunguaire.

We hear Seamus is back in town, have you seen him?"

Paddy O'Brien looked puzzled. "No, not yet. Maybe he went home first."

Teagan grinned and kicked Conor under the table. "Aye," she said. "Maybe he went home." She raised her mug and clicked it against those held by the men, including Paddy O'Brien, who had decided the absent Seamus Hogan would not begrudge him a pint. She could see that White Patrick was getting more comfortable. *Perhaps if Conor had not come along, I would have worn down under Mother Boyle's determined campaign, and accepted Whitey as a husband. I told Conor I hope he thrives here, and I want to see what changes there are in him now that he's not tied down by the power of his mother's will. Certainly she has worn my father down, but maybe now she'll just concentrate on him and leave her son alone.*

Conor was lifting his mug when the peace of the room was broken by a red and white tornado. Sea Dog did two laps around the table, launched himself into Conor's lap and began to plant sloppy kisses on his face. Ronan Mac Fergal O'Malley followed, slightly more restrained.

"Ronan, get this daft beast off me! And welcome. You know these people?"

"Aye. Teagan, whom I tried to warn you about, White Patrick Boyle, the seawall man from Doolin, and Paddy O'Brien, who has helped with the wool."

He smiled at the sputtering Teagan and pulled a small package out of his pouch. "Since you wouldn't listen to me, I have to believe you are lost to the ranks of single men, so I have brought you both a gift to mark the changes in your lives."

He unwrapped the package and exposed two rings, their gold surfaces glowing a bit in the yellow flicker of lamplight. Each showed a pair of hands clasping a heart under a simple crown.

"My village has two or three goldsmiths who have been making these for the past few years. These are by a man named Richard Joyce, who's getting a lot of credit for creating the rings as a symbol of love and friendship."

He held up the smaller ring and handed it to Conor. "Put this on Teagan's left hand, fourth finger, and let the point of the heart face outward to the fingertips. That has become in the Claddagh a symbol of the wearer's engagement to be married. There. Now Teagan, take the other ring and put it on Conor's left hand the same way. It's less common for men to wear the ring as a symbol of marriage or betrothal, but I'm hoping you'll do it, as a gift from me and a public pledge to Teagan." He showed them the inside of the rings, where the jeweler had marked C+T on the smaller one and T+C on the one Conor would wear.

Teagan placed the ring on his finger and got up to lean across the table and kiss Ronan on the cheek. The young sailor blushed while his dog made a nuisance of himself, dancing around the table and launching spasms of tail-wagging and happy barking. Finally, Paddy got a shallow dish, filled it with ale and set it on the floor. That stopped the barking but not the wagging.

"Now, at the moment of your marriage," Ronan said, "you will each turn your ring around so the heart points toward your wrist. That will signify that you are married, as much as any words a priest might say."

"Ronan, I am touched, more than I can say," Teagan said, while Conor nodded, staring at his new jewelry from different angles as he turned his hand this way and that. "And thanks for your help in rebuilding Malachi Moran's tavern."

A few minutes later Seamus Hogan came in, followed by Deirdre O'Canavan, and when they saw the little gathering around the table, both blushed. Teagan jumped up quickly and ran to embrace her mother-in-law to be.

"Look what Ronan has brought us from the Claddagh! They're making a new style of ring there for love and friendship. Look, my hands hold your heart, or your hands hold my heart, as you wish. And Ronan says if you wear it this way, you're engaged, and if you turn it around, you're married. Isn't it just beautiful?"

Seamus grinned and caught Deirdre's eye. "It may be that soon we'll need another pair of those," he said. She smiled and looked at the group around her. "We have a wagon outside, and we'd like some help unloading it. Can you put down your mugs for a moment, please?"

"Mother, what's going on here?"

"I told you and Teagan that I don't wish to be a widow for the next twenty or thirty years. Seamus and I have discovered we have a lot in common. So my things are outside and I am moving in. And I don't care much . . . how did you put it, Tay?"

Teagan burst into laughter, dissolving the tension in the room. "The weight of a mouse plop. I don't care the weight of a mouse plop."

"Aye, well that's how much I don't care what people might think or what they might say. And knowing the people in this town, they'll have their say."

"But you can't!" Conor tried not to look shocked, but his effort failed. "I mean I like you, Seamus, but this is a scandal."

Deirdre smiled as Seamus came up beside her and put his hand on her shoulder. "It's no more scandalous than you and Teagan sleeping together unmarried." She smiled up at her son. "Among us we will fuel the local gossip mill for years."

They trooped out to the wagon where Conor and Teagan made quite a display of picking up bundles while swapping hugs and smiles with Deirdre and Seamus. As they carried an armload into the tavern, Conor whispered to Teagan. "Now the old ladies will forget about us, and chew on the juicier morsel of the deposed landed lady and the innkeeper, a mere tradesman."

"Conor, my heart," she whispered back. "This will last only until the wedding, and then the gossips will get back to us. Should we tell them that you're wanted for murder in County Clare? Suppose we start with Mother O'Brien. She's the best, right, Paddy?"

"My mother can stir a storm that would make Shakespeare's tempest look like dry leaves twirling in the wind. And she can do it with one fact and a chorus of what-ifs. I suppose that makes her the best in Kinvara. And when she saw Red Dillon's head mounted on a post we learned she has the town's loudest banshee shriek, too."

Conor was still trying to adjust to the lightness of mood among the others. "If she's so good," he said, "she won't need a head start." A few minutes later Teagan and

Conor walked their visitors back to the harbor. Ronan and Sea Dog got aboard the *Moira* and Conor pushed it off into deeper water.

What a lot of my life is reflected in that boat and that man, and even that silly dog.

Learning the longbow, learning the sea, smuggling wool, going into exile, meeting Teagan, almost everything important that's happened to me in this new century has a Ronan connection. He watched the gleioteog *Moira* moving north, leaning to the right, away from the wind that blew in from the mouth of Galway Bay. *Once I thought sailors had to hang onto the mast to keep their balance. Can't see Sea Dog standing the bow watch any more. The boat should be coming about to tack off toward the islands and then south to Doolin. I'd like to see how Malachi is doing, but I don't dare leave Teagan and I can't take her back there. You're rambling, Conor. Hmm. He's not turning, he's going to the Claddagh. I wonder what that's about? Does it have anything to do with Seamus and my mother and those rings Ronan brought us? No, that would be too fanciful.*

He turned away from the water and strolled back to the tavern. There was a new sign posted among the public notices on the board.

The Banns of Marriage are posted for The second time for the bachelor SEAMUS HOGAN of this parish

And for the widow DEIRDRE O'CANAVAN

Of this parish.

Turlough O'Heyn, pastor

Well, that's a surprise. They want a double wedding? Nobody told me. I wonder if Teagan knows about this.

"I don't," she said as they put fresh linens on the bed in their new home. "And I'm not sure I'm happy about it. A woman's wedding day ought to be one of a handful of truly joyous moments in her life. I want that moment to myself. Deirdre has already known that joy once, and it seems to me our wedding should be unique to us. I think she's too thoughtful to deny us our day in the sun. Do you think Seamus is behind this?"

"I'll find out. For now, let's have another truly joyous moment in our own lives."

Conor pulled her to the bed and the more clothing flew off in various directions, the more intense the giggling got until it became little moans and sighs. Teagan almost forgot her little jar of cream. "Every time," the strange woman had said. "No exceptions."

"The training of Seamus Hogan begins now," Deirdre said when Teagan told her the proposed wedding dates might be a conflict and not the co-celebration he intended.

"He's a blank slate, just like your man," she went on with a smile. "But I, we, are definitely not going to step on your day. Another week or so won't matter. In fact," she leaned in to whisper as they sat in the tavern.

"I don't care if we marry at all. I think the sharing of lives, of tears and laughter, and love, is the important thing. But now the proprietor of this place is all concerned about propriety. He's afraid women will scold their men for coming here, and his trade will drop off. So now he's all a-flutter to marry. I think women are more practical about these things. Cormac and I ran wild in the heather for two years before we married, and his mother smiled at us. So I smile and say, 'yes, dear' to Seamus, and on we trudge toward married bliss."

17

Bridie

Teagan found Conor wrestling blocks of stone out of the soft ground with an iron bar. *When he works with his shirt off, he's impressive, even beautiful, so he is, and mine. I think even in the glory days of Tara, never did there beat a heart as full as mine.*

"She didn't exactly say she'd box his ears," she told Conor when he stopped to rest. "But he'll hear quite enough about setting a wedding date without consulting her." She paused to turn one of those sly grins up at him. "I would be shocked if he ever needs to take that lesson again."

◆ ◆ ◆

Ten days before their wedding Teagan sat under the huge oak tree at the edge of Kinvara and played idly with Conor's hand.

"There's no building here that could hold all the people we want to invite," she said. "So why not do it here, under this majestic tree?"

Conor caught the idea and enlarged it. "Aye, limbs begin so high on the trunk it makes a space like the inner vault of a cathedral, and on a more primitive level it cements an old and lasting bond between our people and groves of oaks. I wonder if the old druids ever conducted ceremonies here and if so does any of their magic linger?"

"Must we ask for permission? Who owns this grove, or what's left of it?"

Conor pulled her to her feet. "Whose trees these are, I am aware. His castle lies just yonder there. Let's go and see him now, my dear, and learn if we can wed right here. You should meet him anyway, and you should do the asking, both about the wedding site and about whether he will attend as our guest."

Sir William French was inspecting his garrison when he saw the couple approach along the seaside road. "That's it, Eoin, you can dismiss them," he told the nervous guard commander. "Better than last month." *Not much better. Eoin is a pleasant young man but there's not a trace of soldier in him. Not at all like young Conor here, but he'd be wasted in such a minor post. And that must be his Teagan. Oh, my, she is a breathtaking beauty.*

"A very good morning to you, Conor O'Canavan, and to you as well, young lady. I'm guessing that you are Teagan Ni Moran of Doolin. Conor told me you were smart and pretty. He certainly understated that second part." He watched her blush as if her cheeks could ever match the blaze of red on her head.

"Eoin!" he called. "Tell your mother we'll have mead for three in the West courtyard. Come you two, let us go there and talk."

When they were seated and served, Sir William toasted them and then fell silent. *They want something. How long will it take them to ask me, and which one will do the asking? He is smiling at her, which is easy to do, so she's the one. Look at those eyes, and that hair. Calm down, old man, this Irish rose is blooming way too late in your life.*

"Sir William," Teagan began firmly. "My experience of English lords is mixed at best. We are fugitives in County Clare because of events that began when the heir to Doonagore boasted he would rape me, would kill my father and Conor and burn down my father's tavern in Doolin. He has destroyed the tavern, but it's being rebuilt. Conor tells me the evil man will never touch me. I believe that." She reached for Conor's hand and continued, feeling the reassuring squeeze he provided.

"We will wed next week and we'd be pleased if you could witness our vows."

How can I say no? How can Conor refuse her appeal on any issue she raises? "I would be pleased to witness your wedding, Teagan. Where is it to be?"

"Well, that's our second request. Conor and I would like to marry under that huge oak tree beyond the O'Heyn ruins. He says it's your land, and we'll need your consent. You know, Catholics can't have a church that can seat everyone so we need another site."

"All right, then, we'll do it outside, under the oak. You do know that oak leaves are not rainproof?"

"It will not rain on my wedding. I promise you that."

Sir William was impressed but not convinced. "Young lady, if you can control the Irish weather, you'll be more famous than St. Bridget and Grace O'Malley combined."

Conor spoke up. "She didn't say she would do it, just that it would be done. We've got a little time to figure out how."

On their way home, hand in hand as usual, he said, "All right, Miss wonder-worker, how are you going to assure a dry wedding day in this green land where there's more rain than sun?"

Teagan turned on her most charming smile and said, "I have friends in high places.

Trust me on this one. There will be no rain on our wedding day."

◆ ◆ ◆

Two nights later Conor came home exhausted from a day of shifting stones, and she made love to him until he fell asleep. Then she got up, threw a dark cloak over her gown, and walked into a silver-painted night. At the edge of a pasture not far from the big oak she paused to see if anyone was nearby. She stepped into the bright white light and raised her arms over her head.

Bridie! Mathair Crionna! Can you hear me?

Always, my girl. Why do you summon me?

Oh, give me a moment. I wasn't sure this would work.

I told you it would.

Mathair Crionna, I apologize for the doubts, but I feel so much better now that I have reached you. Where are you?

I am close. Again, child, why do you seek me?

Och, I made a rash promise, so I did. I told Conor and Sir William French it would not rain on my wedding day. We're having the ceremony under that big oak tree over there. But I do not know how to control the rain, and I so want a perfect wedding.

And you want me to assure a perfect day.

Aye. I know it sounds selfish, but I do.

Teagan, boons like this have their costs. Life must be a balance between ups and downs, between joys and sorrows. You will get your perfect sunny day, but downstream in your journey through this life you must pay a price. Are you prepared for that?

But what price?

I cannot say. It will become clear in time, as clear as the day you seek. If I may, I will have a joy for now in exchange for a sorrow later.

You may have your wish.

Thank you. But how do you do that?

Teagan heard laughter. *That's my business, but it is not as hard as you think. Go home now, and tell no one. Nor may you brag when your day dawns bright and clear.*

Thank you. Teagan felt she was alone again and walked home slowly. *I will not consider the future sorrow, but rather the joy of now. Deirdre and I must talk about wedding gowns. I wish that were already done, but we still have a week.*

Conor was still deeply asleep and Teagan cuddled into her favorite position beside him, thinking about her wedding dress. *I think green would be nice, maybe with gold trim. I will ask Deirdre, she is such a warm and loving woman, almost like a mother instead of a mother-in-law. Tay, my girl, you are fortunate indeed.*

"Deirdre, when my father and the widow Boyle arrive, can you and Seamus put them up in the inn? The men are longtime friends, but I don't want her under my roof. I'd never have a moment to myself, too busy fending off her ideas on how I ought to run my wedding. I don't want to have to tell her she's not in charge."

Deirdre produced one of her warm smiles. "I can't wait to meet her. I've been told my own willpower is no trifling thing, so if you see smoke rising from the tavern it may be me telling her she's not in charge there either."

◆ ◆ ◆

The wind blew hard from the west on the day before Teagan's wedding. It brought in spates of rain, short bursts of sunshine and dire predictions of disaster at the next day's open-air ceremony. That notion came from the widow O'Brien. She quickly found a kindred spirit in Sinead Boyle, who landed in Kinvara wet, cold, and sour after hours of sailing through heaving waters in Ronan O'Malley's boat. It didn't help that Conor and Seamus led a surge of greeters who swarmed Malachi Moran and pretty much ignored her.

Even her own son seemed happier to see him than her. "Wait, my dear," Mother O'Brien said as they shared a bench and half-pints of ale in the Hogan tavern. "This rain will last, and that hard-headed girl will not listen to my good ideas for an alternate site tomorrow."

"I know how she is," the visitor responded. "She resisted good ideas from me for years, including the suggestion that my Patrick would be a perfect match. She surely didn't get that stubbornness from her father. My Malachi is so easy to manage. Oh, have you seen him?"

"Yes, I saw him walk off with his cane toward the O'Canavan house with Teagan and Conor. That boy is not a native of Kinvara, you know, came from somewhere up beyond Galway City when he was a lad, he and his oh-so-ladylike mother. And did you know this, my new friend? Seamus Hogan, who owns this place, is to be married before the end of the month, to that same Deirdre O'Canavan. It's true."

◆ ◆ ◆

"Come, Papa, let us show you where Conor and I will be nesting, it's a small house a short walk from here, and it's where Conor grew up, from about age nine, his mother Deirdre moved out the other day to go and live with Seamus Hogan, did you know they're getting married in another week or so?"

Conor tried to figure out her non-stop chatter. *She doesn't want to stop long enough to let him to say let's bring Sinead along. She really doesn't like Sinead, and that could get awkward.*

Early on her wedding day Teagan rose to check on Mathair Crionna's promise and was thrilled to see a few puffy clouds, pink in the eastern sky well before sunlight ever hit the ground. Standing in the courtyard she raised her arms to the sky. *Thank you.*

"You're supposed to do that at night, in the full moon."

Teagan spun around to see a small woman sitting on one of the benches under the wall and three stocky men and a much larger man on the others.

"Och, you scared me! How did you get in here? And who are these men?"

"Fear not, my girl. We are not here to spoil your special day but rather to celebrate it. Here is Dennis, and there, Daniel and Donal. They are my brothers. Conor knows them as the family scorekeepers. And that giant is my son, Cormac. We would visit for a few moments before things get busy. Can you wake him, please, and bring him out here?"

"Aye," was all she could say. The three smaller men were dressed in antique costumes and appeared to be wearing swords of bronze. The large man was also fully armed, his steel sword glinting in the early light, while the bronze blades just glowed.

"Good morning, bride," Conor said with a smile when she woke him. "Get dressed," she said. "We have visitors."

"I don't want to see anyone but you. Come back to bed."

"You will want to see these people. Now, up with you."

"Och, nagging already and we're not yet wed."

"Get used to it, husband-almost." Still grumbling, Conor put on fresh clothes and stepped into the brightening light of the courtyard. He was stunned.

"Good morning, my son," Cormac said.

"Happy wedding day," his grandmother said. The brothers smiled happily. "Father, is this a crisis day for me? I last saw you the day Dillon died."

The big man smiled. "Getting married is not a crisis, but an occasion of joy that I wish to share. And if it matters, I approve of your choice in brides."

"None of us will be seen at the ceremony," Mathair Crionna told him. "But we will all be there, wishing you both well." The brothers nodded without speaking.

"Conor, will you tell me what is going on here?" Teagan asked with a distinct alarm note in her voice. "I am not used to being visited by dead people, and ones who just refuse to grow old."

"We are an unusual family," Cormac O'Canavan said to her as she stood holding Conor's hand tightly. "Do not fear us. Our entire reason for being here is to support you, and eventually, your descendants. Precisely why, I may not say, but as spirits go, we are most definitely benign."

"Then why are you armed? What role is there for swords on such a day as this?" She felt a lot less apprehensive but still flabbergasted. *Oh, Teagan, meet your dead father-in-law and these leprechauns right out of Irish folklore, and your husband's grandmother, who looks thirty but may be three hundred or more.*

One of the short men she couldn't name spoke up with a smile. "We are armed because our land is under siege by the Sassenach, just the latest of many conquests, and we never know when they may strike once more to consolidate their domination."

Mathair Crionna spoke again. "Conor, do not go armed to your own wedding. It would be unseemly. But you are a fugitive, doing a very public deed. Give your arms to me and give your other arms to your bride. But if you need your weapons, you will have them instantly."

Conor put his arm around Teagan's waist and feeling her move closer as she spoke. "We are pleased beyond words you are all here, even though you've brought a sober note to what should be a day of gaiety. Conor's father, may I call you Cormac?"

"That's my name, Teagan Dearg Ni Moran."

Conor stirred next to her. "Father, will my mother see you?"

"No, son, she is well launched on a new love with Seamus Hogan, that good man, and I would not risk that to give her a glimpse behind a door that cannot be reopened. We are glad you chose to wed beneath the oak. That makes it easier for us to be there. Now, go with our blessings and greet your guests. We will be among them, but they will not see us. Nor will you." Teagan blinked, and in that time they were gone. She looked around, but they were alone in the courtyard, she and a suddenly pensive Conor.

"Cormac said yours is an unusual family," she said into his shoulder. "We Irish are not used to understatement, but how else to interpret 'unusual'?"

Conor smiled and held her closer. "If I ever get my grandmother figured out, I'll start on how her brothers and my father can even be here.

And the ultimate mystery, my heart, is you. I'll spend a lifetime working on that. But for now, let's begin our magical day. People will be arriving soon at the tavern."

"You go and meet them, Conor. I have a date with Deirdre and an elegant dress."

"Show me."

"Not a chance, boyo. It would be bad luck to see the dress before the wedding, and I'm not starting our life together under a bad luck sign."

18

Promises

Conor changed into his best clothes and walked toward Seamus Hogan's tavern. *Why does so much of life center on inns and pubs? Is it because we can't build churches that we use such places to gather?*

He entered the taproom to find it full of old friends and half-recalled faces.

"Fergal O'Malley! Thanks for coming. And here's Sea Dog. Good to see you too, shipmate." He looked past them to a thin man, slightly bent and clad in gray.

"I am Sean," the man said, trying a tentative smile. Conor's matching grin was brighter. "Ah, my teacher, I must show you how well the bow and I mesh."

"I know what you've done, lad. I'm here to see what's next for you."

Conor saw Sean holding a long staff, longer than the one he had seen as a boy, but similar. *I know there's a bow in there, and somewhere on his back some arrows under that cloak. Someone thinks this day may not pass in peace. That's a grim thought, and if it's true I'm doubly glad he's here. Oh, there's Thomas from Doonagore.*

"Ho, Thomas, and welcome." *And there's Brandon from Doorus and Brendan from Spiddal and a half-dozen more of our wool-smuggling allies.*

The conversational hum dropped as if some giant hand had stopped a waterfall. Sir William French stepped into the silence ahead of Eoin, his garrison chief, who looked nervously at all the Irish faces staring silently at their English overlord.

Conor waved and moved forward. *They can save their spats for tomorrow.*

"Sir William," he called out. "Welcome to my wedding day. We'll be outside for the ceremony and then back in here for the party. Here comes Father Turlough, who will conduct the wedding. He wants to lead us to the oak tree in procession, so if you will drain your mugs, I promise you we won't be gone long, the ale will be here when we return and Seamus told me no one will call, 'Closing time!' on this day"

Turlough O'Heyn looked uncomfortable and unfamiliar to his parishioners wearing his official vestments. *I knew where the stola was because I keep it in my pockets, but some of the robes had been put away so long I thought I'd never find them. And the brass poles with crosses that the altar boys carry had to be dug out from under the stable.*

Oh, there's the oak tree. It doesn't mean anything in the new faith that St. Patrick brought us, but it surely did in the old Celtic worship. I'm not sure these young people have shed the old faith entirely, and in fact most people retain traces of it, especially here in the west of Ireland. Either trees can't talk or maybe it's just that I can't hear them. But I would love to share a dram with this mighty oak, and learn what it has seen in the past few centuries.

In the tree's lower branches a small woman and four men sat in comfort watching the procession approach. One of the men laughed.

Bridie, a butterfly just flew right through you. Did you feel it near your shoulder? No.

Wouldn't you like to be down there instead of up here?

No again. We can do many things as we are now, but mingle with them we cannot do, except under the most special circumstances, and we have pushed the limits on that. Besides, we are here only to observe. Remember?

Donal stirred on his limb and spoke. *Here comes the priest. If he can't sense us then we are safe here. I believe Conor may be aware of us but the others should be without a glimmer. Isn't that true, Bridie?*

Don't discount that Teagan. I think she has potential. I thought so when I met her on the road to Doolin, and the more she's near us, the more sensitive she gets.

Conor walked behind the priest and the altar boys, and ahead of the crowd of townspeople and visitors gathered to watch the ceremony. *Well, some of them are here for the wedding, and others will just put up with it so they can get to the free drinks.*

Here's Sir William French walking beside me, my best man. It's a role I would gladly have given to Rory Donovan, but I'm not sure he was still mobile enough to make this walk, even if he hadn't been murdered. And Ronan backed out when I told him he would have to speak in public. All right, we're here. Where's Teagan?

Deirdre and Teagan left the house as soon as the bride put on her wedding dress. "Why don't I just raise the hood on the robe that hides my dress?" Teagan asked.

"That way we could just slip into the crowd and arrive with everyone else."

"No," Deirdre said, looking her daughter-in-law-to-be in the eye. "It is considered unlucky to walk the same path as the groom to reach the wedding site. You can leave together to go to the tavern, but we must find another way to the tree."

"That's just an old superstition. Nobody believes it any more."

Deirdre smiled and looked into those brown eyes so like her own. "Tay, this is an old land, and as you've seen, things exist here that don't fit the laws of logic. Think of my elusive mother-in-law. No, dear, we'll keep from stepping on old customs. After all, don't we both want a thriving marriage?"

Teagan subsided, but a toss of her head sent red curls flying. Deirdre took that as grudging consent. *She is so like me. It's like seeing myself in a mirror that has no glass.*

◆ ◆ ◆

The two of them, bride and matron of honor, stood behind the massive oak and listened to the crowd approach. Neither realized that benign creatures just above had acted to help them hide until the right moment. The brothers widened the apparent girth of the tree, just a little. Their sister blurred the edge between seen and unseen, just a little.

"When do we go out?" Teagan asked. "Whisht! I'll tell you."

They could hear everything, but they could not see Father Turlough

O'Heyn, tall and stooped, and majestic in his rarely worn finery. The old priest examined the tree. *I feel a presence here. We are not supposed to be able to sense trees, but I do. I must come back here alone.* He gave an almost invisible head shake and turned to look out over the crowd. Slowly, people stopped talking in anticipation of his words.

"We are gathered upon this hallowed site on an auspicious day. Why are we here?" He asked the ritual, rhetorical question.

"To witness a wedding," Sir William French answered, "between Conor Mac Cormac O'Canavan of this barony and parish, and Teagan Ni Moran of the barony and parish of Doolin, in County Clare."

As her name was spoken, Teagan emerged from behind the tree, glowing in her green dress with its gold trim and gauzy veil. Deirdre Ni Reilly O'Canavan followed and stood beside her. *Tay fussed over the semi-transparent veil, saying Conor had already seen her face and every other part of her, but I cited tradition again, and she gave up logic for custom. I hear whispers and gasps in the crowd. I think the dress is a success.*

The old priest looked at the slack-jawed young man beside him and saw him react to the stunning sight of his bride in her finery. O'Heyn's eye flickered to the lovely but nervous girl before him and he smiled encouragement. "Now, who brings this radiant young woman to be married to this fortunate young man?" he asked.

Malachi Moran struggled forward on his cane and took his daughter's arm with a glance so fond it brought a tear to Teagan's eye.

"I have raised this child alone since she was ten, and no one is closer to my heart. I stand here today proud to place her into the care of the finest husband I could have found for her, Conor Mac Cormac O'Canavan." He took her arm from its resting place on his forearm and placed her hand in Conor's. Teagan surprised herself by crying. Conor surprised himself by not crying. This was the symbolic joining he had so desired.

Turlough O'Heyn took his stola from around his neck and wrapped the long thin cloth around their wrists where the hands joined. "This is a ritual older than the faith I serve," he whispered to them. "But we continue because it is such a perfect mirror for the life-bonding we mark on this occasion." *I wish all couples would take this moment in their lives as gravely as these two seem to be doing.*

"Marriage is a self-inflicted sacrament," he intoned solemnly, looking for the faces in the crowd that would react to his words.

"Of all the seven, matrimony is the only one in which those who conduct the ceremony are its beneficiaries. We are all here as witnesses," he said with a broad gesture that embraced the entire landscape. "We are a social people, we Irish, and for the most part we enjoy being in each other's company. We gather for all kinds of occasions, but forgive me for thinking that a wedding is the best of those. This is Conor's day, and Teagan's day, and the rites they are about to perform make this the most solemn day of their lives so far. The rest of us are here simply to say by our presence, we approve of the bonding they undertake, a tying of the knot, if you will," and gestured toward the stola-covered wrists.

"We approve, but you two will perform and will bind yourselves to each other on a level much more profound than the ties on your arms."

He looked out over his audience, knowing most of the faces before him but not all. "The banns of marriage have been published the required three times, and announced from the pulpit as well. Those banns are required that I may speak these words to you: If anyone here knows of a valid reason why Teagan and Conor may not become as one on this day, speak now or never."

The old man stopped and let his arms fall, looking like a craggy statue. People in the crowd cast furtive glances at each other, waiting to be shocked by someone shouting, "They may not wed!" But no one did.

Father O'Heyn took his missal into one hand and placed his other on the ritually bound wrists of his wedding couple. "We use words to glue lives together. Words are the building blocks of ideas, and ideas are the nourishment of the mind. Our idea here is to splice these two lives into one, to borrow an expression from the world of sailors so well represented here."

In the second row Fergal O'Malley raised his hand and Ronan waved beside him.

"So we pay a lot of attention to the words used to seal marriages. Conor and Teagan have asked if they can use their own words, ones they have written to convey the idea that from this day on they are one. I don't often allow that, but these two have thought deeply and written well. Please listen as Conor goes first."

Conor stood with both hands on Teagan's, as they faced each other in front of the priest's weathered face. Her color was high and her eyes wide under the gauzy veil.

"Teagan, you are my heart and I shall love you until my last breath is gone. I shall not command you, for you are a free woman. And when I raise my hand to you, it shall be to feed you, not to strike you. Your face shall be my last vision of the day, your voice shall be my morning rooster, and your touch shall ever heal me. I shall be your shield against want and evil. Never shall we quarrel where others can hear us, and we shall resolve our differences before we sleep. I believe God has moved to bring us together, and I say to you, no man or woman shall ever sunder our bond. These are my promises to you on this our wedding day."

Conor had held Teagan's eyes with his throughout his vows. *She never blinked but she started to cry. Is that even possible? She's so beautiful, and she's about to pledge herself to me forever. Will I cry too?*

"Conor O'Canavan, you have weathered my temper and my silliness alike. But I tell you this as a free woman. I may test your patience but never your love. You are my roof and my walls. You are my joy and my strength. You nurture my heartbeat and my laughter. I am the moon to your sun, the wind at your back, and the shield to your sword. I shall stand with you through darkness and light, and I shall love you until the last breath leaves my body. These are my promises to you on this our wedding day." *He is staring at me so intently and here I am sobbing while making my vows. We are not exactly acting like ourselves, but I think I like the mood in this space. I wonder if those strange people can feel it.*

Aye. revel in it. It is rare. And you have our blessings, dear.

Seamus Hogan watched with pride and apprehension. *Am I going to look as thunderstruck as Conor when I marry his mother?*

Turlough O'Heyn had his own reaction to the vows. *Now I recall why we don't do this much. When they get it right, it stops hearts and starts tears. All right, let's finish.*

"Now, at the end of this ceremony, I unwrap the binding that signaled the hand-fasting between Conor and Teagan. Theirs is no longer a trial union, but a true marriage, so attested by all who came here as witnesses. Now the couple will withdraw from their fingers the rings from the Claddagh that signify their betrothal, and reverse them so the hearts on those rings point upward toward their own hearts. That will signify to all they are no longer single but bound in holy matrimony." *I like this new custom from that village. They seem to be onto something everyone can grasp and honor.*

"Now, young man, you may raise the veil that covers your bride's face. And by the way, I think you'll like what you see there." Conor lifted the gauzy cloth and gazed at Teagan's face, his wide grin overmatched by the glowing smile he saw. He leaned forward and bent a little, finding her willing lips in a tender kiss. Moving his lips to her ear, he whispered. "Pretty tame kiss for us, but we don't want to scandalize the village." Teagan squeezed his hand and giggled, unheard below the applause of the crowd.

"Finally," the old priest said. "With the consent and best wishes of all of us, may you walk together in sunshine, may you always be kind to each other, and may your children be your blessings. We ask this in the name of God, who loves us all. Amen."

Conor and Teagan, walking briskly hand in hand, led a surge of celebrants and witnesses on a beeline path to Seamus Hogan's tavern, where ale and whiskey waited, and where the dancing would soon begin. Seamus and Deirdre walked side by side behind the priest and the lord of Dunguaire. "Are you all right?" he asked as they tried to keep pace with those ahead of them.

"Aye, Seamus. Filled with pride and love for them, and a bit shy of tears for myself. It seems I have used up my allotment today. Oh, do you dance?"

Hogan threw back his head and laughed. "I promise you one twirl around the floor, but only after the crowd thins out. I'm the host of this event, and I must see to my duties."

She smiled, reaching up to tweak his cheek. "You are a slippery fish, Seamus Hogan, a slippery fish indeed. Oh, what's that?"

19

Michael

The bridal couple and their leading escorts stopped abruptly as they turned the last corner leading to the tavern. Before them a large man stood with drawn sword pointed at Conor.

"I am Michael Cole, High Sheriff of County Clare. You are under arrest for the murder of Chester Berry of Ennis at Doonagore. You will place yourself in the hands of my deputies," he said, pointing to five well-armed soldiers behind him.

"You will do no such thing!" A furious French stepped up beside Conor. "I am Sir William French, lord of Dunguaire and the lands all around. In fact, sir, you stand on my land right now and you are not welcome. Now put away that ridiculous parade-ground sword, and march your minions back to Ennis. You are not in County Clare and you have no authority here."

"He is a murderer. He killed an Englishman, and I will see him in chains!"

"Some day you may, but not today. Do you believe in evidence down in County Clare, or do you rely entirely on the rantings of a crazy man who happens to be the heir to Doonagore? If you really want to conduct an inquest into the events surrounding that death, please proceed. Of the five witnesses from the village of Doolin, four are here today. Where is your witness? Where are young Bailey's retainers? Indeed, where is he?"

"I am here!" Arthur Bailey shouted as he came out from behind a broken wall.

"Tay, get behind me!" Conor yelled. "Arthur Bailey, do not spoil my wedding day.

You can't always get what you want even if you are an English heir, and you will never win Teagan's heart. Surely you can see the accident of your birth is not an entitlement to your obsessions."

Bailey stood beside the Sheriff with a stunned look on his face.

"But no one says no to the landed gentry, to the English overlords of this squalid land. Teagan is the only flower on my father's lands, and I must harvest her." His expression twisted into rage and his voice roughened. "And I will have my justice! I will kill him and I will have her!" He held a musket high and glared at Conor and Teagan.

"If that thing goes off you are a dead man," Sir William shouted. "And I don't care whose heir you are! Sheriff, when the Lord enumerates your sins, allowing this demented man to handle firearms is sure to be among them. I meant what I said. If he fires that musket, he will die. And you will too, before you have a chance to note that Arthur Bailey is a half-step ahead of you on the road to Hell."

"I will speak!" Teagan shouted, her hair flying in the wind. "Arthur Bailey, you are lower than a mouse dropping! You are a flyspeck on the tapestry of your time. Think about this. The only reason you are alive today is that my husband once kept you from dragging me into your hands. I would have killed you within a day. I said husband, worm! I am a married woman, wed this day to Conor O'Canavan. I may even be bearing his child, and I am happy. Do you understand me?"

"I hear you, but I don't understand," Bailey said, examining the lace cuffs on his shirt. "I see that this man and I are rivals for your affections, but I should win. I am the heir and it is my destiny. I don't hate this Irish peasant, but I will kill him if he tries to keep me from you."

"Sheriff Cole," French, watching colors and emotions work on Bailey's face. "I am amazed you would allow your office to be bent to the will of this sick man, and even more startled you would force this to a showdown between Clare and Galway, indeed between the provinces of Leinster and Connacht. It could rip the West apart and could affect our control over the restive people we rule in this troubled land. Besides," he added with a gesture to the area behind the sheriff. "I think the time when you might have won this tilt has passed."

Cole grounded his sword and looked over his shoulder. A handful of sheepmen and sailors stood in a row, armed with whatever they could find. Beside them, a gaunt man in a gray cowl pushed arrows point-first into the earth in front of him, ready for rapid fire.

Cole and his men could also see four fully armed warriors, one of them much larger than the others. No one else could see them, but the effect was striking. Some of Cole's detail of soldiers moved closer together and watched their rear.

High Sheriff Cole turned back to see Conor holding his own sword, Teagan trying to hold a musket steady, and Seamus Hogan with a bow in his hand. Further, the six members of the castle garrison and the six members of Conor's Fianna flanked Sir William French and Conor O'Canavan. All were armed and Eoin stood trembling but steady, hoping the moment would pass.

"What say you now, Michael Cole?"

"This is not over, Sir William. There will be another day."

"There may be, but in your jurisdiction," the knight answered. He slid his sword into its scabbard and signaled his men to stand down.

"Before this conference ends, I would speak with the man who has tried to ruin my wedding day," Conor said. "Arthur Bailey, hear this, and the rest of you, mark what I say. Your sick vision of Teagan in your arms, in your bed, is over. She is all that your fevered mind imagined, and more, and you will never, ever have her. Further, I will watch you closely in the future, and this I say to you, Sheriff Cole. I do not fault you for trying to do your duty to the law, but I question your judgment in listening to this man."

He took Teagan by the hand and faced the sheriff. "I am a married man with a job to do here in Kinvara, a man who wishes nothing only to live in peace with his neighbors, be they near or far. But if ever I hear and can prove that Arthur Bailey has taken out his bile on the village of Doolin or anyone there who has annoyed him, I will place his head on the wall outside your own castle. And if that means a new revolt in the West, it will be due to your lack of ability to control a wild beast among you."

High Sheriff Cole looked around him and thought he had never seen a grimmer crowd. He had no doubt that a false move would ignite a slaughter. *This man commands more force than I knew of in this hamlet. And perhaps I should reconsider what I heard from Bailey. The little monster could have started a war, and we would have lost the first battle. I could use a drink.*

Sir William French maintained his position in part by nursing an ability to read faces, and he could read Cole's easily. "Seamus Hogan," he called. "Do you think if this man leaves his escort outside to watch over Arthur Bailey, you could place a pint in his hand? As a gesture of truce, you understand."

Hogan was pretty good at reading faces, too, and saw relief reflected in most of them. All except Teagan, who clearly wanted to shoot Bailey with the musket she didn't know how to use.

"All right, we're late for a wedding party. Let's go. You, too, Sheriff."

◆ ◆ ◆

Inside, where musicians warmed up and the clink of mugs increased, Teagan and Conor stood accepting good wishes from guests. Sea Dog decided Teagan was his new best friend and would not get off her skirts. Sir William took a mug to Paddy O'Brien, who began to fill it. "No, boy," the lord of Dunguaire said. "Not ale. Fill it with that good water of life from up in County Antrim. It's for the sheriff."

Teagan Ni Moran, newly O'Canavan, looked at her groom and got a wink in return. "Do you feel like a married lady?" he asked. She grinned and gave him a little shove. "Don't push me on the lady part, my man, but I surely do feel married. And using my new status, will I be an advisor in this war you're trying to start?"

"What? What war?"

"Conor, you told that sheriff if Arthur Bailey moves against Doolin, you would bring down the fires of Hell on the English. Did you mean that?"

"Tay, you know I make promises, not threats. And yes, I meant what

I said. And yes, if things go to pieces, you will be my best counselor. But for now, suppose you practice being the most beautiful woman I've ever married. Shall we dance, my heart?"

◆ ◆ ◆

"I like it here," Sinead Boyle told Malachi Moran. "It's bigger than Doolin. And Mother O'Brien has become a good friend. Can we stay until the next wedding?"

"Aye, why not?" Malachi said. "Don't you want more time with Patrick?"

"Well, yes, but he'll be coming back to Doolin. I don't think Teagan will."

"Aye, Sinead, I believe you have the truth on your tongue there. But for the moment, we can stay until Deirdre O'Canavan becomes Deirdre Hogan. It's a comfort to me to see my good friend married at last and to a woman who's connected to my daughter's new husband. And wasn't he magnificent facing down that sheriff and that crazy man from Doonagore?"

"Malachi, he scared the devil out of me with all that talk of violence. I hope all that was just to make an impression and he didn't mean it."

"But he did. Couldn't you tell? You were right there. Not everything men say is driven by ale and whiskey. He will fight if he is pushed, and I think that makes it less likely that he will be pushed. And, he is a perfect match for my Tay. Did you see how they look at each other?"

◆ ◆ ◆

"Conor, may I pry you away from this lovely vision in green and red, with gold trim, for a minute or two? Teagan, I'll bring him back soon, and until then there's a line of men awaiting your attention." Sir William French took Conor by the arm and steered him to a table shunned by the crowd because of the man who sat before them. Michael Cole, High Sheriff of County Clare, had worked his way through most of a mug of Irish whiskey with little apparent effect.

"Sheriff Cole and I have agreed we came into peril today, and any small thing could have started a slaughter. Here is our further accord. One, you will stay out of County Clare. Two, he will stay out of Galway. Three, he will provide a suitable dowry for Teagan, which will essentially cover the destruction of Malachi Moran's tavern. That money will be drawn from Doonagore funds. Four, the two of us will visit Sir Edmund Bailey to secure those funds and to persuade him that his disturbed son is a plague on the West. Potentially he's a spark that may ignite another in a sad series of uprisings that serve only to bleed this land of its best men."

Conor raised his mug, ignoring the fact that only fumes remained of the ale that had once filled it. "That is both fair and wise," he said and smiled at Cole. "I would not have believed two Englishmen could reach such an accord, and I will abide by its conditions. But I tell you again, Sheriff, if that animal is allowed to take out his ire on Doolin, all my consents are dissolved, and I will rage through Clare and leave waste in my wake, to borrow a seafaring term. With that exception, I sing praise to your solution. Paddy! We are dry here!"

The young barman quickly brought fresh mugs to the table.

"There is one more thing to say," Conor stated, thinking that he saw a flinch on the sheriff's face. *He thinks I'm going to drive an arrow into his finely crafted diplomacy.*

"I am an Irish man in my own land. I chafe under its seizure by Englishmen, including the two of you. But I am not irrational. I do not lump you together with Neville Morton, who seized my family's land north of Galway, nor with Arthur Bailey, who has nothing positive whatever within him. Please listen when I say I will cooperate with you, but I am not one of you and never will be. Sir William, I am grateful to you for interceding once again on my behalf, and I say that in front of this man."

High Sheriff Michael Cole stirred on his bench. "Sir William, this man could be a very dangerous enemy. Why do you tolerate him, why not just execute him?"

"Well, as he once told me, my new friend, peace is more profitable than strife. Besides, if I kill him I will start a new rebellion. And finally, remember the force he mustered outside a few minutes ago? I'm not sure I could bring him to heel by force without starting an uprising. So I think my course is the right one and sláinte, my companions."

Sheriff Cole trudged off with the protesting Arthur Bailey in the firm grasp of his men and the wedding party dwindled down to close family and chronic drunks. Seamus Hogan had sent a quite impaired Paddy

O'Brien home and was dancing with Deirdre O'Canavan when the bride and groom came to say their farewells. Teagan watched the older couple, not wishing to disturb their moment together. *Somehow I expected her to be graceful, but I didn't think Seamus had any music in him at all and look at the man move.*

Conor embraced them both and opened an arm for Teagan to move in.

"Seamus, you've been good to me ever since we came here, and to my mother as well. We're away now, to explore new mysteries. Tay has heard there's something else that married people are supposed to do, and we'll be off now to try to figure out what that might be."

The women kissed and the men shook hands and parted, leaving Seamus and Deirdre alone with the receding echoes of music that had stopped playing.

"They smile and laugh so easily," Seamus said. "Some day they will learn how fragile the laughter of youth is, and how life erodes that sunniness."

"Don't grow weeds in the garden of your mind," Deirdre chided him. "I remember being that young," she said into his eyes.

"I do, too," he answered. "But it wasn't as joyful as what you remember."

"Then come upstairs and we'll find a trace of whatever you think you missed."

"Not a bad day," he said with a smile and a sigh. "We started a marriage, stopped a war, and now I'm on my way to bed with a woman wiser and lovelier than ever I thought I would find. Aye, my love, not a bad day at all."

◆ ◆ ◆

A few minutes later Teagan realized her new husband was a bit the worse for wear. She got him into the house and undressed him while he aimed a silly grin in her general direction. *Teagan Ni Moran, welcome to your wedding night.* She slipped off the green dress, not bothering to hang it up.

I wonder if he'd still be awake if he knew there was nothing under that greenery but me. She snuggled into bed beside her softly snoring husband and produced a small smile that lasted until sleep found her, too.

20

Pookie

Ronan O'Malley stopped in Kinvara three days after Teagan's wedding and three days before Deirdre's. He noted a role reversal between the women. Tay was now fussing over Deirdre's dress while she swatted at Sea Dog, who was still smitten. He found Malachi behind Hogan's bar, practicing his craft while the widow Boyle watched possessively.

"I'll be running down to Doolin the day after the wedding, my friends. I can pick you up about mid-morning, and it's welcome you'll be."

"No, I will not set one foot on that smelly scow, young Ronan. I will not be on the same boat with that awful dog, and I will not subject my belly to the torture of a horizon that won't stand still. I would rather walk to Doolin. Malachi, I will not go there by sea."

"Ronan, thank you for the offer, it was thoughtful and kind," Malachi said with a smile and a shrug. "I would accept, but we must travel together, so we must, and so we will go by land."

Ronan nodded. *Why would he want to go anywhere with this woman, or pass any time with her at all? Is there some hold she has on Malachi, beyond the notion that she's caring for him? Women like this give women a bad name, and besides, Sea Dog won't go near her, and he has pretty good instincts about people. Anyway, I'll ask Paddy O'Brien if he knows of any land transport. Wait, why is it my job to see them back to Doolin? Maybe*

I just feel sorry for Malachi. Loses his tavern, loses his daughter, takes an

*arrow in the foot, and now is "rewarded" with the attentions of Smothering
Sinead. I'd laugh, except it would be mirth mocking misery.*

◆ ◆ ◆

Conor and Teagan were the first to congratulate Kinvara's latest newly-
weds. He had been best man for Seamus, and she had served as Deirdre's
bridal attendant.

"Do you feel married?" Teagan asked as they toasted after the ceremony. "Yes," Deirdre said with a smile. "And I'll make sure Seamus
does, too."

Conor looked around him, noting he'd seen most of the faces in the
room for more than a decade. "At least we had no invasions from County
Clare, and no crazy people to distract us. Mother and Seamus, Teagan
and I wish you well. I will tell all my friends to patronize your pub."

Seamus laughed, his arm around his new wife. "Och, 'tis a grand gesture, boyo, but everyone you know already comes here, and, there's no
other tavern in the village. But thanks for your support. Now, let's go see
Malachi off. He and Sinead are starting back to Doolin today."

◆ ◆ ◆

"Conor, look!" Deirdre said. "Isn't that the old cart we used to move our
things here when we came to Kinvara so long ago?"

"Aye, and look at the horse, Tay. It's our old friend Pookie."

Malachi looked over his new transport as if it were the royal coach.
"Your man Ronan got Paddy O'Brien to scratch around for a horse and a
cart, and this is what he came up with. I don't think he knew either one
had a history."

Conor handed Sinead up to her seat over the high wheel on the right
side, and Malachi, who admitted being a novice driver, took the reins
on the left.

"Don't worry, Papa," Teagan called as the bundle-laden cart began to
move. "Pookie has a lot of experience at being a horse. He will know
what to do."

The four well-wishers waved until the cart rumbled over a small hill.

"Seeing people off is thirsty work," Seamus declared. Teagan kept her eyes on the spot where the cart had vanished.

"Conor, I felt an odd chill when I kissed my father and I can't explain why. I think he's well and truly trapped by Whitey's mother, who will make him miserable. And I have a fear that I'll never see him again."

Deirdre could see she was near tears and pulled Teagan into a hug. "Tay, sometimes writers come up with a really good idea that just lives in the language. A hundred years ago William Shakespeare had Juliet say to Romeo, 'parting is such sweet sorrow'. Sweet because she anticipated seeing him again, and soon. I think that's where you are with your father. Of course you'll see him again, and soon. Now, my new husband, let us all go in and celebrate our special day."

"You are not permitted behind your bar on your own wedding day," Paddy O'Brien declared as the group entered. "Today you are not the host but the guest of honor. I congratulate you and the new Madam Hogan, I have a toast for you, Seamus. Raise a goblet of good mead for yourself and your lovely bride, and we all say, 'Sláinte!'"

"Sláinte!" came a full roar as the bridal couple smiled and clicked goblets.

"Now!" Paddy called. "Let the dancing begin!" Teagan grabbed Conor and led him to an open space on the floor, where she curtsied and smiled happily at her own new husband as he stumbled through a jig.

◆ ◆ ◆

"How do you know where we're going?" Sinead asked. "It all looks like a wasteland to me, a dull desert of stone."

"Pookie is on a track that runs south and west. Doolin is south and west of Kinvara. We're heading the right way, Sinead."

"But it all looks alike, barren and rocky and hostile. I don't like this place."

Malachi twitched the reins and Pookie ignored him. "Look," he said. You've lived on the edge of the Burren all your life. Have you never explored it?"

"I have always been a village girl," Sinead said. "Not like your daughter, who ran wild in the limestone after her mother died."

"Sinead, if you don't want to find your own way back to Doolin, keep a civil tongue. You take privileges you've not earned, and you're annoying me. Stop it."

"Well, you really know how to flatter a girl, don't you?"

Malachi laughed, but he made the sound as harsh as he could. "The word 'girl' hardly applies here, Sinead. Take a look at yourself, if you can find a mirror big enough. And the next time you say something that maligns Teagan, I will box your ears. Horse, go faster!" Pookie twitched his ears and kept to his pace.

Sinead sat on her side of the cart, fuming. *I told that Widow O'Brien how easy he was to manage. His foot is not much closer to healing, but his confidence is back, and the truth is, I prefer it when there's a little edge to him. Now I have to figure out how to get back on his good side. Maybe there's still a future here.*

Malachi seemed to have recovered his usual placid temperament. "Look, Sinead, you see that upright rock with the spiral design cut into it? It's one of the markers dividing the ancient Irish kingdoms of Leinster and Connacht. It also marks the border between Galway and Clare, and now we're in Clare, just like that. We should get back to Doolin by tomorrow."

"But what about tonight? We can't just sleep on the ground!"

It's probably a sin to enjoy her discomfort so much.

"We'll sleep in the cart," Malachi said. "There's room enough, that is if we don't mind curling up together." After a light supper and a cup of tea over a fire, they got back into the cart. Pookie, staked out near a clump of grass, ignored them. Heavily swathed in her clothes, Sinead turned onto her back and stared upward.

"Mallie, there's a lot of stars up there."

"Don't call me Mallie. I'm not a puppy. As to the stars, whenever you expand your horizons, a lot of new things become visible. You may be beyond your place of comfort, Sinead, but there is a sense of peace and order out here."

"It makes me feel very small," she said.

Good. It must be the first time in years. What am I going to do about her when we get back? I needed some care when Teagan and Conor left, and I'm glad she was there for that, but the trip has put us together much more intimately than I wanted. I'm sure her expectations are high, now that she's seen two weddings back to back. Every time she looks at me I feel as if she's measuring me for a collar. All I want to do is run my pub and try to make my village a better place to live. I just can't see where Smothering Sinead fits into that. She's like an old rose. The petals are gone and so is the sweetness, but the thorns are still there and still sharp.

◆ ◆ ◆

Tavern-keepers are not by nature morning people. Malachi was annoyed when the birds went to work as the new day brightened from gray to silver. *Silly birds are trying to sing some color into the morning. I like color, but this early I don't like noise. Is that odd?*

As the morning sun moved high and swung south over the Burren, Malachi's musings over his long-term future collided with his short-term future. Pookie stopped short and the dozing driver almost lost his seat.

A man stood in the roadway next to a saddled horse whose reins trailed on the ground. He held a musket pointed at the cart and wore a sword at his hip. Malachi came awake quickly.

"Arthur Bailey, get out of the road! You are blocking our passage."

"I will stand where I please. No one tells me what to do, least of all a peasant publican. I am on my way back to Kinvara to kill your son-in-law and to seize your daughter once and for all."

"You will do no such thing!" Sinead stood in the cart and yelled at Bailey.

"Sinead, sit down and shut your mouth, if you would live. He has a musket, and he's crazy enough to use it. Now, young Bailey, you must be planning an ambush, because in a free fight Conor would squash you like a cockroach."

"I am the equal of any man and better than most. I will win. It's my destiny." Malachi shook off Sinead's restraining hand, his anger burying his caution.

"Arthur Bailey, you are, as my Teagan said, lower than a mouse dropping. You are a disgrace to your father and to the Bailey family name. I cannot understand how even an Englishman could be so dishonorable."

"Understand this, you Irish animal!"

Bailey, his face mottled and his teeth showing, swung the musket toward Malachi Moran and pulled the trigger.

Malachi cried out and fell backward onto the cart's floor. Bailey staggered and fell from the gun's recoil. Pookie the carthorse reared and took off at a run down the road, the cart jouncing behind him. And Bailey's saddle horse, spooked by the booming noise and by Pookie's reaction to it, ran off in the opposite direction, leaving his rider in the middle of the road examining the heavy gun he had dropped.

◆ ◆ ◆

Sinead Boyle screamed for fifty yards and then cursed for another hundred. Finally she sawed on the reins enough to slow the terrified horse. Trotting at a speed he hadn't sustained in years, Pookie and his burden rattled down the last few miles, and when she saw the Doolin rooflines, she finally dared to glance at Malachi.

She screamed again and urged the horse to go faster. Malachi lay pale and very still on the cart's floor, with blood pouring from a gaping hole in his chest.

The noise brought men out of the tavern as the sweating horse stopped and stamped nervously until someone grabbed his bridle and soothed him. A man shoved a bar towel into Malachi's wound. Other hands lifted him and placed him on the newly rebuilt bar of his tavern. Faces crowded around and Sinead got pushed to the edge of the throng. *They're all acting like bees after someone kicks their hive. I think he's dead.*

Maybe if I hadn't insisted on coming back by land, he would still be alive. When are they going to ask me what happened? I wish Patrick were here. He would take charge. Oh, here's that Thomas, the one who worked for Bailey. Patrick says he's a good man.

Thomas came over to where Sinead sat. He had two mugs of ale in his hands, and put one down gently in front of her.

"Mother Boyle," he said in his flawed Irish. "It must have been horrible."

For the next five minutes Sinead had the rapt attention of a growing number of men. She cried and drank her way through the narrative.

"Cold, he was, cold like the Atlantic in a winter gale. He just cursed poor Malachi and shot him. There was spittle running out of his mouth and his eyes were wild.

Malachi, the poor wee man, he just cried out and fell back. He never moved again. He's dead, isn't he, Thomas?"

"Aye, Mother Boyle, he sits before St. Peter's gates and awaits admission to walk among the saints and angels. I am sorry, lady, he was a good man, and I know you were close to him. Do you want someone to walk you home?"

"Thomas, this is my home now. I will go upstairs and rest. You will have someone go and fetch Patrick, won't you?"

"Aye, and Teagan and Conor, too. We must move quickly, because the poor man will not keep for long in this summer heat."

Thomas looked around the room. "We must plan, Mother Boyle. We must consider very carefully what to do." He rose and crossed the tavern.

"Who has the fastest boat?" Eyes turned toward Kevin Haggerty, who blushed. "Take two men and sail to Kinvara as fast as ever you have. Bring back Teagan and Conor, and White Patrick as well."

One of the men stepped forward and shook his finger. "You are new here, Sassenach. Who gave you the right to issue orders?"

Thomas smiled and touched his heart. "I owe a debt of gratitude to Conor and Teagan for helping me find a place and peace here, and to Whitey for teaching me a useful skill. I am trying, in their absence, to do what must be done. Gladly will I yield that task to anyone among you who wants to do it in my place."

"The tiller is in your hand," the man said. "Kevin, away now, and take Liam and Keith with you. Fart on the sails if you must, but make that boat move."

Three men ducked out and trotted toward the Doolin harbor, not forgetting a bit of ale to wash down the cheese and bread they were given.

Thomas pointed toward a group of four men sitting near the door. "Would you move our Malachi to the wine storage room? It's cooler there. We'll need some help cleaning blood off the bar and off the cart. Move their bags in here and someone go find Mother Milligan to sit with Sinead. Did anyone see to the horse?"

The answer came from somewhere in the crowd. "As soon as we got him off the cart, he headed for his old barn, trailing his reins. Terry went after him and made sure he was fed and watered. By the way, nobody has asked me what I think, but if that should ever happen, I think when Pookie bolted, he saved Sinead's life."

21

Katie

The long summer twilight filtered through the canvas cover above the outdoor tables at Seamus Hogan's tavern in Kinvara. Conor and Teagan sat in a companionable silence with Deirdre and Patrick, while Seamus tended bar.

"The stones were heavier today," Conor said, forking up the last of a slice of cake. The treat was a recent addition to the tavern menu, one traceable to the arrival of Deirdre, newly Hogan, at the tavern. It was wildly popular. "But only at the end of the drinking," one of the regulars declared, and so the cake became the Hogan tavern's closing ritual.

"We'll need more," said White Patrick Boyle. "There won't be enough stone remaining in the old ruin to build the quay."

"There's another rock pile near the castle," Seamus said. "Some say it's old King Guaire's original fortress, but nobody really knows. Let's have a look in the morning."

"Good idea," Whitey said. "Can't have a quay that's not long enough to . . ." He stopped to the sound of running feet, the heavy thump of a man unused to running.

"Kevin Haggerty! Why are you here and in such a rush? Sit you, man and maybe Seamus can find another mug."

"Och, Patrick, it's bad! A dark day down in Doolin, dark as a moonless midnight."

Teagan gripped Conor's hand and said, "Something is deadly wrong here."

Patrick shoved Haggerty into a chair and yelled at him. "If you don't stop raving like Tim Toomey, I will lower my fist to you. Now, what brings you here so breathless?"

The man took in a deep measure of ale and spoke sadly. "Your mother and Teagan's father were no more than three miles from Doolin when Arthur Bailey stopped them in the road and shot Malachi with a musket. The sound scared the horse and he bolted for the village with the cart bouncing along behind. Bailey's horse ran away, too, and we could hear Sinead screaming. When they reached the pub, he was dead. Och, Teagan, I'm so sad to bear such tidings, but it's true. He's laid out in the storage room, but we must get you back there, now."

Teagan had gone pale and leaned heavily into Conor's shoulder, wordless. There was no doubting the truth in Haggerty's tale.

Conor eased her into Deirdre's arms and stood, his face cold. "Mother, go with her to the house for clothing and weapons. Take Seamus with you and meet us at the boat in fifteen minutes. White Patrick and Deirdre and Seamus will go with us and sail through the night. Paddy, round up the Fianna and anyone else willing to fight for justice and follow as you can. We will bury Malachi, we will comfort Sinead and Teagan, and then we will avenge Malachi Moran, that good man. And as we do, we shall see whether the English still control this part of Ireland. You, go get Father Turlough and tell him he's going with us. You, stay here and listen and then go to Dunguaire and tell Sir William whatever you learn about this. Now Kevin, I know this is hard, but we need the full story, as much as you can recall, to help us plan, and to keep the lord of Dunguaire abreast of the tale."

When Haggerty finished his recital, a man rose and left the tavern. "I'll repeat this word for word, as close as I can when I get to Dunguaire. What do you think he'll do?"

"He who?" Seamus asked. "Sir William or the murderer? Arthur told Malachi and Sinead he was coming here to kill Conor and capture Teagan."

Conor stood up. "The lord of Dunguaire will detain the heir of

Doonagore if he comes here. If not, I will hunt him down after we see to Malachi. Ah, Father Turlough, I'm glad you decided to come with us."

"I didn't have much choice," the priest grumbled. "This overgrown gossoon was a lot more polite when he was an altar boy."

"There's a certain urgency about this, Father, and I regret that. We have a body to bury and a murder to avenge. You'll have your part in at least one of those events. Ah, there's Teagan. Come now, the tide soon turns and the sea is fickle."

Two hours into the voyage Conor crept across the boat to where Teagan stared at a horizon that would not brighten.

"I can't sleep," he said, rubbing the stubble on his face.

Teagan laughed and leaned in to whisper in his ear. "I have a fail-safe remedy for that, but I can't share it with you among all these people in an open boat."

Conor grinned, his first since the man from Doolin stormed into the tavern. "It will be a long day, Tay. I just don't want to fall asleep in the middle of it."

She squeezed his hand. "If you nod off, I will breathe in your ear, like this." He quivered and smiled. "That should work, my love."

"Do you have a plan?" she asked.

"Yes, the beginnings of one. Is there anyone in the village who goes to the castle frequently? To deliver food or fuel or to take away waste?"

"Yes, old Katie McManus and her mute husband Hughie drive a cart up there from their stable in Doolin almost every day."

"Can you have someone ask her to come by the tavern in the morning on their way? The idea would be to keep Doonagore up to date on events in the village. Make sure she sees you, and I'll make sure she sees another figure, a wanted man skulking around the inn."

"Oh, she'll talk about that all right. One of the village jokes is that it doesn't matter that Hughie can't speak, because she talks enough for three. If she sees you here, she's likely to whip that old horse to ribbons getting the story to the Baileys."

Conor grinned, but there was no laughter in those blue eyes. "Perfect. And try to find out whether Sir Edmund is there. To my knowledge he's been away ever since this nasty business began. My idea is to lure the son out of the fortress so I can face him. I think if he knows you're here and believes I'm not, he'll come out."

◆ ◆ ◆

Horses are less successful than dogs at showing affection, but they either like or dislike the people who command them. A tired old dun in Doolin answered to the name King Willie when he felt like it and disliked most of the people around him. But he liked Hughie Mac Manus because Hughie never yelled at him. And besides, the man knew just where to scratch.

On the morning after Conor's return to Doolin, King Willie backed willingly between the poles that connected him to the wagon he would pull to Doonagore. His nose told him this time it carried turf and fresh eggs from the village. Hughie checked the straps and buckles around the horse and whistled a little as he worked. King Willie nudged his hand until it found the scratching place and then whuffled contentedly. Katie Mac Manus came out of their cottage talking, as usual. Not for the first time, Hughie wished his ears would stop working, just for a while.

"Come on, Hughie, we're to stop at the tavern. I want to see how they're getting on with the funeral plans. Of course we have to go by there any-how because it's on our way, but it would be good to see what's going on with our own eyes. Himself will want to know, so he will."

Hughie thought she used the word 'himself' to refer to Bailey the younger. *I think he's a poisonous toad, the kind a dog spits out after one bite. And this time I think he has boiled his brain in his own bile. The village won't abide the murder of Malachi Moran, that good man, who poured me many a free pint. Said he liked the pleasure of my company since I didn't chatter the night away, even after a wee dram or two. Och, the Powers protect me, she's talking again.*

"They say Mother Milligan was called to the tavern last night to look after Sinead. Maybe we can catch her there, Hughie. You know how she talks."

Hughie twitched the reins, and King Willie trotted along the road to the tavern.

Out of habit he stopped there. Sometimes there was a carrot or even an apple. Katie jumped off the wagon and headed for the door. She could see someone ducking around the corner, someone who looked young and seemed to fear being seen. She pushed into the main taproom.

"Teagan Dearg, what are you doing here?"

"This is my home, Katie, and my father has been murdered. Sinead and I are preparing his poor body for burial. We came as soon as we heard, and White Patrick, too. And Conor's mother and her new husband Seamus."

"And what of Conor, the fugitive? I saw someone sneaking around the corner as I came in here. Is Conor O'Canavan with you?"

"Katie, on the day we were married, the High Sheriff came to Kinvara and tried to arrest Conor for the death of that friend of Arthur Bailey. He did not succeed. And on that day the Sheriff and Conor made an agreement. Conor stays out of County Clare and the Sheriff stays out of County Galway. They drank to seal the bargain. And my husband keeps his promises."

"So he's not trying to avenge Malachi?"

"I didn't say that. In fact he told the Sheriff that if anything traceable to Arthur Bailey should happen to Malachi or to the tavern, that he, Conor, would mount young Bailey's head on the wall of the Sheriff's own castle in Ennis. And as I said, Conor O'Canavan is a man who keeps his promises. Oh, since you're going to Doonagore, please tell them nobody from there will be welcome here when we lay my father to rest tomorrow. There will be some very angry people at the cemetery, and if they don't want a war, they will stay away."

Teagan watched as Katie Mac Manus hurried out of the building. *She's scuttling, and with those prominent eyes, she looks like a frightened crab. I think she'll rehearse her story to Hughie, the poor wee man, all the way to Doonagore.*

She went outside to see the couple rolling slowly up the road toward the little castle on the hillside. Katie's arms waved in animated speech, and it seemed to Teagan that Hughie's head was hunched even farther than usual into his shoulders. She turned around and grinned at the inn.

"If any fugitive is hiding there come out, come out, whoever you are!"

A smiling Conor emerged from behind the building. "You certainly gave her enough to keep her tongue busy. Did you learn whether Bailey Senior is there?"

"No," she said. "But people here say he's not, that he's been away in Dublin for weeks now. I'll catch her on her way back and try to learn what the mood is up there." She laughed. "It's almost as if she and Hughie are go-betweens, reporting to each side what the other is doing. I'll bet she's never felt so important."

He took her hands and kissed her lightly. "Is everything ready for tomorrow?"

"I think so. Father Turlough has been so helpful and so has Deirdre. I haven't had time to cry yet, but that will come. When it does just hold me, even if I seem to prefer solitude. Let's go into the taproom, I have a question for you."

For the first time since the fire Conor had a chance to look around the inside of the tavern. It was similar to what he remembered of the original structure but not identical.

There were fewer booths and more tables in the open space. There were enough chairs but they didn't match. Bottles stood in rows behind the bar, and a far-from-gleaming mirror made the room look bigger.

Teagan and Conor sat at one of the tables and she sipped at her tea. He took a wooden wedge from the middle of the table and slid it under one of the legs, and the table stopped rocking. Teagan furrowed her brow in concentration. "I think we now own the tavern, but we're not going to live here. What shall we do with it?"

"We? It's yours, Tay."

"You are my husband, and I'm still getting used to saying husband. I like the sound of it, and even more the meaning of it. But in all things, what's mine is also yours, my heart. Didn't I include that in my vows? Well, I meant to."

Conor put down his cup and looked into those bottomless brown eyes.

"I believe we will become real outlaws after I kill Bailey. We must live on the run, and hound the English as we can. We will have help from the Fianna, and more from the village, but we must raise a larger force, one that will not only get their attention but make them consider the cost of suppressing the uprising."

He reached again for her hand. "Tay, we can't stay here, and we can't own the tavern, since they will seize it. Why not sell it to White Patrick Boyle for a low price? Father Turlough can witness the sale, along with some men from Doolin."

"Hah!" she said. "You thought I married you for that magic lance of yours, but there are other reasons as well. One of them is that your mind moves in a straight line. This should work, and we had best do it before the burying." She raised her cup and saluted him with her eyes.

22

Samuel

"It would be so much sadder to bury my father in the rain," Teagan said, dressed in black on a sunny morning. "We buried my mother in the rain and it made a dark day worse."

Whitey took off the back wall of Pookie's cart, and men loaded the late Malachi Moran into the vehicle he had died in, strapping his coffin to the sides.

Hughie Mac Manus, dressed in his only good clothes, stood by the horse's head with one hand on a braided leather rope and waited for the command to start the procession to the graveside. He had helped to scratch out space for Malachi Moran in the crowded cemetery where his ancestors had rested for centuries. The diggers located his wife's grave and placed his next to it.

There was no resident priest in Doolin, so the sad little parade formed behind Turlough O'Heyn. Teagan and Conor walked behind the priest and she guided him in a low voice toward the cemetery. Hughie led his horse by the bridle, and the cart with the body moved sedately along the road. Sinead and White Patrick Boyle followed with Seamus and Deirdre Hogan, and then a group that included Thomas Briggs, Kevin Haggerty, Katie Mac Manus, Mother Milligan, Ronan O'Malley, Conor's Fianna friends from Kinvara and some seamen from the port. Conor spotted a few Aran Islanders led by Finbar Morrigan, the innkeeper of Kilronan.

There were more people by the gravesite, people Conor did not know. A few yards away, three armed men sat quietly on horses and watched the crowd.

"Teagan, stay here. Seamus and Deirdre, keep her here. Father Turlough, come with me." He strode toward the riders. One of them raised a musket but did not aim it. Arthur Bailey was not among them nor was his father.

"You have been told you are not welcome here, not while we lay to rest this good man who was murdered by the heir to Doonagore."

"We are not intruding," the man in the center answered. "But this is Doonagore land and we have a right to be here. Do not try to order us away."

Conor, unarmed, stood straight and tall. "Hear me well, Sassenach. I do not mourn and march on the same day. And on this day no hand will be raised against you. But I tell you this. Arthur Bailey will die for his deed, and by my hand. If you would save him, send him to Dublin or London, or maybe the wild lands beyond Jerusalem. You will recall today as the last day of peace unless young Bailey is removed from here. And if you must do it by force, the sailors here have plenty of rope, and we will gladly lend you enough to bind him from one end to the other."

The horseman glared at Conor and the priest. "What if I just shoot you?"

Turlough O'Heyn laughed harshly. "Look behind you, Sassenach." The leader did not turn but the flanking riders did, and saw six young men, all armed, and a gaunt archer in a gray robe. Others in the funeral crowd drifted toward the horsemen. And the riders saw something else. A very large warrior and three smaller ones, all in old-fashioned armor, held bared swords alongside the others.

One of the outriders leaned toward the man in the center and spoke softly. "Samuel, we are not in a good position here. There are a dozen armed men behind us and more are moving in. Their mood is very hostile and if something starts, we're all dead. That's what I think."

"I don't pay you to think." Samuel's horse felt the tension and stamped nervously.

His rider sawed on the reins. The musket now pointed toward the sky.

"This is not over. We control this land and the peasants who live here. That means you. England is not to be threatened by a dozen rural ruffians who think they have a cause. You, papist, control your people before your flock is slaughtered." He turned his horse and the others followed as the old priest waved them a mocking benediction.

"Take a deep breath, Conor, and let us get about the grim work of this day."

They walked back to the graveside, and Conor comforted a nervous Teagan, with his mother's help. "It's all right, my heart. They're gone."

"For now," she said in a small voice. "Father, can we get on with this now, please?" The old man stepped to the graveside, where Malachi waited in his coffin.

"In nomine Patris, et Filii, et Spiritus Sancti . . . ."

Later, he made the diggers wait until he was sure Teagan and Sinead, being escorted back to the village, could not hear the hollow sound of dirt landing on the lid of Malachi's coffin.

There was a wake of sorts that night at the tavern. Ale flowed and tales unfolded. A dozen people said things about Malachi that would have embarrassed him. It was all in the spirit of "Do not speak ill of the dead," but Teagan and Conor could hear enough sincerity flowing through the words to know her father had been a good man, had left a good mark on his village, and would be sorely missed. Conor saw there was comfort in that for Teagan, whose tears finally came.

Their lovemaking that night was tender and emotional. Teagan did not apply any of Mathair Crionna's magic cream. *For a long time I haven't had a mother and now I don't have a father either. But I do have a husband, and if the Saints and Powers permit, I shall also have a son.*

In the morning Conor was firm. "No horses, no carts, nothing we can't carry on our backs. We are on the run because we are taking this to the enemy, starting today. The English believe conquest conveys the right to treat the conquered as sub-human. In my mind it does not. We are rebels, and as all rebels proclaim, our cause is just."

Teagan's smile was small and fleeting. "All well and good, my crusader husband, but how do we feed ourselves in the Burren, and how do we make a dent in this awful English dominance, just the two of us?"

"First, we get Doolin out from under the thumb of the Baileys. This morning, we will walk to the port and I will board a boat, the one taking

Seamus and Deirdre back to Kinvara. We will pass the Mac Manus cottage and you will let old Katie know you will be alone here, since I am obeying the sheriff's command to stay out of County Clare. The boat will drop me off at that cove where first we made love. By the way, I should build a monument there, and I'll hurry back to get here before Arthur Bailey comes after you."

Her smile broadened and grew colder. "If you don't get here in time, I shall kill him myself. I have my father's dagger and I will use it." He folded her into a close embrace and kissed the top of her head. "One fugitive in the family is enough. Leave him to me, my heart."

Teagan stood with Sinead and White Patrick Boyle at the quayside, waving a white cloth toward the rapidly shrinking boat, which moved north under a wind that blew across the Aran Islands and so to Ireland.

When the voyage was well begun, Katie Mac Manus scuttled on home, where she urged Hughie to hurry and finish hitching King Willie to the wagon. "Come, work quickly," she said with a wave of her hands. "Important things are happening and I must bear the news to Doonagore. Hurry now, Hughie!"

Mac Manus gave his horse a light scratch on the forehead and attached him to the wagon. He did not hurry. *I liked Malachi and I like that pretty girl, and even the man she married. I don't like that Bailey. Even if he were an Irishman he would be a defective human. To have him hold sway over Doolin for decades may be unendurable for people who try live in peace here on the coast of Clare. Katie is going to tell him something he wants to hear, and he'll be after that girl like a crow on carrion. Some day, some day he'll get what is due him, and in my mind the sooner the better. Come on, King Willie; let's go for a little ride.*

◆ ◆ ◆

Arthur Bailey stood in Doonagore's courtyard with Samuel Cotter. "It was a dangerous moment, sir. I don't think some of them cared whether the burial turned into a battle. The young man you spoke of was not armed, but the rest were. My men said some looked like holdovers from the age of armor."

"We must accustom them to our control," Arthur said. "We tried to subdue these people under King William, and nothing changes with Queen Anne on the throne."

"Nonetheless, they are restive, and I think it's personal. After all, it was you who slew the old man they buried. It's a good thing you stayed here."

Arthur scratched his head with a dirty finger.

"Thank you for going. There's no telling what those beasts might get up to under cover of burying one of their own. Oh, was there a red-haired girl there?"

"Yes. She stayed by the graveside. Very pretty girl as I recall, Teagan Dearg they called her. I believe dearg means red in the primitive language these people speak, and she certainly had the reddest hair I've ever seen, as red as a bishop's skullcap. She was married to the young man we were discussing."

"That's temporary," Arthur Bailey said. "She is to be mine, and the husband must die. Here comes that old woman from the village. She tells me everything."

His father never told me about this when I was hired. Samuel Cotter mused on the difficulties of managing Arthur. *It's beyond feeling entitled to bully people. I agree with Thomas Briggs. It's some sort of sickness of the mind, something that leaves him unable to see anything but his own wants. With Thomas gone it's my task to keep Arthur in line, and I don't like it.*

When Bailey approached the cart Hughie Mac Manus developed a sudden interest in the ivy growing on the courtyard wall.

"Good morning, young sir," Katie chirped. "Just now I stood by the quay and saw Conor board a boat and sail off to Kinvara. It seems he has work there."

"And who has stayed with Red Teagan?" Bailey's question held an urgency that unsettled the old woman. "Well, Sinead is there and so is her son Patrick, who's rebuilding the seawall at the port. But she was crying as the boat sailed off."

"She'll be smiling when I show her into her new home," Bailey said, wiping his mouth. Samuel stared. *Was he drooling? Good Lord, this is an odd post. This idiot will get killed thinking he can just run over the Irish whenever he likes.*

"Samuel, get some men together. This day the wench will be mine. Not that I would ever marry a mere Irish girl, but it's my destiny to have her and kill him. One thing at a time," he said and smiled. Samuel thought it a sickly expression but didn't say so.

"Young sir, I remind you again, I am in your father's service, and his orders are quite specific. I am not to desert Doonagore, nor chase around the moors."

Arthur Bailey scowled. "If I could dismiss you, I would. But it doesn't matter. There is no one there who can stop my mission. However, first I shall prepare a nest for her. Where is that woman who does bedding and things?"

23

Thomas

Conor waded ashore on the peninsula, hopping from rock to rock. He trotted back toward Doolin at a steady pace, as fast as he could maintain without exhausting himself. The musket was hidden in Doolin, but he had his bow and arrows and his sword strapped across his back. On his head was a gold circlet with a moonstone inside a four-spoked wheel centered over his forehead. When he got to the tavern, a crowd clustered in the courtyard. A saddled horse stood by the door.

"He's in there, isn't he?"

"Aye, Conor, he's been there about a minute now."

Conor nodded and slammed the door open. Teagan was behind the bar, eyes flashing and dagger in hand. Arthur Bailey pointed his sword at her from the other side of the counter. "I have you now, wench!" he yelled. When Conor appeared, Bailey swung the sword toward him and smiled. "Ha! I kill you and then I bed her, just as I promised."

"Neither of those things will happen," Conor said, adjusting the tiara on his head. "Arthur Bailey, you die this day for the murder of Malachi Moran. There are other reasons to kill you, some quite personal, but that will do. If you intend to use that sword, do so. Otherwise I will simply cut off your head."

Bailey howled something that could never be a word and charged, his sword arcing out ahead. Conor parried the swing, and shoved him so hard he stumbled backward. "You have one chance to live for more than a minute," he said. "Leave here and take your obsession with you. Go off to London or Dublin or the Gates of Hell, and stay there until you grow some brains. Or stay here and die under my hand."

"I shall kill you, peasant! It is my destiny!" He charged, showing some fencing skills as he wove his blade back and forth. Conor, wielding the heavier cutlass, defended easily, and was grateful for all of Old Rory's thrust and parry lessons.

"Tay, show this oaf what he will never have! And keep me between you and him."

"No," she said, blushing.

"Wife, the man is trying to kill me! Do as I ask!"

Teagan came around the bar and slipped her bodice over her head. She cradled a breast in each hand and stepped forward to give Bailey an enticing smile.

The Englishman stared and hesitated. Oisin the Avenger knocked his guard aside, and turning the cutlass sideways, rammed it into the man's chest, feeling the blade glance off a rib. Bailey fell, groaned, and lay still as blood ran on the floor.

A sobbing Teagan threw herself into Conor's arms, her torso still bare. "I was so afraid for you," she whispered. Then she stiffened and leaned back, still holding him. "The dead man saw something I will never show anyone else."

"I don't know—it was a pretty good tactic. Maybe we should hold that little show in reserve for another fight on another day." Conor's heart rate was down to normal as he reached for Teagan's breasts.

"Not now, idiot! There's a dead man staring at us! By the way, any regrets?"

"No. He got every chance to avoid his fate and he chose to fight. And you?"

"I have seen enough of death lately, my husband, but it has been brought upon us.

Oh, what are you doing?"

Conor bent over his work. "Cutting off his head. I promised the sheriff I would mount it at his castle gate, and so we will. You know I keep my promises." He put his grisly trophy in a basket and covered it while Teagan got dressed.

"All right," he said. "There's a crowd outside. We must tell them what has passed in here." He took off his tiara and put it in his pouch. When he opened the door, Teagan preceded him into the courtyard. Twenty people were there, including White Patrick, who cheered as Conor emerged.

"What happened in there?" asked Bad Tidings Toomey. "A man came seeking death and found it," Conor said.

Teagan looked at Katie Mac Manus and spoke sharply. "You are the one who lured him here and told him the tavern was unprotected. You are partly to blame for his death at the hands of a better man. You will now bring your wagon here and load him into the back. Then you can take Arthur Bailey on his last trip to Doonagore."

Conor noticed that old Katie looked uncomfortable and that Hughie Mac Manus did not. He winked at the man and got a gap-toothed grin in return. Hughie turned and went to get his wagon. The others pressed into the tavern, and there was a shriek. Teagan thought it was from Katie Mac Manus.

"He has no head!" Bad Tidings Toomey yelled out through the door.

"Aye, Tim," Whitey called. "That's our Arthur, feckless, luckless, and headless." Teagan turned to Conor. "We must not be here when the body gets to Doonagore."

"Right. Pick up some food and some clothes, get the musket out of hiding, and I will see to the planting of a legend. Between Tim Toomey and Katie Mac Manus anything I say should last for decades."

The crowd had grown until it contained most of the people of Doolin who were not at sea. Barefoot gossoons ran around spooking Hughie's horse and spiking the excitement they felt in the air. Four men, including White Patrick and the former servant Thomas Briggs, carried the body out to the wagon. Women gasped and boys stared silently at the dead man's neck, which had stopped leaking blood. Thomas spoke to Conor.

"I do not think that many who knew young Arthur will blame you for what happened here," he said. "It was long in the making. But for political reasons, they will make it seem as if you had murdered St. Patrick in cold blood. The death of Arthur Bailey may yet become the excuse for more suppression of the Irish. It depends on how his father and the sheriff react to this."

"And if there should be more trouble, where will you stand, Thomas?"

The man smiled. "I took my stand weeks ago, and I have been welcomed. Besides, there's a girl, little Molly Quinn." He blushed. "It's her I'd like to win."

Conor smiled. "I know the feeling, and I think I know the girl. Small and freckled, with black hair and dimples?"

"Aye, and the best smile ever." Thomas was not seeing the faces before him.

"Patrick!" Conor called, and the man came to stand next to Thomas. "When the English come, tell them we have fled, Teagan Dearg and I. Pretend you don't know where we went, but if they pressure you, even a little, let it slip that we think we're safe in Kinvara, and that Seamus Hogan has offered us shelter, and Sir William French has offered protection. Now I'll have a word with the crowd around that wagon."

Conor stepped up beside the wagon and called for attention.

"The Sassenach will come, and your lives will become harder. I regret that and would not willingly bring this upon you. However, we are not a free people these days, and our decisions are sometimes forced upon us." He stopped to look out over the faces that were still and attentive before him.

"A man who seeks to live in peace will endure much to avoid strife. But there are limits to patience, and there are limits to the indignities a free man may tolerate. Malachi was killed because Arthur Bailey was thwarted in his mad effort to rape Teagan and to kill me. Today he tried again, and he failed. The occupiers of our land will accept only that he was one of them, not that his mind was damaged. In the long watches of the night we all know what the basic problem is. The English consider us sub-human and unworthy of the dignities they extend to each other."

Again he paused, noting the men had moved closer to their women.

"I say to you here and now that I find the oppression intolerable. From now on I will treat them as they treat us. Teagan and I will hound them until they kill us, or until they lift their boots from our necks. We have sold the tavern to White Patrick Boyle, and now we have no holdings here in Doolin. That could be important in shaping your future relationship with the Baileys and the sheriff. If we succeed, we will turn Doonagore into a ruin and the Baileys into a bad dream. Katie and Hughie, you must stop being their delivery service, and the village will give you other cargoes to haul. Teagan Dearg and I will not ask for help from any of you, but if you offer it we will accept. Seek counsel from White Patrick, and from Thomas Briggs, who is becoming a better Irishman every day.

And Bad Tidings Toomey, we hope to keep you busy. Now pray for us, to the Saints and Powers alike. Slan anois, and the Lord keep you from the wrath of the foeman."

He shouldered his pack, shook hands with the men and watched his wife kiss half the village. As they left Doolin northbound on the coastal road they could see Hughie Mac Manus driving his wife and his grim burden slowly along the lane to Doonagore.

Arthur Bailey's horse trailed behind, hitched by his reins to the wagon.

"Conor," Teagan said when the village was well behind them. "It seems that every time we walk away from Doolin we leave a dead Englishman behind us. I have a wicked idea. The sun will have warmed our secret pool and I want to stop there and make love just as we did when we were first together."

Conor grinned and kissed her in the middle of the road. "Once you wanted to walk the road naked. Do you still?" Thirty seconds later they did.

◆ ◆ ◆

"When the history of Doolin is written," Thomas Briggs said to White Patrick. "I hope the tale is more of joy than of sorrow, but the writers must reserve a large chapter for the deeds of Red Teagan and her husband Conor O'Canavan."

Within minutes of the delivery of Arthur Bailey's remains to Doonagore a horseman set out at a gallop for Ennis and Sheriff Michael Cole.

Katie Mac Manus sat in her wagon and watched her husband try to clear the stains out of the cargo bay. She motioned to the man Samuel, who seemed to be in charge. "Me and Hughie won't be comin' here no more. Conor said we been makin' it easy for you English by playin' fetch and carry, and he told us to find other cargoes in the village."

"Conor said, did he?" The Englishman's annoyance was obvious. "Conor said! Well, Conor is a fugitive and the Sheriff will hang him within a week."

This is a sour man. I don't owe him anything. "And Arthur Bailey is dead. Not by his own hand, but by his own deeds. Now whose cautions should I heed? Oh, he and Red Teagan have left for Ennis, to decorate the sheriff's castle wall."

◆ ◆ ◆

Michael Cole, High Sheriff of County Clare, gave the messenger from Doonagore a shilling and sent him away. He sat down to think about the young man he'd been unable to arrest two weeks earlier. *I can't blame him for killing that idiot who was trying to steal his wife, but I can't condone it either. After all, the man was English. I'll shed no tears for mad Arthur Bailey but this does complicate my work. I don't have time to chase young O'Canavan around the county, and if I do, I'll turn him into a local legend. But on the other hand, I can't ignore the fact that he has slain a noble. Hah! Some noble. He was about as disgusting a man as I've ever encountered. Back to work now, Michael. Maybe I can catch the young killer if he really comes here to hang the dead man's head. I'll place some men around the building, and maybe the fly will come close enough to the spider . . .*

◆ ◆ ◆

Conor and Teagan found a spot in the Burren where rocks blocked the wind and where tufts of grass softened the ground. She lay on her back and snuggled into Conor's shoulder. "We can't just go strolling up to Castle Clare and say, 'Here, Sheriff! Hang this on your wall.' They'd have us in chains in no time at all."

He enfolded her and smiled. "I've been thinking about that. If you don't have strength, you use stealth. We can sneak up on them even if we can't charge at them. We can draw them into places where the terrain favors us, and we can seek help from the Saints and the Powers." He stopped to chuckle and gave her an extra squeeze. "You know, when I say all that, it makes me think we're in an equal contest here. But never let me believe that."

Conor O'Canavan, again a fugitive, pulled his new wife's warm body even closer and reveled in her giggle.

"I will keep you tethered to reality, my man, except in moments like this."

24

Richard

Richard Hackett was bored. It happened frequently on guard duty, and he knew his mind wandered. But he'd been a soldier long enough to know how few officers were brilliant, and how many duty chores were wasted.

Sheriff Cole is not a bad commander, but what makes him think some Irish peasant is going to spike an Englishman's head on the castle wall? There's too little to do in this garrison, too much time for flights of fancy. It's hard to stay alert. I think old Daniels on the other side of the gate is asleep, and the men watching the back may not even be there. Well, I can't get in trouble for doing my job. But there's nothing to see. At least a few hours ago there were people passing. Not even a stray cat for more than an hour. I remember a cat we had when I was a boy in Bristol. Toughest cat I ever saw. Once he attacked a little dog. I can still remember the yip-yip as it ran away. Hold, what's that?

A figure moved across the open space in front of the castle, a space lit by a growing moon and by a half-dozen torches. The figure paused under the brightest of those and threw back a hood, revealing a tumbling mass of bright red hair.

It's a girl! What is she doing here? Mmm, look at her walk. She doesn't know I'm hiding here. Oh, she's beckoning! She does know. There she goes around the corner. Well, Guardsman, duty calls. You had best go see what that's about.

Hackett rose from his concealment and walked stiffly toward the corner where the girl had gone. To his great surprise she wasn't there when he turned into the street.

Maybe if I walk a little farther, she'll be waiting for me down that way. Three paces into the street something large and heavy knocked him down from behind.

"Keep still if you would live!" The Irish-accented voice was low and harsh. "I do not wish to kill you, this is not personal. But I will if you don't stop wiggling." Hackett stopped wiggling. He was trussed up neatly and quickly, and a clean cloth was stuck into his mouth. Another slid over his eyes.

"I will move you so your legs stick out into the square, and they will find you when the sun rises in about two hours. When you are asked who did this to you, just say Oisin the Avenger. And please wish Michael Cole a lovely day."

Hackett thought he heard two sets of footfalls walking away. He did not see or hear anything when a man in dark clothing stepped up to the castle wall and drove a spike into the crumbled mortar between two stones. Fifteen seconds later something roundish was tied to the spike and the man was gone.

Richard Hackett heard the roosters first, and right behind them the banshee shriek of an early rising housewife. There came the sound of running feet, awestruck exclamations, and loud calls on God and all his Saints to help, but there could be no help for Arthur Bailey. They found Hackett a few minutes later, and when they led him to the wall he saw what he was afraid he would see. There at about eyeball level, its hair tied to a spike, was the head of a man. The unlovely face of the heir to Doonagore seemed to snarl at the stunned onlookers.

◆ ◆ ◆

Michael Cole could not decide whether to punish his guards or admire the man who had duped them and kept his grisly promise. He did not believe three hooded men had overpowered Richard Hackett and dragged him into a side street, or that Martin Daniels had been awake for the entire watch and had seen or heard nothing. *I'll find out as soon as the barracks rumor mill starts grinding.* By the end of the week he had heard that a beautiful red-haired woman, probably a pagan Irish goddess, had bewitched Hackett into leaving his post and getting tied up by invisible hands. Cole interpreted that his own way. *It had to be the girl I saw in Kinvara, the bride at that wedding. Teagan was her name and she was indeed beautiful. No wonder poor Hackett was beguiled. I'll take him off his liquor ration for a month. But the girl and that Canavan, acting together, they could cause me some discomfort. Oosheen, he said his name was. I'll have to find out what that means too.*

◆ ◆ ◆

Two tired figures stood on a low ridge west of Ennis and watched a partly cloudy sky go red and then gold as the sun lifted above the town. Tiny specks began to move around as people started their days. Reports of the orphaned head spread quickly, and the distant watchers could only imagine the impact of that news.

"And now?" Teagan asked as the wind blew her hair toward the town.

Conor took her hand and smiled. "I'm so proud of you. We make a great team. Now that we've kicked the English nest and we've got the bees all buzzing, let's let them fret for a little while. We have to think how to pick our next targets."

"What do you have in mind?" Teagan asked, turning toward a northerly path.

"We'll talk about it on our way," he said. "But I do want to turn Doonagore into an abandoned ruin. Beyond that, we need to build a network of people who will tell us when a specific English occupier does some specific evil to an Irishman or his family. Then we strike to support the victim. We need to figure out how we're going to do that. Do we have any of that good bread and cheese left? If not we'll have to beg our way across some pretty bleak landscape."

◆ ◆ ◆

One week after part of the late Arthur Bailey turned up in the middle of Ennis, the lord of Doonagore returned from Dublin to bury his son and to consolidate control over his extensive holdings in the west of County Clare. One of the ways he did that was to demand more production from his tenant farmers.

The townland of Ballyvara lies just east of Doonagore Castle, and part of it once served as a garden for the fortified house. In the years the Bailey family held the mini-castle, Jeremiah Danaher held the garden. By 1702 the old bachelor had been producing edibles for the castle kitchen for almost four decades. All those years had bent his back and had given him a fine appreciation for the rhythms of nature. *I may be slower than I once was but I can still outrun a cabbage or a carrot. When I said that to the lads at the pub, they laughed and bought me a pint. I'll have to think of something else funny. Maybe they'll buy me another.*

Jeremiah worked his way up and down the rows, a rough-woven bag dragging behind him, filling slowly with pulled weeds. *Must be something going on, with Edmund Bailey back here. And nobody wept when that young man whacked his boy's head off. If I'd known about that, I would have shown him how I hack off the head of a cabbage. That Arthur was manure on legs. But now the lord wants more work from all of us. That little bastard Jonathan Harvey brought his pompous self out here yesterday to tell me that. I piss on him. Och, here he comes again.*

"I see no change in what you're doing," Harvey said. "I said speed it up."

Jeremiah stood up stiffly, massaging his back with one dirt-encrusted hand. "A gardener must work at Nature's pace. I told you that yesterday, mister."

"Insolence will get you a flogging, old man," the overseer shouted, brandishing a whip. "Now get you busy!"

Jeremiah Danaher stood as straight as his back would allow. "I been doing this ere you was born, Sassenach. I know more about gardenin' than you about grumblin'. Now be off with you and leave me be." He turned his back on the Englishman in a gesture that was not missed.

Jonathan Harvey swung his whip handle, striking Jeremiah in the back of the head.

The old man cried out and fell across a row of carrots. Harvey kicked him twice in the ribs and stalked off in search of another Irish laborer to encourage.

The castle cook found Jeremiah bleeding from the back of his scalp and breathing in a shallow pattern that he hoped would ease the pain in his ribs. She bound him up and got men to help the old gardener to his little room outside the castle wall. Then she had a quiet word with a man who was going down to Doolin. "Find White Patrick Boyle and tell him exactly what happened here. Then stay you away from Jonathan Harvey, for his cruelty has doomed him."

Ten days later Harvey did not come back from a ride he had taken to bully Irish workers into being more productive. A search party found him on the road from the nearby market town of Ennistymon. He was on his back with a black arrow in his chest. A paper wrapped around the shaft contained a word the searchers did not know: Oisin.

◆ ◆ ◆

In the last week of August a churchless priest told the civil authorities in Drumcurreen an English overseer was beating him for the few pence his congregants could afford to give, and so he, the priest was therefore destitute. In the third week of September that overseer was found dead in his bed of a stab wound to the chest. The word "Oisin" was carved into his forehead.

A half-mile east of the seacoast town of Kilkee the townland of Lisdeen sits beside the road to Kilrush. One early autumn morning Teagan and Conor tried to see the Atlantic from that road and failed. There had been a forcible eviction in Lisdeen, not because the Irish tenants were late paying their rent, but because an Englishman wanted the land, and got it in a legalized grab.

Matthew Slater burned all the evicted tenant's property except the farming tools he kept to rent out to a more pliant tenant. The last one, a man named O'Brien, had to be whipped off the land his family had held since before records were kept.

Slater thought he could get enough rent to repay his investment within a few years.

First, he'd have to find a tenant. That search became much harder after the arrow was found driven into the wall of his barn. If he had found it, he would have destroyed it. But an Irishman found it, worse, one who could read. Slater looked at the note wrapped around the black arrow he held. "You shall not profit from an Irishman's misery. Oisin." *Word*

has gotten around about this Oosheen, whatever that is, and I think the
locals are using the name to scare me. That is not going to be easy for them.

From a distance Teagan watched the man work in his barnyard. "Man of my heart, does it ever bother you that when you say, 'annoying the English,' what you mean is killing them?"

"No. If I could negotiate dignity in their behavior toward us, I would. But I can't and they won't permit a better life for the Irish. I'm left with few choices. Besides we're being especially careful to make sure the ones we select have behaved especially badly. Maybe this one will heed the warning and not exploit the land. I don't get pleasure out of this, but nor do I shrink from it."

Matthew Slater died three days later of an arrow in the heart. It was marked Oisin.

◆ ◆ ◆

At the end of October a man and a woman walked into Malachi's Pub, noting that White Patrick Boyle had not changed the tavern's name. The old woman who had sheltered them early in the summer in Lissateeaun would have recognized the couple. He was somewhat bent, and her work-worn hands echoed a face that Nature had not blessed.

"Ale for two, please." Conor made the request while sitting where he could see both the door and the passage to the kitchen.

"The place seems to be doing well," Teagan noted, automatically counting the customers. "They have a harper and a fife player. My father used to say musicians would drink more than their arts are worth. I'm going to order some food, are you hungry?"

"Tay, I'm always hungry these days, but I'll save a little room for dessert. Here comes Whitey, let's see if we can get away with this."

"Supper? I have kidney pie tonight, and people say it's good."

"I hope so," Conor said. "We'll have some. And have you any bed space left?"

"Well," he said, looking sorrowful. "I heard some old friends would be here tonight, but I don't see them, and it's getting late. If they're not here by the time you finish supper, then the room is yours."

"We are here, Whitey" Teagan said with a smile, watching astonishment stretch across his face. "It's just not in our interest to look like us right now. We don't know who your customers are and how anxious they might be to turn Teagan Dearg and Oisin over to the authorities."

"Well, there is a reward," Boyle said, and wiped his hands on a small towel tucked into his waistline. "Fifty shillings for the witch and a hundred for the warrior."

"Unfair!" Teagan said. "I'm worth at least as much as he is."

Conor sipped his ale and sighed gratefully. "Whitey, I need to thank you for tipping us to the man who beat old Jeremiah."

White Patrick's mobile face registered discomfort. "Truth is, Conor, I've been troubled by that. The man is dead because of what I said."

"No, my friend. He is dead because of what he did."

Halfway through their kidney pie supper, the musicians began to play a medley of traditional tunes that might have dated from the days when bards performed for High Kings in the storied halls of Tara. White Patrick came back to the table with three mugs of ale. He pulled out a chair and sat, raising his mug. "Here's to the witch and the warrior, Teagan Dearg and Oisin the Avenger."

As they sipped he added, "There's a new ballad going around. They played it here last night, and I've asked the harper to do it again. I hope you like it."

The music changed in tempo and key and rose to fill the room. The harper spoke. "Something important is happening these days in the west of Ireland, and this is our effort to share it with all of you. It's called *The Ballad of Red Teagan.*" The music rose again in a cascade of harp notes. Teagan thought it sounded like the tinkling of a small waterfall.

The trained voice easily captured the room as Conor and Teagan stared at White Patrick, open-mouthed.

Out in the oceanside village of Doolin
Lived the young maiden, Red Teagan Moran.
Brown-eyed and fire-haired, the fairest colleen.

Now comes the warrior, in from the sea.
Banished from Galway for murder, they say,
Conor O'Canavan swept the girl's heart away.

But a Sassenach lordling would not stand aside.
He slew Teagan's father with a cruel musket ball.

"I'll kill the young man and she'll be my bride!"
Young Conor told Teagan, "Fear not, he must fall."

He took up his weapons, his sword and his bow.
And mad Arthur Bailey, he soon was laid low.

Red Teagan and Conor, they swept through the land,
Seeking out English evil, showing Justice's hand.

So be kind to the Irish, the true folk of Clare.
Red Teagan and Conor are out there somewhere.

Saxon, if you find a bright-haired colleen,
Perfect of figure and lovely of face,
Then you beware if you've pestered our race.
For if it's young Teagan, she'll show you Oisin.

"Whitey, that's astonishing," Teagan said with a smile. Conor looked at Whitey. "Is there anyone in the tavern who's unknown, anyone you don't trust?"

"No," White Patrick said after scanning he room. "They're all known to me and it's reliable they are too, so they are."

"Come on, Tay, I've got an idea." Conor stood and pulled Teagan to her feet. "Let's polish the legend." He led her outside and removed his tiara.

A few seconds later, a fire-haired woman entered the tavern followed closely by a large man bearing arms. The musicians fell silent. All conversation stopped and people held their mugs still, halfway to their mouths. White Patrick Boyle began clapping. Bad Tidings Toomey joined in, and the room filled with cheers and applause. Teagan blushed and held Conor's hand.

"Harper! Play it again! She's here!" Whitey shouted over the din.

The portly musician stood and bowed toward Teagan, and then sat down, his fingers flying over the strings. "This time we'll do the Irish version." *An Bailead ar Teagan Dearg* flowed out over the crowd while its subject sat very still, a tear inching down her cheek when the harper sang of her father's death. At the end she held up a hand to still the lusty cheers.

"Thank you, thank you all," she said. "I'm flattered, but all I do is help my husband, who tries to bring justice where there is tyranny." She pointed to Conor and the cheering resumed.

"This fair land is now captive," Conor said when it faded. "Red Teagan and I are trying to replace the bloody red flag of Albion with the green and gold harp flag of Erin." There were some roars among the cheers, and Conor turned to Teagan. She stood tall next to her husband. "What we do is not for everyone, but thank you for your support."

She and Conor waved at White Patrick and left the tavern. A few minutes later the work-worn couple that had left earlier came back in and sat down without drawing any notice from a crowd that still buzzed about Teagan Dearg and Oisin.

◆ ◆ ◆

"Whitey, we're going up to Kinvara for a week or so. We need to rest a little in a place we feel safe and to plan how to get the remaining Baileys to give up their den." They sat over breakfast in the inn after a night of sound sleep in a real bed.

"If anything happens that we should know about, the Ronan Relay is a pretty good way to get word to Seamus. He'll always know where we are. The sailors will always carry messages. And thank you for being so welcoming."

"It's nothing, my friends. Some day we'll have the time and the peace to go back and finish that quay we started during the summer. Oh, Kevin Haggerty is sailing to Galway in the morning. I'm sure he could drop you off in Kinvara."

25

St. Bridget

Deirdre Hogan wished she had more arms. *I can't squeeze Tay and Conor tightly enough with just two. And here's Seamus trying to get his share too. What they're doing is so dangerous that whenever they leave I wonder if I'll ever see them again. But I can't let them know how I fret.*

"The Atlantic never was an Irish lake," Conor said. He rubbed his hands over the tavern's fireplace, but they still felt cold. "When November begins and the sun is low the sea is very cold. Tay and I knew we weren't going to freeze, but it was a rough trip."

"We emptied the house and brought your things here," Deirdre told Teagan. "We've rented out the house, but there will always be room in the inn for you two."

"Room in the inn," Conor said. "Sounds like the old Christmas story in the Bible. 'There was no room for them in the inn.'"

"They needed a place to give birth to a child," Teagan mused with a far-off look on her face. She reached for Conor's hand and for Deirdre's. "I suppose this is a good time to say it, and I'm bursting with the news."

"You're pregnant!" Deirdre declared.

"Yes!" Teagan squealed, trying to hug everybody.

"I thought so," Deirdre said. "You just look different. You've got that glow."

"What glow?" Conor demanded. "What's changed? She always looks good."

"Oh, Conor, you're a man, you don't know anything. Tay, dear, we'll go to the holy well in the morning, and get you a little flask of St. Bridget's protection."

"Protection against what?" Seamus asked. "Conor and I feel a little left out of this burst of womanish excitement."

"They're all the same, aren't they, dear?" Deirdre was feeling quite proprietary about Teagan's news and instinctively tried to coddle her. "Now you men, listen. Pregnancy is joyous, but not always easy. Childbirth is thrilling but not always successful. And if we can find a bit of leverage against the complications, then we should reach out for it. St. Bridget is a famous patroness of women. We know what we're doing here."

Teagan nodded, though she wasn't sure about that last certainty.

"My father told me I'd have a son, back when I was nine years old," Conor said. "I didn't pay much heed, because he had just told me I would meet a red-haired girl with brown eyes. It never occurred to me he was describing a girl just like my mother. Oh, he also said the son must have a name beginning with the same sound as his name and mine. So how about Kaidan?"

"Warrior?" Seamus asked. "Well, it fits what you've been doing lately. I like it."

Deirdre held up her hand, palm out. "Hold a moment, you two. You're discussing the details of an event that won't even happen until the middle of next summer. Lower your enthusiasm, both of you. And Seamus, my love, I'm glad you like the name, but this is not an election, and even if it were, you don't have a vote. It's for the parents to decide. Now, after saying that, I like the name, too."

Teagan and Conor settled into the room they were told would be theirs whenever they needed it, and she smiled to herself over his boundless excitement.

"A baby! Tay, how wonderful! I always thought I would have a son, but having one with you is so thrilling! I don't dance well, as you know, but I felt like dancing a jig and a hornpipe too when I heard your news."

Teagan smiled and dropped a warm tear onto her favorite headrest on his neck.

Her throat tightened with emotions she would not express by weeping. She swallowed to avoid crying with joy and snuggled deeper into Conor's shoulder.

◆ ◆ ◆

Seamus had bought a few pounds of the new coffee being imported from the Americas, and they tried it out on the morning after learning of Teagan's pregnancy. Conor was doubtful. "I'm not used to drinking liquids I can't see through. And besides, it's bitter. Maybe some honey, or a bit of that cane sugar will tilt the taste a bit."

"Well, my other best friends, what do you think of my new brew?" Seamus asked when their cups were empty.

"I prefer tea," said Deirdre. "Make it tea for two," Tay added.

Conor made a face. "I identify tea with the English, and I'll drink it no more. This stuff is an alternative, even if it is a taste I've yet to acquire."

"Conor, your political ideas war with your sense of taste, and that will cost you some comfort if you keep it up," Deirdre said, an admonishing finger in his face. "If you set yourself apart from everything English, your life may become bleak indeed."

"Mother, how could it be bleak when I have you and Tay and Seamus, and now the little Kaidan, whom I can't wait to meet? And, my heart, in the gray-blue light of dawn I can see the glow the new life within brings to your face. I have never seen you look so alive and so alluring at the same time."

Deirdre laughed. "My son, for a man whose primary skill is smiting people, you are developing a notable eloquence. Where does that come from?"

"From your new daughter, the source of all the laugh lines that are creeping into the corners of my eyes. And as long as I've been caught telling the truth, I never knew how incomplete my life was before I met her."

"You're making me blush," the bride said. Deirdre picked up plates and cups. "Come on, my girl. We have a date with a saint, and neither of these two is at all saintly."

They walked south out of Kinvara, through the scrubby trees of the southern edge of County Galway. Deirdre was sure they walked right over the spot where Conor had killed the brutish soldier Red Dillon.

A casual watcher would have taken them for mother and daughter. Teagan's hair was a little redder and her figure a little slimmer, but they both walked with the grace of dancers and radiated an elegance that couldn't be traced to one trait.

"It should be just along here," Deirdre said, pointing to a low cliff, a capstone outcropping of harder limestone. "Mother O'Brien told me how to get here after she came for some holy water when Rory Donovan was attacked. Did you hear about that?"

"Aye," Teagan said. "I think that assault may have set Conor on a course he still follows, and all before I met him."

"Here we are, dear. I brought some flasks to fill. Why don't you do it, since the water is intended for you?"

The well was more like a spring. Water bubbled up and formed a miniature pond about ten feet across. Teagan knelt on the rocky edge where previous visitors had left weavings of straw known as St. Bridget's crosses. Still thinking about Conor and Red Dillon, Teagan got distracted and dropped her flask into the water. The pool was shallow at its edge and she reached down to about elbow depth to retrieve it.

You carry a new life, Teagan Dearg.

"Deirdre? You already know that."

"Tay, I didn't say anything."

"But I just heard . . ."

Do not speak. Think.

All right. Are you Mathair Crionna?

No.

Can you be St. Bridget?

No. People think I am, but the truth is I am far older. I am Finulla, and I am the spirit of this place.

Can Deirdre hear you?

You must speak aloud to Deirdre.

"I can hear Finulla with my mind, Tay, but for you I need speech. I was born in Connemara and there is Old Irish in my bloodline. I am a little attuned to the Powers."

Teagan sat back and stared at the clear water. *This is a lot to take in. Spirit, Finulla, I was born in Doolin. How can I hear you?*

A month ago, you could not. But now the son within allows you to sense I am here.

With her thoughts swirling, Teagan spoke aloud. "Finulla, I am sure you don't greet every pilgrim who comes here to draw some of your water. Why have you revealed yourself to us?"

Deirdre, do you remember when the old soldier Rory Donovan was so gravely wounded in a cowardly attack in Kinvara?

"Of course. It was unforgettably tragic. Mother O'Brien came here and brought him some of your water. It seemed to help."

I could not save him. The damage was too much. But I did give him a painless and peaceful death. That's important now because you will use my water to ease your discomforts over the next few months. And the birthing will be relatively easy.

"But I don't understand. Why are you taking such an interest in me?"

You are a vital part of a very long-term struggle to restore this land to its true owners, just like Deirdre before you. Her son is moving that process forward and so will yours. More than that I may not say. Just keep in mind that as long as you have some of my water with you, I am with you, too.

"I have never been so shocked," Teagan said as they walked back to the tavern. "I've heard about the Old Powers all my life, even invoked them. But now . . ."

"You are so fortunate, my Tay. I never had such an encounter as this, only the presence of Mathair Crionna, my mother-in-law. Do you believe she and this Finulla are linked somehow?"

"I don't know, but after this morning it's easier to believe than to deny. Oh, my. I'll have to think about all this."

"Tay, I'm not going to tell you how to react to Finulla, but I think this is women's lore, not to be shared with our men."

◆ ◆ ◆

A week stretched into two and then three as the security of Kinvara wrapped itself around the fugitives. "I'm tempted to stay here," Conor said one night after a passionate session of lovemaking. "You're pretty good bait for this old fish."

"Old fish, indeed," Teagan said with a sigh. "You have just loved me into a mass of jelly, so don't talk about old fish. Maybe young lion would be better."

"Rrrr!" said the lion, pretending to devour tender parts of her pleasantly tired body.

"But I have to go back. I heard today that another English overseer from Doonagore has been whipping the farmers who work castle lands, because the harvest has been poor. They never learn anything, do they? But then teaching is a profession that requires patience. Someone told me that when I was a gossoon with a runny nose. You'll be all right staying here with Deirdre and Seamus, won't you?"

"I'm not staying here, boyo, no matter what misguided sense of protection makes you say that. I am fine, and I am going wherever you go. A woman named Ruth once said that to her husband, and she made it stick. So get used to the idea."

Conor laughed and hugged her. "Ruth was a foreigner trying to convince Boaz that she was now attached to him. 'Thy people shall be my people,' she said. If you're going to use quotes in your argument, use them correctly. Now as to going south with me, I . . ."

"I'm going. Someone has to look out for you, my love, or you'll fall into some kind of English trap, and there will be no new verses to *An Bailead ar Teagan Dearg*. I'm going. Are we having our first argument? Oh, I hope not."

The argument, or discussion, ended abruptly when Teagan distracted him with an especially intimate caress. "Unfair," he complained, but weakly.

"Love and war, my dear, love and war. Mathair Crionna once told me all's fair in love and war."

26

John

John Haworth was large and truculent, a man used to getting his way by pushing others out of his way. Sir Edmund Bailey thought he was a good replacement for the late Jonathan Harvey, so he disregarded the cautions raised by his steward Samuel Cotter, and hired the man. The complaints began almost immediately, and one night someone wrote the word *Oisin* on the Doonagore gate. Samuel Cotter showed that to Bailey and got a shrug in return.

"It's a warning, sir. This man killed Harvey, and the Sheriff can't seem to stop him."

"At last report the man was miles from here. I don't fret over an elusive myth. I'm trying to get more work out of these people, and you should be too."

On a cold and misty morning John Haworth got off his horse in front of a thatched cottage on Doonagore land and pounded heavily on the door. It opened and a man stepped out, forcing Haworth to back up a pace. A woman followed, a very pretty woman with bright red hair.

"What do you want?" the man asked.

"Do you know who I am?" Haworth countered. "I am the man who is telling you that if you don't work harder I will whip you. And when I'm done I will take your woman and make you watch, peasant." *He should be very frightened, but he's smiling at me. What's this about?*

"Do you know who I am, Sassenach? I am the man who is telling you that if you ever touch another Irishman in anger, you will die, and by my hand. You will certainly never touch Red Teagan. I am Oisin and I say to you, go away. Leave these lands and improve your manners. And on your way out, tell Sir Edmund Bailey he is not to hire any more heavy-handed enforcers. The people here will not tolerate being abused, and we are here to support them. Now, be gone!" Haworth shook out his whip and raised his arm to strike, rage on his face. Conor ducked and smashed his fist into the man's face, knocking him down. As he tried to rise, Conor kicked him in the ribs and bent to tie his hands.

But Haworth pulled a dagger out of his belt and slashed Conor across his torso. He went down groaning as Red Teagan Moran leaped onto Haworth's back and drove her father's dagger into his ribs. Teagan emerged from a tangle of bleeding bodies and reached for the flask of Finulla water she always carried.

"Tay, watch out. I'm hurt and I can't protect you," Conor whispered, clutching at the red stain on his shirt. She smiled and said, "It's all right. I'm safe. Now let's see if this water really has any magic in it." She opened the flask and poured its water over the long slice in his torso.

"It feels better," he said almost immediately. "What about him?"

"He's down," she said. "Can you get up?"

"I think so. The bleeding seems to have stopped."

Do not fret. He will recover, and soon. Use the rest of my water on the other one. That will be the best way to get him to leave Doonagore. Conor sat up and watched as Teagan used the Finulla water on the wound in Haworth's side. "What are you doing? The man tried to kill me, and almost succeeded."

"It's all right, my heart. I have an idea. Now you, you awful man. You were told to flee this land and you chose to fight. That was not smart, Sassenach. Now you have your life back, but if it's to be a long one, you must spend it elsewhere. You are meddling here in forces you do not understand, and if you make any more bad decisions, I will reverse the healing you feel, and you will die in agony. Now get on your horse, go back to Doonagore, resign, and walk away. And tell Edmund Bailey your life was spared by Red Teagan Ni Moran and Oisin the Avenger."

"I could be dead now and I'm not," Haworth said while examining the wound in his side. "I shall do as you say, goddess, and though it irks me to say this, I must thank you for whatever you did to staunch my wound."

They watched as the man rode slowly away. "This may make a difference," she said. "After this it will be hard for Bailey to hire more help. If this works as it should, the intimidation will stop even as the Bailey holding fails for lack of support by the farmers."

"Speaking of farmers," Conor said. "Let's see how they fared through all this." He stepped to the cottage door and said, "You can come out now, Michael."

A man in his forties emerged from the dark interior. He had a graying beard, was losing his hair and wore fear on his face. Behind him a small woman stood close, clutching her husband's belt. Two young boys peeked from behind her skirt.

"You are safe," Conor said. "He will not return and if we are to gain anything from this, they will not send anyone in his place. Now, Michael, the next time you're in the village you tell White Patrick Red Teagan and Oisin want him to fill your mug as often as you like. And if you should stagger from all that, Hughie Mac Manus will bring you home. Mary, thanks for letting us use your home to face the evil man who is now gone."

"That was bad," Teagan said as they walked off. "The tiara didn't save you."

His grin was rueful. "I wasn't wearing it. I thought it would frighten Michael and his wife. It wasn't my smartest decision. Besides, the man was so quick! I thought I would be too weak to help you. How did you know the water would help?"

"I heard it would help me with the discomforts of pregnancy. I was so afraid I would lose you, and that was the only thing I could think of to do. I know you always try to keep your promises and now it seems that Finulla does, too."

"Who is this Finulla?"

Teagan laughed. "Just woman-lore. It's nothing that would interest a man. Do you see anything nearby that would interest a man?" She flashed him a glimpse of a red-tipped breast that seemed to Conor to be a little bigger and a little rounder these days. "Come on, we're almost back to Malachi's tavern."

◆ ◆ ◆

John Haworth rode slowly into the mini-fortress of Doonagore. "Go fetch Samuel the steward and Sir Edmund. I have tidings for their ears."

Samuel Cotter could see fatigue on the big man's face as they sat over ale in the castle kitchen. Bailey chased the cook out, but she crept back and listened.

"I went to see this Michael like you said, sire, and banged on the door. The man who came out was not Michael, but a bigger, younger man who did not seem to fear me as the others have."

"Was there a girl with him?" Bailey asked.

"Aye, and more of her in a moment. But the man, who said his name was Oosheen or something like that, well, he threatened me and told me to leave Doonagore lands or he would kill me. I started to whip him but he knocked me down. My dagger drew a line across his belly, and he fell. I bent over to finish him and that redheaded devil of a girl jumped on my back and stabbed me. I never felt such pain, lying there on the muddy ground, and at their mercy." He stopped for a three-swallow attack on the mug.

"The woman, I think she must be an Irish goddess of some kind, she poured some water over this Oosheen's wound and pretty soon he sat up. Then she treated me with some of the same water over his objections. The pain went away and I stopped bleeding. She told me: 'Unless you leave Doonagore, I will reverse the healing and you will die in agony.' She wanted me to tell you that my life was spared by Red Teagan Moran and Oosheen the Avenger."

Sir Edmund Bailey gave Haworth a hard look. "Show me where you were stabbed," he ordered. "I do not believe you were as injured as you say."

Haworth opened his shirt, which was dark with dried blood, and the other two examined the right side of his chest. There was a reddish scar about halfway down his ribcage, right where a blade had ripped the shirt.

"I see evidence of an old wound, but nothing to suggest you were stabbed today. I say you lied to us. You are dismissed," Bailey told him.

"You were sent out to horsewhip a peasant farmer, and you come back with this wild tale of magic and goddesses. Rubbish, I say. Take the horse, but you'll get no pay this day." He got up and left the room.

Haworth turned to Samuel. "If I weren't so tired, I would beat him to porridge for suggesting I lied. I'm happy to leave this grim place. Besides, I have orders from the goddess Red Teagan to go away if I wish to live long, and I do."

The steward stalked out and a moment later the castle cook appeared, offered another mug and asked questions. She gave him some provisions and saw him to his horse. Only then did she allow herself a smile and trotted off to tell Jeremiah Danaher the best news he'd heard since the death of Jonathan Harvey.

When a boat carves through still waters its wake forms a V-shaped wedge that fans out on either side of its course and affects the surface for quite a distance. When John Haworth returned to the County Clare shire town of Ennis, half the wake he left was a message that said nothing good about Doonagore or about Sir Edmund Bailey. The other half was a tribute to the newly discovered Irish goddess Red Teagan Moran. Haworth talked on about her beauty and her powers and built up the details of his encounter with the goddess and the avenger. That earned him quite a few mugs of ale along the road and among his old friends in Ennis.

Sheriff Michael Cole called him in as part of his effort to bring his successor up to speed. The next High Sheriff, Henry O'Brien, had what the locals called an Irish name and an English heart. Cole told him the rebel couple were a force he would have to quash, but O'Brien rejected the threat, especially when the man Haworth babbled about the magical powers the pair had shown. All much exaggerated, he thought, and he would crush them in due course. *After all, I am a descendant of the legendary High King Brian Boru, and this is the center of O'Brien influence in Ireland. My ancestor Sean O'Brien owned Doonagore 150 years ago before the Baileys got it, so my roots go as deep into this land as anyone's. Things have gone well for the family since we became Protestants. Yes, these rebels are doomed. I wonder why Michael Cole didn't arrest or kill them on his watch.*

Teagan and Conor told no one about the curative qualities of Finulla's water, and she either shrugged off his questions or found some delightful diversion to send him questing in another direction. The injury was still there, reduced now to a thin white line across his belly, and it raised its own unanswered questions about the borderline between the real world and the parallel realms of legend and myth.

◆ ◆ ◆

"Whitey, we're going back to Kinvara," Conor said. "If that new sheriff ever stirs himself out of Ennis and comes after us, we should not be here. Besides, there's a quay to finish, and some wool gathering to do. Also, I've heard that Sir William French is unwell and I'd like to see him. By the way, how is the tavern doing?"

"Pretty well. We have music several nights a week and the most popular song is still 'The Ballad of Red Teagan.' You may not know this but she's now a bandia, an Irish goddess like Nuala, the daughter of the sea god Lir. This bandia can cure war wounds and can reverse the healing if the injured one misbehaves." He grinned at his married friend. "I just thought you should know the manner of creature you have wed."

"I always thought she was a goddess but I try not to tell her. She already has quite a grand sense of herself. And speaking of girls, how's your pursuit of little Molly Quinn?"

"Wrong man, my friend. It's Thomas who swoons over Miss Molly and looks starstruck whenever she's around. As for me, my day will come but not this day. After all, I'm the owner of a prosperous business, thanks to you and Tay."

The curious have always been drawn to an odd structure in the middle of the Burren, perhaps halfway between Doolin and Kinvara. Upright stones support a huge capstone that rests on a slight angle. Nearby another large flat stone lies on the ground, surrounded by limestone rocks and low grass. There's a wind-bent tree to one side.

"What is this place?" Conor asked as he and Teagan neared the ancient structure.

"It's called Poulnabrone, the Hole of Sorrows," Teagan answered. "My father knew a lot about the old, old marks that men have left on this land. He said this one is older than the Celtic people, older than the Dun Aonghasa we visited so long ago. He said it is a place of great power. I know it's a brooding place but I don't know about the power, how much or what kind. For some reason I've always seen it as a symbol of just how ancient this land is. I think the spirit is benign but I'm not even sure about that."

"And yet you like it, don't you, Tay?"

"Aye, so I do. My father brought me here and told me some of our remote ancestors are buried here. I've always believed that. I just wonder how many generations ago, and what those old people were like. I keep imagining my grandfather Enda's face on that ancestor. I liked my grandfather."

"Tay, we're not sleeping here. I know we've been pushing the edges between the world and Otherworld but this is too odd for me. Let's find a place that's less powerful."

27

Finulla

Teagan and Conor sat on the hard bench Sir William French kept for visitors, across the table from his more comfortable seat. Teagan was a little saddened. *He's changed in recent weeks. He no longer dominates the room as he once did. He's too thin and he looks way too frail.*

"Thanks for seeing us, Sir William," Conor began. "How are you?"

"Why do you ask?"

Teagan laughed. "You're becoming an Irishman. We're the ones who are supposed to answer a question with another question. I think he asked because he likes you, and you can imagine how hard it is for Conor to like an Englishman."

The lord of Dunguaire produced a chilly smile. "If you're concerned that I am not well, the fact is, I am not. Nothing specific, but this body that has served me so well is not serving me so well any more. I'm like an old machine that can only be repaired so often. I think it's the wasting sickness, and I may have less than a year to live. My heirs, especially the Martyn cousins, are already jostling over this little gem."

Teagan scowled. "Can't you select one of them to carry on as you have?"

"I wish I could, my dear. But among them all there's not the value of a cow-plop. The nephews are selfish and venal and true believers in all things English. Whoever the next lord here may be, it's likely that you two will receive no sanctuary and no help. The toll rates on the road will go up and work on the quay may stop. It's a bleak future I see for the links between castle and village. I don't know why I tell you all this. After all, you are fugitives and true justice demands that I hold you for the High Sheriff in Ennis. Do you know who the new one is?"

"Yes," Teagan said. "It's O'Brien, so it is. Henry O'Brien, named after your worst king and our best one. But where will you go? Galway City?"

"No, that's where all the snakes are in spite of the pretty legend about your St. Patrick. No, another cousin has some holdings near Gort, and I'll go there for peace and quiet, probably in about a week."

On the short walk back to the tavern in Kinvara Conor was pensive. "I know we all age, Tay, but it's painful to see a man you admire lose his, what, vitality?"

◆ ◆ ◆

Four people lingered over a late supper in the tavern that night, thinking about the lord of Dunguaire and his impact on their village.

"I never thought I would be heard toasting an Englishman," Seamus Hogan said. "But here's to Sir William French, whom I declare to be a good man and a quiet friend to our people." The musical ting of lightly touching mini-goblets of mead hovered in the still air. "I just wish we could do something for him."

Deirdre caught Tay's eye and raised a brow. "Maybe we can," she said.

◆ ◆ ◆

Two days later the women appeared at the gate of Dunguaire and asked to see Sir William French. Eoin the commander told them he was ill and could see no one.

"Eoin, we know you are a reluctant warrior," Teagan said. "But unless you are prepared to brave the wrath of two red-haired Irishwomen, you will not only admit us but also lead us to him. We have brought comfort to ease his pains. Besides, if you refuse Conor's wife and mother, you will have to deal with him."

Eoin thought about his last confrontation with Conor and opened the gate. They crossed the small courtyard, entered another door in the thick stone wall, and went up two flights of narrow stairs. Down a hallway a small room was well lit by the westering sun and commanded a view of the southeast corner of Galway Bay.

Sir William sat where he could see out, wrapped in a blanket and nursing a small glass of whiskey. "I'm not feeling very spry today, so forgive me if I do not rise to greet you. Thank you, Eoin."

"But sire, I thought perhaps . . ."

"Eoin, I do not need your protection in my own bed-chamber." There was a snappish tone in his voice, and Eoin seemed to recoil at the mild rebuke as he left.

Deirdre looked around and decided no woman had nested in this room for a long time. It projected a monkish austerity. The only light touch was a wall-hung portrait of a smiling young woman standing in front of the castle in the morning sunshine. The man followed Deirdre's gaze.

"That's my Isabel. She came here as a bride and posed for that a few weeks later.

In another year she was gone, taken in childbirth. All that I have accomplished here I have dedicated to the memory of Isabel. She may even be behind the decision to stop that Dillon from molesting you when you first came here years ago. But since she died there's been a gauzy shadow across the sun and the word 'happy' lost its luster for me. Now, fair ladies, what is it that brings you here?"

Teagan responded. "First, please don't punish Eoin for letting us in. We told him he'd have to deal with Conor if he should refuse us."

"Yes, I think I shall have to take Eoin with me when I leave, and his mother, of course. I'd hate to have to cook for myself. I don't think either one would fare well under the next lord here. But, please, back to my question. Why are you brightening my day?"

"Do you recall the death of Rory Donovan, slain by that man Dillon?"

"Of course I do. And I also recall that Dillon himself died a few days later."

Deirdre waved dismissively. "Leaving that aside, sir, Rory was working for me at the time and had retired from teaching the arts of war to my son. They brought him to my house, horribly and fatally wounded. And yet he died a calm and peaceful death. That was possible because of this." She lifted a flask from her bag and put it on the table next to the empty glass.

"Ah, you Irish," the ailing man said with a sigh. "Another magic potion. Forgive my doubts but you are about to tell me, 'Drink this. It will make you well.'"

Deirdre shook her head. "It won't make you well, Sir William, but it may set you free. Our family owes you a boon for the kindness and good sense you have shown us, and this is the best we can do. Yes, we are a people who believe in things the laws of nature don't explain. But what laws apply in this land? What logic rules here? Teagan and I ask only this of you: pour some of this into that goblet and drink it. Your body will tell you whether more will help."

They've got me in a corner. If I don't do this I will seem churlish, and they will be disappointed that their little scheme is rejected. Oh, I suppose it couldn't do me any real harm. He nodded at Deirdre and sat back to watch Teagan pour water into the glass. She handed it to him with a warm smile. *I'm being coddled. They're watching me as if I'm taking a first taste of some exotic food. Well, as they say here, to your good health. Maybe I can take that literally.*

Trying to make the action look routine and casual, Sir William French lifted the small glass and drained it in one gulp. *Now I'm supposed to say I feel better. Hold on. Maybe I do. With my eyes closed I can feel something coursing through my body. Something good. It's like a fresh breeze sweeping clouds out of a July sky.*

His eyes flew open and he sat up straight, looking around the room. "Who are you?" he asked. Teagan and Deirdre glanced at each other and smiled.

Do not speak. Think.

All right, then. Who are you? Are you Isabel?

No. I am not precisely a person, yet I have a name. I am Finulla, and I am the spirit of a holy well here on your own land. This water cannot cure you of the wasting disease. You are going to die, but you need not die in agony. The surge of good feeling you have now will abate, and when the pain gets bad, drink some more. But do not squander the gift. You will never again feel better than you do right now. But you need never feel much worse, even as your time shortens.

The lord of Dunguaire looked at the empty glass in front of him and leaned back in his chair. Teagan could no longer see lines of stress and tension in his face.

"I've been having a conversation, or something like it, with a creature who says she is not a person." He stopped when he caught Deirdre and Teagan smiling at each other. "You know something, don't you?"

"Finulla is an Irish myth. Her origins are so deep in this land that it had yet to be called Erin when she was born to Nuala, daughter of the sea god," Deirdre said. "Apparently she has accepted you into her care, so by definition you are a good man in spite of the accident of birth that made you an Englishman."

"How much of this elixir do you have?" Sir William asked.

"Remember, it's not ours," Deirdre said. "We are only the water carriers for a powerful but benign spirit. We will not tell you the source of this, uh, medication, but we can get you some more and will do so before you leave. Now, I think we're done here, but if you feel up to it, come to the tavern for a free supper one night. After all, I became a pretty good cook in recent years."

On their way home Teagan asked, "Do you think he'll come?"

"No. He might want to since it's the kind of gesture that would appeal to his sense of honor, but Eoin's mother won't permit it."

"What do you mean? He's the lord here and she's the cook. She has no say."

"Tay, for a smart girl, you miss a few things. Eoin was born a year after the lady Isabel died. My guess is that the cook was serving up dessert as well as dinner. No wonder he's planning to take them with him."

Four days later Seamus and Conor slipped a barrel marked "F" into the pile of personal belongings that was destined for transport to Gort. The next morning a crowd gathered at the castle gate to bid farewell to Sir William French, his cook, and his former garrison commander. There was warm applause, and the new steward, Geoffrey Moore, saw it start in a cluster of people that included two red-haired women and some men of military age. *I'll have to keep an eye on that lot. I think the old man got too cozy with his tenants.*

◆ ◆ ◆

The winter of 1702-03 was a bland one by the standards of winter weather in the west of Ireland. On sunny days a small crew of men turned out with horses, wagons and levers. They pried loose the stones that once formed the gable ends of abandoned houses around the village and moved them to the water's edge.

On a morning tempered by a mild south wind they picked through the last of the stones that had once formed the O'Heyn fortress. Conor tried to assess whether the largest blocks would be worth the effort needed to salvage them.

"What is all this?" a loud voice demanded. Conor put down his iron bar and looked up. Castle steward Geoffrey Moore stood before him, backed up by a half-dozen armed men. Conor knew only two of them as members of the Dunguaire garrison during the William French years.

"Who is asking?" Conor countered.

"I am Geoffrey Moore, and I am in charge of the castle and the lands around it, including the place where you lot are standing. And who are you?"

"I am Conor O'Canavan, and I am in charge of clearing this site and using these stones to build a quay that will enable Kinvara to become a better seaport."

"This work stops now," Moore declared. "Castle funds will not be used to push rocks around. The old lord's plans don't apply here any more, and our rule of the village will be strengthened."

"And to what end?" Conor asked mildly. "There has been a friendly and cooperative relationship between town and castle, to the benefit of both. Why change that and start strife where there is none?" His words seemed to have no effect.

"We control this land and the people who live here, mostly illiterate peasants who try to avoid their duties to the castle. I have heard about this place. I have heard tales of agents of the ruling families of Galway who were made to feel unwelcome in Kinvara.

That will stop. No one should have any doubts about who serves here and who rules. Now leave your stones as they lie and disperse, all of you."

"You are making a serious error based on ignorance, hostility, and arrogance. It will cost you and those who sent you."

Geoffrey Moore's face reddened. "All right, you have exceeded the limits of my tolerance. You are now under arrest, O'Canavan."

"For what crime? Speaking the truth?" Conor picked up his iron bar. "How many of your men are you willing to maim in an effort to arrest me that may not even succeed? Look around you. You may want to reconsider."

Moore saw four workers with Conor, all holding iron bars, and as he watched, four more men stepped out from behind the rubble. One was quite large and three were quite short, but they all wore chain-mail tunics and held swords. Three of those blades appeared to be bronze.

Moore blinked. *I don't want to start in this post by ordering a massacre. And I'm not sure I would win if a fight should start.* "I will not clap you in irons today, rebel, but you are banished from Kinvara. I don't care where you go, as long as you cause me no more trouble." He turned his men and walked toward the castle.

◆ ◆ ◆

On the night of Conor's second exile from Kinvara, as on most evenings, four people lingered in the bar of Seamus Hogan's tavern and held a council of war.

"I'm not going to leave," Conor said with granite in his voice. "Tay is due to give birth in a few months, and we can't go back to Doolin."

Seamus raised a cautionary finger. "We haven't a measure of this man Moore. We know nothing about him except that he talks tough. Maybe it's all bluster."

"I don't think so," Deirdre said, reaching out to touch Hogan's arm. "I wish I could agree with my fine new husband on this, but I sense anger in the man, and I don't like the look of the new staff. I think we're going to have a bumpy ride."

Teagan looked inward. "The baby must be safe. That's the only thing that matters, except, your safety, Conor. Let's stay here quietly until summer. The English don't seem to link us to the ballad of Red Teagan, which is now all over County Clare. Conor, can we stay out of trouble here, at least until the baby comes?" *He's nodding. He's deferring what he wants to do in favor of what he should do. And when I met him he could not have done that. Tay, you are a lucky girl.*

◆ ◆ ◆

Within a week everyone in Kinvara knew the past was brighter than the present. Merchants in the marketplace raised their prices to cover higher booth fees. The tolls went up on the road that ran past Dunguaire. Men who did not speak Irish walked around the village watching Turlough O'Heyn and ordering ale at Seamus Hogan's tavern. The same men also kept an eye on the two red-haired women Geoffrey Moore had seen among the of people who applauded Sir William French on his departure. They learned one of those women was Conor O'Canavan's mother and the other his wife. The banished man was not seen in Kinvara, but a work-worn man who appeared to be in his forties was often around the tavern, where he did menial tasks with mop and broom. The watchers never saw that man go upstairs with the younger woman at the end of each day.

"You are so beautiful," he told her whenever he sensed that Teagan was struggling with the changes in her body.

"I don't feel beautiful, my heart. I feel like a whale. I'm slow and I bump into things and my clothes don't fit. Deirdre tells me that's all normal, but I just don't feel like me any more. I'm not going to spill tears over it, but I remember how vibrantly alive I felt when we first fell in love, and I just want that back."

"You will have it. I promise. And you know I keep my promises."

I'm not sure I feel any better, but I am sure my head fits perfectly into the curve between his neck and his shoulder.

28

Kaidan

THe spRiNG of 1703 brought the fifth season of wool smuggling in
County Galway. Conor and Ronan no longer needed Sir William French's
help in arranging for foreign ships to slip into the backwaters of Galway
Bay and the island-spackled Connemara coast. The Claddagh fishermen
now had their pickup sites, and the sheepmen knew where and when to
meet them.

"We're surely not sending a share to Dunguaire this year," Conor told
Ronan one night as the black-hulled, black-sailed *Moira* clawed north
along the Connamara shore.

"The way I see it," Ronan answered with a smile, "that leaves more for
us, quite a lot more. In fact I've been thinking about finding a new cargo
we can export. Galway and London may be healing their rift, according
to the waterfront gossips, and this wool windfall may end in a year or so."

"Something else will present itself," Conor said. "There's no shortage
of ways to discomfort the English and some of them even make money."

"Oh, how is Teagan? I meant to ask earlier, but we got busy."

"She's at about seven months and counting. I can't tell you how aston-
ished she looked the first time she felt the baby kick, and she says I looked
silly when I first felt him. It was indescribable, the first time I really felt
like a father. Scarier than when I faced Red Dillon or Arthur Bailey, but
in a much nicer way. She's doing just fine. She and my mother are fussing

around in what they call the nest, doing mysterious things, and giggling like little girls. You know, sometimes she says she feels heavy and awkward, but she's so thrilled with what's happening she just floats over the top of the discomforts and looks ahead to wonders long foreseen."

"You said 'him.' How do you know it's a boy?"

"It's just a feeling. We've already chosen Kaidan as a name. We'll have a lot of very surprised O'Canavans if we're wrong. Any suggestions for girl names?"

Ronan shook his head. "Last time I named anything, it was Sea Dog." He laughed as the dog moved to the tiller for an ear scratch. "Not original, but he knows who he is and what he is. Suppose your warrior son grows up like Eoin instead of like you? What do you then, start over?"

"I suppose so," Conor said. "Ronan, that never occurred to me. Heavens, maybe he'll even become a sailor. How crushing that would be."

◆ ◆ ◆

Conor's memory of his son's birth was murky at best. He recalled sitting with Seamus and Paddy O'Brien in the inn's taproom while women bustled about up and down the stairs. Once he heard Teagan cry out and tensed as if to go to her.

"Easy, boy," Seamus cautioned. "You can't make this rescue. Only time and the processes of nature can do that. Here, have another ale." Conor never recalled how many he had, but after a long time he heard feet coming down the stairs. Deirdre appeared with a huge smile on her face. "Conor, do you want to come up? Tay has something to show you, something you'll like."

He pushed past his mother and bounded up the steps. Teagan lay on a rumpled bed with the baby on her chest, already suckling. He didn't see the midwife fussing around in a corner, and he didn't see his mother enter the room. He did see Teagan's weary smile, and a few joyful tears he dried with his lips.

"You are magnificent," he whispered.

"Look what I found," she said, as her smile grew wider. She stroked the baby's head softly. The infant had a wealth of hair and a red face. The women had already wrapped him in a swathing of cloth. "He has all the fingers and toes he needs, two eyes, two ears, and a very busy mouth. Would you like to hold him?"

"What if I drop him?"

"You won't. Deirdre will pick him up. Bend your elbow and hold with both hands." Deirdre smiled broadly, watching astonishment spread over he son's face. "Conor, meet Kaidan Mac Conor O'Canavan."

Conor felt his son's slight weight in his arms and looked into the baby's face.

Kaidan was squalling loudly, and Conor looked at his mother with a question in his eyes. She laughed. "It's not you. We stopped his first feast, and he's objecting. You'll get used to the sound."

Conor blinked. *I think I've got a lot to get used to. I never saw so small a person.*

"Conor?" Teagan's voice was very soft. "I love you more than ever, but I need some sleep. Go downstairs and brag about our son." He kissed her gently on the lips and let himself be shooed away. Teagan was asleep when the door closed.

"I'm an ancestor!" Conor shouted as he went into the taproom. Seamus treated the house and wrote on the wall *July 23, 1703.*

◆ ◆ ◆

Over the next few weeks Conor glowed with pride as he watched the bond grow between his wife and his son, watched the grace she brought to motherhood. He learned to change smelly baby garments in the middle of the night while Kaidan objected loudly. " I love you," he said often. "I know this is hard."

"Conor, this is not hard at all. He's very well behaved and healthy. This is what all women experience, as they become mothers. I feel more fierce and more tender at the same time. Does that make sense, my heart?"

◆ ◆ ◆

In the early fall Geoffrey Moore came to the tavern looking for Conor. "I know he's around here somewhere if the rumors are true. The heirs have decided a quay on the Kinvara waterfront would indeed be a boon. If you see him, tell him he can resume work, with pay as it was a year ago."

Seamus treated the man to a pint and negotiated a raise over the old rates. "One more thing," he said. "Booth rents in the marketplace are too high. Rescind half the increase you imposed when you came here." Three days later Conor and some of the Fianna were once again moving rocks to the shoreline.

Pretty soon Kaidan could sit up, and at six months he began to crawl His first words followed. Conor was Papa and Teagan was Mama. Kaidan also recognized his grandparents Deedee and Shamey. And once or twice a month he jumped up and down and crowed when Doggie came bustling in ahead of Ro, who was Papa's friend.

At a year he walked and a few weeks later he started running. Most people in the village would always recall the young Kaidan as the running boy of Kinvara.

◆ ◆ ◆

In the spring of 1704 Conor went to sea with Ronan as another shearing season turned into the annual wool smuggling season. Deep in the summer Conor began feeling restless. Things were going well on the Kinvara harbor project, but White Patrick was funneling to him fresh reports of intimidation and suppression in County Clare, especially around the market village of Ennistymon near Doolin.

"There have been beatings and whippings. People complain to the constable but nothing happens. I should slip into Clare and see what can be done for those people. I'll be back in a couple of days. I'm leaving the tiara with you and Kaidan, because if aught should befall me, it must protect you two."

"I know you must go," Teagan said. "It's been in your face ever since the last boat from Doolin. And by the way, when did you stop confiding in me? I am still Teagan Dearg. I'm still your partner in all things, remember? We can't take Kaidan, he's too young, so you go alone, but be careful. The English may still try to trap you over Bailey's death. You should take the tiara."

"No, my heart, I'll be so stealthy they'll never know I'm there."

◆ ◆ ◆

Three days later Conor walked into a pub in Ennistymon where men he knew tended to gather. He didn't see any of them as he entered, but maybe they would appear. He also didn't see the bartender get a nod from a man who sat in the corner.

Conor was deep into his ale when he noticed the taste was off. When he complained to the barman, he couldn't get the words out. Several men came out of the crowd and knocked him down. He did not remember getting up again.

29

Josiah

FOR ABOUT THE FIFTIETH TIME Conor checked the cell where he'd been kept since his capture. He found nothing new, nothing that might help him escape. It was still six feet by six feet, almost high enough for him to stand up straight, and still had that small window with the four bars in it. Those bars were an inch thick and set firmly in the mortar between the stones. *I have shaken these bars for two weeks, and they don't move any more now than they ever did. Neither do the fittings that hold the door. If I ever get out of here it will be with English consent, and I don't think they will. Oh, they're British now, they say, because they're trying to swallow Scotland and Wales. British, hah! They wear a new name but they play the same game. Keep us down.*

"Ho, prisoner! Stand clear of the door." *I always like that jangling sound the keys make when they open the door. But I hate the same sound when they slam it shut on me.*

"Make yourself presentable. Your trial is today." *Presentable! They won't let me shave or bathe or wash my clothes, which are too big since they don't try hard to feed me.*

◆ ◆ ◆

A guard led Conor to a room with a high ceiling and ample seating. The accused stood in a cage facing the judge and the witness, and jurors sat on both sides of the room.

The judge on the day Conor was summoned was the High Sheriff of County Clare himself, Josiah Butler. In a civil case the complaining party would have argued the facts with the defendant. But in criminal court the judge/sheriff acted as prosecutor. The procedures and the room itself were modeled after the newly designated Old Bailey court in London, where big cases were tried in England's evolving justice system.

"And God save good Queen Anne," the bailiff intoned in the opening ritual.

"Gentlemen of the jury," Butler said. "The defendant is accused of murder and the menacing of good Englishmen working to control rebellious natives. The evidence will show that this Conor O'Canavan did slay the heir to Doonagore Castle, Arthur Bailey.

"You will learn that the same O'Canavan, hiding under the alias 'Oosheen,' has killed several other English citizens whom he accused of excessive force in taming the county's Irish population. The Crown will prove to your satisfaction that Conor O'Canavan is guilty of these charges and deserves the death penalty. I expect you to so find, and to authorize the authorities to hang this man by the neck until he is dead. Now, prisoner, do you have an opening statement?"

"Iss misha Conor Mac Cormac O'Canavan, agus is as Ceann Mhara me."

"The accused will speak English in Her Majesty's court," Judge Butler said, and his voice indicated some irritation.

"That I shall do," Conor said. "Mainly because I don't believe there is a single Irishman on this jury, no one who speaks the tongue of this land. They're all English, all occupiers, exploiters of my land and my people. I ask the court, what became of that new idea, trial by a jury of one's peers?" He waved at the jurors. "These are not my peers but my oppressors."

Judge Butler was getting annoyed. *This lamb is not going peacefully to the slaughter, as he should. This case may yet turn out to be awkward. I wish I could close the trial and keep the rabble out, but that would start a series of protests, maybe even a riot, and I would have to answer for it. Damn these people and their romantic sense of dignity.*

"I am Conor O'Canavan, and I am from Kinvara. I say to this court I object to the makeup of the jury, and I object to the short notice I received. I learned only this morning I'd be on trial for my life this day. I request a delay to gather witnesses who will testify I had every right to defend my wife against assault by the demented Arthur Bailey, who said in my presence several times he would kill me and then rape my new bride. I will need a few days to reach those people. In their absence I cannot mount a real defense."

"This court will be in recess until the morrow while I consider the defendant's request. Bailiff, do not remove the prisoner until I can speak with him."

Conor was led to a nearby room furnished as a retreat for the judge.

"I don't like you and I don't like what you've done," Butler said, sipping from a teacup. He was peeved Conor had refused the tea, claiming it was a colonial symbol. "But fairness demands I permit you to mount a credible defense. How many witnesses?"

"How many charges are you going to press? If you confine the case to the Bailey charge I can save the court a lot of time. Most of the witnesses are in Doolin, some in Kinvara, and two or three are here in Ennis, I believe. The list would include my wife and Michael Cole, who, as you know, was High Sheriff here when the incident occurred."

Butler shifted in his seat until he thought the prisoner might interpret his movements as squirming. "I have trouble with both. Michael Cole prosecuted cases like yours when he served the Crown, and cannot be expected to appear for the defense. And as to your wife, there's an evolving legal theory that a wife should not be coerced into testifying against her husband."

Conor's smile was chilly. "She will not testify against me, I assure you. And Sheriff Cole was present when young Bailey promised to kill me and rape her. At the time, the he was persuaded not to arrest me. We made an agreement. I'd stay out of Clare and he would leave me alone. That worked until Bailey killed my father-in-law, a crime for which he was never tried."

"I will give you a week. And I will send my deputies to serve the witnesses with papers compelling their presence in this court."

"There's one more thing," Conor said. "The next time I appear here, I would like to be shaved, bathed, and properly clothed."

Two days later the sheriff's messenger reached Kinvara and summoned Teagan to court. "Wife of accused is on the witness list in the case of the Crown versus Conor Canavan of Kinvara in County Galway, on trial for the murder of Arthur Bailey of Doonagore," The note was written on parchment paper under an embossed crown.

"Deirdre, look. This explains why I haven't heard from him since he said he was going to Ennistymon more than two weeks ago. Can you watch Kaidan while I'm gone?"

"Of course. Seamus and I will watch him well. Seamus, find this girl a horse."

"Oh, I'm so worried about him. I told him he might get in trouble without me to keep him on course. I've heard that once an Irishman gets into the clutches of the English court system there's no return, no justice. I'm terrified, Deirdre. I can't lose him! I've lost my mother and then my father and now my husband is in mortal peril."

She caught herself sobbing and fell into a hug. *I keep forgetting how comforting a shoulder she has, and how much better I feel with her arms around me, even though nothing has changed. I'm so lucky to have her in my life, and Seamus too.*

"We're changing the plan," Seamus said. "We're going with you. Paddy O'Brien will keep the inn, and we'll move his mother in to see to Kaidan. He's a sturdy little boy and he'll do well in his own setting, especially if the O'Briens bring their busy little dog to play with him."

On Monday morning the ornate room filled early, and there was an audible gasp when Conor came in, shuffling in his leg irons. He recognized about half the people in the room, from Kinvara and from towns around County Clare. Among them were the farmer Michael from Kilkee and the former Doonagore enforcer John Haworth. *There's Jeremiah, the gardener from Doonagore, and Richard Hackett, the soldier we captured in Ennis. And Katie, and Thomas and Whitey and Kevin Haggerty and Ronan O'Malley. I didn't request all these people, but I'm glad they're here. Oh, here's Tay with Mother and Seamus. I've missed her so, and she's so beautiful.*

"Conor? I've been so worried! Are you all right?" He lifted his manacled wrists and enclosed her within. "I am now," he whispered, holding her tight. "How is Kaidan?"

She leaned back a bit and smiled up at him, unaware that many of the jurors were wishing it were their arms around the beautiful woman who was kissing the prisoner.

"Kaidan is well and misses you, so he does. It's hard to tell a child who's just a year old what's happening. Mother O'Brien is thrilled to have him. So, tell me. What is happening here?"

"I may have a chance, Tay. The sheriff is both judge and prosecutor in this case, but I think he's fair. He has threatened me with hanging, but he agreed that the deeds assigned to Oisin are not part of this trial. So the verdict will turn on whether twelve good men and true, as the saying goes, can be made to believe that the death of Arthur Bailey was just. The truth is I have to be optimistic, because otherwise I would despair."

"It's so bad here, then?"

"It's worse than I could have imagined, the shackles on my freedom. I have never thought of myself as a sailor but I dream at night of being at sea, of pointing my craft in any direction I wish to go, or of putting my feet on whatever path I choose, not the one my jailers intend. Losing that choice is worse than being enclosed in a small space and eating swill that would revolt the stomach of a young pig."

Teagan leaked a tear on his best shirt. He lifted her head. "There's one more thing. I miss you more than all the rest of it together."

"Oyez, Oyez, Oyez!" The bailiff's call to order dated back to an era when court proceedings were conducted in Norman French.

"They're starting, my heart. Go sit next to Seamus and mother so I can see your face while this goes on. I'll be all right." *At least I hope I'll be all right.*

"All rise!" the bailiff commanded, "For His Lordship the High Sheriff of County Clare, Judge Josiah Butler."

"You may be seated," Butler said graciously to a scraping of chairs. "Defendant, are you now prepared to face capital murder charges?"

"I am, Your Honor, and I thank the court for allowing me to collect the witnesses who will validate my innocence."

"That remains to be seen. Gentlemen of the jury, the Crown will proceed to prove to you that the defendant Conor O'Canavan did murder and slay an Englishman, one Arthur Bailey, son of Sir Edmund Bailey and heir to Doonagore Castle near Doolin, and all the lands thereabouts." He stopped and looked around. "I call first my predecessor, High Sheriff of Clare in 1702, when the deed in question was done, the distinguished Michael Cole." The retired sheriff sat in the witness chair and swore to tell the truth.

"Sheriff Cole, when did you learn of the death of the victim, Arthur Bailey?"

"I received a messenger from Doonagore, a horseman who reported that this man," and he pointed toward Conor, "had slain young Bailey. The messenger also reported that this O'Canavan had cut off the victim's head and threatened to fasten it to the wall of this very castle. And that deed he did. The rest of the body was returned to his father's castle at Doonagore."

The judge cupped his chin in one hand. "Did you arrest the prisoner?"

"I did not. He and the woman left Doolin on the day of the killing. Nobody in Doolin would tell us where they went. I pressed them a bit and eventually a woman said they had fled to County Galway, beyond my jurisdiction."

Butler frowned at his witness. "Sheriff Cole, have you formed an opinion as to whether defendant O'Canavan was justified in taking the life of Arthur Bailey?"

Cole sat up in his chair. "Judge, we can't govern this land where the people don't love us, if we allow the Irish to slay Englishmen. There is no excuse for that."

"But?"

"But I acknowledge Arthur Bailey was a deeply troubled man, and there is wide agreement he murdered the defendant's father-in-law less than two weeks after O'Canavan's wedding to the Moran girl, who is here in this courtroom."

Teagan sat with Deirdre and Seamus. *The Moran girl, indeed. I am Teagan Dearg O'Canavan, Mister Judge, but nobody on this jury knows what 'dearg' means. They act as if we're all of the same culture, and we're not. We're just not.*

"Prisoner, do you have any questions of this witness?"

Conor stood straight in the dock. "Sheriff, do you recall our first meeting?"

"I do."

"Will you describe the circumstances of that occasion?"

It seemed to Judge Butler that Cole fidgeted in his seat before answering. "It was on this man's wedding day. I had a force of men with me and stopped the wedding party on its way to a reception in an inn. I arrested him for shooting another Englishman at Doonagore, and then firing a forbidden musket when men came out to capture him."

"Were you able to complete that arrest?"

"No. I was stopped by Sir William French, the lord of Dunguaire, who challenged my right to make the arrest in County Galway."

"Was Arthur Bailey among your force?"

"Yes. He hid behind a wall at first, but later came out brandishing a musket."

"Sheriff, this is vital. Do you recall what Arthur Bailey said at that time?" Butler said, "I won't allow that answer. Arthur Bailey is not on trial here."

Conor turned to the judge. "With respect, I wish to appeal your ruling. The court opened this discussion by asking this witness whether the death of Arthur Bailey was justified. That means we must examine Bailey's behavior."

The judge sat silently and thought about that until a man stood up in the crowd and shouted. "I am Sir Edmund Bailey, and it's my son who was murdered by this Irish animal. I say to this court Arthur's behavior had nothing to do with his death, and I object to having that issue raised in this trial."

It seemed to Teagan that the judge stared for a long time at the lord of Doonagore before he spoke. "If Sheriff Cole is willing to answer the defendant's question, I will allow it. Sir Edmund, your objections carry no weight here. I remind you, sir, denying something happened does not make it go away. Sheriff Cole?"

"I will answer. Young Bailey waved a musket around and stared at the bride. In my presence he said he would kill O'Canavan and take the girl against her will. That almost started a war, because in the next moment there were almost a score of armed men around me and my deputies, and even the bride was holding a musket, which is not allowed to the Irish."

"Did you feel yourself to be in danger from me?" Conor asked, palms up.

"No," the ex-sheriff said. "Not after I put young Bailey under guard and joined you and Sir William for a drink in the tavern. Judge Butler, I do recall this. The defendant warned if Arthur Bailey should act out his anger against anyone in Doolin, he would bring down hell upon County Clare. Soon after, Bailey halted the bride's father on the road to Doolin, and shot him dead. We never tried him for that, because O'Canavan killed him in a sword fight before we could arrest him. O'Canavan has a reputation for keeping his promises, including spiking the dead man's head on the wall of Castle Clare, where we sit in trial today."

The judge excused Michael Cole and consulted his list. "I call Timothy Toomey, a resident of the village of Doolin."

Bad Tidings Toomey scuttled to the witness chair, awash in the importance of the moment. He settled himself nervously and looked expectantly at the judge.

"Mr. Toomey, did you witness the death of Arthur Bailey?"

"Almost, your Eminence. I was outside Malachi Moran's tavern, he's the one Bailey shot a few days before on the road from Kinvara. Anyway, your worship, Arthur Bailey arrived armed with a sword and stormed inside the building. He'd been told Teagan was alone in the inn. About a minute later Conor ran up and slammed open the door. I could see Teagan behind the bar, holding a dagger on Bailey, and I could see him waving his sword at her. Conor shut the door and there was some shouting, mostly by Bailey. 'I will kill you and I will have her,' he yelled. 'It is my destiny!' A few seconds later it went quiet in there, and then Conor came out holding something round wrapped in a cloth."

Tim Toomey puffed himself up to a modest full size, and continued. "I said, 'What happened in there?' And Conor said, 'A man came seeking death and found it.' When I examined the body there was a sword wound on the left side of the dead man's chest, and his own sword was still clutched in his hand. I think he was beheaded after his death. As all men know, Bailey's head was on the wall of this castle the next morning."

"Prisoner, do you wish to question this witness?"

"I do not, your honor. Timothy Toomey is known for miles around as Doolin's chief reporter of bad tidings, and I cannot improve upon his story."

Judge Butler dismissed Toomey, who left the witness chair looking somewhat disappointed that his moment had passed so quickly.

Conor faced the judge. "There are many witnesses here who can tell this court that I was indeed justified in scraping Arthur Bailey off the face of the earth, thereby cleansing this world. I need not call any of them, since the question of justified killing turns on one issue, and one alone. Under the Brehon system of law followed for centuries in this land, as well as in the Anglo-Norman law that governs this trial, the justification is clear. A man is permitted to defend his family against threats of peril. And threatening to slay me and to, as he put it, have the woman, certainly created a perilous situation. Teagan, would you please stand up? I ask this of the court and of the men of this jury: Is this woman worth defending from a man who would make her a widow and a rape victim in the same hour?"

Teagan Ni Moran O'Canavan stood and faced the jury, her red hair swirling around her throat, resplendent in her green wedding dress with gold trim. She made eye contact with each of the jury members and smiled at them all.

Conor O'Canavan waited until she had sat down again and turned to the judge. "Judge Butler, I rest my case."

Butler slouched back in his ornate high seat. *This is truly a dangerous man. He has traded on his wife's beauty to sway the jury. On the other hand there's substance to his claim of acting in defense of his bride. On the other hand, I can't just let him walk away. On the other hand this jury is unlikely to convict him. On the other hand Bailey the elder will cause me some trouble if this O'Canavan is not convicted. On the other hand, I must be fair. On the other hand . . . Oh damn, this was going to be so easy.*

"Gentlemen of the jury, I must now instruct you as you begin to weigh this case. You have in your hands the life of another human being, Irishman or not. A man, an Englishman, has been slain and his head severed from his body. Our people do not do that.

These people do, or at least have done in the past. Our laws do indeed protect women against abuse. On the other hand, this one, known as

Red Teagan Moran, has acquired legendary status here in Clare for raging with her husband against English rule. As former Sheriff Cole said,
we cannot, as colonizers of this land, allow our own to be slaughtered
by the natives. You must now consider whether the testimony you have
heard is truthful, and whether the defense offered by the accused is valid.
The bailiff will show you to a room where you can talk out all the issues
you have heard during this proceeding, and where you can take votes
to determine your leanings. Remember, under our system, you must all
agree to convict. The verdict must be unanimous and you may take all
the time you need. Horace Albright, I assign you as jury foreman. In that
office you will lead the jury's deliberations and conduct whatever votes
are taken prior to the reaching of a verdict. Bailiff, show the jury to their
room. This court is in recess pending that verdict.

Guards, take the prisoner out after a moment with his family
and friends."

Butler rapped an ornate wooden gavel on his desk, then rose and left
the room. The jurors filed out as if they were trailing behind a mother
duck. Conor O'Canavan's supporters folded in around the accused with
a babble of optimism.

"Good job, my son, you left them no choice but to acquit you."

"Sea Dog lifted his portside leg to pee last night. That means you'll
go free."

"Deirdre and I believe a man will always have the right to protect
his family."

"I predict *The Ballad of Red Teagan* will soon have some new verses in
the tavern at Doolin, triumphant verses."

Conor shook his head and grinned, with a smiling Teagan snugged
into his shoulder. "I love your cheers, but let's face reality here. An
Englishman is dead and an Irishman is accused. It may be impossible
for them to set that aside. There is a political element to all this, after all,
and don't forget they think I've killed every Englishman who has died
here in the past year, including the one whose heart failed when I faced
him. They may consider me too dangerous to be free, and that I have
brought upon myself."

"Any regrets about that?" Seamus asked.

"Only one: Tay and I have been unable to stir up a broader revolt against the Sassenach. Not even in Doonagore have we been able to turn them out. But perhaps we're not finished."

Wearing expressions of sadness but showing no tears, the little knot of Conor's supporters watched quietly while he was led away to his cell.

"He's right," Seamus said. "They're never going to let him go free."

"But if they don't convict him, if they say the death was justified, don't they have to release him? If he's not proven guilty, isn't he then innocent?" Teagan's questions were based more on optimism than realism and no one answered. *I hope someone else sees the chances as I do. Otherwise we're all just hiding dread.*

30

Edmund

They straggled toward an Irish pub near the government center. Teagan noticed the spot where a chip in the castle wall's mortar had been patched. She was not ready for the steady line of people who came up to her in the pub.

"Are you Bandia Teagan Dearg, the red goddess?" A woman who may once have been pretty leaned over the table, drilling her eyes into Teagan's face.

"I am Teagan Ni Moran, but since I married it's Teagan Bean Ui Canavan."

"You are the goddess who can cure or curse the wounded. Thank you for trying to protect us from the English. I pray to the Saints and Powers for his release from prison."

"Thank you very much. You must know that your support is important to us."

"How often does that happen?" Seamus asked as the woman walked away.

"It started when the ballad spread from Doolin to other towns, so White Patrick and the Doolin harper are responsible for creating the red goddess of Clare." *He's blushing but I think he's proud of his part in spreading this bandia business.*

"It is so intrusive," Deirdre said. "I value my privacy and I think you do, too."

"Of course I do. You know how hard it was for me to prepare for my own wedding. I shivered just thinking about all the people who would see me, even though I knew they were friends. And yet the legend of Bandia Teagan Dearg is now the most tangible sign of what Conor is trying to do. It rings true to people who feel oppressed. And Conor told me you can't be a symbol if you can't be seen. I try to be gracious and to deflect the idea that I can do wondrous things."

When Ronan O'Malley burst in they were sitting quietly, reflecting on the events that had brought them to such a hinge moment in Conor's life. "We have to go back," he told them. "I was there when a man said the jury is about to return."

"They haven't been gone very long," Teagan noted. "Is that good for Conor or good for the Crown?" Nobody had an answer as they walked back to Castle Clare.

◆ ◆ ◆

"All rise!" the bailiff called, and Judge Butler re-entered the courtroom.

"Bring the defendant in," he ordered, and a few minutes later Teagan and Deirdre came close to tears as they watched Conor shuffle into the room in his hand and leg shackles. An angry-looking Sir Edmund Bailey sat with a knot of retainers near the front of the public seats. Conor's witnesses sat as far away from Bailey as they could. Bad Tidings Tim Toomey looked smugly around him, noting that his was the only testimony heard except for the former sheriff.

"All rise!" the bailiff called again, and chairs scraped as people rose in a gesture of respect for the jurors as they filed in.

"Can you read their faces?" Deirdre whispered to Teagan and Seamus. "It's a mix," he said, as Teagan leaned in to hear from Deirdre's other side. "Some of them look stressed and some look angry. I don't think they're in accord."

Judge Butler leaned forward. "Foreman Albright, has the jury reached a verdict?"

"No, Judge, we have not. We honor a man's right to defend his own, but the fact is an Irishman has slain an Englishman. I must tell the court I feel a personal sense of failure. I have been unable to lead my colleagues to unanimity in resolving this case."

"Do you believe that further deliberation will break the deadlock?" Butler asked. *I think I know the answer. They are truly stuck between clashing values.*

"With respect, I do not think so. Our differences are lodged in opposing principals more than in points of law or the credibility of witnesses."

Judge Butler leaned back in his seat and scanned the jurors through half-closed eyes. He had learned that doing so could reveal nervousness or uncertainty in a jury panel, but he saw none. *He's right. There's no weak link in this chain.* "Foreman, without pointing or revealing names, how many of your colleagues are now resistant to convicting the accused?"

"Five of them, Judge. They all have either young wives or daughters of an age to wed. And let me say I don't believe we would be conflicted as we are if the court had refused to allow that woman, Red Teagan, to bewitch so many of us."

Butler answered quickly. "Jurymen, let me remind you I set the rules in this courtroom and I try to be consistent. Besides, we no longer throw the word *witch* around as casually as we did a decade ago. Let's hope we have moved beyond that. I will concede she was a powerful witness for the defense, even though she did not speak. Now, let's see where that leaves us."

Butler sat up straight in his chair and tried to look judicial. *I don't think I have a good face for this. It's too round and cheerful-looking to be truly stern, even with these ridiculous robes and wig helping the illusion. The crowd is buzzing and murmuring.*

Some of them sense what I'm going to have to do.

"I want to address everyone in this court. We English believe our system of law is the world's best, because we try very hard to avoid going straight from accusation to conviction. What you have seen today is a perfect illustration that the system works the way it was designed. A substantial minority of the jury were not convinced by the Crown's evidence, and cling to the belief that the death of Arthur Bailey was justified as portrayed in the testimony, which they found truthful. I wish to thank Foreman Albright and the other solid citizens who took seriously their duty to sit in judgment on Conor O'Canavan and to determine his fate based on the evidence. You are excused with the thanks of this court and of the Crown."

Sir Edmund Bailey leaped to his feet, red-faced. "Are you letting him go? He killed my son! He must hang. Do your duty, man!"

Judge Butler rapped his gavel hard on the desk. "Sir Edmund, this is my courtroom, and you will sit down and control yourself. This court is about to impose conditions on the prisoner that will remove him from your concern."

"I will not sit down, and I will not be a silent witness to this travesty of justice." He shook off the restraining hands that reached for his arms. "I will show you justice, you and the rest of these timid sheep." Bailey reached into an inner pocket of his waistcoat and pulled out one of the new pistols that were coming into common use. He pointed it at Conor and pulled the trigger.

Women screamed and men flinched at the sound. Teagan saw Conor fall with blood streaming from his head. Butler, suddenly a sheriff again, bellowed at his staff. "Detain that man. If his retainers resist, strike them down. And try to find a doctor for this man."

The courtroom swirled in action as deputies rescued Bailey from Ronan O'Malley, who was methodically punching his face to pulp. Seamus had a grip on Bailey's steward, who was trying to free a sword. Only the judge noticed that Red Teagan had slipped to the side of the prisoners' dock where Conor lay, and was pouring a small vial of water into his wound.

"Clear the courtroom!" Butler shouted, and Bad Tidings Toomey was swept out over his vigorous objections. Conor lay quite still, the center of a knot of anxious people, and deputies struggled to shackle the lord of Doonagore. "Put him where O'Canavan was," Butler ordered. "Tell him to practice patience. I will not see to him for some time."

He came down from his perch and forced his way through a knot of Conor's would-be comforters. "Madam O'Canavan, does he live?"

"He does, and he will. The man who's now most in danger of death is that Bailey."

"Lady, he is in the very cell where your husband awaited this trial. He complains of a broken nose." The judge raised an eyebrow and looked her in the eye. "I am not sympathetic. I must move to assure that this kind of outrage never happens again in my court, and to you I say I'm sorry it did. Now, what about your man?"

"The ball hit the side of the head, and as you may know, head wounds bleed freely.

It looks worse than it is, but I must say that one more inch to the left and I would be a widow at the hands of a Bailey, just as the son had schemed. Conor will recover, and may I assume that he can do so in his own space, and not in custody?"

She is smart and tough, and so beautiful. No wonder so many jurors ruled the death justified. I'm not sure I could refuse her request, even if I were inclined to do so. "You may take him to the tavern in Doolin, but he must remain in County Clare at least until all this settles down. I'll have his shackles removed."

Teagan smiled and rose to her feet. "Thank you," she said, and kissed him on the cheek. Before he could blush, she had turned away, calling one of the men. "Whitey, see if you can find Hughie. I suspect he has King Willie and the cart. We are free to go back to Doolin. Conor is no longer in custody."

Judge Butler collected a smattering of nods and a "thank you" from the people around the fallen man. He singled out one of them. "You, sailor. I know you enjoyed striking Bailey, but if you ever do something like that again I will have you in irons for life. As for you others, do not believe a hung jury is a victory. We still rule here and those who cross us will rue their choices. Now go and live quietly if you can, and the farther from here the better."

◆ ◆ ◆

Butler stood by the Castle Clare gates, watching a litter-laden wagon move slowly along the road that led west out of Ennis. A large escort of people on foot went with it. *I think we will lose Doonagore. The people of Doolin will probably shun that little castle until it may as well be under military siege. Why did O'Canavan and Moran come into my orbit at the worst moment? And what am I going to do with Bailey? Maybe I can banish him to Dublin. I'm grateful I have only four months left in this post, and I can bequeath the issues of Doolin and Doonagore and O'Canavan and Red Teagan to the next sheriff, who has yet to be appointed. Maybe*

I'll recommend that the job be divided between enforcement and judgment.
Two functions, two faces.

◆ ◆ ◆

Conor regained his senses about halfway to Doolin. "Tay? The world is moving."

"No, my heart, you are moving. King Willie and Hughie are taking us back to Doolin as gently as possible. Just when the judge said you were free to go, Sir Edmund Bailey stood up in the courtroom and shot you with a pistol. The ball grazed your head enough to make you bleed buckets, but there was no break in your skull. Oh, Ronan had to be pulled off of Bailey after beating his face into raw meat. I treated you with a little healing water and you will recover quickly, but I don't want you on your feet now raging at the English. Butler already thinks he's mistaken in letting you go. Besides, we must go and see to Kaidan. I miss him as much as I missed you while you were in prison."

◆ ◆ ◆

Late on the day after the trial, Teagan and Ronan O'Malley helped a bandaged Conor into the *Moira*. Seamus and Deirdre boarded to be welcomed exuberantly by Sea Dog. A gentle westerly breeze nudged them along toward Kinvara.

"We'll be there an hour after sunset," Ronan said. "And there will be just enough light to reach the tavern. We can be unnoticed, that is if you ladies will cover your hair."

"Good," Seamus nodded. "We must hold a council. How do we deal with Bailey, and what about these English restrictions on where you two can be?"

Deirdre shook her head. "The old holy book talks about a season to every task, and now is not the season for a war conference. Maybe tomorrow, but I haven't been a mother all these years without learning the signs of exhaustion on my son's face. Those new American colonies keep slipping new words into the language, and one I've heard is 'pow-wow.' Do you know what that is? It's a serious conference. The word comes from one of the Red Indian tongues. We'll have no pow-wows until Conor's head heals a bit."

"Drink this," Teagan said firmly as Conor slid into their bed on the tavern's second floor. He stared at it suspiciously. "Is this part of your woman magic, my love?"

Teagan smiled and shrugged. "If it works, you can call it magic. Now go to sleep.

I'll see to Kaidan and be right back."

◆ ◆ ◆

An hour after sunrise Deirdre Hogan placed a sign, *Dunta*, in the tavern's window to discourage patrons who had begun to come in early for a light breakfast. Father Turlough O'Heyn entered anyway. "Why is the tavern closed? I'm now accustomed to breaking my fast after Mass with a little pastry and a hot sip or two of that coffee Seamus keeps pushing on me."

"Family conference," she said. "Stay with us. There will be coffee and pastries, unless you'd like tea." She laughed when he made a face. "You and Conor."

In the taproom Seamus shoved tables together. O'Heyn saw how slowly Conor walked, and that the bandage on his head still showed red. Teagan looked a bit less stunning than usual and the priest decided that was because she had the child glued to her hip.

Deirdre came in from the kitchen with a platter heaped high with fresh rolls. And finally Ronan O'Malley came in behind a wiggling red and white blur. Sea Dog thought Kaidan was trying to give him the slice of toast in his fist. He tried to help the toddler and knocked him down in the process. Kaidan bounced up and went after the toast, only to see it vanish behind the ivory fence of Sea Dog's teeth.

"Toast!" he yelled, swatting at the dog. O'Heyn hid a grin. *The daft beast thinks the boy is trying to pet him.*

"Sea Dog, sit!" Ronan ordered, and the dog strolled over and lay under the table, his nose and eyes alert for whatever blessings might fall.

"This is the meeting I wanted to have last night," Seamus said with a fond glance at Deirdre. "But I was overruled. In essence, we have a problem to solve, maybe two. First, we assume the new power in the castle is hostile to us, and certainly to Conor. Father Turlough is being watched to be sure he doesn't overstep the limits on his work imposed by the penal laws, and Conor has been banished from Kinvara again. That's three banishments so far, and you're violating the sheriff's order by being here at all. Luckily, the word is out that you were very grievously wounded, and so if no one sees you for a few days in Doolin, it will be all right."

The pow-wow lasted until Deirdre's conscience would not let her keep the tavern closed, but did not resolve the long-term problem of how to keep annoying the English while working around their restrictions.

◆ ◆ ◆

Two days later Conor and Teagan got into Ronan's boat and sailed back to Doolin. Once again they arrived after dark and slipped unseen into Malachi's tavern.

31

Bronagh

"The sheriff says we have to stay in Doolin, Patrick. Is there room here?"

"Of course, Tay. it's yours, except for the wee make-believe that keeps it out of English hands. Any room, any time. Next time, bring that jolly little boy."

"What have you been hearing, Whitey, since I went to the sheriff's prison?"

"Well, things are fairly quiet but for Doonagore. Bailey's overseer is still pushing the tenants, even though the harvest is mostly over. They're being drafted for construction projects and other work, and the explanation is that since the crops were so poor, the landlord's share doesn't cover the castle's expenses. That's just not true, the harvest has been pretty good this year."

"How have the workers been treated?" Conor asked.

"Not badly at first, but it's gone from tolerable to terrible. The whips came out when little Mickey Monahan balked at an order to clean out the castle sewage pit."

Teagan shook her head. "Now that Bailey is in prison, have things changed?"

"Well, he's not in prison any more. A traveler from Ennis told me yesterday Sheriff Butler had Bailey escorted to Dublin the day after he shot you. At least he's gone, but the odds of charging him with shooting you go down every day."

"They never learn, do they," Conor said with a trace of bitterness. "Whitey, how many people here are on the castle staff?"

"Hmm, I'd have to make a list. I'll think it over and tell you in the morning."

◆ ◆ ◆

Bronagh Cafferty had made the walk from Doolin to Doonagore every day for more than thirty years. She was the castle cook who had found the injured Jeremiah Danaher in the garden, and the one who learned of Haworth's adventure with Bandia Teagan Dearg Ni Moran. She was thinking about the day's menu as she walked through the village.

"May I stop you for a moment?" The voice came from behind her. Bronagh turned to see a hooded woman whose face was obscured. The woman threw back her hood and Bronagh gasped.

"Bandia Teagan Dearg!"

"Do not be alarmed. I am the same little girl who once pestered you for the secrets of mutton stew, and sweet pastries."

"No, my lady, you're not that girl. You are the bandia. What do you want of me?"

"I'm not your lady, I'm Tay. But that aside, I want you to see White Patrick."

"But I already know Whitey. I know you and he were children together and his mother hoped he would marry you."

Teagan smiled, and Bronagh watched the wind play with her hair. "Well, that didn't happen. You have heard I am married to Oisin the Avenger, and we have a son together. Kaidan was a year old in July. But the reason I want you to see Whitey is that he is in search of a cook. He owns my father's tavern now, and he wants to expand its services.

He believes, and I agree, the new breakwater in the harbor will make Doolin the logical launch point for trips to the Aran Islands, and a full-service kitchen would help him attract lodgers before and after such voyages."

"But Teagan, I have a station. I'm the cook at Doonagore as well you know."

"And how is that going? It seems to me a humorless place. It must be hard to find the joy you once told me is a part of cooking. And if you'll pardon the reference, Doonagore is a place that justifies the idea of sorrow that inspires your name, Bronagh."

"Aye, I have felt more sorrow than joy in recent years, so I have. The castle is now a heartless place, and on many days I wish for wings, just to fly away from there."

"Bronagh, I offer wings in a way. Go see Whitey before you walk up to the castle.

Open your mind to his offer. You need never again enter the darkness of Doonagore."

"I will go," she said and angled off toward the tavern.

◆ ◆ ◆

Jeremiah Danaher sat in his favorite spot late in the evening just outside Doonagore's western wall. He looked northwest and watched the sun go down on Galway Bay. *Only some root vegetables remain in the castle garden, and I will get those tomorrow, unless this pink sunset produces a soft morning, the kind that hovers between mist and real rain.*

"Pretty nice view, so it is." The voice startled the old bachelor, who was more accustomed to solitude than to company.

"Aye," he said, trying to see who was backlit by the sun. "Who are you?"

"You may know me as Oisin," Conor said, stepping to the side and sitting next to Jeremiah on a crudely crafted wooden bench against the sunny wall.

"Aye, the Avenger." The old man squinted at Conor. "You stepped in when that foreman kicked my ribs. Thank you for that. An' I spose I owe you a favor."

Conor grinned. *This old bachelor is so attuned to being alone that he doesn't know much about conversing with people.*

"I don't keep score," Conor said. "But I do come bearing an idea. You should know Bronagh Cafferty will leave the Doonagore staff to cook for White Patrick Boyle in Malachi's tavern. Whitey will set aside a plot for you and enrich it with seaweed and horse dung. And you can move into a better space just behind the inn's main structure."

"Why you doin' this?"

Conor looked grim. "Because I promised to turn Doonagore into a ruin, and so Teagan Dearg and I are telling the staff there will be no more work here. You are the last of that staff, and all have agreed to leave."

"Not safe for you to be here at the castle," Jeremiah decided. "I will grow greens an' other things for White Patrick, an' I will leave the Baileys. They's no Baileys here no more anyways."

"I know that. Tay and I will visit Samuel Cotter and tell him that he too is out of work at Doonagore. We will give him three days to leave, and after that we will kill anyone who stays. The Sassenach must learn the wrath of the Irish is real."

"My son, they do not learn well," Jeremiah said.

"We shall see. And thanks for going to my trial in Ennis."

◆ ◆ ◆

Over supper at Malachi's Tavern Teagan and Conor went over the list of Doonagore retainers who were Irish and lived in Doolin. "That's all of them," she said. "Old Megan Quinn the housekeeper has already left what she called a stable."

"Ah, an idea! Tay, can you ride a horse?"

"Yes, I learned as a child, before those wretched penal laws kept us from owning a horse worth more than five pounds."

"So did I. Whitey, can you find some horses? We're going up to Doonagore tomorrow, and I've noticed that the English, or British, or whoever they want to be this year, anyway, they seem to respect people on horses more than those on foot. That's why they've been trying to keep us on the ground with these new laws."

32

Doonagore

When Conor and Teagan rode up to the closed castle gate, Samuel Cotter opened it, flanked by two other Englishmen. There were no local staffers in sight.

"Good morning," Conor said with a smile. He and Teagan did not dismount. "What do you want?" Cotter asked with a hint of malice in his voice.

"You seem a bit out of sorts, Steward Cotter. Are you not well staffed today?"

The man glared. "For the past few days the Irish have fled as if they were rats and this a sinking ship. We have listed open jobs in the village, but no one comes. Do you know aught of this?"

"Aye," Conor said. He was about to continue when Teagan spoke for the first time. "Red Teagan and Oisin the Avenger have told the people of Doolin that when it comes to working at Doonagore, no Irish need apply."

"This is indeed a sinking ship," Conor said, waving around at the empty courtyard. "The three of you cannot sustain this holding by yourselves, and the locals will not work for you. When you think about it you have no choice but to leave and tell Sir Edmund in Dublin he needs to find another home. And so do all of you. Doonagore is closed and you have three days to pack up and leave."

Cotter was furious. "You can't evict me! Suppose I just shoot you?"

Conor grinned and glanced at Teagan, who laughed. "Listen, Sassenach," she said. "Your master tried that, and it didn't work. You were there to see it. And his son tried to kill Oisin with a sword, and that didn't work either. You may eventually learn this man, this legend, is very hard to kill." She smiled fetchingly at Cotter. "So you see, you really have no choice in this. It's time for the smaller vermin to rule here."

Conor sidestepped his horse a little. "In a few minutes it will occur to you, this is such a minor holding, the big dogs among the English will not bother to fight over it, and then it will occur to them you were in charge here when Doonagore was lost. That is not good for your next effort to find a post. Red Teagan and I will not stay here until your anger goads you into doing something stupid. But just know this. If you are still here when the sun rises on Thursday you will die by my hand and so will your minions. Good day, Samuel Cotter."

Conor and Teagan backed their horses while keeping four eyes on the men at the gate. When it slammed, they turned and rode back to Doolin, holding hands.

"Do you think they will leave?" she asked, with a bit of anxiety in her voice. "Aye, so I do. They are not stupid, or at least Cotter is not, and we shall see."

◆ ◆ ◆

On Wednesday afternoon a small boy ran breathlessly into the tavern.

"Teagan Dearg, Teagan Dearg! Oisin! They're gone! Three men just rode out of Doonagore, and they left the gate open. There may be things there we can use."

"No, boyo," Teagan said. "No one from Doolin will go there, now or ever. Doonagore is a ruin, starting now, shunned and abandoned. It will become a symbol of our resistance, and we will leave it to molder. Do you understand that?"

"Aye, my lady," the boy said.

"Good," Conor said. "Because if we learn anyone has been poking around up there, Bandia Teagan Dearg and the Avenger will be angry. Do you understand that too?"

"Aye, sir."

Conor searched among some things he had brought from Kinvara and found a green cloth with a gold harp embroidered on it. "This is the Irish flag that once flew over my boyhood home near Galway City. My father said my grandfather got it from the great Irish rebel Owen Roe O'Neill about sixty years ago. Tomorrow and from that day on, it will fly over Doonagore."

◆ ◆ ◆

Samuel Cotter led his men to Castle Clare and sought out High Sheriff Butler. "We were forced out of Doonagore," he said, bitterness thickening his voice.

"Let me guess," Butler said. "O'Canavan and his woman have scared the local staff away, and then told you to leave."

"That's what happened, sir. Can we get it back?"

Butler leaned back in his chair. "Let me tell you a dirty little secret, Cotter. I will deny saying this if I ever hear it with my name attached. It's just this: we are spread too thinly here in the West to impose our rule everywhere by force. In the end, that rule depends on whether the locals put up with us. And if they balk, there's not much we can do about it. Doonagore is lost to us for as long as the Irish want to keep it as a trophy.

And I did not say that. As for you and your men, stay here overnight, and then begin the journey to report to your master in Dublin."

First the hinges began squealing in the rain as wind drove the main gate open and shut. Then the hinges froze open in a rictus of lockjaw. Wild grasses, freed from the notice of beast or blade, covered the bare spots in the courtyard and erased the paths of human passage from gate to tower. The stone walls endured. Their presence nourished the new legend of Doonagore as the castle the Irish reclaimed and then shunned.

33

Francis

William Butler sat in the ornate room he called his chambers, and re-read the note his staff had brought him. The night watchman had found it early in the morning, tucked into a crack in the Castle Clare wall..

December 7, 1704

Dear Sheriff Butler:

I remain in Doolin as per your instructions at the end of my trial. I seem to be recovered from the gunshot wound I suffered in your courtroom. Teagan and I have a son, Kaidan, in Kinvara, and I would like to see him.

However, when Sir William French retired from Dunguaire due to ill health, I was banished from the town. I am still uncertain of my status here, and what your intentions are toward further legal action against me.

Will you grant safe passage to me and to my wife to visit Ennis and resolve these issues with you?

Your Obedient Servant,
Conor Mac Cormac O'Canavan

Butler crumpled the paper and started to throw it in the fireplace, and then changed his mind. He wrote back to Conor and agreed to a meeting in two weeks. Then he wrote to Francis Gore, who would become the High Sheriff in a month, asking him to attend the same meeting.

◆ ◆ ◆

On their borrowed horses, a large man and a red-haired woman rode up to the castle gate in Ennis and told the guard they wanted to see Sheriff Butler.

"Is he expecting you?"

"Aye, that he is, and at this hour of the morning."

"Wait here, I'll send someone to see if he's available."

Teagan's horse stamped, feeling his rider's tension. "What an officious little man!"

"Aye," Conor agreed. "The less power some men have, the more they need to wave it around. It may be that working for a public official just makes it worse."

The messenger returned quickly and took the horses. "I know where to go," Conor said and led Teagan into the building. "It's not like my last visit here."

Teagan wore a green cape that set off her hair, and Conor wore a blue one. The garments swirled around them as they entered Butler's office.

The sheriff had a guest. "What's that thing on your head?" the man asked.

"It's a good-luck charm," Conor said. "Supposed to ward off misfortune." He smiled at Butler. "Too bad I wasn't wearing it when your men pounced on me."

Butler waved toward the man in the other chair. "This is Francis Gore, who will be the next High Sheriff here. I thought he should listen to our discussion, since he will have to deal with the aftermath of whatever accord we may reach."

"Why is the woman here?" Gore asked with disapproval clear in his voice.

Teagan produced the most insincere smile Conor had seen since the early days of their courtship. "Because I am a bandia," she simpered. "The goddess Teagan Dearg Ni Moran. At least the Irish people say so. What do you say, Sheriff-to-be?"

"I say this is men's business, and women have no part in it," Gore answered.

Conor produced his own insincere smile and nodded toward Butler. "I'm not sure the present sheriff agrees. Sheriff Butler, does Teagan's presence offend you?"

Butler frowned and then smiled. *He's a clever man, this O'Canavan, using words as weapons.* "It does not, young man. Madam O'Canavan, you are welcome." *She warms the very stones of this room by her presence. I don't know this Gore very well but he seems to be a dour man. A sense of humor has served me well in this post, and I wonder how he'll do without one.*

"So be it, for now," Gore said. "But my wife has stayed home in Clonroad."

"Let's talk about staying home," Conor said. "Teagan and I depend on Sheriff Butler for permission to stay in Doolin, and now we have no right to go elsewhere."

"I've been pondering your request," Butler said. "Why not bring your son to Doolin? After all, you have trouble with the law in Kinvara as well."

"Kaidan is with his grandmother and his step-grandfather. You may know that my father was banished from Ireland in 1691. My mother and I were thrown off our lands north of Galway, and moved as refugees to Kinvara, where I grew up. Our son has a stable home there, surrounded by loving people." Conor let his gaze drift from Butler to Gore, who was glaring at him.

"I am a man who wishes to live in peace. As I have told Sheriff Butler, I resist the English occupation of my land in Galway and more broadly of my country. As a peaceful man I am asking the sheriff to release me from the parole that binds me to Doolin. As you may know, I was tried for murder in the death of Arthur Bailey of Doonagore and was not found guilty. I survived an attempted assassination by the dead man's father, right in the courtroom. I would like to be treated as a free man, so I would, bound by no legal shackles in County Clare."

"And what about Doonagore?" Gore demanded, on his feet and shouting.

"Doonagore is a ruin," Teagan said, her eyes on Gore's red face. "The English fled, leaving the gate open, and now grass grows in the courtyard and small animals shelter there. I have told the local Irish to stay away, and they do. And an Irish flag now flies over the Doonagore tower."

"This is an outrage," Gore said, settling into his chair. "A revolt against the Crown. If I were sheriff now, I would have you in irons for treason. Both of you!"

Butler stirred in his seat. "I'm going to lift your parole, and you may travel where you will. It's clear you will not thrive in Clare while Francis Gore is the High Sheriff. So take your leave, and stay away for a while. Now Francis, as to Doonagore, there is no English lord to take it over, and the local Irish won't staff it. Blame the sour Bailey legacy for the fate of the castle."

"My family's roots in that castle go back more than a hundred years," Gore said. "And I will not see Doonagore abandoned."

"I will say this to you, Sheriff-to-be. Conor and I will leave, and thanks to Sheriff Butler." Teagan got up and walked around the table, standing behind Gore. "You can't see me, and so you fear what I might do, knowing there are reasons the local Irish think I am a bandia, a goddess. I will do nothing today. However, if you try to resettle Doonagore you will fear again, because you will not see me. But I promise you I will act. Leave Doonagore alone, and I will leave you alone." She went back to her seat, fixing an unsmiling gaze on Gore, who was red with anger.

"Josiah, how can you sit here and listen to this? This woman, this mere woman, is actually threatening me! It's treason or sedition; name your crime! There must be a charge you can bring against her. Against both of them!"

"Francis, my friend, set aside worry over a small holding that your family sold decades ago. In releasing them I am removing the most dangerous people in Clare from your concern. It's a favor. If they stay there will be a clash between you and men will die. And in truth, we can't afford to lose more men, so thinly are we spread here in the West." He stood, ending the meeting.

"Conor O'Canavan, Red Teagan, go and live in peace if you can, but not here."

◆ ◆ ◆

Back on their horses and riding away, Conor and Teagan reacted to waves from people in the streets of Ennis. Butler and Gore watched from a window.

"Your term will be easier without him, Francis, and, she is as dangerous as he is."

"I can't believe you are letting them go. Imagine, Irish peasants pushing around English gentry. It surpasses understanding."

"Your understanding, true, and I regret having to say this again. Conor O'Canavan is probably the most fearsome warrior in the west of Ireland. The local people think his wife is some kind of bandia, or goddess. If they demand an uprising it will happen, and it will be bloody and it will occur during your time as sheriff. By letting them go I am keeping you from learning for yourself just how fierce they really are."

On the ride back to Doolin Teagan thought about the people who had cheered them. "You know, we have a lot of support. Suppose we call a revolt?"

Conor shrugged and smiled. "I enjoy my life too much to toss it away on a whim. If the English get serious about running over us we can't stop them. Butler invented an elegant disengagement for Gore and for us, too. Let's go back to Kinvara and see what happens. There's a sturdy little boy waiting there for us."

◆ ◆ ◆

Teagan and Conor walked through the familiar quiet streets from the waterside to Seamus Hogan's tavern. It was dark but not late and they had had a cold voyage from Doolin.

Teagan had wept a bit on their departure from Doolin, realizing she was unlikely to return to her home village any time soon.

"Be strong, my heart. Our son and our lives and our best days are in Kinvara," Conor said, his arm around her as the *Moira* thrust through bumpy seas on its way to Kinvara and that future.

Conor opened the tavern door and heard conversations die as Teagan and he swept into the taproom. She turned to Seamus, the green cloak flaring around her.

"There is a rumor in the village that one of the wee people is haunting this inn. We are here to tame the leprechaun, and our price is two mugs of ale."

Hogan grinned and drew two pints. "The creature you seek is in the upper chamber, where he usually makes his presence known. My most reliable pixie chaser has a very watchful eye on him. And welcome back."

They took their mugs and went quickly up the stairs. A moment later Seamus could hear the squealing sounds of happy greetings and the smile lingered on his lips. Seamus would always remember Kaidan O'Canavan running around the living quarters on Christmas day handing out little sketches to the family.

"What's this?" Seamus asked.

"It's a horsie!" Seamus looked at the untidy lines. "Of course it is! Well done, Kaidan."

Deirdre would always remember a nimble little boy with a stick in his hand, fencing with his father, who held an identical stick. *How Rory Donovan would have loved seeing this. He's just past three, but I can already see traces of his father and even his grandfather in the way he moves, and the way he thinks.*

◆ ◆ ◆

When he was four Kaidan soaked up the ancient legends of Ireland. Mama brought in a small woman in dark clothing who visited once a month and told the most wonderful tales of old heroes and the legends they created. He called her Bridie and did not notice that each of her stories was about a great warrior, or that one of those was his own father.

When he was five he started learning about the English. Kaidan never cried when he fell and scraped his knees in the middle of a headlong rush, but he shed angry tears when Conor told him how his grandfather was exiled and how Deedee and Papa had been forced off their land.

"I will get it back," he promised, his bright red hair falling in front of his eyes.

At six he taught other little boys in the village that teasing him over that red hair carried a cost often expressed in black eyes and bruises.

At seven he was leading those boys around the village on imaginary quests for honor and glory. Their favorite place was a huge old oak tree on the edge of Kinvara.

"When Conor was a boy," Deirdre said one day while she and Teagan watched a small herd of running boys sweep past the tavern. "The pack of boys were Finn McCool's Fianna and he was Oisin the leader."

"So that's where the name came from," Teagan said with a smile.

"Yes, but it worked because the old legend was so strong in young minds, and still is," Deirdre reminded her.

34

EZRA

In 1710 when John Ivers was High Sheriff of County Clare, the British tightened their control over the Irish west. They granted cross-border jurisdictional authority to high sheriffs, enabling them to arrest fugitives who had fled, in cooperation with officials in the counties of refuge.

Ivers sifted through the files of unsolved cases and found several deaths of Englishmen in 1702 and 1703 that all pointed toward a mysterious rebel and a red-haired woman. He soon learned of Oisin the Avenger and the beautiful goddess Red Teagan Moran, who could cure wounds or make them fatal. He also learned Conor O'Canavan had been found not guilty in the death of an Englishman and had left Clare for the Galway town of Kinvara.

Being a practical man, Sheriff Ivers decided the tales were just superstitious Irish nonsense, and that Oisin/O'Canavan was just a local rebel leader who could be executed both for murder and for treason against the Crown. He sent his new chief deputy to have a quiet word with Geoffrey Moore, who was still holding Dunguaire on behalf of the squabbling heirs of the late Sir William French.

"I thought he was a threat when I came here," Moore told the emissary. "But later he worked hard to improve our harbor, and I think he has personally kept petty crime and extortion out of Kinvara. I know nothing of his record in Clare."

"That is why we have this new accord," the visitor said. "It is precisely to keep vermin like this O'Canavan from fleeing across county lines to avoid justice."

Ezra Smith reached into his pouch and pulled out a sheet of parchment that had been extensively sealed and stamped. "This warrant has been signed and certified by the High Sheriff of Clare and his counterpart in Galway. And as you saw, I have a squad of soldiers from Galway, since Kinvara is in their jurisdiction. Will you help arrest this dangerous man, or will you be a problem?"

Moore thought about that. *I don't like this pompous ass. He's straight from Dublin and knows nothing of the West. But the papers seem to be in order, and if I'm not at least neutral, I could lose my post, which I've enjoyed. I'm not going to tell this Smith my son and Conor's run in the same pack of little boys. But neither will I tell him . . . yes I will.*

"My friend, there's a cost to this move. This O'Canavan is the real leader of the Irish in Kinvara, especially since their old priest died. His wife is a power in herself. If we execute him, we're going to have big problems, here and in your village of Doolin."

"Piffle. Doolin is nothing and so is Kinvara. Surely we can find the force to squash these bugs easily. So let's get on with it. Do you know where to find him?"

"He's usually around the tavern, Hogan's tavern. Without a Catholic church here that's where the Irish in Kinvara gather. Do you want to go there now?"

"Yes. I'll alert the soldiers."

Geoffrey Moore watched the man disappear down the castle stairs calling his troops. *This is not going to end well.*

◆ ◆ ◆

The thump of marching feet echoed through Kinvara and people stuck their heads out to see what was happening. Ezra Smith strutted down the street ahead of a column of twenty soldiers in red coats, marching two by two and holding muskets. A small boy told patrons in the tavern there was a parade outside. Conor and Seamus went out to see it.

Smith halted his soldiers and shouted. "I seek the traitor O'Canavan."

"Iss misha Conor Mac Cormac O'Canavan. Conas ata tu?"

"That's the man," Smith said. "Shoot him if he flees."

"I have nothing to flee from, Sassenach," Conor said. "Why are you making such a show of being important?"

"I am Ezra Smith, Chief Deputy High Sheriff of County Clare. I have here the legal writ to hold you for murder and treason. Men, bind him."

"Hold!" Conor called in a commanding voice. "You are risking the peace of this village. I have done no treason, and I do not submit to seizure." *Where are my weapons when I need them? Where is my tiara? Oh, damn, here comes my family.*

Teagan paled when she saw the soldiers pointing weapons at Conor. She gripped Kaidan with one hand and Deirdre with the other. She heard Mathair Crionna's voice. *There's a price to pay for such boons as a sunny wedding day and the accounting is due.* Teagan leaned into Deirdre and thought she would fall.

Smith called out again. "Men, shackle the prisoner. Second rank, if he resists, shoot the women with red hair and the red-haired boy."

Conor, fearful for Teagan, told her, "Do nothing. I will go with these men. This is a mistake that can be cleared up. Now you, Deputy Smith. I will go with you but I will not be bound in front of my home. You may even escort me. Where do you want to go?"

Smith's jaw dropped. *Captives do not give orders. They cry or they run, but nothing like this. He is too dangerous to walk free.* "Take him, I say!" Conor went down under a wedge of red-coated bodies. When they stood him up he was chained hand and foot.

He saw Kaidan struggle to get free and kick Smith hard in the shins. The man cried out and ordered his soldiers to shoot the boy. No one moved. Two of them smiled at their temporary commander's discomfort. Teagan saw them. *They don't like him either.* She stepped in front of the man while Seamus kept a firm grip on Kaidan.

"I am Bandia Teagan Dearg Ni Moran," she told him, eyes flashing. "That means the red goddess of Clare. If you harm Conor you will die before dark, and by my hand. I will cut off your head and mount it on the pole that holds up the shade over these tables."

She was so fierce that Smith backed up among his soldiers, and some of them snickered. Teagan went on. "And if you harm my son I will muster all the wrath of this abused land and flay the skin off your living body and drape it over a pig!"

Even Deirdre paled at that. Smith and his whole escort backed up a pace, and behind them, men could be heard muttering. "Do it! Do it!"

Smith gathered his wits and formed his men into a square with Conor in the middle and marched off at the head of a large crowd.

"Go home, vermin!" he shouted.

"Go home to Satan, Saxon," a man called. "We will see where you take him."

"Mama, why don't the Fianna rescue Papa? They are all great warriors."

Seamus answered. "We have always had great warriors, and still do, Kaidan, as your very name suggests. One-on-one our warriors can beat theirs. But their fighting force is organized as an army. They are not warriors but soldiers, and they fight in formation, not as individual champions. It is a fatal flaw for us, based on the way minds work differently in the two cultures. Besides, they have firearms."

The escort marched Conor into Dunguaire Castle and slammed the gate. Through the bars the watchers could see him led into the stone fortress.

Geoffrey Moore was waiting inside. "Conor, are you all right?"

He smiled, a very thin smile. "Surely. I always walk around shackled hand and foot, haven't you noticed?"

Ezra Smith pushed forward. "Moore, have you a dungeon?"

"No, but I have a storeroom that can be locked." He turned to the soldiers and said, "It's that way. Here's the key. Conor, I will see what I can do for you."

Smith was livid. "Lieutenant, put Moore in the same cell." The man shook his head.

"Our orders are to help you arrest O'Canavan, and only him. Moore is the castle-keeper and is beyond your writ. If you wish him penned up, you must do it yourself."

"All right then. Twenty lashes for the prisoner."

"I have been convicted of nothing," Conor said. "Your entire system of justice is based on keeping a space open between accusation and punishment."

"You are a traitor to the Crown and you are in chains. You have no rights."

Geoffrey Moore made a decision. "You will not torture this man under my roof. You will not act on the fear that his wife strikes in your heart. Dunguaire has never been an evil place, and it will not become one today."

"Thank you," Conor said.

"Remove the prisoner," Smith ordered, and Conor was marched off. "You are walking on thin ice here, Moore," Smith growled.

"No, you are, Deputy. Do not take on more power than is yours and do not do it within my walls. Your authority is limited here, and all you need do to upset this inter-county agreement on arrests is to come in here so heavy-handed your quest goes sour. And I tell you this. If a revolt starts here I will lay the blame squarely on you."

Smith turned back to the redcoats. "Escort this man to his quarters and post a man to make sure he stays there. He is not to hinder the workings of justice."

◆ ◆ ◆

During the night the sound of distant carpentry carried over still waters to the village streets. In the first gray light of a new day Paddy O'Brien banged on the tavern door and ran around waking the villagers.

"They've built a gallows!" he shouted. "And Conor is in there."

Villagers surged toward the castle, none faster than Kaidan O'Canavan, the running boy of Kinvara. They paused in astonishment to see three of the Galway soldiers holding their muskets on the castle garrison, who were seated in a circle on the ground in front of their squad room.

"Are you all right?" Seamus called to one of them.

"We dare not move," the man answered. "And Geoffrey Moore is confined in his quarters. It is not of our doing, this evil thing." More soldiers stood behind the bars, keeping the crowd out and trying to ignore the anger of fist-shaking villagers.

Conor stood on a platform about seven feet above the courtyard, his arms bound behind him and a noose around his neck. There were bloody streaks on his shirt. Ezra Smith stood there, too, with a soldier who held a rope that ran down through the floor.

"Conor O'Canavan," the deputy sheriff called out in a loud voice.

"You have committed treason against the Crown, and you have slain Englishmen doing their work in this foul and pestilent land. Therefore I sentence you to be hanged by the neck until you are dead. Do you have any last words before you die?"

"Indeed I have. I speak for those who cannot. I speak for the oppressed, the ones who are ground down by the daily indignities of occupation by a foreign power. And I say this to the people without. Do not avenge yourself on Geoffrey Moore or on this castle. He has been a quiet friend in recent years. Rather go after the ones who believe that might is always right, who think they can force their will on us no matter how twisted that will may be." He paused for a moment to seek out the eyes of his family.

"And I say this to you, Ezra Smith. Your name will be a stain on the English language from now on and will never be spoken again in Kinvara or in Dunguaire. You are trying to extinguish the idea of light by blowing out a candle. That cannot be done. You are trying to crush the idea of freedom by snuffing out its advocates. That cannot be done either. And there's one more thing, Sassenach. I piss on you. For the lashes you have dealt me, for the assault on the peace of Kinvara and for this travesty of the vaunted English justice, you will die before my body cools."

Conor looked directly into those gold-flecked brown eyes pressed against the castle gate, and said, "Red Teagan, continue our . . ."

Smith, enraged, gestured to the executioner, who pulled on his rope. The trapdoor fell away and Conor dropped out of sight.

◆ ◆ ◆

He sat up and looked around at the huge oak tree at the edge of Kinvara. He could smell last year's acorns. There were clouds, and dappled sunlight angled in from the east.

"How do you feel?" The voice came from behind him, and Conor got to his feet looking around. Cormac O'Canavan was smiling at him.

"What are you doing here?" Conor asked.

"The same thing as you, son. You could say that we're both ghosts now."

"You mean I'm dead?"

"Aye, my son, so you are."

"That's odd. I felt nothing after they pulled the floor out from under me."

"I know. They wanted you to strangle at the end of the rope, but I added some weight to you, and the fall broke your neck. How does it feel now?"

Conor put his hand up and rotated his neck in several directions, and grinned. "It still works, I think. What do we do now?"

"We wait. There is a lot of waiting on this side of the line you just crossed."

"Aye, but what do we do here?"

"Well, Teagan will kill Ezra Smith tonight in that tavern in Ennistymon where you were drugged. We will scare off anyone who may help him. Are you ready for that?"

"Aye. It will take us a long time to get to Ennistymon."

"You'd be surprised. Things are a little different here. Space and time are not the absolutes they once were. You'll get used to it."

35

David

When Conor disappeared at the end of a suddenly taut rope, a howling crowd surged against the castle gate. Thrown rocks struck two soldiers in red coats and a pike thrust through the bars in the castle gate stabbed one townsman.

A crowd of young men led by Paddy O'Brien overwhelmed the red-coats guarding the castle garrison. One was shot with his own musket and the other two fell to knives and clubs. All three died. Men dragged the bodies to the castle gate and the weapons vanished. Lieutenant David Jones, leading the British squad, was furious. He faced a smug-looking Smith, pistol in hand.

"You slimy little bastard," he shouted. "You have cost me three men and we're not even out of here. We are leaving now, and if you don't want to be torn to pieces you will come with us, right now. You have handled this matter so badly I will tell my commanders never again should Galway cooperate with the bloodthirsty officials from County Clare. By the way, my protection is only good on the road to Galway City, where you will not be welcome. When you strike out for Ennis, you will be on your own and I don't care whether you get there or not."

"You can't speak to me in that manner. You are a mere soldier, a very junior officer, and I am the Chief Deputy High Sheriff of County Clare pursuing justice."

The sergeant's laugh was harsh. "If this were about justice I would turn you over to that crowd. They'd pull you apart in so many pieces the carrion eaters could find nothing to feast on, not that they would touch you. When you ordered my men to shoot that child, you lost what little respect I had for you. When you ordered the prisoner flogged and penned up, it got worse. Now hold your tongue and stay away from me while I try to get us out of here alive."

Jones released Geoffrey Moore from his quarters, briefed him on the morning's events and asked him to try to disperse the crowd of angry townsmen.

"You know," the young officer said. "Smith had the prisoner flogged over your objections, and then they hanged him at sunrise without a trace of legal process. O'Canavan spoke to the crowd just before he died and asked them not to take out their wrath on you. So I'm asking you to try to disperse them. I have already lost three men, and I'd like to get the rest of them home alive."

"What about Smith? He's behind all this."

"So he is," Jones said. "But I don't have the authority to shoot him, much as I'd like to do it. We'll take him with us, at least until we're clear of Kinvara."

"I'll do what I can, but I make no promises. The man was much loved in Kinvara, and half the people here think his wife is a goddess. My own view is that she is exceptionally beautiful and just as dangerous. If she should call for revolt this area could be in flames before you can march back to Galway City."

Moore stepped away from the soldier and went to the gate, which had been opened to retrieve the bodies of dead soldiers, and was now barred again. He stared through those bars at Teagan and her supporters.

"I am so sorry," he said. "I am ashamed my holding was used for such a base purpose. It's my hope now to prevent a massacre in the wake of a sanctioned lynching."

"Conor told us not to take out our rage on you or on Dunguaire, and we shall not," Teagan said. "But he promised Ezra Smith would die before his body is cold, and that will be my task. The soldiers will be safe on their way back to Galway, but Smith shall not reach Ennis alive." She stopped while the men around her nodded.

"Geoffrey Moore, you had a poor start in Kinvara, but you have improved. I ask of you this favor. Please hold Conor's body until I return for it tomorrow. We will lay him to rest in a place that's full of Irish magic, a magic that is ancient, and yet will be strengthened by his presence." She stepped away and then turned back.

"Kaidan's eighth birthday is Friday, and your Charles will be welcome at a little party for him. One last thing. I'll need a horse. May I take one of yours?"

Moore watched her leave in a cluster of the village's best people. *She has such a presence. No wonder the people here love her so much. But what I told the soldier is true, too. As far as British rule is concerned, she is exceptionally dangerous. I would never want to be Ezra Smith but especially not today.*

◆ ◆ ◆

After leaving her son with Deirdre Teagan rode south, trying to figure out the road Smith would take to Ennis. As she passed the standing stone marking the Galway-Clare border, she got some help. Three short men met her at a curve.

"You have seen us before, on the morning of your wedding. Now you see us on the morning of your widowhood. As you may know, we are the family scorekeepers. I am Donal, and there is Dennis and Daniel." He stopped while the others doffed their old-fashioned caps and bowed politely to her.

"Normally, the death of Ezra Smith would be our duty. But you, Bandia Teagan Dearg, are the most powerful woman in the family since Bridie and we cede our duty to you. The Inn of the Three Codfish is your destination in Ennistymon. Inside you will find the man you seek."

"We know you haven't decided exactly how to do this," Donal said. "And we look forward to witnessing your deed."

"Aye, lass, do it with flair and style. Do it so the people will shiver for generations when they tell the story," Dennis said with a benign smile. Teagan smiled, too. "Thanks, my uncles. Your support is so vital to me. I'll remember."

The awkwardly named Inn of the Three Codfish boasted a hanging shield that showed three images of the Atlantic's most important food fish, one over another, facing left. "It's a family thing," said the owner, a man named Dubhslainey.

A handful of patrons sipped ale, away from the two obvious Englishmen in the center of the room. Three small men stood together unseen, and Conor saw the drinkers walk around the space they occupied without knowing why. He and Cormac, also unseen, stood nearby. *How do we get rid of Smith's aide?* Conor asked.

Watch. When Teagan comes in, he will discover that he has to pee and will go out to relieve himself. There is no one else here who is likely to interfere.

A woman entered, drawing the eyes of most of the men in the room, including Ezra Smith. She looked around before locking eyes with the Englishman.

"You are dressed better than those others," she said, approaching his table. "So you are probably more able to furnish the help I need."

The man sitting with Smith got up and excused himself, and the deputy offered his chair to the woman. *She is tall and dark, and not quite young any more, but bonny in her own way. I wonder what she needs?*

"How may I help you?" Smith asked.

"I am fallen on difficult days," the woman said with a small shrug that he found charming. She looked him in the eye. "My husband has just died, and I am left to provide for my son." She reached up and took off a tiara he hadn't noticed, and placed it on the table. "My husband said this has been in the family a long time and may have value. What think you, kind sir?"

Smith reached for the golden trinket and picked it up, noting that it seemed to tingle in his hand. There was a four-spoked wheel in the front with a large moonstone in its center. "Jeremy," he called to his returning aide. "What do you think of this?" He put it on his head. Surprise and terror raced across his face. Ezra Smith leaped to his feet and clawed the device off his head. Teagan picked it off the floor.

Smith screamed, grabbed for his head, and foamed at the mouth. He fell, spasming and shrieking, his wildly kicking legs knocking over chairs and his hands digging at his belly. Men jumped to their feet, and only a few noticed the strange woman who smiled as she held the crownlet in her hands.

When Smith stopped moving and lay still, she stood, putting on the tiara. She was younger and her hair flashed bright red in the subdued light.

"Hear me!" she called out. "I am Bandia Teagan Dearg and this man is dead. He tortured and murdered Oisin the Avenger, and justice has found him. Ezra Smith's body bears no marks, and as you saw, I did not touch him. He is dead because of the accumulated evil within him. There is no healing for Ezra Smith." She glanced at the body and turned to the inn's patrons.

"You will all remember this day and this moment. May you also remember what justice comes to those who oppress us in our own land. This man," she said, and pointed to the aide Jeremy. "This man is to live, to bear the tale to Ennis."

Teagan stepped forward and let the green cloak swirl around her. "One more thing. My husband once came here to meet some men over British colonial excesses. Someone here betrayed him and he was caught. Who was that man?"

Several men in the room looked hard at the body on the floor and tried to become very small. One man in the corner jumped up to run out of the room but he tripped over something unseen and fell, slamming his head into a table leg.

Teagan's eyes tracked him while a grim smile worked its way onto her face. She glared around. "You know who he is, and he knows who put the drug in my husband's ale. You will deal with them." She knelt and sawed at Smith's neck with a dagger.

Son, you know something of this process. Can we help her?

Aye. I seem to be able to make the sinews part.

"Innkeeper, a cloth bag, if you please. And if Red Teagan returns to this room it will not be good for your trade."

She turned on her heel and strode out with her trophy, hair and cape flying. A moment later the sound of a walking horse filtered into the room and broke a shock-fueled stillness. Two unseen men traded big grins. *I'm glad she's on our side,* the older one said.

That was fun. Rory told me once that an old woman in Kinvara said the tiara could smite evil men. And it didn't seem she needed much help from us. So, what next?

Do you know the ancient gravesite at Poulnabrone? Aye, I was once there with Teagan.

You will get to know it a lot better. I spoke to the man who was first buried there thousands of years ago. He says you're a welcome addition to the bodies that lie near his.

But I wanted to look in on Kaidan's birthday party.

You will. And then we watch while Teagan and White Patrick raise your son.

White Patrick Boyle? What's that about?

Conor, think it through. Tay is twenty-seven years old and Kaidan is eight. She can't just shut down her life, and he needs a man's presence. Besides, Whitey has felt free since Sinead died last year, and he's a good man. Also, he's always been in love with Teagan.

It'll take some adjustment, but it's like when you died and I was little, isn't it?

Pretty close, and I know they'll do a good job, with help from Ronan and Deirdre and Seamus. And they'll need our help too, so they will.

What kind of help?

That's what we await. We wait a lot here, so be patient. You'll get used to it.

36

Donal

The first crossroads she reached on her way from the inn where Ezra Smith died presented Teagan Dearg with a choice. As she approached it, three familiar short men appeared on the road, brightly lit in the side-slanting light of late afternoon.

"Whither now, my lady?" The voice startled Teagan. *I've been mulling over the way Smith died, the way I gloated over his suffering, and the emptiness of my road ahead. Life without Conor seems grim indeed.* She mustered a smile for the trio of leprechauns.

"It's a timely question, my uncles." *Actually Conor's great-uncles, as I understand the complex relationships among the members of his family.* "I don't want to go left to Doolin, or right to Gort, so that leaves us with Kinvara, straight ahead, more or less. By the way, I have done what I came here for. Oh, which one are you?" She asked with a small shrug. *I should know; I have seen them before.*

"I am Donal, and there is Dennis, and the smiling one is Daniel. We are here to escort you home, and if needed, to terrify any who might pursue."

"Let's hope there are none. I think I did enough terrifying to keep pursuers at a distance for a while. As for today, I don't think anyone in that inn wants to face down Bandia Teagan Dearg in the deepening dusk." They grinned and doffed their old-style hats.

"And a good job it was. So it's off to Hogan's tavern then, my lady. Daniel will pick out our path, while Dennis and I keep pace with you."

"But you have no horses."

Daniel laughed. "Our legs are longer than they look."

Teagan tried walking her horse, noting that Donal and Dennis kept pace easily while appearing to proceed at a stroll. On a whim, she urged the horse to a trot. Without seeming to walk faster, the brothers still moved alongside without apparent effort. *How do they do that? What an odd family I married into. Well, at least the horse seems to think all this eccentricity is normal. What do horses know?*

"Donal, are you and your brothers trying to keep me entertained, trying to keep me from brooding over Conor's death while we ride back to claim his body?"

"Aye, in part, Teagan Dearg, but mostly it's because we want to keep you safe. After all, you're a significant player in the reawakening of this land."

"Everyone who's not normal keeps telling me that, from you to Mathair Crionna to Finulla, but no one really tells me anything. Why not?"

Donal shrugged in the blue-tinted light that seemed to stream back from Daniel to a few feet behind the horse. "It's a complex tapestry, lady, and you are changing the weave of it. All the power was supposed to flow down the male side, and no one knew you would prove to be so strong. You are bending the spirals in ways we could not anticipate, but it's positive, and we're all trying to adjust to it." The new widow's "uncle" smiled and pride showed in his face. "You know you're halfway now to being one of us."

Teagan was shocked. "You mean . . ."

"Aye. You could be among us for a very long time. Bridie's going to be annoyed at me for letting that out, but you deserve to know what lies before you. That knowledge will affect almost all of your choices and decisions. Daniel! Make the light more yellow!"

"You can still hear my mind, can't you?"

"Of course I can. We all can, and you'll get better at it, too. Now, let's get you home to Kinvara and some very special people."

Teagan rode in silence, thinking about what she had just heard. As the night deepened she realized the leprechauns had the journey in hand,

and all she needed to do was hold onto the saddle. *Let's see if I can do that with my eyes closed, just for a moment.*

"Oh, there's the tavern. I didn't realize we were so close."

"Och, lass, blame that on us," Dennis said. "When you fell asleep we kept you upright and fiddled with things a bit. The horse didn't like it very much, but here we are."

Only the welcome lamp burned outside the building and no glimmers came from within. In a moment the door creaked open and a small face framed in red hair peered around the doorpost and then shot across the patio laughing and crying at the same time.

"Kaidan, why are you up and about so late?"

"I woke up and I knew you were here," the boy said. "How did you know?"

"I don't know, I just knew."

Donal, did you have aught to do with this?

Nay, my girl, that's all his doing. The boy is, after all, your son, and Conor's. It suggests an interesting future. Give us the head, and we will post it where all can see. Now let them bundle you in and fuss over you, and insist on some sleep. You have some serious decisions to make when the sun is high.

◆ ◆ ◆

The sun was higher than Teagan thought it should be when she awoke to realize the other half of her bed was empty, and always would be. She stifled the urge to cry, dressed quickly, and went down to the bustle of the inn's kitchen. Hot tea came with a hug from Seamus and toasted bread came with a hug from Deirdre.

"Has anyone been outside yet?" Teagan asked. "No? I'll be right back." She walked out to the patio and looked around. There on top of the pole that held up the canvas sunshades was the head of Ezra Smith, mouth open and eyes bulging in a silent echo of his death scream. A few flies had found it. *This is not supposed to feel satisfying, but it does.* Teagan heard Mathair Crionna's voice. *There is always satisfaction in justice, my dear. That's why we value it so highly.*

The new widow smiled briefly and went back inside, where Deirdre turned the talk to tasks pending. "Yesterday you asked Geoffrey Moore to keep Conor's body until you could come for it," she said as they lingered at their favorite table.

"That will happen today," Teagan said. "And we will take him to Poulnabrone."

37

Charles

Kaidan Mac Conor O'Canavan flinched when the sunshine tickled his eyelids through the bedroom window in Seamus Hogan's tavern. *I'm late. Something important is going to happen today and maybe it already has. I've got to get downstairs.* A minute later he burst into the kitchen, his eyes eager for the next adventure. Exciting things happen every day when you're almost eight.

"Go pack some clothes for a couple of days. I'll help you after breakfast," Teagan Dearg O'Canavan told her son from the kitchen table.

"Where are we going? To Doolin again?"

"No, my son. We're taking your father to be buried at Poulnabrone, the Hole of Sorrows in the Burren. Seamus thinks we should rename it the Hall of Heroes."

"We should," said the innkeeper, bringing Kaidan a glass of milk. "First we make room for Oisin the Avenger, and then maybe we find out where Fionn Mac Cumhaill is, and Cuchulain, and Diarmid, and move them there too."

Deirdre O'Canavan Hogan sipped tea and smiled at her husband and her grandson. "Everyone needs an imagination," she told Kaidan. "But some, like Seamus, have imagination without limit. We call those people dreamers when we speak kindly of them."

The boy watched as Hogan smiled fondly at his grandmother. *This room sees a lot of smiles and hears a lot of kindly teasing. It's the center of my family's life. I learned to walk here. There's Mom with her bright red hair lighting up the room, and Dad's mom, Deirdre. I called her DeeDee when I was little, and Seamus Hogan her new husband was Shamey. Dad's friend Ronan comes here sometimes and brings Sea Dog with him. Sea Dog is in love with Mom. Almost everybody is in love with Mom except the ones who are afraid of her, and there are a lot of those. That's everybody. My dad's not here because the British hanged him yesterday, and my mom went after the man who ordered him hanged. I guess I'll hear that story pretty soon, but not from her. Not sure what this room will be like without my dad.*

"Kaidan!" Teagan called, pulling her son back from thoughts that dwelt on yesterday's chaotic hanging. "Why don't you run up to the castle and see if Charles wants to go with us today on the trek to Poulnabrone?"

The boy was lunging into his shoes before the question ended. "Two or three days," Teagan called after his vanishing back. In a moment he was back, eyes wide. "Mama, Mama! That man's head is up on a pole over the patio!" Everyone went out to see and to hear the neighbor women mutter about the Powers and Bandia Teagan Dearg. They had all heard her threaten Smith two days ago. Teagan shooed Kaidan off on his errand and went back inside.

Most people in the village thought of Kaidan as the running boy of Kinvara. They had gotten used to seeing him speeding through the streets, usually at the head of a pack of small boys off on secret adventures. Charles Moore was one of those boys. His father Geoffrey was the castle keeper at Dunguaire.

Kaidan covered the distance to Dunguaire Castle before his mother's tea cooled. *Geoffrey Moore tried to protect my father from being lashed after he was arrested, and Mom told people not to turn their anger on him. I hope Charles can go with us.*

Geoffrey Moore directed the men of his small garrison as they demolished the gallows where Conor Mac Cormac O'Canavan died just over twenty-four hours ago on the orders of a Deputy High Sheriff from the adjacent County Clare. *I still have a sour feeling about that. But that bastard Smith got the soldiers to pen me up, and then whipped Conor before staging a blatantly non-legal hanging. O'Canavan was a champion of Irish resistance to the excesses of British rule, but he didn't deserve this.*

All I can do now is clean away the traces of treachery and cruelty and hope yesterday's trouble doesn't ignite a general uprising in the Irish west. Oh, here comes the boy, Kaidan, sprinting as usual.

"Good morning to you, sir," Kaidan said in English.

"And to you, too, young man," Moore said, wondering why the little boy was not breathless after his run from the village. "Your father is resting in a cool space within. We have honored his body, and I say to you that I am sorry about his death. Do you know what became of the man Smith, the deputy sheriff from Ennis? Your mother borrowed a horse from me yesterday to go after him."

"You must ask her that question, Castle-keeper, but this morning his head is mounted above Seamus Hogan's tavern. My mother and some others are coming here today to collect the body of Oisin the Avenger. We will take him for burial to a place in County Clare called Poulnabrone. Do you know aught of that location?"

"I have heard stories that it is a place of power in Irish mythology. It is alone out in the Burren, and men say it is old, very old. I would like to see it some day."

Moore saw Kaidan shift from foot to foot, almost hopping in his eagerness to speak, but unwilling to interrupt.

"I came here to ask if Charles can come with us to Poulnabrone. It would be nice to have another boy along. And if you want to go, you must ask for yourself."

"That I will do, Kaidan." Moore turned toward the blocky tower and shouted. "Charles! Kaidan is here!"

Charles Moore popped out of the tower door so quickly that Kaidan wondered if he had slid down a rope from the living quarters. "Charles!" he called. "There's to be a real adventure today and you're invited. We're off to Poulnabrone to bury my father and my mother asks if you want to come with us for two or three days."

"Aye," Charles shouted around his biggest grin. "Tell the goddess I will be ready when the journey begins. I can go, can't I, father?"

"Yes, son, you may. I want to go myself, to honor a good man. And by the way, Kaidan's mother is not a goddess." He smiled inwardly at the flickers of doubt that suddenly showed on both small faces. "Tell your mother I will have a cart for the body and a draft horse to pull it. And until we all return she can keep the horse she rode yesterday."

Kaidan jumped in the air and exchanged grins and a not-so-secret handshake with Charles and sped off at his usual pace. Geoffrey Moore watched him go with a small smile and turned to his son. "She's not, you know."

"Not what?"

"Not a goddess, my boy. Don't believe everything you hear."

"All right, but everybody in Kinvara thinks Teagan Dearg, or Red Teagan, is magical. There's even a harper song called The Ballad of Red Teagan. Have you heard it?"

My son's face is so eager that his beliefs be his truths. But goddesses are out of style these days, however useful they may be in the politics of resistance. "I have heard of it, but I don't shape what I believe out of myths and legends that float in the wind. Go now and gather clothing for a few days, and remember protection against the rain."

Goddess indeed. I remember the first time I saw her. She was in the crowd that came to bid farewell to Sir William French when he retired to Gort. She was the most beautiful woman I had ever seen. Still is. That blazing red hair and those golden brown eyes set her apart. Yesterday morning, with her husband's body still warm under the gallows she took command of the crowd at the gate and I believe she alone averted a massacre. She and Conor worked in tandem as leaders of the Irish in Kinvara, and from what I hear, even more strongly down in County Clare. I wonder what she'll do now, and where. Maybe I can learn what happened to that self-important snake Ezra Smith.

He turned to the commander of the castle garrison. "Tell the man on watch I want to know when he sees people coming from the village. And move the good wagon into the shade where we can load O'Canavan's body on it. I'll have a draft horse for the wagon and the bay gelding for myself. I'll be gone for maybe three days and while I'm away you will be in charge here. Collect the rents and the road tolls but do nothing that may stir up wrath in the village. One crisis at a time among these people is quite enough, Jerome."

38

GEOFFREY

When a beehive is busy, its residents shuttle in and out with bewildering speed but there's a pattern to the activity. When a beehive is agitated, its residents buzz around the entrance nervously and without purpose. On the morning after Conor O'Canavan's hanging, Kaidan and Sea Dog provided the agitation in the beehive that was Seamus Hogan's tavern, the boy pointing at Ezra Smith's head and the dog running in aimless circles and getting thoroughly under foot while everyone prepared for the trip to Poulnabrone.

Everyone wanted to go. Seamus Hogan complained about that to Ronan O'Malley, Conor's sailor friend from the Claddagh fishing village near Galway City. "I asked Paddy O'Brien to run the tavern while I'm gone but he refused. Said he's one of Conor's original Fianna warriors and he's going, no matter what."

"Would you trust my cousin, Liam Reilly?" Ronan asked. "He sailed here with me and he has no ties to Conan. He's already planning to stay here and look after the *Moira*."

Seamus shook his head. "Trust a sailor to mind a pub? Ask a fox to guard a henhouse. Thanks, Ronan. I'll say yes, and tell him to remove the head while we're gone. Where is he?"

"On the boat. I'll go get him. And I'll leave Sea Dog with him. No telling what he'd get into if he gets loose in the Burren. It's so far from the ocean he'd be confused."

◆ ◆ ◆

Kaidan watched a growing crowd swirl around the tavern, ready to go but unwilling to leave before Teagan. *All these people are here to honor my father. Now they wait for my mother to lead them. They don't see the widow but they do see the bandia.*

When she came out dressed in black with her bright hair resting on her green cloak, the procession formed behind her. Teagan mounted her borrowed horse and reined it toward the castle. An opal fronted the gold circlet shining on her head.

Seamus, Deirdre and Kaidan walked behind the horse, followed by Ronan O'Malley and the six young men of Conor's Fianna and then dozens of Kinvara residents. There was sadness among them, a mood the horse reflected. Usually spirited and high stepping, the mare walked sedately on the improved road to the castle and the mourners shuffled along behind.

Geoffrey Moore sat on his own horse at the castle gate, behind the wagon that held Conor's body and beside the restless figure of young Charles. *His mother didn't want him to go. I don't think she likes it here on the edge of Ireland. But Charles does. It will be interesting to see how he deals with the cultural differences when he's older.*

Castle-keeper Moore watched the slow-moving clot of villagers approach. *More people than I expected, but then I should have expected more people. Conor was, in an old-fashioned sense, the chief of this village, and I think the goddess Red Teagan will inherit that role.*

A crippled man dragged his bad leg up to the horse. "Have you assigned a driver for the wagon Connor's body is on?"

"Who are you?" Moore asked.

"I am Eamon O'Shaughnessy, and Conor was a benefactor to me years ago. I would be honored to drive his remains to the gravesite." He did not say he was crippled by the beatings he was given after the English caught him poaching deer.

"I thought someone from the village would drive," Moore said. The man smiled. "I am from the village. It just takes me a while to get anywhere."

"The horse and wagon are mine, but the decision is Madam O'Canavan's." Kaidan O'Canavan trotted up grinning. "Good morning, Eamon O'Shaughnessy."

"You know this man, Kaidan?"

"Aye, sir, he is the venison man of Kinvara. My father told me he met Eamon when he was fifteen or sixteen years old and has tried to help him ever since. Eamon, why are you here?"

"I want to drive the wagon that carries your father's body."

"Wait," said Kaidan. "I will ask her." And he sped off toward the approaching procession. A minute later he was back, well ahead of the others and smiling.

"She says Eamon can't walk to Poulnabrone, so he'll ride with reins in his hands." Geoffrey Moore looked at the cripple. "What did a beardless youth do for you?"

"He kept me from starving after I was injured."

Moore's attention shifted to the roadway. "Good morning, Madam O'Canavan. I am sorry to greet you on such a sad day."

"Sad indeed, Castle-Keeper, but I hope to make this day a celebration of his life." She turned a brilliant smile on O'Shaughnessy. "Eamon, your offer to drive is thoughtful, so it is. And my Conor will be in good hands."

"Thank you, Bandia. I will try to keep pace. And Kaidan, if you ever need to rest those legs, you can ride too."

Eamon struggled up to the driver's seat, picked up the reins and looked expectantly at Teagan, who was talking to Moore. "My son told me you would like to go with us. You are welcome but you should know there will be no other English, and some of the people here are very angry with the English, so they are."

"Thank you for the caution, Madam, but I will go, both to honor a good man, and to see a place of legend I've always wanted to visit."

She nodded and was about to turn the horse when she thought of something. "We are not all as fit and fleet as Kaidan and Charles. We will move slowly and it will take about five hours to walk there, maybe a bit longer. Before we start I must say it's important to take food, water and bedding with you, since the gifts of the Burren are sparse."

Moore smiled. "That was a thoughtful suggestion. I have enough for myself and the boy, and perhaps a little more. We are prepared and will follow your lead."

"Eamon, we'll start now and only Paddy will precede you. He knows the way."

Eamon O'Shaughnessy smiled and twitched the reins. The horse began to move and so did the people, stretching out behind the wagon. Kaidan and Charles darted ahead and swirled around the walkers and the wagon like dragonflies.

◆ ◆ ◆

As time crept on and distance shrank slowly Teagan thought about her decision to bury Conor at Poulnabrone. *How do I know he'll be welcome? When he saw the place he was a bit spooked by the somber mood of Poulnabrone. I hope I'm not making a mistake.*

You are not.

Teagan started in her saddle and the mare sidestepped for a few paces.

Who are you?

I am Kerbasi.

Aye, but who are you?

In a language older than yours my name means warrior.

My son Kaidan's name also means warrior.

That is fitting. Teagan thought there was a hint of rustiness in the ideas that flowed into her head from this Kerbasi.

You are very old, is it not so?

I am. Once I ruled this land long before the Sons of Mil made it a Celtic island.

My retainers brought me to the place you call Poulnabrone and strove for a long time to build a tomb. It is loki burugazi, temple of chiefs, not hole of sorrows. That misses the whole point of my grave. Your mate is welcome here, not just for his deeds, but also for the spirit behind them.

Teagan felt a tugging at her foot.

"Mother?" She saw Kaidan's worried face. "Mom, something strange is happening. It's like there's another person here, but I can't see who and I can't hear anything."

She smiled and tousled his hair. "It's all right, there's no danger. Why don't you and Charles get out ahead and make sure Paddy's choosing the

smoothest way west and south." Kaidan's face cleared, and the boys trotted off in their new role as scouts. *I'm sure they'll have lots of suggestions
for Paddy O'Brien. And isn't it curious how he can almost but not quite
sense Kerbasi? How shall I guide that gift?*

◆ ◆ ◆

The cortege plodded west toward the Atlantic, passing not far from the
inn at Lissateeaun, where Teagan and Conor had sheltered in their flight
from Doolin. *We told the old lady the fugitives were bound for Poulnabrone,
and now we go there without being chased.*

"Come on, Charles, I'll race you to those rocks ahead." Charles shook
his head with a sheepish grin. "I have to talk to my father," he said. He
trotted to where Geoffrey Moore rode along in the middle of the pack
of mourners. The man gave his son a hand up to the saddle and noted
how tired he looked. "Is he wearing you out, son?"

"He never stops. Now he wants to race to those rocks. It's about the
fourth challenge. I'm glad I'm here, but keeping up with the running boy
of Kinvara is not easy."

Geoffrey grinned. "Then stay here for a while. By the way those stones
mark the border between County Galway and County Clare. There are
supposed to be some very old spirals carved on those rocks. Pretty soon
we'll swing more to the south and stop for a bit of rest. And don't look
now but the running boy is riding, up on the wagon with that cripple,
Eamon O'Shaughnessy."

Eamon looked at the boy on the seat beside him and saw exhaustion.
"Kaidan, are you running to avoid thinking, because thinking hurts?"

The boy gave him a small grin and brushed a trickle of sweat away
from his eyes. "Aye, Eamon, that I am. I worry for my mother, who will
not weep, and for myself because I don't know how to care for her, or
what to do without my father. So my heart hurts, and now Charles won't
even run with me any more."

"He will, after a rest. Would you like to drive? The horse's name is Laidir."

"Strong?" The boy smiled. "Well, he's a draft horse. He has to be strong."

"You are right, lad, so you are. Look, Paddy is calling a stop near those
trees." But Kaidan was already gone, exploring the rest area.

Teagan slid off the mare and stretched to work some of the stiffness out of her body. "Mother O'Brien, how are you faring?"

"I am well, Teagan Dearg, so I am. I say this to you, goddess. I will not be the last of us to reach Poulnabrone." She smiled and stood up straight, one hand on her back.

Teagan smiled and gripped the woman's hands in hers. "I have no doubt. Maybe you should challenge Kaidan to a race."

The widow's smile widened as she shook her head. "I'd need your horse, my dear. No, I won't challenge the running boy. Can I do anything for you, Teagan?"

"No, I don't think so. I have been to Poulnabrone with my father and with my husband. Now my father is gone, my husband is gone, and my son is in pain. I've never felt so dark making this journey. I must lead but I so want to cry."

Mother O'Brien shrugged her narrow shoulders. "So then, cry." Teagan smiled briefly. "But it's not that easy, is it."

The new widow turned away and found Paddy and the rest of the Fianna. She greeted each of them and called them together.

"We're about halfway and the road is pretty clear from here on. Paddy, you and the others please press ahead to find a place near the tomb where we can camp and build some fires. Most of you have brought wood. There is some to be found along the way, and there's more on the wagon. I want to select Conor's resting place myself, and I'll do it as soon as I get there. But we must also have a welcoming site for weary walkers."

She was chatting with Deirdre and Seamus when Kaidan bustled up.

"Mother, the Fianna are going ahead to prepare a place for the crowd. Can I go? Please?" She met Deirdre's eyes and got a grin. "He is who he is," his grandmother said. "Aye, you can go. And tell Paddy that I said he must keep an eye on you."

39

Paddy

In a landscape devoid of tall trees and the works of man, Poulnabrone dominated the skyline for quite a distance, even though less than a dozen feet high. Charles sat on the wagon, riding with Eamon O'Shaughnessy.

"Look, Eamon, a little bump on the horizon. Is that where we're going?"

"I think so. There are footprints along the path before us. One set is quite small. I think those were left by Kaidan and the Fianna."

◆ ◆ ◆

The ground around Poulnabrone was a mix of grass and limestone, as if a scattering of gray marshmallows were afloat in a bowl of green pudding. That combination formed a platform a foot or so higher than the surrounding land and served as a pedestal for the structure it supported. Kaidan and the quick-stepping Fianna warriors arrived well ahead of the main procession and halted in silence and stillness before the ancient dolmen. The boy reached out to touch one of the upright slabs that supported the great capstone. "Paddy," he said in what was for him a small voice. "Can you feel anything odd here? It's not like this thing is breathing, but power abides here. It's almost vibrating like a harp string. Can you feel it?"

Paddy O'Brien had to look twice to decide that Kaidan was not teasing, not this time. He clapped the boy on a shoulder. "Nay, lad. There's nothing magical or eerie here. It's very solemn but not enchanted." Kaidan was not sure about Paddy's dismissal. He felt quite small after realizing the journey had a very dark core.

"I love the adventure of coming here, but not the reason," he told his mother when she got to the gravesite. "This is a forever thing, isn't it?"

"Yes, son. We've talked about other things that happen. Birthdays are a one-day thing. Festivals last a few days. From one full moon to another is a month and then it's over. Even winter comes to an end. But death is forever, my son. Like when Father Turlough died. You simply don't see those people any more and so you hold inside yourself an open space where you celebrate your memories of them. It's one of the hardest things you'll ever have to do, to heal a hole in your heart." *I'm not telling him the forever rule is apparently not absolute in this family. We'll get to that, but not now. For now it's right that the running boy of Kinvara is sitting, and mourning. I think I'll ask Seamus to come over and sit with him.*

◆ ◆ ◆

As the day faded she stood beside the dolmen and watched the sunset paint its vertical walls in shades of pink and then purple. *The later it gets the darker the color. I think that very darkness is eating into me, owning me. Yesterday I became a widow at twenty-seven.*

I was younger even than Deirdre was when Cormac was lost. My Conor will never again hold me; never make a brother or sister for Kaidan. And how will I deal with the darkness I see in my son? I think it will get worse. Ahhh. But now to the duty of the moment, something I never thought I would do alone.

You are not alone.

Bridie?

Aye, and Cormac, and here my brothers. You are not alone, will never be alone as you go through these next years. Now what do you think about finding a place for Oisin the Avenger, here in this solemn and sacred place?

The large warrior turned and pointed his sword to the east. *Not under the capstone, that space is taken. But look over here, where the morning sun will light the walls. I think this would be appropriate. So does Kerbasi.*

You know him, Cormac?

We have talked. He likes you, and he thinks you have power. My uncles, please mark off this space, and then tomorrow we dig, and complete our task here.

Teagan looked around at the dancing points of firelight that flickered off the faces of those who had come so far to honor her man. *I am so lucky to have this handful of spirits in my life. But my life itself is so joyless now, except for Kaidan.*

40

Nevan

That night the flames leapt highest at the center of a circle of fires where ale and tears flowed together. No one was surprised when the evening floated on songs of bravery and toasting, and all the stories began with "I remember when Conor . . ."

Ronan O'Malley set the tone. "I remember when Conor and I surveyed the Galway Bay shoreline and the Connemara coast for places to load bales of wool into fishing boats. It was Conor's first trip with Sea Dog as a crewmember, so it was. Sea Dog always liked Conor and wanted to show him what a good sailor he was. So here's Conor, trying to figure out how to be useful aboard the boat and keep his lunch in his belly. And here comes Sea Dog, showing off his latest achievement. He dropped a well-chewed rat at Conor's feet and waited for his praise. Instead Conor threw up all over the rat and got some on Sea Dog, too. I told him Conor would get better and then I couldn't stop laughing." A man raised the dregs of a mug of ale. "I wish I had seen Sea Dog's face when that happened." He wandered off in search of more ale, still trying to tamp down his chuckles.

◆ ◆ ◆

"I remember when Conor first formed a raggle-taggle bunch of boys into the Fianna," a quiet man named Niall added. "I thought I would not be allowed in because one of my eyes wanders off and away from where the other is looking. But Conor said if I brought a good heart and a will to work hard, then my lazy eye would not deny me a place among them. I never thanked Conor for preventing me from being an outcast in my own village. Now I do that by being here on this day."

Teagan nodded and smiled. "Nevan," she prompted. "You told me you wanted to say something tonight."

"When I was a boy I cried a lot," the youth said. "My father had died and my mother was too shaken to look after me. Conor was about eighteen or nineteen. He brought me a puppy he got from the fishermen in Galway. He said it was time for me to turn my mind to something beyond myself. So meet Quigley, my best friend." The huge dog sat up and thumped his tail twice on the ground. Wiry hair covered his eyes. "I hear they bred these dogs to fight wolves," Teagan said. "And I think the dogs won." She looked over the gathering, warmed by the rows of faces she knew.

"It's getting late, my dear friends, and we have much to do when the dawn comes.

I want to make sure each of you knows how deeply grateful I am, and Kaidan is, and Deirdre and Seamus, to see you all here. I believe your presence is an expression of love and respect. I also believe we're not here to mark a death we could not prevent, but to mark the achievements only Conor could carry out. So this is not just a burial. It is the beginning of a tradition, of calling on the ancient spirits who rule here and asking them to take up our crusade for the freedom of this land, a freedom that must be sought and can be won. Conor once said the English do not rule here, we do. He was right. We hold Doonagore Castle as a symbol of Irish ascendancy in Doolin. We hold Kinvara a bit less directly, and by the way, enfold Geoffrey Moore and his son Charles, who sleeps now in his father's lap. The Dunguaire castle-holder is a friend, and is not to be shunned for the accident of his birth."

Teagan brought out the moonstone tiara and placed it on her head. "This comes to me from my husband's family. I think of it as a very Irish symbol of our long struggle for this land. For this land," she called out, pointing toward the dolmen, which reflected firelight onto faces in the crowd.

"We struggle for Poulnabrone, where Oisin the Avenger will lie among heroes. We struggle for Doolin!" Men in the crowd reacted. "Aye!"

"For Kinvara!"

"Aye!"

"For the Aran Islands and Galway!"

"Aye!" They were on their feet now, clapping and waving in a call-and-response chant. And leading them was not the innkeeper's girl from Doolin or the new widow from Kinvara, but a regal and striking woman, Bandia Teagan Dearg Ni Moran, the red goddess of Clare.

"We struggle for Connaught, for Munster and Leinster!"

"Aye!"

"We struggle for Dublin, for Ulster and for Tara! We struggle, my friends, for this land, for Ireland! And we will win!"

Teagan seemed to realize belatedly that she was sparking a political rally as much as a memorial for her husband. *I don't want this to get out of hand. The last thing we need is to turn a burial into a brawl.*

As the crowd drifted off, Seamus and Geoffrey Moore made sure the fire was out. "She can start a rising on a whim," Moore said, his tone reflecting concern.

"She won't," Seamus assured him. "But you have just seen that there is a strong current, a yearning for freedom flowing in these people. I think she was struck by the intensity of their mood and will do nothing else to get them fired up. Besides, she specifically told these people not to villainize you and Charles."

"It's not the boy who concerns me, or myself either. It is that this little corner of Ireland could start something that can't be contained here in the west of this island."

"Look, my friend. You are the agent of an occupying power, and you should not be surprised if the people you dominate do not love you."

◆ ◆ ◆

Teagan snuggled into her blankets next to the pile of bedding that was the sleeping Kaidan. *What a day! Conor once said he didn't want to sleep here, and said we should find a place less powerful. Oh, I hope I didn't make a mistake when I decided to honor Conor by bringing him here.*

You did not.

Kerbasi?

Aye. Trust your heart. Poulnabrone is able to enfold additions. I will not speak to you tomorrow; your son is too close to sensing my presence. I will meet him when he is older, and we two shall talk again. Sleep well tonight, and may tomorrow go well.

41

Hughie

At the equator the sun seems to dive below the horizon when it sets, and to leap aloft when it rises. The turn from night to day is stark and sudden.

In the high latitudes that transition is subtle and slow. On a summer morning the skies over Poulnabrone gave up their dark cloak reluctantly. But there came a moment when Kaidan could see the underside of the great capstone was darker than the sky surrounding it.

I want to get up because I might miss something, but I don't want to get up just as much. This is the day men will shovel dirt over my father's body, and I won't see him ever again. If I cry now maybe no one will see. Besides, no one else seems to be stirring this early. I'll wait. He snuggled in closer to the blankets where his mother lay and quickly fell asleep again.

The sun continued its leisurely arrival, sidling upward toward the Burren skyline and stimulating internal alarms among early rising sleepers. Here and there cocoons of cloaks and blankets shuddered and parted. Men and women rose quietly, reoriented themselves in the gray pre-dawn light, and stretched kinks out of their bodies. The smell of coffee rode a soft wind across the site and kindled hunger pangs among the mourners.

Teagan Dearg the red widow walked with the six young men of Conor's Fianna to the far side of the dolmen, still unlit by the emerging sun.

"You are the best of Conor's Kinvara friends," she told them. "And to you falls the honor and the duty of making a space for him in this rocky landscape."

The Fianna stood on the ground that had been marked in yesterday's last light, with shovels and picks at hand. Three short men and one tall one marched out from behind the standing stones and faced the others. One of the short ones spoke.

"We are Conor's family," he said. "And we will do the task that lies before us. We shall be the gravediggers. Ye shall be the pallbearers and bring the body here when we are done." There was a tone of firmness in his speech that discouraged any dissent, even from the normally disputatious Paddy O'Brien.

He stood by the dolmen wall, now colored by the early sun, and watched. *Conor's family, the little man said. Oisin had no brothers or sisters, so I don't know how to place them among the relatives, but sure they know how to dig.*

Paddy and his friends leaned back to watch the work. He felt drowsy and didn't notice the immense volume of gravel and small rocks that came very quickly out of the deepening hole. And nobody noticed the short man who was so good at moving larger rocks they seemed to nuzzle under his extended hand.

"I am Daniel," one of the short men said to Paddy O'Brien. "There are stones enough here to cover the grave and we have left them close at hand. Now, you must not hurry this. There are people coming from Doolin, people important to the life of Oisin the Avenger. Please ask Teagan to wait a little longer." Daniel turned and walked behind the portal grave. When Paddy went after him to get more details, he wasn't there.

The Fianna leader found the widow O'Canavan sitting by a dying fire, staring at the smoke that blew toward the grave.

"Teagan Dearg," he said. "There was a man here, a little man who said we should wait for some people from Doolin to arrive. He seemed pretty sure they're coming, but he didn't say when and now I can't find him."

She mustered a small smile. "I think I know the man. And I do hope that some of our friends from Doolin can be here. By the way, is there a priest among the crowd?"

"I don't know, lady, they haven't replaced Father Turlough, even though he's been dead almost a year. And Doolin doesn't have a priest at all. I recall hearing Father Turlough went there to bury your father."

"Aye, Paddy, that he did. We must have someone to conduct a ceremony for Conor, and I must think over who best can do it."

◆ ◆ ◆

King Willie trotted sedately along the path that led north and east from Doolin. He felt the light sure touch of Hughie Mac Manus on the reins and heard the endless chatter of Katie Mac Manus behind him. He knew one of the other two men in the wagon. White Patrick Boyle was a frequent source of apples and carrots when King Willie and the wagon went to Malachi's tavern.

The fourth man was a stranger to the old horse. He was small and lean with a face that closed in on itself. He wore sandals and a long black robe but he did not look priestly. His hair was long and needed washing, as did the hand that bore a moonstone ring on his fourth finger.

"Belenus," White Patrick said, nudging the dozing man. "What makes you so certain that Teagan Dearg will accept a druidic rite at her husband's burial. After all, a priest married them and she has never even seen you."

"I do not flaunt myself. I have seen her and she is a woman of surprising power, power that is growing. My ceremony is needful on a larger scale to cement the seal between this land and its heroes. The faith of Patrick grows ever stronger here but it is not the only way to light up the spirit that sets this green and troubled Erin apart."

It was mid-morning when King Willie stopped gratefully before another person he knew, the red-haired woman from the tavern in Doolin.

Teagan, her eyes filling, kissed Hughie, hugged Katie, and held both hands out to White Patrick Boyle, her childhood friend and now owner of the inn that was still called Malachi's. She found the perfect scratching spot on King Willie's forehead, and only then turned her golden brown eyes to the last person in the wagon.

"Welcome. I don't know who you are but I know what you are, and we must talk. Whitey, would you find Seamus and Deirdre and meet us back here?"

"You are a woman of power," the man said. "And you are getting stronger. I am Belenus, and I hold to the old faith. I hope you will let me honor your husband as he is laid among the heroes in this place of power."

"That's what we'll discuss," she said with a smile, climbing into the driver's seat while Hughie led King Willie away to be fed and watered.

For the next thirty minutes passing people noticed an intense conversation among the people in the wagon. But none of them spoke loudly enough to inform the curious.

When they dispersed, Belenus walked with a limp toward the dolmen and bowed deeply toward the capstone. *You are older than the gods I serve and I honor you. I hope you accept my being here on this day.*

Be at ease, druid. I do not reject those who can sense my presence. You are a boon to this moment and so you are welcome among the admirers of Oisin the Avenger.

42

Belenus

The last of the stragglers from Doolin arrived just before high noon at Poulnabrone. The crowd clustered around the newly dug grave with many eyes measuring how Teagan Dearg and Kaidan were behaving. Seamus Hogan, standing with Conor's mother, his widow and his son, noticed the harper who often performed the Ballad of Teagan Dearg, Thomas Briggs, the Englishman who had joined the Irish community in the village, and Kevin the sailor who'd brought tragic news to Kinvara. They were standing with White Patrick Boyle and the Mac Manuses.

At the head of the grave, Belenus the druid stood absolutely still in a gray robe with the cowl pulled up over his head. All eyes turned to the wagon that held Conor's body. The six members of Conor's Fianna stepped to the rear and slid the casket out of the wagon bed. Seamus watched them try to walk in step as they carried it toward the raw hole in the stony ground.

Seamus watched as they moved to begin the burial. *They're being very careful, and it's clear that they don't like doing this, at all. Paddy O'Brien looks as if he's about to cry. Deirdre is already crying and I think Kaidan may be next. I wish Teagan would weep too, but she won't allow herself to do that, not yet.* The Fianna put down their burden at one end of the grave and stood stiffly beside it, three on one side and three on the other.

Kaidan, standing between his mother and his grandmother, became the central link in a chain of bowed red heads.

Belenus raised his arms and nodded to the Doolin harper who strummed one multi-note chord that flowed over the crowd and stopped all the small talk.

"I call upon Eriu," the druid intoned in a voice that reached the edges of the gathering. "I call upon Fodla. I call upon Banb." Everyone knew of the triad of ancient Celtic goddesses.

"I call upon Lugh. I call upon Manannan Mac Lir. I call upon The Dagda!" Seamus shivered. *They are this land's oldest and most powerful deities.*

"I call upon all the gods and goddesses who have shaped this land and the people who dwell herein." The voice took on a chant rhythm and the harpist adorned it with pulses of sound. The crowd stood utterly still.

"I call on all the gods and goddesses, to witness that we meet, in this place of power, to honor them. We are also here, to honor the newest hero, this land has produced, Conor Mac Cormac O'Canavan, who flowed into legend, as Oisin the Avenger!"

Geoffrey Moore stood in the second rank with Charles, feeling quite alone. *I wish I could understand Irish, but what I'm getting is intense. Not hostile but very intense.*

"This is a place of power, power of the spirit," the old druid intoned. "And so it has been on this site, for age upon age. We add to that power, on this sunny day, as we place the body, of Oisin the Avenger, among the heroes here enshrined." He stopped to look at Teagan, standing with Kaidan, Deirdre, Seamus and White Patrick Boyle.

"There is no magic potion, no spell nor charm, that can ease the pain of the loss, of one so loved as Conor O'Canavan. They say time helps, but it only dulls that pain. There simply is no dissolving it, as salt dissolves in water." Belenus wasn't sure his meaning was clear to her. "Death is a permanent separation, and yet we do not believe, it is the end of the one who was taken. We believe the spirit, the life-force of the departed, lives on.

We have always believed that, as most men do. Our people have held to that truth, since long before the great Patrick, brought a new way, to look at this world, and to fathom Otherworld."

Again, the old man paused and glanced around him, gauging the effect his words were having on his listeners.

"We know the ocean lies beyond the land because we have seen it. We cannot see it from here but we know it's there. We know Tir na nOg lies beyond the line, where sea and sky meet, in the western ocean. We cannot see the Land of Youth, but we have always known it's out there, somewhere. And as we bury the shell that carried Oisin on his adventures, his life-force, his spirit, abides beyond our reach. And that is the source of our comfort on this day, such as it is. Now, with honor and with dignity, let us complete the task that brought us here."

Belenus stepped back from the edge of the grave. The Fianna bent in unison and raised the casket on three ropes they had passed under it from side to side. Sidestepping with care, they straddled the open hole and slowly lowered Conor's remains into the ground and dropped their ends of the ropes on top of the casket. Again Belenus raised his thin arms and spoke loudly enough to be heard at the back of the crowd.

"To Conor I say, I beseech the Powers, to make you welcome, in your new place. To his family I say, the part of him that is here, has already been welcomed, by the spirits that rule here. And to all here present I say, we are done here. We have launched Oisin the Avenger, into Otherworld, as well as we could. Now we depart from Poulnabrone, to cherish his memory, and to polish his legend."

Seamus stepped between the grave and the widow and touched Teagan's shoulder. "Come, Tay and Kaidan, we're done here. Let's go, there's water on Hughie's wagon."

"Wait." Teagan resisted the tug on her arm. "They're not done yet."

Deirdre pulled Teagan and Kaidan into an expansive hug. "My dear, you told me once you were haunted by the sound of dirt falling on your mother's casket, and you will not hear it today. That sound need not be your last memory of my son. I don't want to hear it either, and it would not be good for Kaidan. There are times when Seamus is right, and this is one of those times."

Teagan Dearg pivoted with a last glance at the Fianna standing stiffly over the grave. She took Kaidan and Deirdre by the hand and walked slowly away from the still-open hole. Seamus and White Patrick Boyle followed at the leading edge of a general movement away from the standing stones of Poulnabrone.

The Fianna and the druid stood beside the grave and did not move until the people they knew were blended by distance into an amorphous moving mass.

Paddy O'Brien raised his shovel, nudged it into the gritty dirt and flipped the soil off the blade and into the grave. Small stones rattled off the casket lid and there was a *whump* as smaller particles hit bottom in the grave. The five other Fianna warriors followed O'Brien's lead and swung their own shovels until the grave was almost full. Paddy stopped to wipe his brow and when he looked up those short men were standing there.

"We will place the stones over his grave. It's a family thing for us. We will create a small cairn over the site and as the mound subsides the traces of Oisin the Avenger's presence will linger only in our minds. Well done, young men, and go you now to the people you serve so well. They are not so far away."

The man stood alone at the head of the grave. Paddy could not find the druid or anyone else except for the distant crowd drifting off to the north and east toward Kinvara. The Fianna gathered up their things from the site of last night's camp and trotted after the faraway figures.

43

Sea Dog

The stragglers from Poulnabrone had overwhelmed Liam the stand-in bartender when Seamus and Deirdre entered the tavern. He slipped behind the bar and began drawing ale while Deirdre made room among the tables for the rest of her family. She gave Kaidan a glass of milk and some pastries and poured a glass of the good whiskey from County Antrim for Teagan, who raised an eyebrow when Deirdre placed it in front of her.

"Drink, you need it," Conor's mother said. "Fatigue and grief are at war within you and this will diminish that struggle." Teagan began to push the glass and its amber liquid away from her but Deirdre stayed her hand. "It will not harm you to do as you're told, just this once. Here and now you need make no more decisions this day, my dear."

"I've always known what comes next in my life, especially since I met Conor," Teagan said. "But now I have no star to steer by, no goal before me, and a small boy to raise." She smiled and took a sip. "I think it's all catching up with me." They glanced at Kaidan, who was sleeping, his head on his arms at the table.

Ronan O'Malley came in with Sea Dog, who trotted over to Teagan without his usual bounce and put his head in her lap. The Irish people of Clare and Galway asked each other whether Teagan was indeed a goddess, but the dog had no doubt. He gazed adoringly at her as she absently scratched his ear in just the right place.

Teagan sipped at her whiskey without tasting it. Every time the door opened she swiveled in her chair and looked in hopes of seeing Conor sweep through the entrance with that grin dancing between his mouth and his eyes. *I know better. I know he's not coming through that door. I know he's gone, but yet . . . I can't seem to accept the fact of his death. He's too much a part of this inn, of this town. His absence is surrounding me in an embrace I don't want. Do want. Damn, I'm so confused. Whatever would I do without Kaidan and Deirdre? And all these people who think the goddess is going to lead them to happiness and freedom, what do I do about them?*

Sea Dog stirred under Teagan's hand and put his head on her knee. *Daft beast is trying to comfort me. Maybe he's smarter than I thought. Maybe a lot smarter. I think I know what I have to do, but it'll hold until morning.*

◆ ◆ ◆

Morning came late to Seamus Hogan's tavern, where on a normal day robins were not the only early birds. Sea Dog stood up and faced the door when Deirdre came into the taproom. She smiled and let him out, keeping an ear open for the scratching he would do to get back in. She was busy harvesting the oven when she heard Red Teagan's voice.

"I can't stay here, Deirdre. It hurts to say so, but this place, this town, is just too full of Conor. He's behind every door, he's every unseen sound, he's every movement in the corner of my eye. It's all too much." And in Deirdre's kitchen Teagan Dearg wept for the first time since becoming a widow. She leaned into Deirdre's shoulder and sobbed, her body shaking. Seamus started to come in and was shooed back out.

"I know," Deirdre whispered. "It's a good thing, looking back, that Conor and I were evicted from our home soon after Cormac was exiled, because I had the same feelings of drowning in the familiarity of a setting that would never again echo his voice or reflect his image. So Kinvara was a fresh start for me, and a healthy change. Dear one, I know you must leave and I know why, but I don't have to like it. Surely I don't. Where will you go? To America, perhaps? Or England?"

Teagan smiled a little and shook her head. "I will not leave Ireland, but beyond that I don't know. Maybe we'll go to Doolin for a while, and of course I'll take the Ben Mullagh tiara with me. In Doolin my memories are all of new love and fresh promise, none of the sorrow that filters into my warm memories of Kinvara. Besides, Kaidan knows the village and most of the people there."

44

Doolin

Kaidan sat on the stones when his world got complicated. He'd learned that these stones were the ones his father had helped to place in the Doolin harbor to make it safer for boats to shelter there. When the wind was lively, the Atlantic surge splashed off the stone quay and into his face. That made him laugh except when the salt water got into his eyes.

Does that only happen when my troubles pile up like a spring tide or do I only notice it then? But now it's not the water acting up. It's the air. A soft day, Whitey says. Less water than when it rains but it's a lot wetter than sunshine.

Kaidan Mac Conor O'Canavan stared out to sea at the westernmost outpost of the Celtic world, out to where the Aran Islands crouched like guardians in the mouth of Galway Bay beyond the rocky coast of County Clare.

Mom took me there when we first moved here from Kinvara. I didn't like the boat much but the cart ride from Kilronan to Dun Aonghasa was fun. The fort was scary though. It was all dark rock and penned-in space at the top of a cliff. Mom told me Dad was afraid she'd fall off and grabbed her away from the edge when they went there years ago. I think she liked it when he did that, and when we went there she acted strangely. It was like she was sharpening her memories of her visit there with Dad, reaching out and grabbing those moments. That visit must have been very important to her.

The mist thickened over a quiet sea and he watched it reduce the islands to silhouettes in gray and then erase them entirely in a silver haze that shimmered in thin sunshine.

When we came here in Ronan's boat I watched the town of Kinvara disappear in the distance. It wasn't the same as this mist but it still disappeared. Kinvara is home, not this Doolin. Besides, there's no one my own age here except for a clot of girls and that boy who runs around telling my mother what goes on here.

Kaidan picked up some limestone chips and scaled them into the harbor, annoying some sea gulls. He thought once again that most people in Doolin were a little afraid of his mother. *They all think she's a goddess and they whisper that she will save them from the British. And they treat me as if I have powers, too, All I want to do is be an ordinary boy like I was in Kinvara. I wonder how old I'll be when they say I'm old enough to go back there on my own?*

Epilogue

Braxton

"We should have gone to Paris and Vienna. This is supposed to be a grand tour, and, my new husband, I find nothing grand about this Ennis. It's Ireland, Braxton, it's not even civilized! This is your idea of a romantic excursion?"

Braxton Hawkins watched the hostler ready their carriage. *Three weeks and already the sour side of young Anne is emerging. My brother warned me, but I didn't listen.*

"Is this horse well trained?" The tone of Anne's question suggested serious doubt.

The man patted his horse on the neck. "Best horse I've got, Madam. Her name is Grace, named after Grace O'Malley. She's smart and gentle. It's sure I am that yer husband can manage her out and back."

Anne looked unconvinced. "This is supposed to be a sightseeing ride. Tell me, horse man. What sights are to be seen around here? Keeping in mind, of course, that we must be back here for tea with the Everetts this afternoon. And by the way, do I know this Grace O'Malley?"

Liam O'Hara allowed himself a small smile. *I don't like these Sassenachs, especially her. Grainne O Maille, I'm about to polish your legend.*

"Grace O'Malley was the famous pirate queen of Connemara, back in the days of your Queen Elizabeth. She seized English estates, married and discarded English nobles, and once sat in the queen's own palace, where the two of them conducted a conversation in Latin. She's an Irish folk hero. Oh, and by the by, there is a famous site not far from here. It could be one of the oldest tombs in the world."

"I have no interest in visiting dead people," Anne said with a dismissive wave.

Liam patted his horse again. "Madam Hawkins, this grave may be as old as the pyramids. What remains after thousands of years is one of the world's unique samples of primitive architecture. Grace knows the way; she's been there many times. All right, Mr. Hawkins? Right, up you go, madam. Now you, sir, and here are the reins. Turn left, then right at the High Street, and out along the road north."

Braxton Hawkins relished the near-silence on his high seat, with the horse providing a cloppity cadence to the turning of the wheels. It didn't last.

"This isn't much of a road, Braxton. Be careful you don't spill me out of this cart."

"It's not a cart, Anne, but a nice little carriage. And as to the road, we have bad roads in the center of London as well. You are grumbling because you don't want to be here. Well, I do, and I invite you to find something to enjoy out here." Anne flounced in her seat and huffed a little. She subsided for a few minutes.

"It's a wasteland out here, Braxton. No trees, no cattle, no anything. How could that awful man have sent us out here? Is he trying to kill us by getting us lost in a hostile wilderness? I tell you, husband, I have little liking for this place or for this country."

He was annoyed and felt the horse could sense his mood. "Look, Mrs. Hawkins, you are three weeks into a new life, and already I have heard a lifetime's collection of complaints, mostly about your presumed discomforts. You are pretty but you are selfish, and I tell you this. Right now I don't care if you think your life is unjust or too taxing. If you cannot be pleasant company, at least be silent for the next hour."

There was an open-mouthed stare and a flounce, followed by a sulky silence. *I don't think anyone has ever spoken to her this way. Interesting.*

In less than an hour Braxton spotted something starkly vertical on the horizon. "Look, Anne, that must be it, off to the right."

Anne, who had been about to say it didn't look like much to her, caught herself. "We'll know more when we get closer," she said, trying to push just a little interest into her answer.

"There must be people here, because I can see smoke rising from behind that flat stone," she said a few minutes later, with a real hint of curiosity in her words.

Braxton pulled off the modest road and stopped the horse in front of an odd structure. Stone slab walls held aloft an enormous capstone that may have covered fifteen square feet. Almost at once a very old man came out from behind the stonework and waved at the newcomers. He wore the tattered remnants of an old-fashioned military uniform and he held a rusted pike, its lethal end waggling above their heads as the ancient warrior tried to hold it still and vertical.

"Dia dhuit, aGranuile," he greeted the horse. "Who are you?" Braxton asked.

"And what is this place?" Anne said.

"Iss misha Padraig O'Brien," the old man answered.

"Don't you speak English?" Anne Hawkins asked sharply, as if she expected everyone in this subdued island to speak the language of the colonists. The man's smile showed a bitter edge, but he answered in Irish-accented English.

"I do not speak it by choice, or among friends, lady. But yes, I do speak the tongue of the Sassenach, of the Saxons. And as to what this place is, it is the gravesite of Oisin the Avenger, rebel against English rule over this land. I am the last of the Fianna, Oisin's warrior companions. And on the days marking his death and burial, we come here to honor him. At least, we used to. As I have said, I am the last of the Celtic warriors, and I do not think I will be able to come back next year."

Braxton Hawkins had been listening closely and looked around. "I think this place is far too old to have been built in your lifetime."

The old man smiled, his nose and chin flirting in a space once owned by teeth. "Aye, young man, ye've a hold on the truth of it. The wise men say this thing is called a dolmen grave. They don't know when it was built, but they say it's older than Jaysus, maybe older than Moses. And nobody knows who was buried here first in the dawn of time. Now, boy, on rare occasions our people decide a man has earned the highest of honors during his life, and that honor is to be buried here, here among the valiant."

Paddy O'Brien stood as tall as he could, and said again as if reciting a prayer. "Here, among the valiant. The last time that happened was fifty-two years ago, in 1710. The man was Conor O'Canavan, but to we of the Fianna, his companions, he was Oisin the Avenger, a figure right out of Irish legend."

Braxton noticed his bride had lost her sulk and was looking around with interest.

"You're not going to like this part of the story," O'Brien said with a shake of his bony forefinger. "But here you are. The English orphaned young Conor, killed first his mentor, then his new father-in-law. Oisin and the goddess Teagan Dearg, Red Teagan, the two of them raged through County Clare avenging the oppression of Irishmen by the English, the British. Eventually they hanged him, and Red Teagan brought him here. We all came here, all the Fianna, and we scratched out a place for him here in Poulnabrone. It means Hole of Sorrows, but it should mean Hall of Honors. And on the 18th of July every year, we have come back here to honor him. His son Kaidan carried on the resistance, but the British expelled him, and we think he was lost in the unknown wilds of North America years ago. But I am grateful that you are here to learn the story of Oisin the Avenger."

The old man stopped, looking stricken. His pike fell away and he clutched his chest before falling in what Braxton thought was slow motion. The visitor jumped out of his carriage and knelt over O'Brien.

"I told you I would not be back next year," the old warrior said with a ghastly grin.

"Step back, please, I'll attend him," Braxton heard. He looked up to see the most beautiful woman he'd ever beheld. Bright red hair flowed out from under a golden tiara centered on a moonstone and cascaded over a green cloak. She knelt beside the fallen man, held his hand, and poured a bit of water over his head.

"Go in peace, Paddy," she said in Irish. "Your duty here is done. And we thank you, the Avenger and I. Kaidan, too, from somewhere on the American frontier."

O'Brien produced a better smile, closed his eyes, and lay very still. Three short men and a tall one, all in old-fashioned military uniforms, came out from behind the stone wall, lifted the body and went back where they came from.

Anne sat in the carriage, open-mouthed, and silent. Braxton spoke to the strange woman when she got to her feet. "I'm not sure what you said, but I think you were trying to comfort him. But who are you, and where did you come from, you and those others?"

"I am Bandia Teagan Dearg Ni Moran, wife to Oisin the Avenger who is buried here. This is the day we celebrate his life, and the day of his death."

Braxton was stunned. "But Madam, you are far too young to be the wife of a man who's five decades dead. Are you then, as the old man said, a goddess?"

She smiled at him, a dazzling smile that made her lovelier than ever.

"Mr. Hawkins, you are a stranger in a land where the rules you know do not always hold. Do not inquire too deeply into what you cannot know. It would be best if you leave now. Thank you for trying to help Paddy, but it was his time. Oh, and make no investments in Ireland. Your people cannot hold it in the long view."

She walked over to the horse and bestowed a soft pat on her neck. "Grace O'Malley, please take these people back to Ennis. They have a long and happy life to share."

The horse turned and trotted off toward her distant stable. A few minutes later Anne Hawkins spoke for the first time.

"Husband, what just happened?"

"I think we'll never know, but I've never been through anything like it. Those old warriors, that woman, they just appeared and then they were gone. We're going back to England, and you will not tell this tale to any of your friends. I think this land is truly different and some very strange things happen here. And I tell you this. The woman said, do not invest in Ireland, and I shall not. Instead, I think the prospects for British interests are better in the Americas, and I have a friend in Boston who writes to say that colonial town is prosperous and peaceful and better yet, welcoming to English investors. Let us go there to seek our fortune."

Glossary

Aran—as "Aaron." Three rocky islands at the mouth of Galway Bay

Bandia—Ban-DEE-ah, woman god, goddess

Banshee—Female spirit in Irish mythology, often credited with shrieking just before the death of a prominent man

Ben Brack—One of the Twelve Bens (small mountains) of Connemara

Ben Cullagh—one of the Twelve Bens, perhaps the most remote

Burren, the—Burr-en, limestone landscape in County Clare

Breantas—BREN-tass, funky, smelly

Brehon—BRAY-hone Traditional Irish magistrates, arbiters. Their system of law flourished until early in the Eighteenth Century when English law superseded it

Brian Boru—BRY-en Bo-ROO, first king to unify Ireland, died 1015. By legend, the ancestor of all O'Briens

Ceann Mhara—Kinvara, southern County Galway town Claddagh, the CLOD-doch (as in loch) ancient Galway fishing village

"Conas a ta tu?"—CO-nas uh TAH-too?, "How are you?"

Connemara—CON-nuh-MARR-rah. Large, lightly populated peninsula forming the western half of County Galway

Deirdre—DEAR-Druh, female name. In legend a great beauty who endured great suffering

Dearg—Red

Dia dhuit—DJIA rritch formal Irish hello. Literally, "God with you"

Doolin—DOO-linn, coastal village in County Clare

Drumcurreen—Village east of Doolin in County Clare

Doonagore—Doo-na-GORE, small castle near Doolin in County Clare

Dun Aonghasa—Dun Angus. Iron Age, maybe Bronze Age stone for-
    tress on a clifftop on Inishmor in the Aran Islands. Abandoned for
    centuries, somewhat restored in the 1880's.

Dunguaire—Dun (fortress) + GOO-i-reh, (ancient king), castle near
    Kinvara, seat of English power in southern County Galway

Eamon—A- (as in hay) mun, male name

Ennis—Shire town of County Clare, southeast of Doolin

Ennistymon—Ennis-Tee-MOAN, Market town 10 miles southeast of
    Doolin

Eoin—Owen

Fergal—FERR-uh-gall. Male name

Fianna—FEE-innah. Finn Mac Cool's warrior band.

Finbar—FINN-bar, male name

Finulla—Finn-OO-lah, mythical Irish naiad, protector of Teagan

Fionn Mac Cumhaill—Finn McCool, legendary Irish hero

Gleoiteog—GLAW-tug, sailing boat that evolved on Galway Bay.

Gossoon—Young boy, often a servant

Inisheer—IN-ish (as in finish) ear, smallest of the Aran Islands

Inishmaan—IN-ish (as in finish)-mon, middle one of the Aran Islands

Inishmor—IN-ish (as in finish) Island + Mor (More) big. Largest of the
    three Aran Islands in Galway Bay

"Iss misha . . ."—Ish (as in fish) misha, "I am . . ."

Kaidan—KAY-dan, male name meaning warrior

Kilkee—Coastal town in southern County Clare

Kilronan—Kill-ROE-nun, largest Aran Island village.

Kilrush—market town in southwest County Clare

Kinvara—Sometimes Kinvarra. Coastal town in southern County Galway. Anglicized from Ceann Mhara

Lisdeen—Townland east of Kilkee in County Clare

Lissateeaun—Leesa-tee-oon, ancient earthen fortification in northeast County Clare, near the present-day Lisdoonvarna

Lofa—LOW-fah, crap

Mac—Mac, surname prefix for male children

Maeve—Mave, female name, traceable to an ancient queen

Malachi—MAL-a-kye, male name

Mathair Crionna—Mother Cree-OH-nah. Translates best as "wise mother"

Moher—MOE-her, High sheer cliffs south of Doolin, Co. Clare

Moran—Mo-RAN, Irish surname

Ni—Nee, surname prefix for a girl-child

O'—Oh, surname prefix for grandson of . . . or descendant of. Thus: Conor Mac Cormac O'Canavan

O'heyn—O'Hain, Irish surname. Modern spelling Hanes.

Oisin—OH-shin, Finn McCool's son, war leader of the Fianna.

Pookie—Irish pixie. Like a leprechaun but less benign

Poulnabrone—Pool-nuh-brone(as in minestrone), dolmen grave in the Burren, may pre-date 3500 BC.

Ronan—ROE-nun, male name

Sassenach—SASS-uh-noch (as in loch). Saxon, derogatory term for Englishman

Sean—Shawn, male name, as in Connery

Shaughnessy—SHAWN-ess-see, surname common in the Irish west

Sidhe—Shee, the Little People of Irish legend

Sinead—Shin-AID, female name

"Slan anois!"—Slahn Anish, "Bye for now!"

Sláinte—SLONT-cha, Irish drinking toast

"Ta me go maith"—"TAH may guh MOY," "It goes well with me." "All right."

Teagan—TAY-gan, as in Reagan

Townland—smallest division of land in old Ireland, sometimes just a few hundred acres

Tuam—Toom, large town in north central County Galway

Tuatha de Danaan—TOO-ah de DAN-an, legendary pre-Celtic Irish race, thought to have paranormal powers. Perhaps ancestors of leprechauns.

Turlough—TUR-loch, Irish male name

About the Author

Steve Delaney, a Vermonter since 1988, is a fifty-year broadcast journalist who has covered politics in Washington, finance in New York, and wars on three continents. He has won national honors for two NBC White Paper television documentaries, and for radio documentaries and news programs produced for Vermont Public Radio, where his distinctive voice has been heard for a decade.

He is also the author of *Vermont Seasonings: Reflections on the Rhythms of a Vermont Year* and The Nilesburgh Chronicles trilogy.

Acknowledgments

A book begins as an idea, an intellectual orphan. It thrives when good people take it in hand to polish and grind. Publishing, like journalism, is a collaborative effort. My fifth book benefits enormously from the careful edits done by Ann Wicker in Charlotte. Kirsty Walker of Hobblebush Books lent craft and skill to shaping the manuscript into a book, and Judi Calhoun did wonders with the cover art. My old friend Frank Dobisky has been endlessly encouraging.

Finally and most importantly, George Geers at Plaidswede Publishing set new records for patience in undertaking a project that may have been beyond his comfort zone and in staying with it to bring the idea to life. To all of them I am enormously indebted.

Steve Delaney
Milton, Vermont, May 2017